SWORD SONG

Bernard Cornwell was born in London, raised in Essex and now lives mostly in the USA.

Visit www.AuthorTracker.co.uk for exclusive updates on Bernard Cornwell.

PLACE NAMES

The spelling of place names in Anglo-Saxon England was an uncertain business, with no consistency and no agreement even about the name itself. Thus London was variously rendered as Lundonia, Lundenberg, Lundenne, Lundene, Lundenwic, Lundenceaster and Lundres. Doubtless some readers will prefer other versions of the names listed below, but I have usually employed whichever spelling is cited in either the *Oxford* or the *Cambridge Dictionary of English Place-Names* for the years nearest or contained within Alfred's reign, AD 871–899, but even that solution is not foolproof. Hayling Island, in 956, was written as both Heilincigae and Hæglingaiggæ. Nor have I been consistent myself; I spell England as Englaland, but have preferred the modern form Northumbria to Norðhymbralond to avoid the suggestion that the boundaries of the ancient kingdom coincide with those of the modern county. So this list, like the spellings themselves, is capricious.

Æscengum	Eashing, Surrey
Arwan	River Orwell, Suffolk
Beamfleot	Benfleet, Essex
Bebbanburg	Bamburgh, Northumberland
Berrocscire	Berkshire
Cair Ligualid	Carlisle, Cumbria
Caninga	Canvey Island, Essex

Cent	Kent
Cippanhamm	Chippenham, Wiltshire
Cirrenceastre	Cirencester, Gloucestershire
Cisseceastre	Chichester, Sussex
Coccham	Cookham, Berkshire
Colaun, River	River Colne, Essex
Contwaraburg	Canterbury, Kent
Cornwalum	Cornwall
Cracgelad	Cricklade, Wiltshire
Dunastopol	Dunstable (Roman name Durocobrivis), Bedfordshire
Dunholm	Durham, County Durham
Eoferwic	York, Yorkshire
Ethandun	Edington, Wiltshire
Exanceaster	Exeter, Devon
Fleot	River Fleet, London
Frankia	Germany
Fughelness	Foulness Island, Essex
Grantaceaster	Cambridge, Cambridgeshire
Gyruum	Jarrow, County Durham
Hastengas	Hastings, Sussex
Horseg	Horsey Island, Essex
Hothlege	River Hadleigh, Essex
Hrofeceastre	Rochester, Kent
Hwealf	River Crouch, Essex
Lundene	London
Mædes Stana	Maidstone, Kent
Medwæg	River Medway, Kent
Oxnaforda	Oxford, Oxfordshire
Padintune	Paddington, Greater London
Pant	River Blackwater, Essex
Scaepege	Isle of Sheppey, Kent
Sceaftes Eye	Sashes Island (at Coccham)
Sceobyrig	Shoebury, Essex

Scerhnesse	Sheerness, Kent
Sture	River Stour, Essex
Sutherge	Surrey
Suthriganaweorc	Southwark, Greater London
Swealwe	River Swale, Kent
Temes	River Thames
Thunresleam	Thundersley, Essex
Wæced	Watchet, Somerset
Wæclingastræt	Watling Street
Welengaford	Wallingford, Oxfordshire
Werham	Wareham, Dorset
Wiltunscir	Wiltshire
Wintanceaster	Winchester, Hampshire
Wocca's Dun	South Ockenden, Essex
Wodenes Eye	Odney Island (at Coccham)

BERNARD CORNWELL

Sword Song

HARPER

Harper
An Imprint of HarperCollins*Publishers*
77–85 Fulham Palace Road,
Hammersmith, London W6 8JB

www.harpercollins.co.uk

Special overseas edition 2008

1

First published in Great Britain by
HarperCollins 2007

A catalogue record for this book is
available from the British Library

ISBN: 978-0-00-726935-8

Set in Meridien by Palimpsest Book Production Limited,
Grangemouth, Stirlingshire

Printed and bound in Great Britain by
Clays Ltd, St Ives plc

Sword Song is voor Aukje,
mit liefde:
Er was eens . . .

Contents

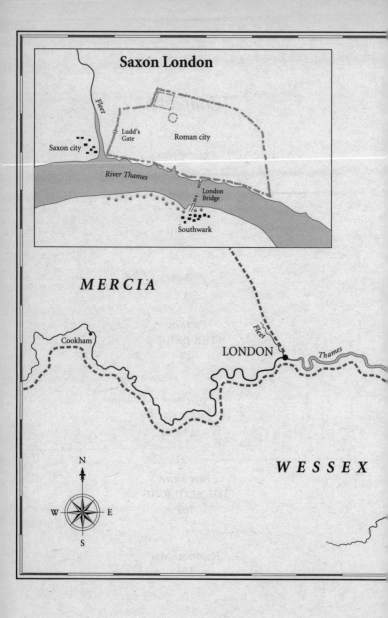

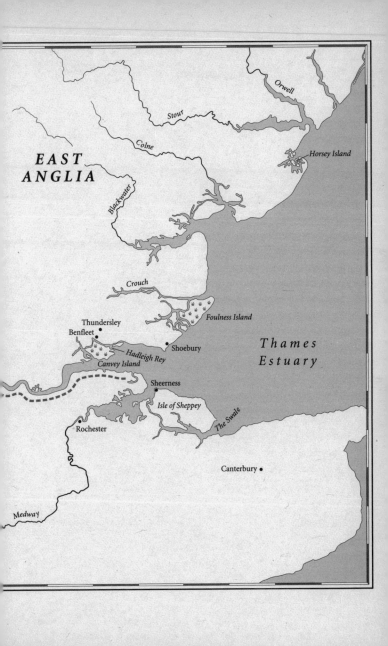

PROLOGUE

Darkness. Winter. A night of frost and no moon.

We floated on the River Temes, and beyond the boat's high bow I could see the stars reflected on the shimmering water. The river was in spate as melted snow fed it from countless hills. The winterbournes were flowing from the chalk uplands of Wessex. In summer those streams would be dry, but now they foamed down the long green hills and filled the river and flowed to the distant sea.

Our boat, which had no name, lay close to the Wessex bank. North across the river lay Mercia. Our bows pointed upstream. We were hidden beneath the leafless, bending branches of three willow trees, held there against the current by a leather mooring rope tied to one of those branches.

There were thirty-eight of us in that nameless boat, which was a trading ship that worked the upper reaches of the Temes. The ship's master was called Ralla and he stood beside me with one hand on the steering-oar. I could hardly see him in the darkness, but knew he wore a leather jerkin and had a sword at his side. The rest of us were in leather and mail, had helmets and carried shields, axes, swords or spears. Tonight we would kill.

Sihtric, my servant, squatted beside me and stroked a whetstone along the blade of his short-sword. 'She says she loves me,' he told me.

'Of course she says that,' I said.

He paused, and when he spoke again his voice had brightened, as though he had been encouraged by my words. 'And I must be nineteen by now, lord! Maybe even twenty?'

'Eighteen?' I suggested.

'I could have been married four years ago, lord!'

We spoke almost in whispers. The night was full of noises. The water rippled, the bare branches clattered in the wind, a night creature splashed into the river, a vixen howled like a dying soul, and somewhere an owl hooted. The boat creaked. Sihtric's stone hissed and scraped on the steel. A shield thumped against a rower's bench. I dared not speak louder, despite the night's noises, because the enemy ship was upstream of us and the men who had gone ashore from that ship would have left sentries on board. Those sentries might have seen us as we slipped downstream on the Mercian bank, but by now they would surely have thought we were long gone towards Lundene.

'But why marry a whore?' I asked Sihtric.

'She's . . .' Sihtric began.

'She's old,' I snarled, 'maybe thirty. And she's addled. Ealhswith only has to see a man and her thighs fly apart! If you lined up every man who'd tupped that whore you'd have an army big enough to conquer all Britain.' Beside me Ralla sniggered. 'You'd be in that army, Ralla?' I asked.

'Twenty times over, lord,' the shipmaster said.

'She loves me,' Sihtric spoke sullenly.

'She loves your silver,' I said, 'and besides, why put a new sword in an old scabbard?'

It is strange what men talk about before battle. Anything except what faces them. I have stood in a shield wall, staring

4

at an enemy bright with blades and dark with menace, and heard two of my men argue furiously about which tavern brewed the best ale. Fear hovers in the air like a cloud and we talk of nothing to pretend that the cloud is not there.

'Look for something ripe and young,' I advised Sihtric. 'That potter's daughter is ready to wed. She must be thirteen.'

'She's stupid,' Sihtric objected.

'And what are you, then?' I demanded. 'I give you silver and you pour it into the nearest open hole! Last time I saw her she was wearing an arm ring I gave you.'

He sniffed, said nothing. His father had been Kjartan the Cruel, a Dane who had whelped Sihtric on one of his Saxon slaves. Yet Sihtric was a good boy, though in truth he was no longer a boy. He was a man who had stood in the shield wall. A man who had killed. A man who would kill again tonight. 'I'll find you a wife,' I promised him.

It was then we heard the screaming. It was faint because it came from very far off, a mere scratching noise in the darkness that told of pain and death to our south. There were screams and shouting. Women were screaming and doubtless men were dying.

'God damn them,' Ralla said bitterly.

'That's our job,' I said curtly.

'We should . . .' Ralla started, then thought better of speaking. I knew what he was going to say, that we should have gone to the village and protected it, but he knew what I would have answered.

I would have told him that we did not know which village the Danes were going to attack, and even if I had known I would not have protected it. We might have shielded the place if we had known where the attackers were going. I could have placed all my household troops in the small houses and, the moment the raiders came, erupted into the street with sword, axe and spear, and we would have killed some of them, but

5

in the dark many more would have escaped and I did not want one to escape. I wanted every Dane, every Norseman, every raider dead. All of them, except one, and that one I would send eastwards to tell the Viking camps on the banks of the Temes that Uhtred of Bebbanburg was waiting for them.

'Poor souls,' Ralla muttered. To the south, through the tangle of black branches, I could see a red glow that betrayed burning thatch. The glow spread and grew brighter to lighten the winter sky beyond a row of coppiced trees. The glow reflected off my men's helmets, giving their metal a sheen of red, and I called for them to take the helmets off in case the enemy sentries in the large ship ahead saw the reflected glimmer.

I took off my own helmet with its silver wolf crest.

I am Uhtred, Lord of Bebbanburg, and in those days I was a lord of war. I stood there in mail and leather, cloaked and armed, young and strong. I had half my household troops in Ralla's ship while the other half were somewhere to the west, mounted on horses and under Finan's command.

Or I hoped they were waiting in the night-shrouded west. We in the ship had enjoyed the easier task, for we had slid down the dark river to find the enemy, while Finan had been forced to lead his men across night-black country. But I trusted Finan. He would be there, fidgeting, grimacing, waiting to unleash his sword.

This was not our first attempt in that long wet winter to set an ambush on the Temes, but it was the first that promised success. Twice before I had been told that Vikings had come through the gap in Lundene's broken bridge to raid the soft, plump villages of Wessex, and both times we had come downriver and found nothing. But this time we had trapped the wolves. I touched the hilt of Serpent-Breath, my sword, then touched the amulet of Thor's hammer that hung around my neck.

Kill them all, I prayed to Thor, kill them all but one.

It must have been cold in that long night. Ice skimmed the dips in the fields where the river had flooded, but I do not remember the cold. I remember the anticipation. I touched Serpent-Breath again and it seemed to me that she quivered. I sometimes thought that blade sang. It was a thin, half-heard song, a keening noise, the song of the blade wanting blood; the sword song.

We waited and, afterwards, when it was all over, Ralla told me I had never stopped smiling.

I thought our ambush would fail, for the raiders did not return to their ship till dawn blazed light across the east. Their sentries, I thought, must surely see us, but they did not. The drooping willow boughs served as a flimsy screen, or perhaps the rising winter sun dazzled them because no one saw us.

We saw them. We saw the mail-clad men herding a crowd of women and children across a rain-flooded pasture. I guessed there were fifty raiders and they had as many captives. The women would be the young ones from the burned village, and they had been taken for the raiders' pleasure. The children would go to the slave market in Lundene and from there across the sea to Frankia or even beyond. The women, once they had been used, would also be sold. We were not so close that we could hear the prisoners sobbing, but I imagined it. To the south, where low green hills swelled from the river's plain, a great drift of smoke dirtied the clear winter sky to mark where the raiders had burned the village.

Ralla stirred. 'Wait,' I murmured, and Ralla went still. He was a grizzled man, ten years older than I, with eyes reduced to slits from the long years of staring across sun-reflecting seas. He was a shipmaster, soldier and friend. 'Not yet,' I said softly, and touched Serpent-Breath and felt the quiver in the steel.

Men's voices were loud, relaxed and laughing. They shouted as they pushed their prisoners into the ship. They forced them to crouch in the cold flooded bilge so that the overloaded craft would be stable for its voyage through the downriver shallows, where the Temes raced across stone ledges and only the best and bravest shipmasters knew the channel. Then the warriors clambered aboard themselves. They took their plunder with them, the spits and cauldrons and ard-blades and knives and whatever else could be sold or melted or used. Their laughter was raucous. They were men who had slaughtered, and who would become rich on their prisoners and they were in a cheerful, careless mood.

And Serpent-Breath sang soft in her scabbard.

I heard the clatter from the other ship as the oars were thrust into their rowlocks. A voice called out a command. 'Push off!'

The great beak of the enemy ship, crowned with a monster's painted head, turned out into the river. Men shoved oar-blades against the bank, pushing the boat farther out. The ship was already moving, carried towards us by the spate-driven current. Ralla looked at me.

'Now,' I said. 'Cut the line!' I called, and Cerdic, in our bows, slashed through the leather rope tethering us to the willow. We were only using twelve oars and those now bit into the river as I pushed my way forward between the rowers' benches. 'We kill them all!' I shouted. 'We kill them all!'

'Pull!' Ralla roared, and the twelve men heaved on their oars to fight the river's power.

'We kill every last bastard!' I shouted as I climbed onto

the small bow platform where my shield waited. 'Kill them all! Kill them all!' I put on my helmet, then pushed my left forearm through the shield loops, hefted the heavy wood, and slid Serpent-Breath from her fleece-lined scabbard. She did not sing now. She screamed.

'Kill!' I shouted. 'Kill, kill, kill!' and the oars bit in time to my shouting. Ahead of us the enemy ship slewed in the river as panicked men missed their stroke. They were shouting, looking for shields, scrambling over the benches where a few men still tried to row. Women screamed and men tripped each other.

'Pull!' Ralla shouted. Our nameless ship surged into the current as the enemy was swept towards us. Her monster's head had a tongue painted red, white eyes, teeth like daggers.

'Now!' I called to Cerdic and he threw the grapnel with its chain so that it caught on the enemy ship's bow and he hauled on the chain to sink the grapnel's teeth into the ship's timber and so draw her closer.

'Now kill!' I shouted, and leaped across the gap.

Oh the joy of being young. Of being twenty-eight years old, of being strong, of being a lord of war. All gone now, just memory is left, and memories fade. But the joy is bedded in the memory.

Serpent-Breath's first stroke was a back-cut. I made it as I landed on the enemy's bow platform where a man was trying to tug the grapnel free, and Serpent-Breath took him in the throat with a cut so fast and hard that it half severed his head. His whole skull flopped backwards as blood brightened the winter day. Blood splashed on my face. I was death come from the morning, blood-spattered death in mail and black cloak and wolf-crested helmet.

I am old now. So old. My sight fades, my muscles are weak, my piss dribbles, my bones ache and I sit in the sun and fall asleep to wake tired. But I remember those fights,

9

those old fights. My newest wife, as pious a piece of stupid woman who ever whined, flinches when I tell the stories, but what else do the old have, but stories? She protested once, saying she did not want to know about heads flopping backwards in bright spraying blood, but how else are we to prepare our young for the wars they must fight? I have fought all my life. That was my fate, the fate of us all. Alfred wanted peace, but peace fled from him and the Danes came and the Norsemen came, and he had no choice but to fight. And when Alfred was dead and his kingdom was powerful, more Danes came, and more Norsemen, and the Britons came from Wales and the Scots howled down from the north, and what can a man do but fight for his land, his family, his home and his country? I look at my children and at their children and at their children's children and I know they will have to fight, and that so long as there is a family named Uhtred, and so long as there is a kingdom on this windswept island, there will be war. So we cannot flinch from war. We cannot hide from its cruelty, its blood, its stench, its vileness or its joy, because war will come to us whether we want it or not. War is fate, and wyrd bi∂ ful āræd. Fate is inescapable.

So I tell these stories so that my children's children will know their fate. My wife whimpers, but I make her listen. I tell her how our ship crashed into the enemy's outside flank, and how the impact drove that other ship's bows towards the southern bank. That was what I had wanted, and Ralla had achieved it perfectly. Now he scraped his ship down the enemy's hull, our impetus snapping the Dane's forward oars as my men jumped aboard, swords and axes swinging. I had staggered after that first cut, but the dead man had fallen off the platform to impede two others trying to reach me, and I shouted a challenge as I leaped down to face them. Serpent-Breath was lethal. She was, she is, a lovely blade, forged in the north by a Saxon smith who had known his trade. He had taken seven rods, four of iron and three of steel, and he had heated them and hammered them into one long two-edged blade with a leaf-shaped point. The four softer iron rods had been twisted in the fire and those twists survived in the blade as ghostly wisps of pattern that looked like the curling flame-breath of a dragon, and that was how Serpent-Breath had gained her name.

A bristle-bearded man swung an axe at me that I met with my out-thrust shield and slid the dragon-wisps into his belly. I gave a fierce twist with my right hand so that his dying flesh and guts did not grip the blade, then I yanked her out, more blood flying, and dragged the axe-impaled shield across my body to parry a sword cut. Sihtric was beside me, driving his short-sword up into my newest attacker's groin. The man screamed. I think I was shouting. More and more of my men were aboard now, swords and axes glinting. Children cried, women wailed, raiders died.

The bows of the enemy ship thumped onto the bank's mud while her stern began to swing outwards in the river's grip. Some of the raiders, sensing death if they stayed aboard, jumped ashore, and that started a panic. More and more leaped for the bank, and it was then Finan came from the west. There was a small mist on the river meadows, just a pearly skein drifting over the iced puddles, and through it came Finan's bright horsemen. They came in two lines, swords held like spears, and Finan, my deadly Irishman, knew his business and galloped the first line past the escaping men to cut off their retreat and let his second line crash into the enemy before he turned and led his own men back to the kill.

'Kill them all!' I shouted to him. 'Kill every last one!'

A wave of a blood-reddened sword was his reply. I saw

11

Clapa, my big Dane, spearing an enemy in the river's shallows. Rypere was hacking his sword at a cowering man. Sihtric's sword hand was red. Cerdic was swinging an axe, shouting incomprehensibly as the blade crushed and pierced a Dane's helmet to spill blood and brains on the terrified prisoners. I think I killed two more, though my memory is not certain. I do remember pushing a man down onto the deck and, as he twisted around to face me, sliding Serpent-Breath into his gullet and watching his face distort and his tongue protrude from the blood welling past his blackened teeth. I leaned on the blade as the man died and watched as Finan's men wheeled their horses to come back at the trapped enemy. The horsemen cut and slashed, Vikings screamed and some tried to surrender. One young man knelt on a rower's bench, axe and shield discarded, and held his hands to me in supplication. 'Pick up the axe,' I told him, speaking Danish.

'Lord . . .' he began.

'Pick it up!' I interrupted him, 'and watch for me in the corpse-hall.' I waited till he was armed, then let Serpent-Breath take his life. I did it fast, showing mercy by slicing his throat with one quick scraping drag. I looked into his eyes as I killed him, saw his soul fly, then stepped over his twitching body, which slipped off the rower's bench to collapse bloodily in the lap of a young woman who began to scream hysterically. 'Quiet!' I shouted at her. I scowled at all the other women and children screaming or weeping as they cowered in the bilge. I put Serpent-Breath into my shield hand, took hold of the mail collar of the dying man, and heaved him back onto the bench.

One child was not crying. He was a boy, perhaps nine or ten years old, and he was just staring at me, mouth agape, and I remembered myself at that age. What did that boy see? He saw a man of metal, for I had fought with the face-plates of my helmet closed. You see less with the plates hinged

12

across the cheeks, but the appearance is more frightening. That boy saw a tall man, mail-clad, sword bloody, steel-faced, stalking a boat of death. I eased off my helmet and shook my hair loose, then tossed him the wolf-crested metal. 'Look after it, boy,' I told him, then I gave Serpent-Breath to the girl who had been screaming. 'Wash the blade in river water,' I ordered her, 'and dry it on a dead man's cloak.' I gave my shield to Sihtric, then stretched my arms wide and lifted my face to the morning sun.

There had been fifty-four raiders, and sixteen still lived. They were prisoners. None had escaped past Finan's men. I drew Wasp-Sting, my short-sword that was so lethal in a shield wall fight when men are pressed close as lovers. 'Any of you,' I looked at the women, 'who wants to kill the man who raped you, then do it now!'

Two women wanted revenge and I let them use Wasp-Sting. Both of them butchered their victims. One stabbed repeatedly, the other hacked, and both men died slowly. Of the remaining fourteen men, one was not in mail. He was the enemy's shipmaster. He was grey-haired with a scanty beard and brown eyes that looked at me belligerently. 'Where did you come from?' I asked him.

He thought about refusing to answer, then thought better. 'Beamfleot,' he said.

'And Lundene?' I asked him. 'The old city is still in Danish hands?'

'Yes.'

'Yes, lord,' I corrected him.

'Yes, lord,' he conceded.

'Then you will go to Lundene,' I told him, 'and then to Beamfleot, and then to anywhere you wish, and you will tell the Northmen that Uhtred of Bebbanburg guards the River Temes. And you will tell them they are welcome to come here whenever they wish.'

13

That one man lived. I hacked off his right hand before letting him go. I did it so he could never wield a sword again. By then we had lit a fire and I thrust his bleeding stump into the red-hot embers to seal the wound. He was a brave man. He flinched when we cauterised his stump, but he did not scream as his blood bubbled and his flesh sizzled. I wrapped his shortened arm in a piece of cloth taken from a dead man's shirt. 'Go,' I ordered him, pointing downriver. 'Just go.' He walked eastwards. If he were lucky he would survive the journey to spread the news of my savagery.

We killed the others, all of them.

'Why did you kill them?' my new wife asked once, distaste for my thoroughness evident in her voice.

'So they would learn to fear,' I answered her, 'of course.'

'Dead men can't fear,' she said.

I try to be patient with her. 'A ship left Beamfleot,' I explained, 'and it never went back. And other men who wanted to raid Wessex heard of that ship's fate. And those men decided to take their swords somewhere else. I killed that ship's crew to save myself having to kill hundreds of other Danes.'

'The Lord Jesus would have wanted you to show mercy,' she said, her eyes wide.

She is an idiot.

Finan took some of the villagers back to their burned homes where they dug graves for their dead while my men hanged the corpses of our enemies from trees beside the river. We made ropes from strips torn from their clothes. We took their mail, their weapons and their arm rings. We cut off their long hair, for I liked to caulk my ships' planks with the hair of slain enemies, and then we hanged them and their pale naked bodies twisted in the small wind as the ravens came to take their dead eyes.

Fifty-three bodies hung by the river. A warning to those who might follow. Fifty-three signals that other raiders were risking death by rowing up the Temes.

Then we went home, taking the enemy ship with us.

And Serpent-Breath slept in her scabbard.

PART ONE

The Bride

One

'The dead speak,' Æthelwold told me. He was sober for once. Sober and awed and serious. The night wind snatched at the house and the rushlights flickered red in the wintry draughts that whipped from the roof's smoke-hole and through the doors and shutters.

'The dead speak?' I asked.

'A corpse,' Æthelwold said, 'he rises from the grave and he speaks.' He stared at me wide-eyed, then nodded as if to stress that he spoke the truth. He was leaning towards me, his clasped hands fidgeting between his knees. 'I have seen it,' he added.

'A corpse talks?' I asked.

'He rises!' He wafted a hand to show what he meant.

'He?'

'The dead man. He rises and he speaks.' He still stared at me, his expression indignant. 'It's true,' he added in a voice that suggested he knew I did not believe him.

I edged my bench closer to the hearth. It was ten days after I had killed the raiders and hanged their bodies by the river, and now a freezing rain rattled on the thatch and beat on the barred shutters. Two of my hounds lay in front of

19

the fire and one gave me a resentful glance when I scraped the bench, then rested his head again. The house had been built by the Romans, which meant the floor was tiled and the walls were of stone, though I had thatched the roof myself. Rain spat through the smoke-hole. 'What does the dead man say?' Gisela asked. She was my wife and the mother of my two children.

Æthelwold did not answer at once, perhaps because he believed a woman should not take part in a serious discussion, but my silence told him that Gisela was welcome to speak in her own house and he was too nervous to insist that I dismiss her. 'He says I should be king,' he admitted softly, then gazed at me, fearing my reaction.

'King of what?' I asked flatly.

'Wessex,' he said, 'of course.'

'Oh, Wessex,' I said, as though I had never heard of the place.

'And I should be king!' Æthelwold protested. 'My father was king!'

'And now your father's brother is king,' I said, 'and men say he is a good king.'

'Do you say that?' he challenged me.

I did not answer. It was well enough known that I did not like Alfred and that Alfred did not like me, but that did not mean Alfred's nephew, Æthelwold, would make a better king. Æthelwold, like me, was in his late twenties, and he had made a reputation as a drunk and a lecherous fool. Yet he did have a claim to the throne of Wessex. His father had indeed been king, and if Alfred had possessed a thimbleful of sense he would have had his nephew's throat sliced to the bone. Instead Alfred relied on Æthelwold's thirst for ale to keep him from making trouble. 'Where did you see this living corpse?' I asked, instead of answering his question.

He waved a hand towards the north side of the house. 'On the other side of the street,' he said. 'Just the other side.'

'Wæclingastræt?' I asked him, and he nodded.

So he was talking to the Danes as well as to the dead. Wæclingastræt is a road that goes north-west from Lundene. It slants across Britain, ending at the Irish Sea just north of Wales, and everything to the south of the street was supposedly Saxon land, and everything to the north was yielded to the Danes. That was the peace we had in that year of 885, though it was a peace scummed with skirmish and hate. 'Is it a Danish corpse?' I asked.

Æthelwold nodded. 'His name is Bjorn,' he said, 'and he was a skald in Guthrum's court, and he refused to become a Christian so Guthrum killed him. He can be summoned from his grave. I've seen it.'

I looked at Gisela. She was a Dane, and the sorcery that Æthelwold described was nothing I had ever known among my fellow Saxons. Gisela shrugged, suggesting that the magic was equally strange to her. 'Who summons the dead man?' she asked.

'A fresh corpse,' Æthelwold said.

'A fresh corpse?' I asked.

'Someone must be sent to the world of the dead,' he explained, as though it were obvious, 'to find Bjorn and bring him back.'

'So they kill someone?' Gisela asked.

'How else can they send a messenger to the dead?' Æthelwold asked pugnaciously.

'And this Bjorn,' I asked, 'does he speak English?' I put the question for I knew that Æthelwold spoke little or no Danish.

'He speaks English,' Æthelwold said sullenly. He did not like being questioned.

21

'Who took you to him?' I asked.

'Some Danes,' he said vaguely.

I sneered at that. 'So some Danes came,' I said, 'and told you a dead poet wanted to speak to you, and you meekly travelled into Guthrum's land?'

'They paid me gold,' he said defensively. Æthelwold was ever in debt.

'And why come to us?' I asked. Æthelwold did not answer. He fidgeted and watched Gisela, who was teasing a thread of wool onto her distaff. 'You go to Guthrum's land,' I persisted, 'you speak to a dead man, and then you come to me. Why?'

'Because Bjorn said you will be a king too,' Æthelwold said. He had not spoken loudly, but even so I held up a hand to hush him and I looked anxiously at the doorway as if expecting to see a spy listening from the darkness of the next room. I had no doubt Alfred had spies in my household and I thought I knew who they were, but I was not entirely certain that I had identified all of them, which was why I had made sure all the servants were well away from the room where Æthelwold and I talked. Even so it was not wise to say such things too loudly.

Gisela had stopped spinning the wool and was staring at Æthelwold. I was too. 'He said what?' I asked.

'He said that you, Uhtred,' Æthelwold went on more quietly, 'will be crowned King of Mercia.'

'Have you been drinking?' I asked.

'No,' he said, 'only ale.' He leaned towards me. 'Bjorn the Dead wishes to speak to you also, to tell you your fate. You and me, Uhtred, will be kings and neighbours. The gods want it and they sent a dead man to tell me so.' Æthelwold was shaking slightly, and sweating, but he was not drinking. Something had scared him into sobriety, and that convinced me he spoke the truth. 'They want to know if you are willing to meet the dead,' he said, 'and if you are then they will send for you.'

I looked at Gisela who merely looked back at me, her face expressionless. I stared back at her, not waiting for a response, but because she was beautiful, so beautiful. My dark Dane, my lovely Gisela, my bride, my love. She must have known what I was thinking, for her long, grave face was transformed by a slow smile. 'Uhtred is to be king?' she asked, breaking the silence and looking at Æthelwold.

'The dead say so,' Æthelwold said defiantly. 'And Bjorn heard it from the three sisters.' He meant the Fates, the Norns, the three sisters who weave our destiny.

'Uhtred is to be King of Mercia?' Gisela asked dubiously.

'And you will be the queen,' Æthelwold said.

Gisela looked back to me. She had a quizzical look, but I did not try to answer what I knew she was thinking. Instead I was reflecting that there was no king in Mercia. The old one, a Saxon mongrel on a Danish leash, had died, and there was no successor, while the kingdom itself was now split between Danes and Saxons. My mother's brother had been an ealdorman in Mercia before he was killed by the Welsh, so I had Mercian blood. And there was no king in Mercia.

'I think you had better hear what the dead man says,' Gisela spoke gravely.

'If they send for me,' I promised, 'I will.' And so I would, because a dead man was speaking and he wanted me to be a king.

Alfred arrived a week later. It was a fine day with a pale blue sky in which the midday sun hung low above a cold land. Ice edged the sluggish channels where the River Temes

23

flowed about Sceaftes Eye and Wodenes Eye. Coot, moorhen and dabchicks paddled at the edge of the ice, while on the thawing mud of Sceaftes Eye a host of thrush and black-birds hunted for worms and snails.

This was home. This had been my home for two years now. Home was Coccham, at the edge of Wessex where the Temes flowed towards Lundene and the sea. I, Uhtred, a Northumbrian lord, an exile and a warrior, had become a builder, a trader and a father. I served Alfred, King of Wessex, not because I wished to, but because I had given him my oath.

And Alfred had given me a task; to build his new burh at Coccham. A burh was a town turned into a fortress and Alfred was riveting his kingdom of Wessex with such places. All around the boundaries of Wessex, on the sea, on the rivers and on the moors facing the wild Cornish savages, the walls were being built. A Danish army could invade between the fortresses, but they would discover still more strongholds in Alfred's heartland, and each burh held a garrison. Alfred, in a rare moment of savage elation, had described the burhs to me as wasps' nests from which men could swarm to sting the attacking Danes. Burhs were being made at Exanceaster and Werham, at Cisseceastre and Hastengas, at Æscengum and Oxnaforda, at Cracgelad and Wæced, and at dozens of places between. Their walls and palisades were manned by spears and shields. Wessex was becoming a land of fortresses, and my task was to make the little town of Coccham into a burh.

The work was done by every West Saxon man over the age of twelve. Half of them worked while the other half tended the fields. At Coccham I was supposed to have five hundred men serving at any one time, though usually there were fewer than three hundred. They dug, they banked, they cut timber for walls, and so we had raised a stronghold on the banks of the Temes. In truth it was two strongholds, one on the river's southern bank and the other on Sceaftes Eye, which was an island splitting the river into two channels, and in that January of 885 the work was nearly done and no Danish ship could now row upstream to raid the farms and villages along the river's bank. They could try, but they must pass my new ramparts and know that my troops would follow them, trap them ashore and kill them.

A Danish trader called Ulf had come that morning, tying his boat at the wharf on Sceaftes Eye where one of my officials prodded through the cargo to assess the tax. Ulf himself, grinning toothlessly, climbed up to greet me. He gave me a piece of amber wrapped in kidskin. 'For the Lady Gisela, lord,' he said. 'She is well?'

'She is,' I said, touching Thor's hammer that hung around my neck.

'And you have a second child, I hear?'

'A girl,' I said, 'and where did you hear of her?'

'Beamfleot,' he said, which made sense. Ulf was a northerner, but no ships were making the voyage from Northumbria to Wessex in the depth of this cold winter. He must have spent the season in southern East Anglia, on the long intricate mudflats of the Temes estuary. 'It isn't much,' he said, gesturing at his cargo. 'I bought some hides and axe blades in Grantaceaster and thought I'd come upriver to see if you Saxons have any money left.'

'You came upriver,' I told him, 'to see whether we'd finished the fortress. You're a spy, Ulf, and I think I'll hang you from a tree.'

'No, you won't,' he said, unmoved by my words.

'I'm bored,' I said, putting the amber into my pouch, 'and watching a Dane twitch on a rope would be amusing, wouldn't it?'

25

'You must have been laughing when you hanged Jarrel's crew then,' he said.

'Was that who it was?' I asked. 'Jarrel? I didn't ask his name.'

'I saw thirty bodies,' Ulf said, jerking his head downstream, 'maybe more? All hanging from trees and I thought, that looks like Lord Uhtred's work.'

'Only thirty?' I said, 'there were fifty-three. I should add your miserable corpse, Ulf, to help make up the numbers.'

'You don't want me,' Ulf said cheerfully, 'you want a young one, because young ones twitch more than us old ones.' He peered down at his boat and spat towards a red-haired boy who was staring vacantly across the river. 'You could hang that little bastard. He's my wife's oldest boy and nothing but a piece of toad gristle. He'll twitch.'

'So who's in Lundene these days?' I asked.

'Earl Haesten's in and out,' Ulf said, 'more in than out.'

I was surprised by that. I knew Haesten. He was a young Dane who had once been my oath-man, but who had broken his oath and now aspired to be a warrior lord. He called himself an earl, which amused me, but I was surprised he had gone to Lundene. I knew he had made a walled camp on the coast of East Anglia, but now he had moved much closer to Wessex, which suggested he was looking for trouble. 'So what's he doing?' I asked scornfully, 'stealing his neighbours' ducks?'

Ulf drew in a breath and shook his head. 'He's got allies, lord.'

Something in his tone made me wary. 'Allies?'

'The Thurgilson brothers,' Ulf said, and touched his hammer amulet.

The name meant nothing to me then. 'Thurgilson?'

'Sigefrid and Erik,' Elf said, still touching the hammer. 'Norse earls, lord.'

26

That was something new. The Norse did not usually come to East Anglia or to Wessex. We often heard tales of their raids in the Scottish lands and in Ireland, but Norse chieftains rarely came close to Wessex. 'What are Norsemen doing in Lundene?' I asked.

'They got there two days ago, lord,' Ulf said, 'with twenty-two keels. Haesten went with them, and he took nine ships.'

I whistled softly. Thirty-one ships was a fleet and it meant the brothers and Haesten together commanded an army of at least a thousand men. And those men were in Lundene and Lundene was on the frontier of Wessex.

Lundene was a strange city back then. Officially it was part of Mercia, but Mercia had no king and so Lundene had no ruler. It was neither Saxon nor Dane, but a mix of both, and a place where a man could become rich, dead, or both. It stood where Mercia, East Anglia and Wessex met, a city of merchants, tradesmen and seafarers. And now, if Ulf was right, it had an army of Vikings within its walls.

Ulf chuckled. 'They've got you stopped up like a rat in a sack, lord.'

I wondered how a fleet had gathered and ridden the tide upstream to Lundene without my finding out long before it sailed. Coccham was the nearest burh to Lundene and I usually knew what happened there within a day, but now an enemy had occupied the city and I had known nothing about it. 'Did the brothers send you to tell me this?' I asked Ulf. I was assuming that the Thurgilson brothers and Haesten had only captured Lundene so that someone, probably Alfred, would pay them to go away. In which case it served their interest to let us know of their arrival.

Ulf shook his head. 'I sailed as they arrived, lord. Bad enough having to pay you duty without giving half my goods to them.' He shuddered. 'The Earl Sigefrid's a bad man, lord. Not someone to do business with.'

'Why didn't I know they were with Haesten?' I asked.

'They weren't. They've been in Frankia. Sailed straight across the sea and up the river.'

'With twenty-two ships of Norsemen,' I said bitterly.

'They've got everything, lord,' Ulf said. 'Danes, Frisians, Saxons, Norse, everything. Sigefrid finds men wherever the gods shake out their shit-pots. They're hungry men, lord. Masterless men. Rogues. They come from all over.'

The masterless man was the worst kind. He owed no allegiance. He had nothing but his sword, his hunger and his ambition. I had been such a man in my time. 'So Sigefrid and Erik will be trouble?' I suggested mildly.

'Sigefrid will,' Ulf said. 'Erik? He's the younger. Men speak well of him, but Sigefrid can't wait for trouble.'

'He wants ransom?' I asked.

'He might,' Ulf said dubiously. 'He's got to pay all those men, and he got nothing but mouse droppings in Frankia. But who'll pay him ransom? Lundene belongs to Mercia, doesn't it?'

'It does,' I said.

'And there's no king in Mercia,' Ulf said. 'Isn't natural, is it? A kingdom without a king.'

I thought of Æthelwold's visit and touched my amulet of Thor's hammer. 'Have you ever heard of the dead being raised?' I asked Ulf.

'The dead being raised?' He stared at me, alarmed, and touched his own hammer amulet. 'The dead are best left in Niflheim, lord.'

'An old magic, perhaps?' I suggested. 'Raising the dead?'

'You hear tales,' Ulf said, now gripping his amulet tightly.

'What tales?'

'From the far north, lord. From the land of ice and birch. Strange things happen there. They say men can fly in the darkness, and I did hear that the dead walk on the frozen

28

seas, but I never saw such a thing.' He raised the amulet to his lips and kissed it. 'I reckon they're just stories to scare children on winter nights, lord.'

'Maybe,' I said, and turned as a boy came running along the foot of the newly raised wall. He jumped the timbers that would eventually make the fighting platform, skidded in a piece of mud, clambered up the bank and then stood, panting too hard to be able to speak. I waited until he caught his breath. '*Haligast*, lord,' he said, '*Haligast!*'

Ulf looked at me quizzically. Like all traders he spoke some English, but haligast puzzled him. 'The Holy Ghost,' I translated into Danish.

'Coming, lord,' the boy gasped excitedly and pointed upriver. 'Coming now!'

'The Holy Ghost is coming?' Ulf asked in alarm. He probably had no idea what the Holy Ghost was, but he knew enough to fear all spectres, and my recent question about the living dead had scared him.

'Alfred's ship,' I explained, then turned back to the boy. 'Is the king on board?'

'His flag's flying, lord.'

'Then he is,' I said.

Ulf pulled his tunic straight. 'Alfred? What does he want?'

'He wants to discover my loyalties,' I said drily.

Ulf grinned. 'So you might be the one who twitches on a rope, eh, lord?'

'I need axe-heads,' I told him. 'Take your best ones to the house and we'll discuss a price later.'

I was not surprised by Alfred's arrival. In those years he spent much of his time travelling between the growing burhs to inspect the work. He had been to Coccham a dozen times in as many months, but this visit, I reckoned, was not to examine the walls, but to find out why Æthelwold had come

29

to see me. The king's spies had done their work, and so the king had come to question me.

His ship was coming fast, carried by the Temes's winter flow. In the cold months it was quicker to travel by ship, and Alfred liked the *Haligast* because it enabled him to work on board as he journeyed along the northern frontier of Wessex. The *Haligast* had twenty oars and room enough for half Alfred's bodyguard and the inevitable troop of priests. The king's banner, a green dragon, flew from the masthead, while two flags hung from the cross spar, which would have held a sail if the ship had been at sea. One flag showed a saint, while the other was a green cloth embroidered with a white cross. At the ship's stern was a small cabin that cramped the steersman, but provided Alfred a place to keep his desk. A second ship, the *Heofonhlaf*, carried the rest of the bodyguard and still more priests. *Heofonhlaf* meant bread of heaven. Alfred never could name a ship.

Heofonhlaf berthed first and a score of men in mail, carrying shields and spears, clambered ashore to line the wooden wharf. The *Haligast* followed, her steersman thumping the bow hard on a piling so that Alfred, who was waiting amidships, staggered. There were kings who might have disembowelled a steersman for that loss of dignity, but Alfred seemed not to notice. He was talking earnestly with a thin-faced, scrape-chinned, pale-cheeked monk. It was Asser of Wales. I had heard that Brother Asser was the king's new pet, and I knew he hated me, which was only right because I hated him. I still smiled at him and he twitched away as if I had just vomited down his robe, bending his head closer to Alfred who could have been his twin, for Alfred of Wessex looked much more like a priest than a king. He wore a long black cloak and a growing baldness gave him the tonsured look of a monk. His hands, like a clerk's, were always ink-stained, while his bony face was lean and serious and earnest and pale. His beard was thin. He often went clean-shaven, but now had a beard streaked thick with white hairs.

Crewmen secured the *Haligast*, then Alfred took Asser's elbow and stepped ashore with him. The Welshman wore an oversized cross on his chest and Alfred touched it briefly before turning to me. 'My lord Uhtred,' he said enthusiastically. He was being unusually pleasant, not because he was glad to see me, but because he thought I was plotting treason. There was little other reason for me to sup with his nephew Æthelwold.

'My lord King,' I said, and bowed to him. I ignored Brother Asser. The Welshman had once accused me of piracy, murder, and a dozen other things, and most of his accusations had been accurate, but I was still alive. He shot me a dismissive glance, then scuttled off through the mud, evidently going to make certain that the nuns in Coccham's convent were not pregnant, drunk or happy.

Alfred, followed by Egwine, who now commanded the household troops, and by six of those troops, walked along my new battlements. He glanced at Ulf's ship, but said nothing. I knew I had to tell him of the capture of Lundene, but I decided to let that news wait until he had asked his questions of me. For now he was content to inspect the work we had been doing and he found nothing to criticise, nor did he expect to. Coccham's burh was far more advanced than any of the others. The next fort west on the Temes, at Welengaford, had scarcely broken ground, let alone built a palisade, while the walls at Oxnaforda had slumped into their ditch after a week of violent rain just before Yule. Coccham's burh, though, was almost finished. 'I am told,' Alfred said, 'that the fyrd is reluctant to work. You have not found that true?'

The fyrd was the army, raised from the shire, and the fyrd not only built the burhs, but formed their garrisons. 'The fyrd are very reluctant to work, lord,' I said.

'Yet you have almost finished?'

I smiled. 'I hanged ten men,' I said, 'and it encouraged the rest to enthusiasm.'

He stopped at a place where he could stare downriver. Swans made the view lovely. I watched him. The lines on his face were deeper and his skin paler. He looked ill, but then Alfred of Wessex was always a sick man. His stomach hurt and his bowels hurt, and I saw a grimace as a stab of pain lanced through him. 'I heard,' he spoke coldly, 'that you hanged them without benefit of trial?'

'I did, lord, yes.'

'There are laws in Wessex,' he said sternly.

'And if the burh isn't built,' I said, 'then there will be no Wessex.'

'You like to defy me,' he said mildly.

'No, lord, I swore an oath to you. I do your work.'

'Then hang no more men without a fair trial,' he said sharply, then turned and stared across the river to the Mercian bank. 'A king must bring justice, Lord Uhtred. That is a king's job. And if a land has no king, how can there be law?' He still spoke mildly, but he was testing me, and for a moment I felt alarm. I had assumed he had come to discover what Æthelwold had said to me, but his mention of Mercia, and of its lack of a king, suggested he already knew what had been discussed on that night of cold wind and hard rain. 'There are men,' he went on, still staring at the Mercian bank, 'who would like to be King of Mercia.' He paused and I was certain he knew everything that Æthelwold had said to me, but then he betrayed his ignorance. 'My nephew Æthelwold?' he suggested.

I gave a burst of laughter that was made too loud by my relief. 'Æthelwold!' I said. 'He doesn't want to be King of Mercia! He wants your throne, lord.'

'He told you that?' he asked sharply.

'Of course he told me that,' I said. 'He tells everyone that!'

'Is that why he came to see you?' Alfred asked, unable to hide his curiosity any longer.

'He came to buy a horse, lord,' I lied. 'He wants my stallion, Smoca, and I told him no.' Smoca's hide was an unusual mix of grey and black, thus his name, Smoke, and he had won every race he had ever run in his life and, better, was not afraid of men, shields, weapons or noise. I could have sold Smoca to any warrior in Britain.

'And he talked of wanting to be king?' Alfred asked suspiciously.

'Of course he did.'

'You didn't tell me at the time,' he said reproachfully.

'If I told you every time Æthelwold talked treason,' I said, 'you'd never cease to hear from me. What I tell you now is that you should slice his head off.'

'He is my nephew,' Alfred said stiffly, 'and has royal blood.'

'He still has a removable head,' I insisted.

He waved a petulant hand as if my idea were risible. 'I thought of making him king in Mercia,' he said, 'but he would lose the throne.'

'He would,' I agreed.

'He's weak,' Alfred said scornfully, 'and Mercia needs a strong ruler. Someone to frighten the Danes.' I confess at that moment I thought he meant me and I was ready to thank him, even fall to my knees and take his hand, but then he enlightened me. 'Your cousin, I think.'

'Æthelred!' I asked, unable to hide my scorn. My cousin was a bumptious little prick, full of his own importance, but he was also close to Alfred. So close that he was going to marry Alfred's elder daughter.

'He can be ealdorman in Mercia,' Alfred said, 'and rule with my blessing.' In other words my miserable cousin would govern Mercia on Alfred's leash and, if I am truthful, that was a better solution for Alfred than letting someone like me take Mercia's throne. Æthelred, married to Æthelflaed, was more likely to be Alfred's man, and Mercia, or at least that part of it south of Wæclingastræt, would be like a province of Wessex.

'If my cousin,' I said, 'is to be Lord of Mercia, then he'll be Lord of Lundene?'

'Of course.'

'Then he has a problem, lord,' I said, and I confess I spoke with some pleasure at the prospect of my pompous cousin having to deal with a thousand rogues commanded by Norse earls. 'A fleet of thirty-one ships arrived in Lundene two days ago,' I went on. 'The Earls Sigefrid and Erik Thurgilson command them. Haesten of Beamfleot is an ally. So far as I know, lord, Lundene now belongs to Norsemen and Danes.'

For a moment Alfred said nothing, but just stared at the swan-haunted floodwaters. He looked paler than ever. His jaw clenched. 'You sound pleased,' he said bitterly.

'I do not mean to, lord,' I said.

'How in God's name can that happen?' he demanded angrily. He turned and gazed at the burh's walls. 'The Thurgilson brothers were in Frankia,' he said. I might never have heard of Sigefrid and Erik, but Alfred made it his business to know where the Viking bands were roving.

'They're in Lundene now,' I said remorselessly.

He fell silent again, and I knew what he was thinking. He was thinking that the Temes is our road to other kingdoms, to the rest of the world, and if the Danes and the Norse block the Temes, then Wessex was cut off from much of the world's trade. Of course there were other ports and other rivers, but the Temes is the great river that sucks in vessels from all the wide seas. 'Do they want money?' he asked bitterly.

'That is Mercia's problem, lord,' I suggested.

'Don't be a fool!' he snapped at me. 'Lundene might be in Mercia, but the river belongs to both of us.' He turned around again, staring downriver almost as though he expected to see the masts of Norse ships appearing in the distance. 'If they will not go,' he said quietly, 'then they will have to be expelled.'

'Yes, lord.'

'And that,' he said decisively, 'will be my wedding gift to your cousin.'

'Lundene?'

'And you will provide it,' he said savagely. 'You will restore Lundene to Mercian rule, Lord Uhtred. Let me know by the Feast of Saint David what force you will need to secure the gift.' He frowned, thinking. 'Your cousin will command the army, but he is too busy to plan the campaign. You will make the necessary preparations and advise him.'

'I will?' I asked sourly.

'Yes,' he said, 'you will.'

He did not stay to eat. He said prayers in the church, gave silver to the nunnery, then embarked on *Haligast* and vanished upstream.

And I was to capture Lundene and give all the glory to my cousin Æthelred.

The summons to meet the dead came two weeks later and took me by surprise.

Each morning, unless the snow was too thick for easy travel, a crowd of petitioners waited at my gate. I was the ruler in Coccham, the man who dispensed justice, and Alfred had granted me that power, knowing it was essential if his burh was to be built. He had given me more. I was entitled to a tenth part of every harvest in northern Berrocscire, I was given pigs and cattle and grain, and from that income I paid for the timber that made the walls and the weapons that guarded them. There was opportunity in that, and Alfred suspected me, which is why he had given me a sly priest called Wulfstan, whose task was to make sure I did not steal too much. Yet it was Wulfstan who stole. He had come to me in the summer, half grinning, and pointed out that the dues we collected from the merchants who used the river were unpredictable, which meant Alfred could never estimate whether we were keeping proper accounts. He waited for my approval and got a thump about his tonsured skull instead. I sent him to Alfred under guard with a letter describing his dishonesty, and then I stole the dues myself. The priest had been a fool. You never, ever, tell others of your crimes, not unless they are so big as to be incapable of concealment, and then you describe them as policy or statecraft.

I did not steal much, no more than another man in my position would put aside, and the work on the burh's walls proved to Alfred that I was doing my job. I have always loved building and life has few ordinary pleasures greater than chatting with the skilled men who split, shape and join timbers. I dispensed justice too, and I did that well, because my father, who had been Lord of Bebbanburg in Northumbria, had taught me that a lord's duty was to the folk he ruled, and that they would forgive a lord many sins so long as he protected them. So each day I would listen to misery, and some two weeks after Alfred's visit I remember a morning of spitting rain in which some two dozen folk knelt to me in the mud outside my hall. I cannot remember all the petitions now, but doubtless they were the usual complaints of boundary stones being moved or of a marriage-price unpaid. I made my decisions swiftly, gauging my judgments by the demeanour of the petitioners. I usually reckoned a defiant petitioner was probably lying, while a tearful one elicited my pity. I doubt I got every decision right, but folk were content enough with my judgments and they knew I did not take bribes to favour the wealthy.

I do remember one petitioner that morning. He was solitary, which was unusual, for most folk arrived with friends or relatives to swear the truth of their complaints, but this man came alone and continually allowed others to get ahead of him. He plainly wanted to be the last to talk to me, and I suspected he wanted a lot of my time and I was tempted to end the morning session without granting him audience, but in the end I let him speak and he was mercifully brief.

'Bjorn has disturbed my land, lord,' he said. He was kneeling and all I could see of him was his tangled and dirt-crusted hair.

For a moment I did not recognise the name. 'Bjorn?' I demanded. 'Who is Bjorn?'

'The man who disturbs my land, lord, in the night.'

'A Dane?' I asked, puzzled.

'He comes from his grave, lord,' the man said, and I understood then and hushed him to silence so that the priest who noted down my judgments would not learn too much.

I tipped up the petitioner's head to see a scrawny face. By his tongue I reckoned him for a Saxon, but perhaps he was a Dane who spoke our tongue perfectly, so I tried him in Danish. 'Where have you come from?' I asked.

'From the disturbed ground, lord,' he answered in Danish, but it was obvious from the way he mangled the words that he was no Dane.

'Beyond the street?' I spoke English again.

'Yes, lord,' he said.

'And when does Bjorn disturb your land again?'

'The day after tomorrow, lord. He will come after moonrise.'

'You are sent to guide me?'

'Yes, lord.'

We rode next day. Gisela wanted to come, but I would not allow her for I did not wholly trust the summons, and because of that mistrust I rode with six men; Finan, Clapa, Sihtric, Rypere, Eadric and Cenwulf. The last three were Saxons, Clapa and Sihtric were Danes, and Finan was the fiery Irishman who commanded my household troops, and all six were my oath-men. My life was theirs as theirs was mine. Gisela stayed behind Coccham's walls, guarded by the fyrd and by the remainder of my household troops.

We rode in mail and we carried weapons. We went west and north first because the Temes was winter swollen and we had to ride a long way upstream to find a ford shallow enough to be crossed. That was at Welengaford, another burh, and I noted how the earth walls were unfinished and how the timber to make the palisades lay rotting and untrimmed in the mud. The commander of the garrison, a man named Oslac, wanted to know why we crossed the river, and it was his right to know because he guarded this part of the frontier between Wessex and lawless Mercia. I said a fugitive had fled Coccham and was thought to be skulking on the Temes's northern bank, and Oslac believed the tale. It would reach Alfred soon enough.

The man who had brought the summons was our guide. He was called Huda and he told me he served a Dane named Eilaf who had an estate that bordered the eastern side of Wæclingastræt. That made Eilaf an East Anglian and a subject of King Guthrum. 'Is Eilaf a Christian?' I asked Huda.

'We are all Christians, lord,' Huda said, 'King Guthrum demands it.'

'So what does Eilaf wear about his neck?' I asked.

'The same as you, lord,' he said. I wore Thor's hammer because I was no Christian and Huda's answer told me that Eilaf, like me, worshipped the older gods, though to please his king, Guthrum, he pretended to a belief in the Christian god. I had known Guthrum in the days when he had led great armies to attack Wessex, but he was getting old now. He had adopted his enemy's religion and it seemed he no longer wanted to rule all Britain, but was content with the wide fertile fields of East Anglia as his kingdom. Yet there were many in his lands who were not content. Sigefrid, Erik, Haesten, and probably Eilaf. They were Norsemen and Danes, they were warriors, they sacrificed to Thor and to Odin, they kept their swords sharp and they dreamed, as all Northmen dream, of the richer lands of Wessex.

We rode through Mercia, the land without a king, and I noted how many farmsteads had been burned so that the only trace of their existence was now a patch of scorched earth where weeds grew. More weeds smothered what had been ploughland. Hazel saplings had invaded the pastures. Where folk did still live, they lived in fear and when they saw us coming they ran to the woodlands, or else shut themselves behind palisades. 'Who rules here?' I asked Huda.

'Danes,' he said, then jerked his head westwards, 'Saxons over there.'

'Eilaf doesn't want this land?'

'He has much of it, lord,' Huda said, 'but the Saxons harass him.'

According to the treaty between Alfred and Guthrum this land was Saxon, but the Danes are land hungry and Guthrum could not control all his thegns. So this was battle land, a place where both sides fought a sullen, small and endless war, and the Danes were offering me its crown.

I am a Saxon. A northerner. I am Uhtred of Bebbanburg, but I had been raised by the Danes and I knew their ways.

I spoke their tongue, I had married a Dane, and I worshipped their gods. If I were to be king here then the Saxons would know they had a Saxon ruler while the Danes would accept me because I had been as a son to Earl Ragnar. But to be king here was to turn on Alfred and, if the dead man had spoken truly, to put Alfred's drunken nephew on the throne of Wessex, and how long would Æthelwold last? Less than a year, I reckoned, before the Danes killed him, and then all England would be under Danish rule except for Mercia where I, a Saxon who thought like a Dane, would be king. And how long would the Danes tolerate me?

'Do you want to be a king?' Gisela had asked me the night before we rode.

'I never thought I did,' I answered cautiously.

'Then why go?'

I had stared into the fire. 'Because the dead man brings a message from the Fates,' I told her.

She had touched her amulet. 'The Fates can't be avoided,' she said softly. Wyrd bi∂ ful āræd.

'So I must go,' I said, 'because fate demands it. And because I want to see a dead man talk.'

'And if the dead man says you are to be a king?'

'Then you will be a queen,' I said.

'And you will fight Alfred?' Gisela asked.

'If the Fates say so,' I said.

'And your oath to him?'

'The Fates know that answer,' I said, 'but I don't.'

And now we rode beneath beech-covered hills that slanted east and north. We spent the night in a deserted farm and one of us was always awake. Nothing disturbed us and, in the dawn, under a sky the colour of sword-steel, we rode on. Huda led, mounted on one of my horses. I talked to him for a while to discover that he was a huntsman and that he had served a Saxon lord killed by Eilaf, and that he reckoned himself content under the Dane's lordship. His replies became surlier and shorter as we neared Wæclingastræt so, after a while, I dropped back to ride beside Finan. 'Trust him?' Finan asked, nodding at Huda.

I shrugged. 'His master does Sigefrid and Haesten's bidding,' I said, 'and I know Haesten. I saved his life and that means something.'

Finan thought about it. 'You saved his life? How?'

'I rescued him from some Frisians. He became my oathman.'

'And broke his oath?'

'He did.'

'So Haesten can't be trusted,' Finan said firmly. I said nothing. Three deer stood poised for flight at the far side of a bare pasture. We rode on an overgrown track beside a hedgerow where crocuses grew. 'What they want,' Finan went on, 'is Wessex. And to take Wessex they must fight. And they know you are Alfred's greatest warrior.'

'What they want,' I said, 'is the burh at Coccham.' And to get it they would offer me the crown of Mercia, though I had not revealed that offer to Finan or to any other man. I had only told Gisela.

Of course they wanted much more. They wanted Lundene because it gave them a walled town on the Temes, but Lundene was on the Mercian bank and would not help them invade Wessex. But if I gave them Coccham then they were on the river's south bank and they could use Coccham as a base to raid deep into Wessex. At the very least Alfred would pay them to leave Coccham and so they would make much silver even if they failed to dislodge him from the throne.

But Sigefrid, Erik and Haesten, I reckoned, were not after mere silver. Wessex was the prize, and to gain Wessex they needed men. Guthrum would not help them, Mercia was riven between Dane and Saxon and could supply few men willing to leave their homes unguarded, but beyond Mercia was Northumbria, and Northumbria had a Danish king who commanded the loyalty of a great Danish warrior. The king was Gisela's brother and the warrior, Ragnar, was my friend. By buying me they believed they could bring Northumbria into their war. The Danish north would conquer the Saxon south. That was what they wanted. That was what the Danes had wanted all my life. And all I needed to do was break my oath to Alfred and become king in Mercia, and the land that some called England would become Daneland. That, I reckoned, was why the dead man had summoned me.

We came to Wæclingastræt at sunset. The Romans had strengthened the road with a gravel bed and stone edges, and some of their masonry still showed through the pale winter grass beside which a moss-grown milestone read Durocobrivis V. 'What's Durocobrivis?' I asked Huda.

'We call it Dunastopol,' he said with a shrug to indicate that the place was negligible.

We crossed the street. In a well-governed country I might have expected to see guards patrolling the road to protect travellers, but there were none in sight here. There were just crows flying to a nearby wood and silvered clouds stretching across the western sky while ahead of us the darkness lay swollen and heavy above East Anglia. Low hills lay to the north, towards Dunastopol, and Huda led us towards those hills and up a long shallow valley where bare apple trees stood stark in the gloom. Night had fallen by the time we reached Eilaf's hall.

Eilaf's men greeted me as though I were already a king. Servants waited at the gate of his palisade to take our horses, and another knelt at the doorway of the hall to offer me a bowl of washing water and a cloth to dry my hands. A steward took my two swords, the long-bladed Serpent-Breath

42

and the gut-ripper called Wasp-Sting. He took them respectfully, as if he regretted the custom that no man could carry
a blade inside a hall, but that was a good custom. Blades
and ale do not mix well.

The hall was crowded. There were at least forty men
there, most in mail or leather, standing either side of the
central hearth where a great fire blazed to fill the beamed
roof with smoke. Some of the men bowed as I entered, others
just stared at me as I walked to greet my host, who stood
with his wife and two sons beside the hearth. Haesten was
beside them, grinning. A servant brought me a horn of ale.

'Lord Uhtred!' Haesten greeted me loudly so that every man
and woman in the hall would know who I was. Haesten's grin
was somehow mischievous, as if he and I shared a secret joke
in this hall. He had hair the colour of gold, a square face,
bright eyes and was wearing a tunic of fine wool dyed green,
above which hung a thick chain of silver. His arms were heavy
with rings of silver and gold, while silver brooches were pinned
to his long boots. 'It is good to see you, lord,' he said, and
gave me a hint of a bow.

'Still alive, Haesten?' I asked, ignoring my host.

'Still alive, lord,' he said.

'And no wonder,' I said, 'the last time I saw you was at
Ethandun.'

'A rainy day, lord, as I remember,' he said.

'And you were running like a hare, Haesten,' I said.

I saw the shadow cross his face. I had accused him of
cowardice, but he deserved an attack from me for he had
sworn to be my man and had betrayed his oath by deserting
me.

Eilaf, sensing trouble, cleared his throat. He was a heavy
man, tall, with hair the brightest red I have ever seen. It was
curly, and his beard was curly, and both were flame-coloured.
Eilaf the Red, he was called, and though he was tall and

heavy-set, he somehow seemed smaller than Haesten, who had a sublime confidence in his own abilities. 'You are welcome, Lord Uhtred,' Eilaf said.

I ignored him. Haesten was watching me, his face still clouded, but then I grinned. 'Yet all Guthrum's army ran that day,' I said, 'and the ones who didn't are all dead. So I am glad that I saw you run.'

He smiled then. 'I killed eight men at Ethandun,' he said, eager for his men to know that he was no coward.

'Then I am relieved I did not face your sword,' I said, recovering my earlier insult with insincere flattery. Then I turned to the red-headed Eilaf. 'And you,' I asked, 'were you at Ethandun?'

'No, lord,' he said.

'Then you missed a rare fight,' I said. 'Isn't that so, Haesten? A fight to remember!'

'A massacre in the rain, lord,' Haesten said.

'And I still limp from it,' I said, which was true, though the limp was small and hardly inconvenient.

I was named to three other men, three Danes. All of them were dressed well and had arm rings to show their prowess. I forget their names now, but they were there to see me, and they had brought their followers with them. I understood as Haesten made the introductions that he was showing me off. He was proving that I had joined him, and that it was therefore safe for them to join him. Haesten was brewing rebellion in that hall. I drew him to one side. 'Who are they?' I demanded.

'They have lands and men in this part of Guthrum's kingdom.'

'And you want their men?'

'We must make an army,' Haesten said simply.

I gazed down at him. This rebellion, I thought, was not just against Guthrum of East Anglia, but against Alfred of

Wessex, and if it was to succeed then all Britain would need be roused by sword, spear and axe. 'And if I refuse to join you?' I asked him

'You will, lord,' he said confidently.

'I will?' I asked.

'Because tonight, lord, the dead will speak to you.' Haesten smiled, and just then Eilaf intervened to say that all was ready. 'We shall raise the dead,' Haesten said dramatically, touching the hammer amulet about his neck, 'and then we shall feast.' He gestured towards the door at the back of the hall. 'This way, if you will, lord. This way.'

And so I went to meet the dead.

Haesten led us into the darkness and I remember thinking how easy it was to say the dead rose and spoke if the thing was done in such darkness. How would we know? We could hear the corpse perhaps, but not see him, and I was about to protest when two of Eilaf's men came from the hall with burning brands that flared bright in the damp night. They led us past a pen of pigs and the beasts' eyes caught the firelight. It had rained while we were in the hall, just a passing winter shower, but water still dripped from the bare branches. Finan, nervous at the sorcery we were about to witness, stayed close to me.

We followed a path downhill to a small pasture beside what I took to be a barn, and there the torches were thrust into waiting heaps of wood that caught the fire fast so that the flames leaped up to illuminate the barn's wooden wall and wet thatch. As the light brightened I saw that it was not a pasture at all, but a graveyard. The small field was dotted with low earth heaps, and was well fenced to stop animals rooting up the dead.

'That was our church,' Huda explained. He had appeared beside me and nodded at what I had assumed was the barn.

'You're a Christian?' I asked.

'Yes, lord. But we have no priest now.' He made the sign of the cross. 'Our dead go to their rest unshriven.'

'I have a son in a Christian graveyard,' I said, and wondered why I had said it. I rarely thought of my dead infant son. I had not known him. His mother and I were estranged. Yet I remembered him on that dark night in that wet place of the dead. 'Why is a Danish skald buried in a Christian grave?' I asked Huda. 'You told me he was no Christian.'

'He died here, lord, and we buried him before we knew that. Maybe that is why he is restless?'

'Maybe,' I said, then heard the struggle behind me and wished I had thought to ask for my swords before I left Eilaf's hall.

I turned, expecting an attack, and instead saw that two men were dragging a third towards us. The third man was slight, young and fair-haired. His eyes looked huge in the flamelight. He was whimpering. The men who dragged him were much bigger and his struggles were useless. I looked quizzically at Haesten.

'To raise the dead, lord,' he explained, 'we have to send a messenger across the gulf.'

'Who is he?'

'A Saxon,' Haesten said carelessly.

'He deserves to die?' I asked. I was not squeamish about death, but I sensed Haesten would kill like a child drowning a mouse and I did not want a man's death on my conscience if that man had not deserved to die. This was not battle, where a man stood a chance of going to the eternal joys of Odin's hall.

'He's a thief,' Haesten said.

46

'Twice a thief,' Eilaf added.

I crossed to the young man and lifted his head by raising his chin, and so saw that he had the brand-mark of a convicted robber burned into his forehead. 'What did you steal?' I asked him.

'A coat, lord,' he spoke in a whisper. 'I was cold.'

'Was that the first theft?' I asked, 'or the second?'

'The first was a lamb,' Eilaf said behind me.

'I was hungry, lord,' the young man said, 'and my child was starving.'

'You stole twice,' I said, 'which means you must die.' That was the law even in this lawless place. The young man was weeping, yet still stared at me. He thought I might relent and order his life spared, but I turned away. I have stolen many things in my life, almost all of them more valuable than any lamb or coat, but I steal while the owner is watching and while he can defend his property with his sword. It is the thief who steals in the dark who deserves to die.

Huda was making the sign of the cross again and again. He was nervous. The young thief shouted incomprehensible words at me until one of his guards slapped him hard across the mouth, and then he just hung his head and cried. Finan and my three Saxons were clutching the crosses they wore about their necks.

'You are ready, lord?' Haesten asked me.

'Yes,' I said, trying to sound confident, yet in truth I was as nervous as Finan. There is a curtain between our world and the lands of the dead and part of me wished that curtain to stay closed. I instinctively felt for Serpent-Breath's hilt, but of course she was not with me.

'Put the message in his mouth,' Haesten ordered. One of the guards tried to open the young man's mouth, but the prisoner resisted until a knife stabbed at his lips and then he opened wide. An object was pushed onto his tongue. 'A harp string,' Haesten explained to me, 'and Bjorn will know its meaning. Kill him now,' he added to the guards.

'No!' the young man shouted, spitting out the coiled string. He started screaming and weeping as the two men dragged him to one of the earth mounds. They stood either side of the mound, holding their prisoner over the grave. The moon was silvering a gap in the clouds. The churchyard smelt of new rain. 'No, please, no,' the young man was shaking, crying. 'I have a wife, I have children, no! Please!'

'Kill him,' Eilaf the Red ordered.

One of the guards pushed the harp string back into the messenger's mouth, then held the jaw shut. He tilted the young man's head back, hard back, exposing his throat and the second Dane slit it with a quick, practised thrust and a wrenching pull. I heard a stifled, guttural sound and saw the blood flicker black in the flamelight. It spattered the two men, fell across the grave and slapped wetly onto the damp grass. The messenger's body twitched and struggled for a while as the blood flow became weaker. Then, at last, the young man slumped between his captors who let his last blood drops spurt weakly onto the grave. Only when no more blood flowed did they drag him away, dropping his corpse beside the graveyard's wooden fence. I was holding my breath. None of us moved. An owl, its wings astonishingly white in the night, flew close above me and I instinctively touched my hammer amulet, convinced I had seen the thief's soul going to the other world.

Haesten stood close to the blood-soaked grave. 'You have blood, Bjorn!' he shouted. 'I have given you a life! I have sent you a message!'

Nothing happened. The wind sighed on the church's thatch. Somewhere a beast moved in the darkness and then went still. A log collapsed in one of the fires and the sparks flew upwards.

'You have blood!' Haesten shouted again. 'Do you need more blood?'

I thought nothing was going to happen. That I had wasted a journey.

And then the grave moved.

Two

The grave mound shifted.

I remember a coldness gripping my heart and terror consuming me, but I could neither breathe nor move. I stood fixed, watching, waiting for the horror.

The earth fell in slightly, as though a mole was scrabbling out of its small hill. More soil shifted and something grey appeared. The grey thing lurched and I saw the earth was falling away faster as the grey thing rose from the mound. It was in half darkness, for the fires were behind us and our shadows were cast across the phantom that was born out of that winter earth, a phantom that took shape as a filthy corpse that staggered out of its broken grave. I saw a dead man who twitched, half fell, struggled to find his balance and finally stood.

Finan gripped my arm. He had no idea he did such a thing. Huda was kneeling and clutching the cross at his neck. I was just staring.

And the corpse gave a coughing, choking noise like a man's death rattle. Something spat from his mouth, and he choked again, then slowly unbent to stand fully upright and, in the shadowed flamelight, I saw that the dead man was dressed in a soiled grey winding sheet. He had a pale face streaked with dirt, a face untouched by any decay. His long hair lay lank and white on his thin shoulders. He breathed, but had trouble breathing, just as a dying man has trouble breathing. And that was right, I remember thinking, for this man was coming back from death and he would sound just as he had when he had taken his journey into death. He gave a long moan, then took something from his mouth. He threw it towards us and I took an involuntary step backwards before seeing that it was a coiled harp string. I knew then that the impossible thing I saw was real, for I had seen the guards force the harp string into the messenger's mouth, and now the corpse had shown us that he had received the token. 'You will not leave me in peace,' the dead man spoke in a dry half-voice and beside me Finan made a sound that was like a despairing moan.

'Welcome, Bjorn,' Haesten said. Alone among us Haesten seemed unworried by the corpse's living presence. There was even amusement in his voice.

'I want peace,' Bjorn said, his voice a croak.

'This is the Lord Uhtred,' Haesten said, pointing at me, 'who has sent many good Danes to the place where you live.'

'I do not live,' Bjorn said bitterly. He began grunting and his chest heaved spasmodically as though the night air hurt his lungs. 'I curse you,' he said to Haesten, but so feebly that the words had no threat.

Haesten laughed. 'I had a woman today, Bjorn. Do you remember women? The feel of their soft thighs? The warmth of their skin? You remember the noise they make when you ride them?'

'May Hel kiss you through all time,' Bjorn said, 'till the last chaos.' Hel was the goddess of the dead, a rotting corpse of a goddess, and the curse was dreadful, but Bjorn again

51

spoke so dully that this second curse, like the first, was empty. The dead man's eyes were closed, his chest still jerked and his hands made grasping motions at the cold air.

I was in terror and I do not mind confessing it. It is a certainty in this world that the dead go to their long homes in the earth and stay there. Christians say our corpses will all rise one day and the air will be filled with the calling of angels' horns and the sky will glow like beaten gold as the dead come from the ground, but I have never believed that. We die and we go to the afterworld and we stay there, but Bjorn had come back. He had fought the winds of darkness and the tides of death and he had struggled back to this world and now he stood before us, gaunt and tall and filthy and croaking, and I was shivering. Finan had dropped to one knee. My other men were behind me, but I knew they would be shaking as I shook. Only Haesten seemed unaffected by the dead man's presence. 'Tell the Lord Uhtred,' he commanded Bjorn, 'what the Norns told you.'

The Norns are the Fates, the three women who spin life's threads at the roots of Yggdrasil, the tree of life. Whenever a child is born they start a new thread, and they know where it will go, with what other threads it will weave and how it will end. They know everything. They sit and they spin and they laugh at us, and sometimes they shower us with good fortune and sometimes they doom us to hurt and to tears.

'Tell him,' Haesten commanded impatiently, 'what the Norns said of him.'

Bjorn said nothing. His chest heaved and his hands twitched. His eyes were closed.

'Tell him,' Haesten said, 'and I will give you back your harp.'

'My harp,' Bjorn said pathetically, 'I want my harp.'

'I will put it back in your grave,' Haesten said, 'and you can sing to the dead. But first speak to Lord Uhtred.'

52

Bjorn opened his eyes and stared at me. I recoiled from those dark eyes, but made myself stare back, pretending a bravery I did not feel.

'You are to be king, Lord Uhtred,' Bjorn said, then gave a long moan like a creature in pain. 'You are to be king,' he sobbed.

The wind was cold. A spit of rain touched my cheek. I said nothing.

'King of Mercia,' Bjorn said in a sudden and surprisingly loud voice. 'You are to be king of Saxon and of Dane, enemy of the Welsh, king between the rivers and lord of all you rule. You are to be mighty, Lord Uhtred, for the three spinners love you.' He stared at me and, though the fate he pronounced was golden, there was a malevolence in his dead eyes. 'You will be king,' he said, and the last word sounded like poison on his tongue.

My fear passed then, to be replaced by a surge of pride and power. I did not doubt Bjorn's message because the gods do not speak lightly, and the spinners know our fate. We Saxons say wyrd biđ ful āræd, and even the Christians accept that truth. They might deny that the three Norns exist, but they know that wyrd biđ ful āræd. Fate is inexorable. Fate cannot be changed. Fate rules us. Our lives are made before we live them, and I was to be King of Mercia.

I did not think of Bebbanburg at that moment. Bebbanburg is my land, my fortress beside the northern sea, my home. I believed my whole life was dedicated to recovering it from my uncle, who had stolen it from me when I was a child. I dreamed of Bebbanburg, and in my dreams I saw its rocks splintering the grey sea white and felt the gales tear at the hall thatch, but when Bjorn spoke I did not think of Bebbanburg. I thought of being a king. Of ruling a land. Of leading a great army to crush my enemies.

And I thought of Alfred, of the duty I owed him and the

promises I had made him. I knew I must be an oath-breaker to be a king, but to whom are oaths made? To kings, and so a king has the power to release a man from an oath, and I told myself that as a king I could release myself from any oath, and all this whipped through my mind like a swirl of wind gusting across a threshing floor to spin the chaff up into the sky. I did not think clearly. I was as confused as the chaff spinning in the wind, and I did not weigh my oath to Alfred against my future as a king. I just saw two paths ahead, one hard and hilly, and the other a wide green way leading to a kingdom. And besides, what choice did I have? Wyrd bið ful āræd.

Then, in the silence, Haesten suddenly knelt to me. 'Lord King,' he said, and there was unexpected reverence in his voice.

'You broke an oath to me,' I said harshly. Why did I say that then? I could have confronted him earlier, in the hall, but it was by that opened grave I made the accusation.

'I did, lord King,' he said, 'and I regret it.'

I paused. What was I thinking? That I was a king already? 'I forgive you,' I said. I could hear my heartbeat. Bjorn just watched and the light of the flaming torches cast deep shadows on his face.

'I thank you, lord King,' Haesten said, and beside him Eilaf the Red knelt and then every man in that damp grave-yard knelt to me.

'I am not king yet,' I said, suddenly ashamed of the lordly tones I had used to Haesten.

'You will be, lord,' Haesten said. 'The Norns say so.'

I turned to the corpse. 'What else did the three spinners say?'

'That you will be king,' Bjorn said, 'and you will be the king of other kings. You will be lord of the land between the rivers and the scourge of your enemies. You will be king.' He stopped suddenly and went into spasm, his upper body jerking forward and then the spasms stopped and he stayed motionless, bent forward, retching drily, before slowly crumpling onto the disturbed earth.

'Bury him again,' Haesten said harshly, rising from his knees and speaking to the men who had cut the Saxon's throat.

'His harp,' I said.

'I will return it to him tomorrow, lord,' Haesten said, then gestured towards Eilaf's hall. 'There is food, lord King, and ale. And a woman for you. Two if you want.'

'I have a wife,' I said harshly.

'Then there is food, ale and warmth for you,' he said humbly. The other men stood. My warriors looked at me strangely, confused by the message they had heard, but I ignored them. King of other kings. Lord of the land between the rivers. King Uhtred.

I looked back once and saw the two men scraping at the soil to make Bjorn's grave again, and then I followed Haesten into the hall and took the chair at the table's centre, the lord's chair, and I watched the men who had witnessed the dead rise, and I saw they were convinced as I was convinced, and that meant they would take their troops to Haesten's side. The rebellion against Guthrum, the rebellion that was meant to spread across Britain and destroy Wessex, was being led by a dead man. I rested my head on my hands and I thought. I thought of being king. I thought of leading armies.

'Your wife is Danish, I hear?' Haesten interrupted my thoughts.

'She is,' I said.

'Then the Saxons of Mercia will have a Saxon king,' he said, 'and the Danes of Mercia will have a Danish queen. They will both be happy.'

I raised my head and stared at him. I knew him to be clever and sly, but that night he was carefully subservient and genuinely respectful. 'What do you want, Haesten?' I asked him.

'Sigefrid and his brother,' he said, ignoring my question, 'want to conquer Wessex.'

'The old dream,' I said scornfully.

'And to do it,' he said, disregarding my scorn, 'we shall need men from Northumbria. Ragnar will come if you ask him.'

'He will,' I agreed.

'And if Ragnar comes, others will follow.' He broke a loaf of bread and pushed the greater part towards me. A bowl of stew was in front of me, but I did not touch it. Instead I began to crumble the bread, feeling for the granite chips that are left from the grindstone. I was not thinking about what I did, just keeping my hands busy while I watched Haesten.

'You didn't answer my question,' I said. 'What do you want?'

'East Anglia,' he said.

'King Haesten?'

'Why not?' he said, smiling.

'Why not, lord King,' I retorted, provoking a wider smile.

'King Æthelwold in Wessex,' Haesten said, 'King Haesten in East Anglia, and King Uhtred in Mercia.'

'Æthelwold?' I asked scornfully, thinking of Alfred's drunken nephew.

'He is the rightful King of Wessex, lord,' Haesten said.

'And how long will he live?' I asked.

'Not long,' Haesten admitted, 'unless he is stronger than Sigefrid.'

'So it will be Sigefrid of Wessex?' I asked.

Haesten smiled. 'Eventually, lord, yes.'

'What of his brother, Erik?'

'Erik likes to be a Viking,' Haesten said. 'His brother takes Wessex and Erik takes the ships. Erik will be a sea king.'

So it would be Sigefrid of Wessex, Uhtred of Mercia and Haesten in East Anglia. Three weasels in a sack, I thought, but did not let the thought show. 'And where,' I asked instead, 'does this dream begin?'

His smile went. He was serious now. 'Sigefrid and I have men. Not enough, but the heart of a good army. You bring Ragnar south with the Northumbrian Danes and we'll have more than enough to take East Anglia. Half of Guthrum's earls will join us when they see you and Ragnar. Then we take the men of East Anglia, join them to our army, and conquer Mercia.'

'And join the men of Mercia,' I finished for him, 'to take Wessex?'

'Yes,' he said. 'When the leaves fall,' he went on, 'and when the barns are filled, we shall march on Wessex.'

'But without Ragnar,' I said, 'you can do nothing.'

He bowed his head in agreement. 'And Ragnar will not march unless you join us.'

It could work, I thought. Guthrum, the Danish King of East Anglia, had repeatedly failed to conquer Wessex and now had made his peace with Alfred, but just because Guthrum had become a Christian and was now an ally of Alfred did not mean that other Danes had abandoned the dream of Wessex's rich fields. If enough men could be assembled, then East Anglia would fall, and its earls, ever eager for plunder, would march on Mercia. Then Northumbrians, Mercians and East Anglians could turn on Wessex, the richest kingdom and the last Saxon kingdom in the land of the Saxons.

Yet I was sworn to Alfred. I was sworn to defend Wessex. I had given Alfred my oath and without oaths we are no better than beasts. But the Norns had spoken. Fate is inexorable, it cannot be cheated. That thread of my life was already in place, and I could no more change it than I could make the sun go backwards. The Norns had sent a messenger across the black gulf to tell me that my oath must be broken, and that I would be a king, and so I nodded to Haesten. 'So be it,' I said.

'You must meet Sigefrid and Erik,' he said, 'and we must make oaths.'

'Yes,' I said.

'Tomorrow,' he said, watching me carefully, 'we leave for Lundene.'

So it had begun. Sigefrid and Erik were readying to defend Lundene, and by doing that they defied the Mercians, who claimed the city as theirs, and they defied Alfred, who feared Lundene being garrisoned by an enemy, and they defied Guthrum, who wanted the peace of Britain kept. But there would be no peace.

'Tomorrow,' Haesten said again, 'we leave for Lundene.'

We rode next day. I led my six men while Haesten had twenty-one companions, and we followed Wæclingastræt south through a persistent rain that turned the road's verges to thick mud. The horses were miserable, we were miserable. As we rode I tried to remember every word that Bjorn the Dead had said to me, knowing that Gisela would want the conversation recounted in every detail.

'So?' Finan challenged me soon after midday. Haesten had ridden ahead and Finan now spurred his horse to keep pace with mine.

'So?' I asked.

'So are you going to be king in Mercia?'

'The Fates say so,' I said, not looking at him. Finan and I had been slaves together on a trader's ship. We had suffered, frozen, endured and learned to love each other like brothers, and I cared about his opinion.

'The Fates,' Finan said, 'are tricksters.'

'Is that a Christian view?' I asked.

He smiled. He wore his cloak's hood over his helmet, so I could see little of his thin, feral face, but I saw the flash of teeth when he smiled. 'I was a great man in Ireland,' he said, 'I had horses to outrun the wind, women to dim the sun, and weapons that could outfight the world, yet the Fates doomed me.'

'You live,' I said, 'and you're a free man.'

'I'm your oath-man,' he said, 'and I gave you my oath freely. And you, lord, are Alfred's oath-man.'

'Yes,' I said.

'Were you forced to make your oath to Alfred?' Finan asked.

'No,' I confessed.

The rain was stinging in my face. The sky was low, the land dark. 'If fate is unavoidable,' Finan asked, 'why do we make oaths?'

I ignored the question. 'If I break my oath to Alfred,' I said instead, 'will you break yours to me?'

'No, lord,' he said, smiling again. 'I would miss your company,' he went on, 'but you would not miss Alfred's.'

'No,' I admitted, and we let the conversation drift away with the wind-blown rain, though Finan's words lingered in my mind and they troubled me.

We spent that night close to the great shrine of Saint Alban. The Romans had made a town there, though that town had now decayed, and so we stayed at a Danish hall just to the east. Our host was welcoming enough, but he was cautious in conversation. He did admit to hearing that

Sigefrid had moved men into Lundene's old town, but he neither condemned nor praised the act. He wore the hammer amulet, as did I, but he also kept a Saxon priest who prayed over the meal of bread, bacon and beans. The priest was a reminder that this hall was in East Anglia, and that East Anglia was officially Christian and at peace with its Christian neighbours, but our host made certain that his palisade gate was barred and that he had armed men keeping watch through the damp night. There was a shiftless air to this land, a feeling that a storm might break at any time.

The rainstorm ended in the darkness. We left at dawn, riding into a world of frost and stillness, though Wæclingastræt became busier as we encountered men driving cattle to Lundene. The beasts were scrawny, but they had been spared the autumn slaughter so they could feed the city through its winter. We rode past them and the herdsmen dropped to their knees as so many armed men clattered by. The clouds cleared to the east so that, when we came to Lundene in the middle of the day, the sun was bright behind the thick pall of dark smoke that always hangs above the city.

I have always liked Lundene. It is a place of ruins, trade and wickedness that sprawls along the northern bank of the Temes. The ruins were the buildings the Romans left when they abandoned Britain, and their old city crowned the hills at the city's eastern end and were surrounded by a wall made of brick and stone. The Saxons had never liked the Roman buildings, fearing their ghosts, and so had made their own town to the west, a place of thatch and wood and wattle and narrow alleys and stinking ditches that were supposed to carry sewage to the river, but usually lay glistening and filthy until a downpour of rain flooded them. That new Saxon town was a busy place, stinking with the smoke from smithy fires and raucous with the shouts of tradesmen, too busy, indeed, to bother making a defensive wall. Why did they need a wall, the Saxons argued, for the Danes were content to live in the old city and had showed no desire to slaughter the inhabitants of the new. There were palisades in a few places, evidence that some men had tried to protect the rapidly growing new town, but enthusiasm for the project always died and the palisades rotted, or else their timbers were stolen to make new buildings along the sewage-stinking streets.

Lundene's trade came from the river and from the roads that led to every part of Britain. The roads, of course, were Roman, and down them flowed wool and pottery, ingots and pelts, while the river brought luxuries from abroad and slaves from Frankia and hungry men seeking trouble. There was plenty of that, because the city, which was built where three kingdoms met, was virtually ungoverned in those years.

To the east of Lundene the land was East Anglia, and so ruled by Guthrum. To the south, on the far bank of the Temes, was Wessex, while to the west was Mercia to which the city really belonged, but Mercia was a crippled country without a king and so there was no reeve to keep order in Lundene, and no great lord to impose laws. Men went armed in the alleyways, wives had bodyguards and great dogs were chained in gateways. Bodies were found every morning, unless the tide carried them downriver towards the sea and past the coast where the Danes had their great camp at Beamfleot from where the Northmen's ships sailed to demand customs payments from the traders working their way up the wide mouth of the Temes. The Northmen had no authority to impose such dues, but they had ships and men and swords and axes, and that was authority enough.

Haesten had exacted enough of those illegal dues, indeed he had become rich by piracy, rich and powerful, but he was still nervous as we rode into the city. He had talked incessantly as we neared Lundene, mostly about nothing, and he laughed too easily when I made sour comments about his inane words. But then, as we passed between the half-fallen towers either side of a wide gateway, he fell silent. There were sentries on the gate, but they must have recognised Haesten for they did not challenge us, but simply pulled aside the hurdles that blocked the ruined arch. Inside the arch I could see a stack of timbers that meant the gate was being rebuilt.

We had come to the Roman town, the old town, and our horses picked a slow path up the street that was paved with wide flagstones between which weeds grew thick. It was cold. Frost still lay in the dark corners where the sun had not reached the stone all day. The buildings had shuttered windows through which woodsmoke sifted to be whirled down the street. 'You've been here before?' Haesten broke his silence with the abrupt question.

'Many times,' I said. Haesten and I rode ahead now.

'Sigefrid,' Haesten said, then found he had nothing to say.

'Is a Norseman, I hear,' I said.

'He is unpredictable,' Haesten said, and the tone of his voice told me that it was Sigefrid who had made him nervous. Haesten had faced a living corpse without flinching, but the thought of Sigefrid made him apprehensive.

'I can be unpredictable,' I said, 'and so can you.'

Haesten said nothing to that. Instead he touched the hammer hanging at his neck, then turned his horse into a gateway where servants ran forward to greet us. 'The king's palace,' Haesten said.

I knew the palace. It had been made by the Romans and was a great vaulted building of pillars and carved stone, though it had been patched by the kings of Mercia so that thatch, wattle and timber filled the gaps in the half-ruined walls. The great hall was lined with Roman pillars and its walls were of brick, but here and there patches of marble facing had somehow survived. I stared at the high masonry and marvelled that men had ever been able to make such walls. We built in wood and thatch, and both rotted away, which meant we would leave nothing behind. The Romans had left marble and stone, brick and glory.

A steward told us that Sigefrid and his younger brother were in the old Roman arena that lay to the north of the palace. 'What is he doing there?' Haesten asked.

'Making a sacrifice, lord,' the steward said.

'Then we'll join him,' Haesten said, looking at me for confirmation.

'We will,' I said.

We rode the short distance. Beggars shrank from us. We had money, and they knew it, but they dared not ask for it because we were armed strangers. Swords, shields, axes and spears hung beside our horses' muddy flanks. Shopkeepers bowed to us, while women hid their children in their skirts. Most of the folk who lived in the Roman part of Lundene were Danes, yet even these Danes were nervous. Their city had been occupied by Sigefrid's crewmen who would be hungry for money and women.

I knew the Roman arena. When I was a child I was taught the fundamental strokes of the sword by Toki the Shipmaster, and he had given me those lessons in the great oval arena that was surrounded by decayed layers of stone where wooden benches had once been placed. The tiered stone layers were almost empty, except for a few idle folk who were watching the men in the centre of the weed-choked arena. There must have been forty or fifty men there, and a score of saddled horses were tethered at the far end, but what surprised me most as I rode through the high walls of the entrance, was a Christian cross planted in the middle of the small crowd.

'Sigefrid's a Christian?' I asked Haesten in astonishment.

'No!' Haesten said forcefully.

The men heard our hoofbeats and turned towards us. They were all dressed for war, grim in mail or leather and armed with swords or axes, but they were cheerful. Then, from the centre of that crowd, from a place close to the cross, stalked Sigefrid.

I knew him without having to be told who he was. He was a big man, and made to look even bigger for he wore a great cloak of black bear's fur that swathed him from neck to ankles. He had tall black leather boots, a shining mail coat, a sword belt studded with silver rivets, and a bushy black beard that sprang from beneath his iron helmet that was chased with silver patterns. He pulled the helmet off as he strode towards us and his hair was as black and bushy as his beard. He had dark eyes in a broad face, a nose that had been broken and squashed, and a wide slash of a mouth that gave him a grim appearance. He stopped, facing us, and set his feet wide apart as though he waited for an attack.

'Lord Sigefrid!' Haesten greeted him with forced cheerfulness.

'Lord Haesten! Welcome back! Welcome indeed.' Sigefrid's voice was curiously high-pitched, not feminine, but it sounded odd coming from such a huge and malevolent-looking man. 'And you!' he pointed a black-gloved hand towards me, 'must be the Lord Uhtred!'

'Uhtred of Bebbanburg,' I named myself.

'And you are welcome, welcome indeed!' He stepped forward and took my reins himself, which was an honour, and then he smiled up at me and his face, that had been so fearsome, was suddenly mischievous, almost friendly. 'They say you are tall, Lord Uhtred!'

'So I am told,' I said.

'Then let us see who is taller,' he suggested genially, 'you or I?' I slid from the saddle and eased the stiffness from my legs. Sigefrid, vast in his fur cloak, still held my reins and still smiled. 'Well?' he demanded of the men nearest to him.

'You are taller, lord,' one of them said hastily.

'If I asked you who was the prettiest,' Sigefrid said, 'what would you say?'

The man looked from Sigefrid to me and from me to Sigefrid and did not know what to say. He just looked terrified.

'He fears that if he gives the wrong answer,' Sigefrid confided to me in an amused voice, 'that I would kill him.'

'And would you?' I asked.

'I would think about it. Here!' he called to the man, who came nervously forward. 'Take the reins,' Sigefrid said, 'and walk the horse. So who's taller?' This last question was to Haesten.

'You are the same height,' Haesten said.

'And just as pretty as each other,' Sigefrid said, then laughed. He put his arms around me and I smelt the rank stench of his fur cloak. He hugged me. 'Welcome, Lord Uhtred, welcome!' He stepped back and grinned. I liked him at that moment because his smile was truly welcoming. 'I have heard much of you!' he declared.

'And I of you, lord.'

'And doubtless we were both told many lies! But good lies. I also have a quarrel with you.' He grinned, waiting, but I offered him no response. 'Jarrel!' he explained, 'you killed him.'

'I did,' I said. Jarrel had been the man leading the Viking crew I had slaughtered on the Temes.

'I liked Jarrel,' Sigefrid said.

'Then you should have advised him to avoid Uhtred of Bebbanburg,' I said.

'That is true,' Sigefrid said, 'and is it also true that you killed Ubba?'

'I did.'

'He must have been a hard man to kill! And Ivarr?'

'I killed Ivarr too,' I confirmed.

'But he was old and it was time he went. His son hates you, you know that?'

'I know that.'

Sigefrid snorted in derision. 'The son is a nothing. A piece of gristle. He hates you, but why should the falcon care about the sparrow's hate?' He grinned at me, then looked at Smoca, my stallion, who was being walked about the arena so he could cool slowly after his long journey. 'That,' Sigefrid said admiringly, 'is a horse!'

'It is,' I agreed.

'Maybe I should take him from you?'

'Many have tried,' I said.

He liked that. He laughed again and put a heavy hand on my shoulder to lead me towards the cross. 'You're a Saxon, they tell me?'

'I am.'

'But no Christian?'

'I worship the true gods,' I said.

'May they love and reward you for that,' he said, and he squeezed my shoulder and, even through the mail and leather, I could feel his strength. He turned then. 'Erik! Are you shy?'

His brother stepped out of the crowd. He had the same black bushy hair, though Erik's was tied severely back with a length of cord. His beard was trimmed. He was young, maybe only twenty or twenty-one, and he had a broad face with bright eyes that were at once full of curiosity and welcome. I had been surprised to discover I liked Sigefrid, but it was no surprise to like Erik. His smile was instant, his face open and guileless. He was, like Gisela's brother, a man you liked from the moment you met him.

'I am Erik,' he greeted me.

'He is my adviser,' Sigefrid said, 'my conscience and my brother.'

'Conscience?'

'Erik would not kill a man for telling a lie, would you, brother?'

'No,' Erik said.

'So he is a fool, but a fool I love.' Sigefrid laughed. 'But don't think the fool is a weakling, Lord Uhtred. He fights like a demon from Niflheim.' He slapped his brother on the shoulder, then took my elbow and led me on towards the incongruous cross. 'I have prisoners,' he explained as we neared the cross, and I saw that five men were kneeling with their hands tied behind their backs. They had been stripped of cloaks, weapons and tunics so that they wore only their trews. They shivered in the cold air.

The cross had been newly made from two beams of wood that had been crudely nailed together and then sunk into a hastily dug hole. The cross leaned slightly. At its foot were some heavy nails and a big hammer. 'You see death by the cross on their statues and carvings,' Sigefrid explained to me, 'and you see it on the amulets they wear, but I've never seen the real thing. Have you?'

'No,' I admitted.

'And I can't understand why it would kill a man,' he said with genuine puzzlement in his voice. 'It's only three nails! I've suffered much worse than that in battle.'

'Me too,' I said.

'So I thought I'd find out!' he finished cheerfully, then jerked his big beard towards the prisoner nearest to the foot of the cross. 'The two bastards at the end there are Christian priests. We'll nail one of them up and see if he dies. I have ten pieces of silver that say it won't kill him.'

I could see almost nothing of the two priests except that one had a big belly. His head was bowed, not in prayer, but because he had been beaten hard. His naked back and chest were bruised and bloody, and there was more blood in the tangle of his brown curly hair. 'Who are they?' I asked Sigefrid.

'Who are you?' he snarled at the prisoners and, when none answered, he gave the nearest man a brutal kick in the ribs. 'Who are you?' he asked again.

The man lifted his head. He was elderly, at least forty years old, and had a deep lined face on which was etched the resignation of those who knew they were about to die. 'I am Earl Sihtric,' he said, 'counsellor to King Æthelstan.'

'Guthrum!' Sigefrid screamed, and it was a scream. A scream of pure rage that erupted from nowhere. One moment he had been affable, but suddenly he was a demon. Spittle flew from his mouth as he shrieked the name a second time. 'Guthrum! His name is Guthrum, you bastard!' He kicked Sihtric in the chest, and I reckoned that kick was hard enough to break a rib. 'What is his name?' Sigefrid demanded.

'Guthrum,' Sihtric said.

'Guthrum!' Sigefrid shouted, and kicked the old man again. Guthrum, when he made peace with Alfred, had become a Christian and taken the Christian name Æthelstan as his own. I still thought of him as Guthrum, as did Sigefrid, who now appeared to be trying to stamp Sihtric to death. The old man attempted to evade the blows, but Sigefrid had driven him to the ground from where he could not escape. Erik seemed unmoved by his brother's savage anger, yet after a while he stepped forward and took Sigefrid's arm and the bigger man allowed himself to be pulled away. 'Bastard!' Sigefrid spat back at the moaning man. 'Calling Guthrum by a Christian name!' he explained to me. Sigefrid was still shaking from his sudden anger. His eyes had narrowed and his face was contorted, but he seemed to control himself as he draped a heavy arm around my shoulder. 'Guthrum sent them,' he said, 'to tell me to leave Lundene. But it's none of Guthrum's business! Lundene doesn't belong to East Anglia! It belongs to Mercia! To King Uhtred of Mercia!' That was the first time anyone had used that title so formally, and I liked the sound of it. King Uhtred. Sigefrid turned back to Sihtric who now had blood at his lips. 'What was Guthrum's message?'

'That the city belongs to Mercia, and you must leave,' Sihtric managed to say.

'Then Mercia can throw me out,' Sigefrid sneered.

'Unless King Uhtred allows us to stay?' Erik suggested with a smile.

I said nothing. The title sounded good, but strange, as if it defied the strands coming from the three spinners.

'Alfred will not permit you to stay.' One of the other prisoners dared to speak.

'Who gives a turd about Alfred?' Sigefrid snarled. 'Let the bastard send his army to die here.'

'That is your reply, lord?' the prisoner asked humbly.

'My reply will be your severed heads,' Sigefrid said.

I glanced at Erik then. He was the younger brother, but clearly the one who did the thinking. He shrugged. 'If we negotiate,' he explained, 'then we give time for our enemies to gather their forces. Better to be defiant.'

'You'll pick war with both Guthrum and Alfred?' I asked.

'Guthrum won't fight,' Erik said, sounding very certain. 'He threatens, but he won't fight. He's getting old, Lord Uhtred, and he would prefer to enjoy what life is left to him. And if we send him severed heads? I think he will understand the message that his own head is in danger if he disturbs us.'

'What of Alfred?' I asked.

'He's cautious,' Erik said, 'isn't he?'

'Yes.'

'He'll offer us money to leave the city?'

'Probably.'

'And maybe we'll take it,' Sigefrid said, 'and stay anyway.'

'Alfred won't attack us till the summer,' Erik said, ignoring his brother, 'and by then, Lord Uhtred, we hope you will have led Earl Ragnar south into East Anglia. Alfred can't ignore that threat. He will march against our combined armies, not against the garrison in Lundene, and our job is to kill Alfred and put his nephew on the throne.'

'Æthelwold?' I asked dubiously. 'He's a drunk.'

'Drunk or not,' Erik said, 'a Saxon king will make our conquest of Wessex more palatable.'

'Until you need him no longer,' I said.

'Until we need him no longer,' Erik agreed.

The big-bellied priest at the end of the line of kneeling prisoners had been listening. He stared at me, then at Sigefrid, who saw his gaze. 'What are you looking at, turd?' Sigefrid demanded. The priest did not answer, but just looked at me again, then dropped his head. 'We'll start with him,' Sigefrid said, 'we'll nail the fat bastard to a cross and see if he dies.'

'Why not let him fight?' I suggested.

Sigefrid stared at me, unsure he had heard me correctly. 'Let him fight?' he asked.

'The other priest is skinny,' I said, 'so much easier to nail to the cross. That fat one should be given a sword and made to fight.'

Sigefrid sneered. 'You think a priest can fight?'

I shrugged as though I did not care one way or the other. 'It's just that I like seeing those fat-bellied ones lose a fight,' I explained. 'I like seeing their bellies slit open. I like watching their guts spill out.' I was staring at the priest as I spoke and he looked up again to gaze into my eyes. 'I want to see yards of gut spilled out,' I said wolfishly, 'and then watch as your dogs eat his intestines while he's still alive.'

'Or make him eat them himself,' Sigefrid said thoughtfully. He suddenly grinned at me. 'I like you, Lord Uhtred!'

'He'll die too easily,' Erik said.

'Then give him something to fight for,' I said.

'What can that fat pig of a priest fight for?' Sigefrid demanded scornfully.

I said nothing, and it was Erik who supplied the answer. 'His freedom?' he suggested. 'If he wins then all prisoners go free, but if he loses then we crucify them all. That should make him fight.'

'He'll still lose,' I said.

'Yes, but he'll make an effort,' Erik said.

Sigefrid laughed, amused by the incongruity of the suggestion. The priest, half naked, big-bellied and terrified, looked at each of us in turn but saw nothing but amusement and ferocity. 'Ever held a sword, priest?' Sigefrid demanded of the fat man. The priest said nothing.

I mocked his silence with laughter. 'He'll only flail around like a pig,' I said.

'You want to fight him?' Sigefrid asked.

'He wasn't sent as an envoy to me, lord,' I said respectfully. 'Besides, I've heard there is no one to match your skill with a blade. I challenge you to make a cut straight across his belly button.'

Sigefrid liked that challenge. He turned to the priest. 'Holy man! You want to fight for your freedom?'

The priest was shaking with fear. He glanced at his

71

companions, but found no help there. He managed to nod his head. 'Yes, lord,' he said,

'Then you can fight me,' Sigefrid said happily, 'and if I win? You all die. And if you win? You can ride away from here. Can you fight?'

'No, lord,' the priest said.

'Ever held a sword, priest?'

'No, lord.'

'So are you ready to die?' Sigefrid asked.

The priest looked at the Norseman and, despite his bruises and cuts, there was a hint of anger in his eyes that was belied by the humility in his voice. 'Yes, lord,' he said, 'I'm ready to die and meet my Saviour.'

'Cut him free,' Sigefrid ordered one of his followers. 'Cut the turd free and give him a sword.' He drew his own sword that was a long two-edged blade. 'Fear-Giver,' he named the blade with fondness in his voice, 'and she needs exercise.'

'Here,' I said, and I drew Serpent-Breath, my own beautiful blade, and I turned her so that I held her by the blade and I tossed the sword to the priest whose hands had just been cut free. He fumbled the catch, letting Serpent-Breath fall among the pale winter weeds. He stared at the sword for a moment as though he had never seen such a thing before, then stooped to pick her up. He was unsure whether to hold her in his right hand or left. He settled for the left and gave her a clumsy experimental stroke that caused the watching men to laugh.

'Why give him your sword?' Sigefrid asked.

'He'll do no good with it,' I said scornfully.

'And if I break it?' Sigefrid asked forcefully.

'Then I'll know the smith who made it didn't know his business,' I said.

'It's your blade, your choice,' Sigefrid said dismissively, then turned to the priest who was holding Serpent-Breath

72

so that her tip rested on the ground. 'Are you ready, priest?' he demanded.

'Yes, lord,' the priest said, and that was the first truthful answer he had given to the Norseman. For the priest had held a sword many times before and he did know how to fight and I doubted he was ready to die. He was Father Pyrlig.

If your fields are heavy and damp with clay then you can harness two oxen to an ard blade, and you can goad the beasts bloody so that the blade ploughs your ground. The beasts must pull together, which is why they are yoked together, and in life one ox is called Fate and the other is named Oaths.

Fate decrees what we do. We cannot escape fate. Wyrd bið ful āræd. We have no choices in life, how can we? Because from the moment we are born the three sisters know where our thread will go and what patterns it will weave and how it will end. Wyrd bið ful āræd.

Yet we choose our oaths. Alfred, when he gave me his sword and hands to enfold in my hands did not order me to make the oath. He offered it and I chose. But was it my choice? Or did the Fates choose for me? And if they did, why bother with oaths? I have often wondered about this and even now, as an old man, I still wonder. Did I choose Alfred? Or were the Fates laughing when I knelt and took his sword and hands in mine?

The three Norns were certainly laughing on that cold bright day in Lundene, because the moment I saw that the big-bellied priest was Father Pyrlig I knew that nothing was simple. I had realised in that instant that the Fates had not spun me a golden thread leading to a throne. They were laughing from the roots of Yggdrasil, the tree of life. They had made a jest and I was its victim, and I had to make a choice.

Or did I? Maybe the Fates had made the choice, but at that moment, overshadowed by the gaunt stark makeshift cross, I believed I had to choose between the Thurgilson brothers and Pyrlig.

Sigefrid was no friend, but he was a formidable man, and with his alliance I could become king in Mercia. Gisela would be a queen. I could help Sigefrid, Erik, Haesten and Ragnar plunder Wessex. I could become rich. I would lead armies. I would fly my banner of the wolf's head, and at Smoca's heels would ride a mailed host of spearmen. My enemies would hear the thunder of our hooves in their nightmares. All that would be mine if I chose to ally myself with Sigefrid.

While by choosing Pyrlig I would lose all that the dead man had promised me. Which meant that Bjorn had lied, yet how could a man sent from his grave with a message from the Norns tell a lie? I remember thinking all that in the heartbeat before I made my choice, though in truth there was no hesitation. There was not even a heartbeat of hesitation.

Pyrlig was a Welshman, a Briton, and we Saxons hate the Britons. The Britons are treacherous thieves. They hide in their hill fastnesses and ride down to raid our lands, and they take our cattle and sometimes our women and children, and when we pursue them they go ever deeper into a wild place of mists, crags, marsh and misery. And Pyrlig was also a Christian, and I have no love for Christians. The choice would seem so easy! On one side a kingdom, Viking friends and wealth, and on the other a Briton who was the priest of a religion that sucks joy from this world like dusk swallowing daylight. Yet I did not think. I chose, or fate chose, and I chose friendship. Pyrlig was my friend. I had met him in Wessex's darkest winter, when the Danes seemed to have conquered the kingdom, and Alfred with a few followers had been driven to take refuge in the western marshes. Pyrlig had been sent as an emissary by his Welsh king to discover and perhaps exploit Alfred's weakness, but instead he had sided with Alfred and fought for Alfred. Pyrlig and I had stood in the shield wall together. We had fought side by side. We were Welshman and Saxon, Christian and pagan, and we should have been enemies, but I loved him like a brother.

So I gave him my sword and, instead of watching him nailed to a cross, I gave him the chance to fight for his life.

And, of course, it was not a fair fight. It was over in a moment! Indeed, it had hardly begun before it ended, and I alone was not astonished by its ending.

Sigefrid was expecting to face a fat, untrained priest, yet I knew that Pyrlig had been a warrior before he discovered his god. He had been a great warrior, a killer of Saxons and a man about whom his people had made songs. He did not look like a great warrior now. He was half naked, fat, dishevelled, bruised and beaten. He waited for Sigefrid's attack with a look of horrified terror on his face and with the tip of Serpent-Breath's blade still resting on the ground. He backed away as Sigefrid came closer, and began making mewing noises. Sigefrid laughed and swung his sword almost idly, expecting to knock Pyrlig's blade out of his path and so expose that big belly to Fear-Giver's gut-opening slash.

And Pyrlig moved like a weasel.

He lifted Serpent-Breath gracefully and danced a backwards pace so that Sigefrid's careless swing went under her blade, and then he stepped towards his enemy and brought Serpent-Breath down hard, all wrist in that stroke, and sliced her against Sigefrid's sword arm as it was still swinging outwards. The stroke was not powerful enough to break the mail armour, but it did drive Sigefrid's sword arm further out and so opened the Norseman to a lunge. And Pyrlig lunged. He was so fast that Serpent-Breath was a silver blur that struck hard on Sigefrid's chest.

Once again the blade did not pierce Sigefrid's mail. Instead it pushed the big man backwards and I saw the fury come into the Norseman's eyes and saw him bring Fear-Giver back in a mighty swing that would surely have decapitated Pyrlig in a red instant. There was so much strength and savagery in that huge cut, but Pyrlig, who seemed a heartbeat from death, simply used his wrist again. He did not seem to move, but still Serpent-Breath flickered up and sideways.

Serpent-Breath's point met that death-swing on the inside of Sigefrid's wrist and I saw the spray of blood like a red fog in the air.

And I saw Pyrlig smile. It was more of a grimace, but there was a warrior's pride and a warrior's triumph in that smile. His blade had ripped up Sigefrid's forearm, slicing the mail apart and laying open flesh and skin and muscle from wrist to elbow, so that Sigefrid's mighty blow faltered and stopped. The Norseman's sword arm went limp, and Pyrlig suddenly stepped back and turned Serpent-Breath so he could cut downwards with her and at last he appeared to put some effort into the blade. She made a whistling noise as the Welshman slashed her onto Sigefrid's bleeding wrist. He almost severed the wrist, but the blade glanced off a bone and took the Norseman's thumb instead, and Fear-Giver fell to the arena floor and Serpent-Breath was in Sigefrid's beard and at his throat.

'No!' I shouted.

Sigefrid was too appalled to be angry. He could not believe what had happened. He must have realised by that moment that his opponent was a swordsman, but still he could not believe he had lost. He brought up his bleeding hands as if to seize Pyrlig's blade, and I saw the Welshman's blade twitch and Sigefrid, sensing death a hair's breadth away, went still.

'No,' I repeated.

'Why shouldn't I kill him?' Pyrlig asked, and his voice was a warrior's voice now, hard and merciless, and his eyes were warrior's eyes, flint-cold and furious.

'No,' I said again. I knew that if Pyrlig killed Sigefrid then Sigefrid's men would have their revenge.

Erik knew it too. 'You won, priest,' he said softly. He walked to his brother. 'You won,' he said again to Pyrlig, 'so put down the sword.'

'Does he know I beat him?' Pyrlig asked, staring into Sigefrid's dark eyes.

'I speak for him,' Erik said. 'You won the fight, priest, and you are free.'

'I have to deliver my message first,' Pyrlig said. Blood dripped from Sigefrid's hand. He still stared at the Welshman. 'The message we bring from King Æthelstan,' Pyrlig said, meaning Guthrum, 'is that you are to leave Lundene. It is not part of the land ceded by Alfred to Danish rule. Do you understand that?' He twitched Serpent-Breath again, though Sigefrid said nothing. 'Now I want horses,' Pyrlig went on, 'and Lord Uhtred and his men are to escort us out of Lundene. Is that agreed?'

Erik looked at me and I nodded consent. 'It is agreed,' Erik said to Pyrlig.

I took Serpent-Breath from Pyrlig's hand. Erik was holding his brother's wounded arm. For a moment I thought Sigefrid would attack the unarmed Welshman, but Erik managed to turn him away.

Horses were fetched. The men in the arena were silent and resentful. They had seen their leader humiliated, and they did not understand why Pyrlig was allowed to leave with the other envoys, but they accepted Erik's decision.

'My brother is headstrong,' Erik told me. He had taken me aside to talk while the horses were saddled.

'It seems the priest knew how to fight after all,' I said apologetically.

Erik frowned, not with anger, but puzzlement. 'I am curious about their god,' he admitted. He was watching his brother, whose wounds were being bandaged. 'Their god does seem to have power,' Erik said. I slid Serpent-Breath into her scabbard and Erik saw the silver cross that decorated her pommel. 'You must think so too?'

'That was a gift,' I said, 'from a woman. A good woman. A lover. Then the Christian god took hold of her and she loves men no more.'

Erik reached out and touched the cross tentatively. 'You don't think it gives the blade power?' he asked.

'The memory of her love might,' I said, 'but power comes from here.' I touched my amulet, Thor's hammer.

'I fear their god,' Erik said.

'He's harsh,' I said, 'unkind. He's a god who likes to make laws.'

'Laws?'

'You're not allowed to lust after your neighbour's wife,' I said.

Erik laughed at that, then saw I was serious. 'Truly?' he asked with disbelief in his voice.

'Priest!' I called to Pyrlig. 'Does your god let men lust after their neighbours' wives?'

'He lets them, lord,' Pyrlig said humbly as if he feared me, 'but he disapproves.'

'Did he make a law about it?'

'Yes, lord, he did. And he made another that says you mustn't lust after your neighbour's ox.'

'There,' I said to Erik. 'You can't even wish for an ox if you're a Christian.'

'Strange,' he said thoughtfully. He was looking at Guthrum's envoys who had so narrowly escaped losing their heads. 'You don't mind escorting them?'

'No.'

'It might be no bad thing if they live,' he said quietly. 'Why give Guthrum cause to attack us?'

'He won't,' I said confidently, 'whether you kill them or not.'

'Probably not,' he agreed, 'but we agreed that if the priest won, then they would all live, so let them live. And you're sure you don't mind escorting them away?'

'Of course not,' I said.

'Then come back here,' Erik said warmly, 'we need you.'

'You need Ragnar,' I corrected him.

'True,' he confessed, and smiled. 'See those men safe out of the city, then come back.'

'I have a wife and children to fetch first,' I said.

'Yes,' he said, and smiled again. 'You are fortunate in that. But you will come back?'

'Bjorn the Dead told me so,' I said, carefully evading his question.

'So he did,' Erik said. He embraced me. 'We need you,' he said, 'and together we can take this whole island.'

We left, riding through the city streets, out through the western gate that was known as Ludd's Gate, and then down to the ford across the River Fleet. Sihtric was bent over his saddle's pommel, still suffering from the kicking he had received from Sigefrid. I looked behind as we left the ford, half expecting that Sigefrid would have countermanded his brother's decision and sent men to pursue us, but none appeared. We spurred through the marshy ground and then up the slight slope to the Saxon town.

I did not stay on the road that led westwards, but instead turned onto the wharves where a dozen ships were moored.

79

These were river boats that traded with Wessex and Mercia. Few shipmasters cared to shoot the dangerous gap in the ruined bridge that the Romans had thrown across the Temes, so these ships were smaller, manned by oarsmen, and all of them had paid dues to me at Coccham. They all knew me, because they did business with me on every trip.

We forced our way through heaps of merchandise, past open fires and through the gangs of slaves loading or unloading cargoes. Only one ship was ready to make a voyage. She was named the *Swan* and I knew her well. She had a Saxon crew, and she was nearly ready to leave because her oarsmen were standing on the wharf while the ship-master, a man called Osric, finished his business with the merchant whose goods he was carrying. 'You're taking us too,' I told him.

We left most of the horses behind, though I insisted that room was found for Smoca, and Finan wanted to keep his stallion too, and so the beasts were coaxed into the *Swan*'s open hold where they stood shivering. Then we left. The tide was flooding, the oars bit, and we glided upriver. 'Where am I taking you, lord?' Osric the shipmaster asked me.

'To Coccham,' I said.

And back to Alfred.

The river was wide, grey and sullen. It flowed strongly, fed by the winter rains against which the incoming tide gave less and less resistance. The *Swan* made hard work of the early rowing as the ten oarsmen fought the current and I caught Finan's eye and we exchanged smiles. He was remembering, as I was, our long months at the oars of a slave-rowed trading ship. We had suffered, bled and shivered, and we had thought that only death could release us from that

80

fate, but now other men rowed us as the *Swan* fought around the great swooping bends of the Temes that were softened by the wide floods that stretched into the water meadows.

I sat on the small platform built in the ship's blunt bow and Father Pyrlig joined me there. I had given him my cloak, which he clutched tight around him. He had found some bread and cheese, which did not surprise me because I have never known a man eat so much. 'How did you know I'd beat Sigefrid?' he asked.

'I didn't know,' I said. 'In fact I was hoping he'd beat you, and that there would be one less Christian.'

He smiled at that, then gazed at the waterfowl on the flood water. 'I knew I had two or three strokes only,' he said, 'before he realised I knew what I was doing. Then he'd have cut the flesh off my bones.'

'He would,' I agreed, 'but I reckoned you had those three strokes and they'd prove enough.'

'Thank you for that, Uhtred,' he said, then broke off a lump of cheese and gave it to me. 'How are you these days?'

'Bored.'

'I hear you're married?'

'I'm not bored with her,' I said hurriedly.

'Good for you! Me, now? I can't stand my wife. Dear God, what a tongue that viper has. She can split a sheet of slate just by talking to it! You've not met my wife, have you?'

'No.'

'Sometimes I curse God for taking Adam's rib and making Eve, but then I see some young girl and my heart leaps and I think God knew what he was doing after all.'

I smiled. 'I thought Christian priests were supposed to set an example?'

'And what's wrong with admiring God's creations?' Pyrlig asked indignantly. 'Especially a young one with plump round tits and a fine fat rump? It would be sinful of me to ignore such signs of his grace.' He grinned, then looked anxious. 'I heard you were taken captive?'

'I was.'

'I prayed for you.'

'Thank you for that,' I said, and meant it. I did not worship the Christian god, but like Erik I feared he had some power, so prayers to him were not wasted.

'But I hear it was Alfred who had you released?' Pyrlig asked.

I paused. As ever I hated to acknowledge any debt to Alfred, but I grudgingly conceded that he had helped. 'He sent the men who freed me,' I said, 'yes.'

'And you reward him, Lord Uhtred, by naming yourself King of Mercia?'

'You heard that?' I asked cautiously.

'Of course I heard it! That great oaf of a Norseman bawled it just five paces from my ear. Are you King of Mercia?'

'No,' I said, resisting the urge to add 'not yet'.

'I didn't think you were,' Pyrlig said mildly. 'I'd have heard about that, wouldn't I? And I don't think you will be, not unless Alfred wants it.'

'Alfred can piss down his own throat for all I care,' I said.

'And of course I should tell him what I heard,' Pyrlig said.

'Yes,' I said bitterly, 'you should.'

I leaned against the curving timber of the ship's stem and stared at the backs of the oarsmen. I was also watching for any sign of a pursuing ship, half expecting to see some fast warship swept along by banks of long oars, but no mast showed above the river's long bends, which suggested Erik had successfully persuaded his brother against taking an instant revenge for the humiliation Pyrlig had given him. 'So whose idea is it,' Pyrlig asked, 'that you should be king in Mercia?' He waited for me to answer, but I said nothing. 'It's Sigefrid, isn't it?' he demanded. 'Sigefrid's crazy idea.'

'Crazy?' I asked innocently.

'The man's no fool,' Pyrlig said, 'and his brother certainly isn't. They know Æthelstan's getting old in East Anglia, and they ask who'll be king after him? And there's no king in Mercia. But he can't just take Mercia, can he? The Mercian Saxons will fight him and Alfred will come to their aid, and the Thurgilson brothers will find themselves facing a fury of Saxons! So Sigefrid has this idea to rally men and take East Anglia first, then Mercia, and then Wessex! And to do all that he really needs Earl Ragnar to bring men from Northumbria.'

I was appalled that Pyrlig, a friend of Alfred's, should know all that Sigefrid, Erik and Haesten planned, but I showed no reaction. 'Ragnar won't fight,' I said, trying to end the conversation.

'Unless you ask him,' Pyrlig said sharply. I just shrugged. 'But what can Sigefrid offer you?' Pyrlig asked, and, when I did not respond again, provided the answer himself. 'Mercia.'

I smiled condescendingly. 'It all sounds very complicated.'

'Sigefrid and Haesten,' Pyrlig said, ignoring my flippant comment, 'have ambitions to be kings. But there are only four kingdoms here! They can't take Northumbria because Ragnar won't let them. They can't take Mercia because Alfred won't let them. But Æthelstan's getting old, so they could take East Anglia. And why not finish the job? Take Wessex? Sigefrid says he'll put that drunken nephew of Alfred's on the throne, and that'll help calm the Saxons for a few months until Sigefrid murders him, and by then Haesten will be King of East Anglia and someone, you perhaps, King of Mercia. Doubtless they'll turn on you then and divide Mercia between them. That's the idea, Lord

Uhtred, and it's not a bad one! But who'd follow those two brigands?'

'No one,' I lied.

'Unless they were convinced that the Fates were on their side,' Pyrlig said almost casually, then looked at me. 'Did you meet the dead man?' he asked innocently, and I was so astonished by the question that I could not answer. I just stared into his round, battered face. 'Bjorn, he's called,' the Welshman said, putting another lump of cheese into his mouth.

'The dead don't lie,' I blurted out.

'The living do! By God, they do! Even I lie, Lord Uhtred,' he grinned at me mischievously, 'I sent a message to my wife and said she'd hate being in East Anglia!' He laughed. Alfred had asked Pyrlig to go to East Anglia because he was a priest and because he spoke Danish, and his task there had been to educate Guthrum in Christian ways. 'In fact she'd love it there!' Pyrlig went on. 'It's warmer than home and there are no hills to speak of. Flat and wet, that's East Anglia, and without a proper hill anywhere! And my wife's never been fond of hills, which is why I probably found God. I used to live on hilltops just to keep away from her, and you're closer to God on a hilltop. Bjorn isn't dead.'

He had said the last three words with a sudden brutality, and I answered him just as harshly. 'I saw him.'

'You saw a man come from a grave, that's what you saw.'

'I saw him!' I insisted.

'Of course you did! And you never thought to question what you saw, did you?' The Welshman asked the question harshly. 'Bjorn had been put in that grave just before you came! They piled earth on him and he breathed through a reed.'

I remembered Bjorn spitting something out of his mouth

84

as he staggered upright. Not the harp string, but something else. I had thought it a lump of earth, but in truth it had been paler. I had not thought about it at the time, but now I understood that the resurrection had all been a trick and I sat on the foredeck of the *Swan* and felt the last remnants of my dream crumbling. I would not be king. 'How do you know all this?' I asked bitterly.

'King Æthelstan's no fool. He has his spies.' Pyrlig put a hand on my arm. 'Was he very convincing?'

'Very,' I said, still bitter.

'He's one of Haesten's men, and if we ever catch him he'll go properly to hell. So what did he tell you?'

'That I would be king in Mercia,' I said softly. I was to be king of Saxon and Dane, enemy of the Welsh, king between the rivers and lord of all I ruled. 'I believed him,' I said ruefully.

'But how could you be King of Mercia?' Pyrlig asked, 'unless Alfred made you king?'

'Alfred?'

'You gave him your oath, did you not?'

I was ashamed to tell the truth, but had no choice. 'Yes,' I admitted.

'Which is why I must tell him,' Pyrlig said sternly, 'because a man breaking an oath is a serious matter, Lord Uhtred.'

'It is,' I agreed.

'And Alfred will have the right to kill you when I tell him.'

I shrugged.

'Better you keep the oath,' Pyrlig said, 'than be fooled by men who make a corpse from a living man. The Fates are not on your side, Lord Uhtred. Trust me.'

I looked at him and saw the sorrow in his eyes. He liked me, yet he was telling me I had been fooled, and he was right, and the dream was collapsing around me. 'What choice do I have?' I asked him bitterly. 'You know I went to Lundene to join them, and you must tell Alfred that, and he will never trust me again.'

'I doubt he trusts you now,' Pyrlig said cheerfully. 'He's a wise man, Alfred. But he knows you, Uhtred, he knows you are a warrior, and he needs warriors.' He paused to pull out the wooden cross that hung about his neck. 'Swear on it,' he said.

'Swear what?'

'That you will keep your oath to him! Do that and I will keep silent. Do that and I will deny what happened. Do that and I will protect you.'

I hesitated.

'If you break your oath to Alfred,' Pyrlig said, 'then you are my enemy and I'll be forced to kill you.'

'You think you could?' I asked.

He grinned his mischievous grin. 'Ah, you like me, lord, even though I am a Welshman and a priest, and you'd be reluctant to kill me, and I'd have three strokes before you woke up to your danger, so yes, lord, I would kill you.'

I put my right hand on the cross. 'I swear it,' I said.

And I was still Alfred's man.

Three

We reached Coccham that evening and I watched Gisela, who had as little love for Christianity as I did, warm to Father Pyrlig. He flirted with her outrageously, complimented her extravagantly and played with our children. We had two then, and we had been lucky, for both babies had lived, as had their mother. Uhtred was the oldest. My son. He was four years old with hair as golden-coloured as mine and a strong little face with a pug nose, blue eyes and a stubborn chin. I loved him then. My daughter Stiorra was two years old. She had a strange name and at first I had not liked it, but Gisela had pleaded with me and I could refuse her almost nothing, and certainly not the naming of a daughter. Stiorra simply meant 'star', and Gisela swore that she and I had met under a lucky star and that our daughter had been born under the same star. I had got used to the name by now and loved it as I loved the child, who had her mother's dark hair and long face and sudden mischievous smile. 'Stiorra, Stiorra!' I would say as I tickled her, or let her play with my arm rings. Stiorra, so beautiful.

I played with her on the night before Gisela and I left for Wintanceaster. It was spring and the Temes had subsided so that the river meadows showed again and the world was hazed with green as the leaves budded. The first lambs wobbled in fields bright with cowslips, and the blackbirds filled the sky with rippling song. Salmon had returned to the river and our woven willow traps provided good eating. The pear trees in Coccham were thick with buds, and just as thick with bullfinches, which had to be scared away by small boys so that we would have fruit in the summertime. It was a good time of year, a time when the world stirred, and a time when we had been summoned to Alfred's capital for the wedding of his daughter, Æthelflaed, to my cousin, Æthelred. And that night, as I pretended my knee was a horse and that Stiorra was the horse's rider, I thought about my promise to provide Æthelred with his wedding gift. The gift of a city. Lundene.

Gisela was spinning wool. She had shrugged when I had told her she was not to be Queen of Mercia, and she had nodded gravely when I said I would keep my oath with Alfred. She accepted fate more readily than I did. Fate and that fortunate star, she said, had brought us together despite all that the world had done to keep us apart. 'If you keep your oath to Alfred,' she said suddenly, interrupting my play with Stiorra, 'then you must capture Lundene from Sigefrid?'

'Yes,' I said, marvelling as I often did that her thoughts and mine were so often the same.

'Can you?' she asked.

'Yes,' I said. Sigefrid and Erik were still in the old city, their men guarding the Roman walls that they had repaired with timber. No ship could now come up the Temes without paying the brothers their toll, and that toll was huge, so that the river traffic had stopped, as merchants sought other ways to bring goods to Wessex. King Guthrum of East Anglia had threatened Sigefrid and Erik with war, but his threat had proved empty. Guthrum did not want war, he just wanted to persuade Alfred that he was doing his best to keep the peace treaty, so if Sigefrid was to be removed, then it would be the West Saxons who did the work, and I who would be responsible for leading them.

I had made my plans. I had written to the king and he, in turn, had written to the ealdormen of the shires, and I had been promised four hundred trained warriors along with the fyrd of Berrocscire. The fyrd was an army of farmers, foresters and labourers, and though it would be numerous it would also be untrained. The four hundred trained men would be the ones I relied on, and spies said Sigefrid now had at least six hundred in the old city. Those same spies said that Haesten had gone back to his camp at Beamfleot, but that was not far from Lundene and he would hurry to reinforce his allies, as would those Danes of East Anglia who hated Guthrum's Christianity and wanted Sigefrid and Erik to begin their war of conquest. The enemy, I thought, would number at least a thousand, and all of them would be skilled with sword, axe or spear. They would be war-Danes. Enemies to fear.

'The king,' Gisela said mildly, 'will want to know how you plan to do it.'

'Then I shall tell him,' I said.

She gave me a dubious glance. 'You will?'

'Of course,' I said, 'he's the king.'

She laid the distaff on her lap and frowned at me. 'You will tell him the truth?'

'Of course not,' I said. 'He may be the king, but I'm not a fool.'

She laughed, which made Stiorra echo the laugh. 'I wish I could come with you to Lundene,' Gisela said wistfully.

'You can't,' I said forcefully.

'I know,' she answered with uncharacteristic meekness, then touched a hand to her belly. 'I really can't.'

I stared at her. I stared a long time as her news settled in my mind. I stared, I smiled and then I laughed. I threw Stiorra high into the air so that her dark hair almost touched the smoke-blackened thatch. 'Your mother's pregnant,' I told the happily squealing child.

'And it's all your father's fault,' Gisela added sternly.

We were so happy.

Æthelred was my cousin, the son of my mother's brother. He was a Mercian, though for years now he had been loyal to Alfred of Wessex, and that day in Wintanceaster, in the great church Alfred had built, Æthelred of Mercia received his reward for that loyalty.

He was given Æthelflaed, Alfred's eldest daughter and second child. She was golden haired and had eyes the colour and brightness of a summer's sky. Æthelflaed was thirteen or fourteen years old then, the proper age for a girl to marry, and she had grown into a tall young woman with an upright stance and a bold look. She was already as tall as the man who was to be her husband.

Æthelred is a hero now. I hear tales of him, tales told by firelight in Saxon halls the length of England. Æthelred the Bold, Æthelred the Warrior, Æthelred the Loyal. I smile when I hear the stories, but I do not say anything, not even when men ask if it is true that I once knew Æthelred. Of course I knew Æthelred, and it is true that he was a warrior before sickness slowed and stilled him, and he was also bold, though his shrewdest stroke was to pay poets to be his courtiers so that they would make up songs about his prowess. A man could become rich in Æthelred's court by stringing words like beads.

He was never King of Mercia, though he wanted to be.

Alfred made sure of that, for Alfred wanted no king in Mercia. He wanted a loyal follower to be the ruler of Mercia, and he made sure that loyal follower was dependent on West Saxon money, and Æthelred was his chosen man. He was given the title Ealdorman of Mercia, and in all but name he was king, though the Danes of northern Mercia never recognised his authority. They did recognise his power, and that power came from being Alfred's son-in-law, which was why the Saxon thegns of southern Mercia also accepted him. They may not have liked Ealdorman Æthelred, but they knew he could bring West Saxon troops to confront any southward move by the Danes.

And on a spring day in Wintanceaster, a day bright with birdsong and sunlight, Æthelred came into his power. He strutted into Alfred's big new church with a smile across his red-bearded face. He ever suffered from the delusion that others liked him and perhaps some men did like him, but not me. My cousin was short, pugnacious and boastful. His jaw was broad and belligerent, his eyes challenging. He was twice as old as his bride, and for almost five years he had been commander of Alfred's household troops, an appointment he owed to birth rather than to ability. His good fortune had been to inherit lands that spread across most of southern Mercia, and that made him Mercia's foremost nobleman and, I grudgingly supposed, that sad country's natural leader. He was also, I ungrudgingly supposed, a piece of shit.

Alfred never saw that. He was deceived by Æthelred's flamboyant piety, and by the fact that Æthelred was always ready to agree with the King of Wessex. Yes, lord, no, lord, let me empty your night soil bucket, lord, and let me lick your royal arse, lord. That was Æthelred, and his reward was Æthelflaed.

She came into the church a few moments after Æthelred and she, like him, was smiling. She was in love with love,

91

transported that day to a height of joy that showed like radiance on her sweet face. She was a lithe young woman who already had a sway in her hips. She was long-legged, slender, and with a snub-nosed face unscarred by disease. She wore a dress of pale blue linen sewn with panels showing saints with haloes and crosses. She had a girdle of gold cloth hung with tassels and small silver bells. Over her shoulders was a cape of white linen that was fastened at her throat with a crystal brooch. The cape swept the rushes on the flagstone floor as she walked. Her hair, gold bright, was coiled about her head and held in place with ivory combs. That spring day was the first on which she wore her hair up, a sign of marriage, and it revealed her long thin neck. She was so graceful that day.

She caught my gaze as she walked towards the white-hung altar and her eyes, already filled with delight, seemed to take on a new dazzle. She smiled at me and I had to smile back, and she laughed for joy before walking on towards her father and the man who was to be her husband. 'She's very fond of you,' Gisela said with a smile.

'We have been friends since she was a child,' I said.

'She is still a child,' Gisela said softly as the bride reached the flower-strewn, cross-burdened altar.

I remember thinking that Æthelflaed was being sacrificed on that altar, but if that was true then she was a most willing victim. She had always been a mischievous and wilful child, and I did not doubt that she chafed under her sour mother's eye and her stern father's rules. She saw marriage as an escape from Alfred's dour and pious court, and that day Alfred's new church was filled with her happiness. I saw Steapa, perhaps the greatest warrior of Wessex, crying. Steapa, like me, was fond of Æthelflaed.

There were close to three hundred folk in the church. Envoys had come from the Frankish kingdoms across the sea, and others had come from Northumbria, Mercia, East Anglia and the Welsh kingdoms, and those men, all priests or nobles, were given places of honour close to the altar. The ealdormen and high reeves of Wessex were there too, while nearest to the altar was a dark herd of priests and monks. I heard little of the mass, for Gisela and I were in the back of the church where we talked with friends. Once in a while a sharp command for silence would be issued by a priest, but no one took any notice.

Hild, abbess of a nunnery in Wintanceaster, embraced Gisela. Gisela had two good Christian friends. The first was Hild, who had once fled the church to become my lover, and the other was Thyra, Ragnar's sister, with whom I had grown up and whom I loved as a sister. Thyra was a Dane, of course, and had been raised in the worship of Thor and Odin, but she had converted and come south to Wessex. She dressed like a nun. She wore a drab grey robe with a hood that hid her astonishing beauty. A black girdle encircled her waist, which was normally as thin as Gisela's, but now was plump with pregnancy. I laid a gentle hand on the girdle. 'Another?' I asked.

'And soon,' Thyra said. She had given birth to three children, of whom one, a boy, still lived.

'Your husband is insatiable,' I said with mock sternness.

'It is God's will,' Thyra said seriously. The humour I remembered from her childhood had evaporated with her conversion, though in truth it had probably left her when she had been enslaved in Dunholm by her brother's enemies. She had been raped and abused and driven mad by her captors, and Ragnar and I had fought our way into Dunholm to release her, but it was Christianity that had freed her from the madness and made her into the serene woman who now looked at me so gravely.

'And how is your husband?' I asked her.

'Well, thank you,' her face brightened as she spoke. Thyra had found love, not just of God, but of a good man, and for that I was thankful.

'You will, of course, call the child Uhtred if it's a boy,' I said sternly.

'If the king permits it,' Thyra said, 'we shall name him Alfred, and if she's a girl then she will be called Hild.'

That made Hild cry, and Gisela then revealed that she was also pregnant, and the three women went into an interminable discussion of babies. I extricated myself and found Steapa who was standing head and shoulders above the rest of the congregation. 'You know I'm to throw Sigefrid and Erik out of Lundene?' I asked him.

'I was told,' he said in his slow, deliberate way.

'You'll come?'

He gave a quick smile that I took to be consent. He had a frightening face, his skin stretched tight across his big-boned skull so that he seemed to be perpetually grimacing. In battle he was fearsome, a huge warrior with sword skill and savagery. He had been born to slavery, but his size and his fighting ability had raised him to his present eminence. He served in Alfred's bodyguard, owned slaves himself, and farmed a wide swathe of fine land in Wiltunscir. Men were wary of Steapa because of the anger that was ever-present on his face, but I knew him to be a kind man. He was not clever. Steapa was never a thinker, but he was kind and he was loyal. 'I'll ask the king to release you,' I said.

'He'll want me to go with Æthelred,' Steapa said.

'You'd rather be with the man who does the fighting, wouldn't you?' I asked.

Steapa blinked at me, too slow to understand the insult I had offered my cousin. 'I shall fight,' he said, then laid a huge arm on the shoulders of his wife, a tiny creature with

94

an anxious face and small eyes. I could never remember her name, so I greeted her politely and pushed on through the crowd.

Æthelwold found me. Alfred's nephew had begun drinking again and his eyes were bloodshot. He had been a handsome young man, but his face was thickening now and the veins were red and broken under his skin. He drew me to the edge of the church to stand beneath a banner on which a long exhortation had been embroidered in red wool. 'All That You Ask of God,' the banner read, 'You Will Receive if You Believe. When Good Prayer Asks, Meek Faith Receives.' I assumed Alfred's wife and her ladies had done the embroidery, but the sentiments sounded like Alfred's own. Æthelwold was clutching my elbow so hard that it hurt. 'I thought you were on my side,' he hissed reproachfully.

'I am,' I said.

He stared at me suspiciously. 'You met Bjorn?'

'I met a man pretending to be dead,' I said.

He ignored that, which surprised me. I remembered how affected he had been by his meeting with Bjorn, so impressed indeed that Æthelwold had become sober for a while, but now he took my dismissal of the risen corpse as a thing of no importance. 'Don't you understand,' he said, still gripping my elbow, 'that this is our best chance!'

'Our best chance of what?' I asked patiently.

'Of getting rid of him,' he spoke too vehemently and some folk standing nearby turned to look at us. I said nothing. Of course Æthelwold wanted to be rid of his uncle, but he lacked the courage to strike the blow himself, which is why he was constantly seeking allies like me. He looked up into my face and evidently found no support there, for he let go of my arm. 'They want to know if you've asked Ragnar,' he said, his voice lower.

So Æthelwold was still in contact with Sigefrid? That was interesting, but perhaps not surprising. 'No,' I said, 'I haven't.'

'For God's sake, why not?'

'Because Bjorn lied,' I said, 'and it is not my fate to be king in Mercia.'

'If I ever become king in Wessex,' Æthelwold said bitterly, 'then you had better run for your life.' I smiled at that, then just looked at him with unblinking eyes and, after a while he turned away and muttered something inaudible that was probably an apology. He stared across the church, his face dark. 'That Danish bitch,' he said vehemently.

'What Danish bitch?' I asked, and, for a heartbeat, I thought he meant Gisela.

'That bitch,' he jerked his head towards Thyra. 'The one married to the idiot. The pious bitch. The one with her belly stuffed.'

'Thyra?'

'She's beautiful,' Æthelwold said vengefully.

'So she is.'

'And she's married to an old fool!' he said, staring at Thyra with loathing on his face. 'When she's whelped that pup inside her I'm going to put her on her back,' he said, 'and show her how a real man ploughs a field.'

'You do know she's my friend?' I asked.

He looked alarmed. He had plainly not known of my long affection for Thyra and now tried to recant. 'I just think she's beautiful,' he said sullenly, 'that's all.'

I smiled and leaned down to his ear. 'You touch her,' I whispered, 'and I'll put a sword up your arsehole and I'll rip you open from the crotch to the throat and then feed your entrails to my pigs. Touch her once, Æthelwold, just once, and you're dead.'

I walked away. He was a fool and a drunk and a lecher, and I dismissed him as harmless. In which I was wrong, as it turned out. He was, after all, the rightful King of Wessex, but only he and a few other fools truly believed he should be king instead of Alfred. Alfred was everything his nephew was not; he was sober, clever, industrious and serious.

He was also happy that day. He watched as his daughter married a man he loved almost like a son, and he listened to the monks chanting and he stared at the church he had made with its gilded beams and painted statues, and he knew that by this marriage he was taking control of southern Mercia.

Which meant that Wessex, like the infants inside Thyra and Gisela, was growing.

Father Beocca found me outside the church where the wedding guests stood in the sunshine and waited for the summons to the feast inside Alfred's hall. 'Too many people were talking in the church!' Beocca complained. 'This was a holy day, Uhtred, a sacred day, a celebration of the sacrament, and people were talking as if they were at market!'

'I was one of them,' I said.

'You were?' he asked, squinting up at me. 'Well, you shouldn't have been talking. It's just plain bad manners! And insulting to God! I'm astonished at you, Uhtred, I really am! I'm astonished and disappointed.'

'Yes, father,' I said, smiling. Beocca had been reproving me for years. When I was a child, Beocca was my father's priest and confessor and, like me, he had fled Northumbria when my uncle had usurped Bebbanburg. Beocca had found a refuge at Alfred's court where his piety, his learning and his enthusiasm were appreciated by the king. That royal favour went a long way to stop men mocking Beocca, who was, in all truth, as ugly a man as you could have found in all Wessex. He had a club foot, a squint, and a palsied left hand. He was blind in his wandering eye that had gone as white as his hair, for he was now nearly fifty years old. Children jeered at him in the streets and some folk made the sign of the cross, believing that ugliness was a mark of the devil, but he was as good a Christian as any I have ever known. 'It is good to see you,' he said in a dismissive tone, as if he feared I might believe him. 'You do know the king wishes to speak with you? I suggested you meet him after the feast.'

'I'll be drunk.'

He sighed, then reached out with his good hand to hide the amulet of Thor's hammer that was showing at my neck. He tucked it under my tunic. 'Try to stay sober,' he said.

'Tomorrow, perhaps?'

'The king is busy, Uhtred! He doesn't wait on your convenience!'

'Then he'll have to talk to me drunk,' I said.

'And I warn you he wants to know how soon you can take Lundene. That's why he wishes to speak with you.' He stopped talking abruptly because Gisela and Thyra were walking towards us, and Beocca's face was suddenly transformed by happiness. He just stared at Thyra like a man seeing a vision and, when she smiled at him, I thought his heart would burst with pride and devotion. 'You're not cold, are you, my dear?' he asked solicitously. 'I can fetch you a cloak.'

'I'm not cold.'

'Your blue cloak?'

'I am warm, my dear,' she said, and put a hand on his arm.

'It will be no trouble!' Beocca said.

'I am not cold, dearest,' Thyra said, and again Beocca looked as though he would die of happiness.

All his life Beocca had dreamed of women. Of fair women. Of a woman who would marry him and give him children, and for all his life his grotesque appearance had made him an object of scorn until, on a hilltop of blood, he had met Thyra and he had banished the demons from her soul. They had been married four years now. To look at them was to be certain that no two people were ever more ill-suited to each other. An old, ugly, meticulous priest and a young, golden-haired Dane, but to be near them was to feel their joy like the warmth of a great fire on a winter's night. 'You shouldn't be standing, my dear,' he told her, 'not in your condition. I shall fetch you a stool.'

'I shall be sitting soon, dearest.'

'A stool, I think, or a chair. And are you sure you don't need a cloak? It would really be no trouble to fetch one!'

Gisela looked at me and smiled, but Beocca and Thyra were oblivious of us as they fussed over each other. Then Gisela gave the smallest jerk of her head and I looked to see that a young monk was standing nearby and staring at me. He had obviously been waiting to catch my eye, and he was just as obviously nervous. He was thin, not very tall, brown haired and had a pale face that looked remarkably like Alfred's. There was the same drawn and anxious look, the same serious eyes and thin mouth, and evidently the same piety judging by the monk's robe. He was a novice, because his hair was untonsured, and he dropped to one knee when I looked at him. 'Lord Uhtred,' he said humbly.

'Osferth!' Beocca said, becoming aware of the young monk's presence. 'You should be at your studies! The wedding is over and novices are not invited to the feast.'

Osferth ignored Beocca. Instead, with his head bowed, he spoke to me. 'You knew my uncle, lord.'

'I did?' I asked suspiciously. 'I have known many men,'

I said, preparing him for the refusal I was sure I would offer to whatever he requested of me.

'Leofric, lord.'

And my suspicion and hostility vanished at the mention of that name. Leofric. I even smiled. 'I knew him,' I said warmly, 'and I loved him.' Leofric had been a tough West Saxon warrior who had taught me about war. Earsling, he used to call me, meaning something dropped from an arse, and he toughened me, bullied me, snarled at me, beat me and became my friend and remained my friend until the day he died on the rain-swept battlefield at Ethandun.

'My mother is his sister, lord,' Osferth said.

'To your studies, young man!' Beocca said sternly.

I put a hand on Beocca's palsied arm to hold him back. 'Your mother's name?' I asked Osferth.

'Eadgyth, lord.'

I leaned down and tipped Osferth's face up. No wonder he looked like Alfred, for this was Alfred's bastard son who had been whelped on a palace servant-girl. No one ever admitted that Alfred was the boy's father, though it was an open secret. Before Alfred found God he had discovered the joys of palace maids, and Osferth was the product of that youthful exuberance. 'Does Eadgyth live?' I asked him.

'No, lord. She died of the fever two years ago.'

'And what are you doing here, in Wintanceaster?'

'He is studying for the church,' Beocca snapped, 'because his calling is to be a monk.'

'I would serve you, lord,' Osferth said anxiously, staring up into my face.

'Go!' Beocca tried to shoo the young man away. 'Go! Go away! Back to your studies, or I shall have the novice-master whip you!'

'Have you ever held a sword?' I asked Osferth.

'The one my uncle gave me, lord, I have it.'

'But you've not fought with it?'

'No, lord,' he said, and still he looked up at me, so anxious and frightened, and with a face so like his father's face.

'We are studying the life of Saint Cedd,' Beocca said to Osferth, 'and I expect you to have copied the first ten pages by sundown.'

'Do you want to be a monk?' I asked Osferth.

'No, lord,' he said.

'Then what?' I asked, ignoring Father Beocca who was spluttering protests, but unable to advance past my sword arm that held him back.

'I would follow my uncle's steps, lord,' Osferth said.

I almost laughed. Leofric had been as hard a warrior as ever lived and died, while Osferth was a puny, pale youth, but I managed to keep a straight face. 'Finan!' I shouted.

The Irishman appeared at my side. 'Lord?'

'This young man is joining my household troops,' I said, handing Finan some coins.

'You can't . . .' Beocca began protesting, then went silent when both Finan and I stared at him.

'Take Osferth away,' I told Finan, 'find him clothes fit for a man, and get him weapons.'

Finan looked dubiously at Osferth. 'Weapons?' he asked.

'He has the blood of warriors,' I said, 'so now we will teach him to fight.'

'Yes, lord,' Finan said, his tone suggesting he thought I was mad, but then he looked at the coins I had given him and saw a chance of profit. He grinned. 'We'll make him a warrior yet, lord,' he said, doubtless believing he lied, then he led Osferth away.

Beocca rounded on me. 'Do you know what you've just done?' he spluttered.

'Yes,' I said.

'You know who that boy is?'

101

'He's the king's bastard,' I said brutally, 'and I've just done Alfred a favour.'

'You have?' Beocca asked, still bristling, 'and what kind of favour, pray?'

'How long do you think he'll last,' I asked, 'when I put him in the shield wall? How long before a Danish blade slits him like a wet herring? That, father, is the favour. I've just rid your pious king of his inconvenient bastard.'

We went to the feast.

The wedding feast was as ghastly as I expected. Alfred's food was never good, rarely plentiful and his ale was always weak. Speeches were made, though I heard none, and harpists sang, though I could not hear them. I talked with friends, scowled at various priests who disliked my hammer amulet, and climbed the dais to the top table to give Æthelflaed a chaste kiss. She was all happiness. 'I'm the luckiest girl in all the world,' she told me.

'You're a woman now,' I said, smiling at her upswept woman's hair.

She bit her lower lip, looked shy, then grinned mischievously as Gisela approached. They embraced, golden hair against the dark, and Ælswith, Alfred's sour wife, glowered at me. I bowed low. 'A happy day, my lady,' I said.

Ælswith ignored that. She was sitting beside my cousin, who gestured at me with a pork rib. 'You and I have business to discuss,' he said.

'We do,' I said.

'We do, lord,' Ælswith corrected me sharply. 'Lord Æthelred is the Ealdorman of Mercia.'

'And I'm the Lord of Bebbanburg,' I said with an asperity that matched hers. 'How are you, cousin?'

'In the morning,' Æthelred said, 'I shall tell you our plans.'

'I was told,' I said, ignoring the truth that Alfred had asked me to devise the plans for the capture of Lundene, 'that we were to meet the king tonight?'

'I have other matters for my attention tonight,' Æthelred said, looking at his young bride, and for an eyeblink his expression was feral, almost savage, then he offered me a smile. 'In the morning, after prayers.' He waved the pork rib again, dismissing me.

Gisela and I lay in the principal chamber of the Two Cranes tavern that night. We lay close, my arm around her, and we said little. Smoke from the tavern hearth sifted up through the loose floorboards and men were singing beneath us. Our children slept across the room with Stiorra's nurse, while mice rustled in the thatch above. 'About now, I suppose,' Gisela said wistfully, breaking our silence.

'Now?'

'Poor little Æthelflaed is becoming a woman,' she said.

'She can't wait for that to happen,' I said.

Gisela shook her head. 'He'll rape her like a boar,' she said, whispering the words. I said nothing. Gisela put her head on my chest so that her hair was across my mouth. 'Love should be tender,' she went on.

'It is tender,' I said.

'With you, yes,' she said, and for a moment I thought she was crying.

I stroked her hair. 'What is it?'

'I like her, that is all.'

'Æthelflaed?'

'She has spirit and he has none.' She tilted her face to look at me and in the darkness I could just see the glint of her eyes. 'You never told me,' she said reprovingly, 'that the Two Cranes is a brothel.'

'There are not many beds in Wintanceaster,' I said, 'and

103

not nearly enough for all the invited guests, so we were very lucky to find this room.'

'And they know you very well here, Uhtred,' she said accusingly.

'It's a tavern as well,' I said defensively.

She laughed, then reached out a long thin arm and pushed a shutter open to find the heavens were bright with stars.

The sky was still clear next morning when I went to the palace, surrendered my two swords and was ushered by a young and very serious priest to Alfred's room. I had met him so often in that small, bare chamber that was cluttered with parchments. He was waiting there, dressed in the brown robe that made him look like a monk, and with him was Æthelred who wore his swords because, as Ealdorman of Mercia, he had been granted that privilege within the palace. A third man was in the room, Asser the Welsh monk, who glared at me with undisguised loathing. He was a slight, short man with a very pale face that was scrupulously clean-shaven. He had good cause to hate me. I had met him in Cornwalum where I had led a slaughter of the kingdom where he was an emissary and I had tried to kill Asser too, a failure I have regretted all my life. He scowled at me and I rewarded him with a cheerful grin that I knew would annoy him.

Alfred did not look up from his work, but gestured at me with his quill. The gesture was evidently a welcome. He was standing at the upright desk he used for writing and for a moment all I could hear was the quill spluttering scratchily on the skin. Æthelred smirked, looking pleased with himself, but then he always did.

'De consolatione philosophiae,' Alfred said without looking up from his work.

'Feels as if rain is coming, though,' I said, 'there's a haze in the west, lord, and the wind is brisk.'

He gave me an exasperated look. 'What is preferable,' he asked, 'and sweeter in this life than to serve and to be near to the king?'

'Nothing!' Æthelred said enthusiastically.

I made no answer because I was so astonished. Alfred liked the formalities of good manners, but he rarely wanted obsequiousness, yet the question suggested that he wished me to express some doltish adoration of him. Alfred saw my surprise and sighed. 'It is a question,' he explained, 'posed in the work I am copying.'

'I look forward to reading it,' Æthelred said. Asser said nothing, just watched me with his dark Welsh eyes. He was a clever man, and about as trustworthy as a spavined weasel.

Alfred laid down the quill. 'The king, in this context, Lord Uhtred, might be thought of as the representative of Almighty God, and the question suggests, does it not, the comfort to be gained from a nearness to God? Yet I fear you find no consolation in either philosophy or religion.' He shook his head, then tried to wipe the ink from his hands with a damp cloth.

'He had better find consolation from God, lord King,' Asser spoke for the first time, 'if his soul is not to burn in the eternal fire.'

'Amen,' Æthelred said.

Alfred looked ruefully at his hands that were now smeared with ink. 'Lundene,' he said, curtly changing the subject.

'Garrisoned by brigands,' I said, 'who are killing trade.'

'That much I know,' he said icily. 'The man Sigefrid.'

'One-thumbed Sigefrid,' I said, 'thanks to Father Pyrlig.'

'That I also know,' the king said, 'but I would dearly like to know what you were doing in Sigefrid's company?'

'Spying on them, lord,' I said brightly, 'just as you spied on Guthrum so many years ago.' I referred to a winter night when, like a fool, Alfred had disguised himself as a musician and gone to Cippanhamm when it was occupied by Guthrum in the days when he was an enemy of Wessex. Alfred's bravery had gone badly wrong, and if I had not been there then I dare say Guthrum would have become King of Wessex. I smiled at Alfred, and he knew I was reminding him that I had saved his life, but instead of showing gratitude he just looked disgusted.

'It is not what we heard,' Brother Asser went onto the attack.

'And what did you hear, brother?' I asked him.

He held up one long slender finger. 'That you arrived in Lundene with the pirate Haesten,' a second finger joined the first, 'that you were welcomed by Sigefrid and his brother, Erik,' he paused, his dark eyes malevolent, and raised a third finger, 'and that the pagans addressed you as King of Mercia.' He folded the three fingers slowly, as though his accusations were irrefutable.

I shook my head in feigned wonderment. 'I have known Haesten since I saved his life many years ago,' I said, 'and I used the acquaintance to be invited into Lundene. And whose fault is it if Sigefrid gives me a title I neither want nor possess?' Asser did not answer, Æthelred stirred behind me while Alfred just stared at me. 'If you don't believe me,' I said, 'ask Father Pyrlig.'

'He has been sent back to East Anglia,' Asser said brusquely, 'to continue his mission. But we will ask him. You may be sure of that.'

'I already have asked,' Alfred said, making a calming gesture towards Asser, 'and Father Pyrlig vouched for you,' he added those last words cautiously.

'And why,' I asked, 'has Guthrum not taken revenge for the insults to his envoys?'

'King Æthelstan,' Alfred said, using Guthrum's Christian name, 'has abandoned any claims to Lundene. It belongs to Mercia. His troops will not trespass there. But I have promised to send him Sigefrid and Erik as captives. That is your job.' I nodded, but said nothing. 'So tell me how you plan to capture Lundene?' Alfred demanded.

I paused. 'You attempted to ransom the city, lord?' I asked.

Alfred looked irritated at the question, then nodded abruptly. 'I offered silver,' he said stiffly.

'Offer more,' I suggested.

He gave me a very sour look. 'More?'

'The city will be difficult to take, lord,' I said. 'Sigefrid and Erik have hundreds of men. Haesten will join them as soon as he hears that we have marched. We would have to assault stone walls, lord, and men die like flies in such attacks.'

Æthelred again stirred behind me. I knew he wanted to dismiss my fears as cowardice, but he had just enough sense to keep silent.

Alfred shook his head. 'I offered them silver,' he said bitterly, 'more silver than a man can dream of. I offered them gold. They said they would take half of what I offered if I added one more thing.' He looked at me belligerently. I gave a small shrug as if to suggest that he had rejected a bargain. 'They wanted Æthelflaed,' he said.

'They can have my sword instead,' Æthelred said belligerently.

'They wanted your daughter?' I asked, amazed.

'They asked,' Alfred said, 'because they knew I would not grant their request, and because they wished to insult me.' He shrugged, as if to suggest that the insult was as feeble as it was puerile. 'So if the Thurgilson brothers are to be thrown out of Lundene, then you must do it. Tell me how.'

I pretended to gather my thoughts. 'Sigefrid does not have sufficient men to guard the whole circuit of the city walls,' I said, 'so we send a large attack against the western gate, and then launch the real assault from the north.'

Alfred frowned and sifted through the parchments piled on the windowsill. He found the page he wanted and peered at the writing. 'The old city, as I understand it,' he said, 'has six gates. To which do you refer?'

'In the west,' I said, 'the gate nearest the river. The local folk call it Ludd's Gate.'

'And on the northern side?'

'There are two gates,' I said, 'one leads directly into the old Roman fort, the other goes to the market place.'

'The forum,' Alfred corrected me.

'We take the one that leads to the market,' I said.

'Not the fort?'

'The fort is part of the walls,' I explained, 'so capture that gate and we still have to cross the fort's southern wall. But capture the market place and our men have cut off Sigefrid's retreat.'

I was talking nonsense for a reason, though it was plausible nonsense. Launching an attack from the new Saxon town across the River Fleot onto the old city's walls would draw defenders to Ludd's Gate, and if a smaller, better-trained force could then attack from the north they might find those walls lightly guarded. Once inside the city that second force could assault Sigefrid's men from the rear and open Ludd's Gate to let in the rest of the army. It was, in truth, the obvious way to assault the city, indeed it was so obvious that I was sure Sigefrid would be guarding against it.

Alfred pondered the idea.

Æthelred said nothing. He was waiting for his father-in-law's opinion.

'The river,' Alfred said in a hesitant tone, then shook his head as though his thought was leading nowhere.

'The river, lord?'

'An approach by ship?' Alfred suggested, still hesitant.

I let the idea hang, and it was like dangling a piece of gristle in front of an unschooled puppy.

And the puppy duly pounced. 'An assault by ship is frankly a better idea,' Æthelred said confidently. 'Four or five ships? Travelling with the current? We can land on the wharves and attack the walls from behind.'

'An attack by land will be hazardous,' Alfred said dubiously, though the question suggested he was supporting his son-in-law's ideas.

'And probably doomed,' Æthelred contributed confidently. He was not trying to hide his scorn of my plan.

'You considered a shipborne assault?' Alfred asked me.

'I did, lord.'

'It seems a very good idea to me!' Æthelred said firmly.

So now I gave the puppy the whipping it deserved. 'There's a river wall, lord,' I said. 'We can land on the wharves, but we still have a wall to cross.' The wall was built just behind the wharves. It was another piece of Roman work, all masonry, brick and studded with circular bastions.

'Ah,' Alfred said.

'But of course, lord, if my cousin wishes to lead an attack on the river wall?'

Æthelred was silent.

'The river wall,' Alfred said, 'it's high?'

'High enough, and newly repaired,' I said, 'but of course, I defer to your son-in-law's experience.'

Alfred knew I did no such thing and gave me an irritable look before deciding to slap me down as I had slapped Æthelred. 'Father Beocca tells me you took Brother Osferth into your service.'

'I did, lord,' I said.

'It is not what I wish for Brother Osferth,' Alfred said firmly, 'so you will send him back.'

'Of course, lord.'

'He is called to serve the church,' Alfred said, suspicious of my ready agreement. He turned and stared out of his small window. 'I cannot endure Sigefrid's presence,' he said. 'We need to open the river passage to shipping, and we need to do it soon.' His ink-smeared hands were clasped behind his back and I could see the fingers clenching and unclenching. 'I want it done before the first cuckoo sounds. Lord Æthelred will command the forces.'

'Thank you, lord,' Æthelred said and dropped to one knee.

'But you will take Lord Uhtred's advice,' the king insisted, turning on his son-in-law.

'Of course, lord,' Æthelred agreed untruthfully.

'Lord Uhtred is more experienced in war than you,' the king explained.

'I shall value his assistance, lord,' Æthelred lied very convincingly.

'And I want the city taken before the first cuckoo sounds!' the king reiterated.

Which meant we had perhaps six weeks. 'You will summon men now?' I asked Alfred.

'I shall,' he said, 'and you will each see to your provisions.'

'And I shall give you Lundene,' Æthelred said enthusiastically. 'What good prayers ask, lord, meek faith receives!'

'I don't want Lundene,' Alfred retorted with some asperity, 'it belongs to Mercia, to you,' he gave a slight inclination of his head to Æthelred, 'but perhaps you will allow me to appoint a bishop and a city governor?'

'Of course, lord,' Æthelred said.

I was dismissed, leaving father and son-in-law with the sour-faced Asser. I stood in the sunshine outside and thought about how I was to take Lundene, for I knew that I would have to do it, and do it without Æthelred ever suspecting my plans. And it could be done, I thought, but only by stealth and with good fortune. Wyrd bi∂ ful āræd.

110

I went to find Gisela. I crossed the outer courtyard to see a knot of women beside one of the doors. Eanflæd was among them and I turned to greet her. She had been a whore once, then she had become Leofric's lover, and now she was a companion to Alfred's wife. I doubted that Ælswith knew her companion had once been a whore, though perhaps she did and did not care because the bond between the two women was a shared bitterness. Ælswith resented that Wessex would not call the king's wife a queen, while Eanflæd knew too much of men to be fond of any one of them. Yet I was fond of her and I veered out of my way to speak with her, but, seeing me coming, she shook her head to warn me away.

I stopped then and saw that Eanflæd had her arm about a younger woman who sat on a chair with her head bowed. She looked up suddenly and saw me. It was Æthelflaed and her pretty face was wan, drawn and scared. She had been crying and her eyes were still bright from the tears. She seemed not to recognise me, then she did and offered me a sad reluctant smile. I smiled back, bowed and walked on.

And thought about Lundene.

PART TWO

The City

Four

We had agreed at Wintanceaster that Æthelred would come downriver to Coccham, bringing with him the troops from Alfred's household guard, his own warriors, and whatever men he could raise from his extensive lands in southern Mercia. Once he arrived we would jointly march on Lundene with the Berrocscire fyrd and my own household troops. Alfred had stressed the need for haste, and Æthelred had promised to be ready in two weeks.

Yet a whole month passed and still Æthelred had not come. The year's first nestlings were taking wing among trees that were still not in full leaf. The pear blossom was white, and wagtails flitted in and out of their nests under the thatched eaves of our house. I watched a cuckoo staring intently at those nests, planning when to leave her egg among the wagtail's clutch. The cuckoo had not started calling yet, but it would soon, and that was the time by which Alfred wanted Lundene captured.

I waited. I was bored, as were my household troops, who were ready for war and suffered peace. They numbered just fifty-six warriors. It was a small number, scarcely sufficient to crew a ship, but men cost money and I was hoarding my silver in those days. Five of those men were youngsters who had never faced the ultimate test of battle, which was to stand in the shield wall, and so, as we waited for Æthelred, I put those five men through day after day of hard training. Osferth, Alfred's bastard, was one of them. 'He's no good,' Finan said to me repeatedly.

'Give him time,' I said just as frequently.

'Give him a Danish blade,' Finan said viciously, 'and pray it slits his monkish belly.' He spat. 'I thought the king wanted him back in Wintanceaster?'

'He does.'

'So why don't you send him back? He's no use to us.'

'Alfred has too many other things on his mind,' I said, ignoring Finan's question, 'and he won't remember Osferth.' That was not true. Alfred had a most methodical mind, and he would not have forgotten Osferth's absence from Wintanceaster, nor my disobedience in not sending the youth back to his studies.

'But why not send him back?' Finan insisted.

'Because I liked his uncle,' I said, and that was true. I had loved Leofric and, for his sake, I would be kind to his nephew.

'Or are you just trying to annoy the king, lord?' Finan asked, then grinned and strode away without waiting for an answer. 'Hook and pull, you bastard!' he shouted at Osferth. 'Hook and pull!'

Osferth turned to look at Finan and was immediately struck on the head by an oak cudgel wielded by Clapa. If it had been an axe the blade would have split Osferth's helmet and cut deep into his skull, but the cudgel just half stunned him, so he fell to his knees.

'Get up, you weakling!' Finan snarled. 'Get up, hook and pull!'

Osferth tried to get up. His pale face looked miserable

under the battered helmet that I had given him. He managed to stand, but immediately wobbled and knelt again.

'Give me that,' Finan said, and snatched the axe out of Osferth's feeble hands. 'Now watch! It isn't difficult to do! My wife could do this!'

The five new men were facing five of my experienced warriors. The youngsters had been given axes, real weapons, and told to break the shield wall that opposed them. It was a small wall, just the five overlapping shields defended by wooden clubs, and Clapa grinned as Finan approached.

'What you do,' Finan was speaking to Osferth, 'is hook the axe blade over the top of the enemy bastard's shield. Is that so difficult? Hook it, pull the shield down, and let your neighbour kill the earsling behind it. We'll do it slowly, Clapa, to show how it's done, and stop grinning.'

They made the hook and pull in ludicrously slow motion, the axe coming gently overhand to latch its blade behind Clapa's shield, and Clapa then allowing Finan to pull the shield's top down towards him. 'There,' Finan turned on Osferth when Clapa's body had been exposed to a blow, 'that's how you break a shield wall! Now we'll do it for real, Clapa.'

Clapa grinned again, relishing a chance to clout Finan with the cudgel. Finan stepped back, licked his lips, then struck fast. He swung the axe just as he had demonstrated, but Clapa tilted the shield back to take the axe head on the wooden surface and, at the same time, rammed his cudgel under the shield in a savage thrust at Finan's groin.

It was always a pleasure to watch the Irishman fight. He was the quickest man with a blade that I ever saw, and I have seen many. I thought Clapa's lunge would fold him in two and drive him to the grass in agony, but Finan side-stepped, seized the lower rim of the shield with his left hand and jerked it hard upwards to drive the top iron rim into Clapa's face. Clapa staggered backwards, his nose already red with blood, and the axe was somehow dropped with the speed of a striking snake and its blade was hooked around Clapa's ankle. Finan pulled, Clapa fell back and now it was the Irishman who grinned. 'That isn't hook and pull,' he said to Osferth, 'but it works just the same.'

'Wouldn't have worked if you'd been holding a shield,' Clapa complained.

'That thing in your face, Clapa?' Finan said, 'thing that flaps open and closed? That ugly thing you shovel food into? Keep it shut.' He tossed the axe to Osferth who tried to snatch the handle out of the air. He missed and the axe thumped into a puddle.

The spring had turned wet. Rain sheeted down, the river spread, there was mud everywhere. Boots and clothes rotted. What little grain was left in store sprouted and I sent my men hunting or fishing to provide us with food. The first calves were born, slithering bloodily into a wet world. Every day I expected Alfred to come and inspect Coccham's progress, but in those drenched days he stayed in Wintanceaster. He did send a messenger, a pallid priest who brought a letter sewn into a greased lambskin pouch. 'If you cannot read it, lord,' he suggested tentatively as I slit the pouch open, 'I can . . .'

'I can read,' I growled. I could too. It was not an achievement I was proud of, because only priests and monks really needed the skill, but Father Beocca had whipped letters into me when I was a boy, and the lessons had proved useful. Alfred had decreed that all his lords should be able to read, not just so they could stagger their way through the gospel books the king insisted on sending as presents, but so they could read his messages.

I thought the letter might bring news of Æthelred, perhaps some explanation of why he was taking so long to bring his men to Coccham, but instead it was an order that I was to take one priest for every thirty men when I marched to Lundene. 'I'm to do what?' I asked aloud.

'The king worries about men's souls, lord,' the priest said.

'So he wants me to take useless mouths to feed? Tell him to send me grain and I'll take some of his damned priests.' I looked back to the letter, which had been written by one of the royal clerks, but at the bottom, in Alfred's bold handwriting, was one line. 'Where is Osferth?' the line read. 'He is to return today. Send him with Father Cuthbert.'

'You're Father Cuthbert?' I asked the nervous priest.

'Yes, lord.'

'Well you can't take Osferth back,' I said, 'he's ill.'

'Ill?'

'He's sick as a dog,' I said, 'and probably going to die.'

'But I thought I saw him,' Father Cuthbert said, gesturing out of the open door to where Finan was trying to goad Osferth into showing some skill and enthusiasm. 'Look,' the priest said brightly, trying to be of assistance.

'Very likely to die,' I said slowly and savagely. Father Cuthbert turned back to speak, caught my eye and his voice faltered. 'Finan!' I shouted, and waited till the Irishman came into the house with a naked sword in his hand. 'How long,' I asked, 'do you think young Osferth will live?'

'He'll be lucky to survive one day,' Finan said, assuming I had meant how long Osferth would last in battle.

'You see?' I said to Father Cuthbert. 'He's sick. He's going to die. So tell the king I shall grieve for him. And tell the king that the longer my cousin waits, the stronger the enemy becomes in Lundene.'

'It's the weather, lord,' Father Cuthbert said. 'Lord Æthelred cannot find adequate supplies.'

'Tell him there's food in Lundene,' I said and knew I was wasting my breath.

Æthelred finally came in mid April, and our joint forces now numbered almost eight hundred men, of whom fewer than four hundred were useful. The rest had been raised from the fyrd of Berrocscire or summoned from the lands in southern Mercia that Æthelred had inherited from his father, my mother's brother. The men of the fyrd were farmers, and they brought axes or hunting bows. A few had swords or spears, and fewer still had any armour other than a leather jerkin, while some marched with nothing but sharpened hoes. A hoe can be a fearful weapon in a street brawl, but it is hardly suitable to beat down a mailed Viking armed with shield, axe, short-sword and long blade.

The useful men were my household troops, a similar number from Æthelred's household, and three hundred of Alfred's own guards who were led by the grim-faced, looming Steapa. Those trained men would do the real fighting, while the rest were just there to make our force look large and menacing.

Yet in truth Sigefrid and Erik would know exactly how menacing we were. Throughout the winter and early spring there had been travellers coming upriver from Lundene and some were doubtless the brothers' spies. They would know how many men we were bringing, how many of those men were true warriors, and those same spies must have reported back to Sigefrid on the day we had last crossed the river to the northern bank.

We made the crossing upstream of Coccham, and it took all day. Æthelred grumbled about the delay, but the ford we used, which had been impassable all winter, was running high again and the horses had to be coaxed over, and the supplies had to be loaded on the ships for the crossing, though not on board Æthelred's ship, which he insisted could not carry cargo.

Alfred had given his son-in-law the *Heofonhlaf* to use for the campaign. It was the smaller of Alfred's river ships, and Æthelred had raised a canopy over the stern to make a sheltered spot just forward of the steersman's platform. There were cushions there, and pelts, and a table and stools, and Æthelred spent all day watching the crossing from beneath the canopy while servants brought him food and ale.

He watched with Æthelflaed who, to my surprise, accompanied her husband. I first saw her as she walked the small raised deck of the *Heofonhlaf* and, seeing me, she had raised a hand in greeting. At midday Gisela and I were summoned to her husband's presence and Æthelred greeted Gisela like an old friend, fussing over her and demanding that a fur cloak be fetched for her. Æthelflaed watched the fuss, then gave me a blank look. 'You are going back to Wintanceaster, my lady?' I asked her. She was a woman now, married to an ealdorman, and so I called her my lady.

'I am coming with you,' she said blandly.

That startled me. 'You're coming . . .' I began, but did not finish.

'My husband wishes it,' she said very formally, then a flash of the old Æthelflaed showed as she gave me a quick smile, 'and I'm glad. I want to see a battle.'

'A battle is no place for a lady,' I said firmly.

'Don't worry the woman, Uhtred!' Æthelred called across the deck. He had heard my last words. 'My wife will be quite safe, I have assured her of that.'

'War is no place for women,' I insisted.

'She wishes to see our victory,' Æthelred insisted, 'and so she shall, won't you, my duck?'

'Quack, quack,' Æthelflaed said so softly that only I could hear. There was bitterness in her tone, but when I glanced at her she was smiling sweetly at her husband.

121

'I would come if I could,' Gisela said, then touched her belly. The baby did not show yet.

'You can't,' I said, and was rewarded by a mocking grimace, then we heard a bellow of rage from the bows of *Heofonhlaf*.

'Can't a man sleep!' the voice shouted. 'You Saxon earsling! You woke me up!'

Father Pyrlig had been sleeping under the small platform at the ship's bows, where some poor man had inadvertently disturbed him. The Welshman now crawled into the sullen daylight and blinked at me. 'Good God,' he said with disgust in his voice, 'it's the Lord Uhtred.'

'I thought you were in East Anglia,' I called to him.

'I was, but King Æthelstan sent me to make sure you useless Saxons don't piss down your legs when you see Northmen on Lundene's walls.' It took me a moment to remember that Æthelstan was Guthrum's Christian name. Pyrlig came towards us, a dirty shirt covering his belly where his wooden cross hung. 'Good morning, my lady,' he called cheerfully to Æthelflaed.

'It is afternoon, father,' Æthelflaed said, and I could tell from the warmth in her voice that she liked the Welsh priest.

'Is it afternoon? Good God, I slept like a baby. Lady Gisela! A pleasure. My goodness, but all the beauties are gathered here!' He beamed at the two women. 'If it wasn't raining I would think I'd been transported to heaven. My lord,' the last two words were addressed to my cousin and it was plain from their tone that the two men were not friends. 'You need advice, my lord?' Pyrlig asked.

'I do not,' my cousin said harshly.

Father Pyrlig grinned at me. 'Alfred asked me to come as an adviser.' He paused to scratch a fleabite on his belly. 'I'm to advise Lord Æthelred.'

'As am I,' I said.

'And doubtless Lord Uhtred's advice would be the same as mine,' Pyrlig went on, 'which is that we must move with the speed of a Saxon seeing a Welshman's sword.'

'He means we must move fast,' I explained to Æthelred, who knew perfectly well what the Welshman had meant.

My cousin ignored me. 'Are you being deliberately offensive?' he asked Pyrlig stiffly.

'Yes, lord!' Pyrlig grinned, 'I am!'

'I have killed dozens of Welshmen,' my cousin said.

'Then the Danes will be no problem to you, will they?' Pyrlig retorted, refusing to take offence. 'But my advice still stands, lord. Make haste! The pagans know we're coming, and the more time you give them, the more formidable their defences!'

We might have moved fast had we possessed ships to carry us downriver, but Sigefrid and Erik, knowing we were coming, had blocked all traffic on the Temes and, not counting *Heofonhlaf*, we could only muster seven ships, not nearly sufficient to carry our men and so only the laggards and the supplies and Æthelred's cronies travelled by water. So we marched and it took us four days, and every day we saw horsemen to the north of us or ships downstream of us, and I knew those were Sigefrid's scouts, making a last count of our numbers as our clumsy army lumbered ever nearer Lundene. We wasted one whole day because it was a Sunday and Æthelred insisted that the priests accompanying the army said mass. I listened to the drone of voices and watched the enemy horsemen circle around us. Haesten, I knew, would already have reached Lundene, and his men, at least two or three hundred of them, would be reinforcing the walls.

Æthelred travelled on board the *Heofonhlaf*, only coming ashore in the evening to walk around the sentries I had posted. He made a point of moving those sentries, as if to suggest I did not know my business, and I let him do it. On the last night of the journey we camped on an island that was reached from the north bank by a narrow causeway, and its reed-fringed shore was thick with mud so that Sigefrid, if he had a mind to attack us, would find our camp hard to approach. We tucked our ships into the creek that twisted to the island's north and, as the tide went down and the frogs filled the dusk with croaking, the hulls settled into the thick mud. We lit fires on the mainland that would illuminate the approach of any enemy, and I posted men all around the island.

Æthelred did not come ashore that evening. Instead he sent a servant who demanded that I go to him on board the *Heofonhlaf* and so I took off my boots and trousers and waded through the glutinous muck before hauling myself over the ship's side. Steapa, who was marching with the men from Alfred's bodyguard, came with me. A servant drew buckets of river water from the ship's far side and we cleaned the mud from our legs, then dressed again before joining Æthelred under his canopy at the *Heofonhlaf* 's stern. My cousin was accompanied by the commander of his household guard, a young Mercian nobleman named Aldhelm who had a long, supercilious face, dark eyes and thick black hair that he oiled to a lustrous sheen.

Æthelflaed was also there, attended by a maid and by a grinning Father Pyrlig. I bowed to her and she smiled back, but without enthusiasm, and then bent to her embroidery, which was illuminated by a horn-shielded lantern. She was threading white wool onto a dark grey field, making the image of a prancing horse that was her husband's banner. The same banner, much larger, hung motionless at the ship's mast. There was no wind, so the smoke from the fires of Lundene's two towns was a motionless smear in the darkening east.

124

'We attack at dawn,' Æthelred announced without so much as a greeting. He was dressed in a mail coat and had his swords, short and long, belted at his waist. He was looking unusually smug, though he tried to make his voice casual. 'But I will not sound the advance for my troops,' he went on, 'until I hear your own attack has started.'

I frowned at those words. 'You won't start your attack,' I repeated cautiously, 'until you hear mine has started?'

'That's plain, isn't it?' Æthelred demanded belligerently.

'Very plain,' Aldhelm said mockingly. He treated Æthelred in the same manner that Æthelred behaved to Alfred and, secure in my cousin's favour, felt free to offer me veiled insult.

'It's not plain to me!' Father Pyrlig put in energetically. 'The agreed plan,' the Welshman went on, speaking to Æthelred, 'is for you to make a feint attack on the western walls and, when you have drawn defenders from the north wall, for Uhtred's men to make the real assault.'

'Well I've changed my mind,' Æthelred said airily. 'Uhtred's men will now provide the diversionary attack, and my assault will be the real one.' He tilted up his broad chin and stared at me, daring me to contradict him.

Æthelflaed also looked at me, and I sensed she wanted me to oppose her husband, but instead I surprised all of them by bowing my head as if in acquiescence. 'If you insist,' I said.

'I do,' Æthelred said, unable to conceal his pleasure at gaining the apparent victory so easily. 'You may take your own household troops,' he went on grudgingly, as though he possessed the authority to take them away from me, 'and thirty other men.'

'We agreed I could have fifty,' I said.

'I have changed my mind about that too!' he said pugnaciously. He had already insisted that the men of the Berrocscire fyrd, my men, would swell his ranks, and I had

125

meekly agreed to that, just as I had now agreed that the glory of the successful assault could be his. 'You may take thirty,' he went on harshly. I could have argued and maybe I should have argued, but I knew it would do no good. Æthelred was beyond argument, wanting only to demonstrate his authority in front of his young wife. 'Remember,' he said, 'that Alfred gave me command here.'

'I had not forgotten,' I said. Father Pyrlig was watching me shrewdly, doubtless wondering why I had yielded so easily to my cousin's bullying. Aldhelm was half smiling, probably in the belief that I had been thoroughly cowed by Æthelred.

'You will leave before us,' Æthelred went on.

'I shall leave very soon,' I said, 'I have to.'

'My household troops,' Æthelred said, now looking at Steapa, 'will lead the real attack. You will bring the royal troops immediately behind.'

'I'm going with Uhtred,' Steapa said.

Æthelred blinked. 'You are the commander,' he said slowly, as though he talked with a small child, 'of Alfred's bodyguard! And you will bring them to the wall as soon as my men have laid the ladders.'

'I'm going with Uhtred,' Steapa said again. 'The king ordered it.'

'The king did no such thing!' Æthelred said dismissively.

'In writing,' Steapa said. He frowned, then felt in a pouch and brought out a small square of parchment. He peered at it, not sure which way up the writing went, then just shrugged and gave the scrap to my cousin.

Æthelred frowned as he read the message in the light of his wife's lantern. 'You should have given me this before,' he said petulantly.

'I forgot,' Steapa said, 'and I'm to take six men of my own choosing.' Steapa had a way of speaking that discouraged argument. He spoke slowly, harshly and dully, and managed to convey the impression that he was too stupid to understand any objection raised against his words. He also conveyed the thought that he might just slaughter any man who insisted on contradicting him. And Æthelred, faced with Steapa's stubborn voice, and by the sheer presence of the man who was so tall and broad and skull-faced, surrendered without a fight.

'If the king orders it,' he said, offering back the scrap of parchment.

'He does,' Steapa insisted. He took the parchment and seemed uncertain what to do with it. For a heartbeat I thought he was going to eat it, but then he tossed it over the ship's side and then frowned eastwards at the great pall of smoke that hung above the city.

'Be certain you're on time tomorrow,' Æthelred said to me, 'success depends on it.'

That was evidently our dismissal. Another man would have offered us ale and food, but Æthelred turned away from us and so Steapa and I stripped our legs bare again and waded ashore through the cloying mud. 'You asked Alfred if you could come with me?' I asked Steapa as we pushed through the reeds.

'No,' he said, 'it was the king who wanted me to come with you. It was his idea.'

'Good,' I said, 'I'm glad.' I meant it too. Steapa and I had begun as enemies, but we had become friends, a bond forged by standing shield to shield in the face of an enemy. 'There's no one I'd rather have with me,' I told him warmly as I stooped to pull on my boots.

'I'm coming with you,' he said in his slow voice, 'because I'm to kill you.'

I stopped and stared at him in the darkness. 'You're to do what?'

127

'I'm to kill you,' he said, then remembered there was more to Alfred's orders, 'if you prove to be on Sigefrid's side.'

'But I'm not,' I said.

'He just wants to be sure of that,' Steapa said, 'and that monk? Asser? He says you can't be trusted, so if you don't obey your orders then I'm to kill you.'

'Why are you telling me this?' I asked him.

He shrugged. 'Doesn't matter whether you're ready for me or not,' he said, 'I'll still kill you.'

'No,' I said, amending his words, 'you'll try to kill me.'

He thought about that for quite a long time, then shook his head. 'No,' he said, 'I'll kill you.' And so he would.

We left in the black of night under a sky smothered with clouds. The enemy horsemen who had been watching us had withdrawn to the city at dusk, but I was certain Sigefrid would still have scouts in the darkness and so for an hour or more we followed a track that led north through the marshes. It was hard keeping to the path, but after a while the ground became firmer and climbed to a village where small fires burned inside mud-walled huts piled with great heaps of thatch. I pushed a door open to see a family crouched in terror about their hearth. They were frightened because they had heard us, and they knew nothing moves at night except creatures that are dangerous, sinister and deadly. 'What's this place called?' I asked and for a moment no one answered, then a man bowed his head convulsively and said he thought the settlement was named Padintune. 'Padintune?' I asked, 'Padda's estate? Is Padda here?'

'He's dead, lord,' the man said, 'he died years ago, lord. No one here knew him, lord.'

'We're friends,' I told him, 'but if anyone here leaves their house, we won't be friends.' I did not want some villager running to Lundene to warn Sigefrid that we had stopped in Padintune. 'You understand that?' I asked the man.

'Yes, lord.'

'Leave your house,' I said, 'and you die.'

I assembled my men in the small street and had Finan place a guard on every hovel. 'No one's to leave,' I told him. 'They can sleep in their beds, but no one's to leave the village.'

Steapa loomed from the dark. 'Aren't we supposed to be marching north?' he asked.

'Yes, and we're not,' I retorted. 'So this is when you're supposed to kill me. I'm disobeying orders.'

'Ah,' he grunted, then crouched. I heard the leather of his armour creak and the chink of his chain mail settling.

'You could draw your sax now,' I suggested, 'and gut me in one move? One cut up into my belly? Just make it fast, Steapa. Open my belly and keep the blade moving till it reaches my heart. But just let me draw my sword first, will you? I promise not to use it on you. I just want to go to Odin's hall when I'm dead.'

He chuckled. 'I'll never understand you, Uhtred,' he said.

'I'm a very simple soul,' I told him. 'I just want to go home.'

'Not Odin's hall?'

'Eventually,' I said, 'yes, but home first.'

'To Northumbria?'

'Where I have a fortress by the sea,' I said wistfully, and I thought of Bebbanburg on its high crag, and of the wild grey sea rolling endlessly to break on the rocks, and of the cold wind blowing from the north and of the white gulls crying in the spindrift. 'Home,' I said.

'The one your uncle stole from you?' Steapa asked.

'Ælfric,' I said vengefully, and I thought of fate again. Ælfric was my father's younger brother and he had stayed in Bebbanburg while I had accompanied my father to Eoferwic. I was a child. My father had died in Eoferwic, cut down by a Danish blade, and I had been given as a slave to Ragnar the Older, who had raised me like a son, and my uncle had ignored my father's wishes and kept Bebbanburg for himself. That treachery was ever in my heart, seeping anger, and one day I would revenge it. 'One day,' I told Steapa, 'I shall gut Ælfric from his crotch to his breastbone and watch him die, but I won't do it quickly. I won't pierce his heart. I shall watch him die and piss on him while he struggles. Then I'll kill his sons.'

'And tonight?' Steapa asked. 'Who do you kill tonight?'

'Tonight we take Lundene,' I said.

I could not see his face in the dark, but I sensed that he smiled. 'I told Alfred he could trust you,' Steapa said.

It was my turn to smile. Somewhere in Padintune a dog howled and was quieted. 'But I'm not sure Alfred can trust me,' I said after a long pause.

'Why?' Steapa asked, puzzled.

'Because in one way I'm a very good Christian,' I said.

'You? A Christian?'

'I love my enemies,' I said.

'The Danes?'

'Yes.'

'I don't,' he said bleakly. Steapa's parents had been slaughtered by Danes. I did not respond. I was thinking of destiny. If the three spinners know our fate, then why do we make oaths? Because if we then break an oath, is it treachery? Or is it fate? 'So will you fight them tomorrow?' Steapa asked.

'Of course,' I said. 'But not in the way Æthelred expects. So I'm disobeying orders, and your orders are to kill me if I do that.'

130

'I'll kill you later,' Steapa said.

Æthelred had changed our agreed plan without ever suspecting that I had never intended to keep to it anyway. It was too obvious. How else would an army assault a city, except by trying to draw defenders away from the targeted ramparts? Sigefrid would know our first assault was a feint, and he would leave his garrison in place until he was certain he had identified the real threat, and then we would die under his walls and Lundene would remain a stronghold of the Northmen.

So the only way to capture Lundene was by trickery, stealth and by taking a desperate risk. 'What I'm going to do,' I told Steapa, 'is wait for Æthelred to leave the island. Then we go back there, and we take two of the ships. It will be dangerous, very, because we have to go through the bridge's gap in the dark and ships die there even in daylight. But if we can get through then there is an easy way into the old city.'

'I thought there was a wall along the river?'

'There is,' I said, 'but it's broken in one place.' A Roman had built a great house by the river and had cut a small channel beside his house. The channel pierced the wall, breaking it. I assumed the Roman had been wealthy and he had wanted a place to berth his ship and so he had pulled down a stretch of the river wall to make his channel and that was my way into Lundene.

'Why didn't you tell Alfred?' Steapa asked.

'Alfred can keep a secret,' I said, 'but Æthelred can't. He would have told someone and within two days the Danes would have known what we planned.' And that was true. We had spies and they had spies, and if I had revealed my real intentions then Sigefrid and Erik would have blocked the channel with ships and garrisoned the big house beside the river with men. We would have died on the wharves,

131

and we still might die because I did not know that we could find the gap in the bridge, and if we did find it whether we could shoot through that perilous broken space where the river level dropped and the water foamed. If we missed, if one of the ships was just a half oar's length too far south or north, then it would be swept onto the jagged pilings and men would be tipped into the river and I would not hear them drown because their armour and weapons would drag them under instantly.

Steapa had been thinking, always a slow process, but now he posed a shrewd question. 'Why not land upriver of the bridge?' he suggested. 'There must be gates through the wall?'

'There are a dozen gates,' I said, 'maybe a score, and Sigefrid will have blocked them all, but the last thing he'll expect is for ships to try and run the gap in the bridge.'

'Because ships die there?' Steapa said.

'Because ships die there,' I agreed. I had watched it happen once, watched a trading ship run the gap at slack water, and somehow the steersman had veered too far to one side and the broken pilings had ripped the planks from the bottom of his hull. The gap was some forty paces wide and, when the river was calm with neither tide nor wind to churn the water, the gap looked innocent, but it never was. Lundene's bridge was a killer, and to take Lundene I had to run the bridge.

And if we survived? If we could find the Roman dock and get ashore? Then we would be few and the enemy would be many, and some of us would die in the streets before Æthelred's force could ever cross the wall. I touched Serpent-Breath's hilt and felt the small silver cross that was embedded there. Hild's gift. A lover's gift. 'Have you heard a cuckoo yet?' I asked Steapa.

'Not yet.'

'It's time to go,' I said, 'unless you want to kill me?'

'Maybe later,' Steapa said, 'but for the moment I'll fight beside you.'

And we would have a fight. That I knew. And I touched my hammer amulet and sent a prayer into the darkness that I would live to see the child in Gisela's belly.

Then we went back south.

Osric, who had brought me away from Lundene with Father Pyrlig, was one of our shipmasters, and the other was Ralla, the man who had carried my force to ambush the Danes whose corpses I had hanged beside the river. Ralla had negotiated the gap in Lundene's bridge more times than he could remember. 'But never at night,' he told me that night when we returned to the island.

'But it can be done?'

'We're going to discover that, lord, aren't we?'

Æthelred had left a hundred men to guard the island where the ships lay and those men were under the command of Egbert, an old warrior whose authority was denoted by a silver chain hanging about his neck, and who challenged me when we unexpectedly returned. He did not trust me and believed I had abandoned my northern attack because I did not want Æthelred to succeed. I needed him to give me men, but the more I pleaded the more he bristled with hostility. My own men were boarding the two ships, wading through the cold water and hauling themselves over the sides. 'How do I know you're not just going back to Coccham?' Egbert asked suspiciously.

'Steapa!' I called. 'Tell Egbert what we're doing.'

'Killing Danes,' Steapa growled from beside a campfire. The flames reflected from his mail coat and from his hard, feral eyes.

'Give me twenty men,' I pleaded with Egbert.

He stared at me, then shook his head. 'I can't,' he said.

'Why not?'

'We have to guard the Lady Æthelflaed,' he said. 'Those are the Lord Æthelred's orders. We're here to guard her.'

'Then leave twenty men on her ship,' I said, 'and give me the rest.'

'I can't,' Egbert insisted doggedly.

I sighed. 'Tatwine would have given me men,' I said. Tatwine had been the commander of the household troops for Æthelred's father. 'I knew Tatwine,' I said.

'I know you did. I remember you.' Egbert spoke curtly and the hidden message in his tone was that he did not like me. As a young man I had served under Tatwine for a few months, and back then I had been brash, ambitious and arrogant. Egbert plainly thought I was still brash, ambitious and arrogant, and perhaps he was right.

He turned away and I thought he was dismissing me, but instead he watched as a pale and ghostly shape appeared beyond the campfires. It was Æthelflaed, who had evidently seen our return and had waded ashore wrapped in a white cloak to discover what we did. Her hair was unbound and fell in golden tangles over her shoulders. Father Pyrlig was with her.

'You didn't go with Æthelred?' I asked, surprised to see the Welsh priest.

'His lordship felt he needed no more advice,' Pyrlig said, 'so asked me to stay here and pray for him.'

'He didn't ask,' Æthelflaed corrected him, 'he ordered you to stay and pray for him.'

'He did,' Pyrlig said, 'and as you can see, I am dressed for praying.' He was in a mail coat and had his swords strapped at his waist. 'And you?' he challenged me. 'I thought you were marching to the city's north?'

'We're going downriver,' I explained, 'and attacking Lundene from the wharf.'

'Can I come?' Æthelflaed asked instantly.

'No.'

She smiled at that curt refusal. 'Does my husband know what you're doing?'

'He'll find out, my lady.'

She smiled again, then walked to my side and pulled my cloak aside to lean against me. She wrapped my dark cloak over her white one. 'I'm cold,' she explained to Egbert, whose face showed surprise and indignation at her behaviour.

'We are old friends,' I said to Egbert.

'Very old friends,' Æthelflaed agreed, and she put an arm around my waist and clung to me. Egbert could not see her arm beneath my cloak. I was aware of her golden hair just beneath my beard, and I could feel her thin body shivering. 'I think of Uhtred as an uncle,' she told Egbert.

'An uncle who is going to give your husband victory,' I told her, 'but I need men. And Egbert won't give me men.'

'He won't?' she asked.

'He says he needs all his men to guard you.'

'Give him your best men,' she said to Egbert in a light, pleasant voice.

'My lady,' Egbert said, 'my orders are to . . . '

'You will give him your best men!' Æthelflaed's voice was suddenly hard as she stepped from beneath my cloak into the harsh light of the campfires. 'I am a king's daughter!' she said arrogantly, 'and wife to Mercia's Ealdorman! And I am demanding that you give Uhtred your best men! Now!'

She had spoken very loudly so that men all across the island were staring at her. Egbert looked offended, but said nothing. He straightened instead and looked stubborn. Pyrlig caught my eye and smiled slyly.

'None of you have the courage to fight alongside Uhtred?'

Æthelflaed demanded of the watching men. She was four-teen years old, a slight, pale girl, yet in her voice was the lineage of ancient kings. 'My father would want you to show courage tonight!' she went on, 'or am I to return to Wintanceaster and tell my father that you sat by the fires while Uhtred fought?' This last question was directed at Egbert.

'Twenty men,' I pleaded with him.

'Give him more!' Æthelflaed said firmly.

'There's only room in the boats for forty more,' I said.

'Then give him forty!' Æthelflaed said.

'Lady,' Egbert said hesitantly, but stopped when Æthelflaed held up one small hand. She turned to look at me.

'I can trust you, Lord Uhtred?' she asked.

It seemed a strange question from a child I had known nearly all her life and I smiled at it. 'You can trust me,' I said lightly.

Her face grew harder and her eyes flinty. Perhaps that was the reflection of the fire from her pupils, but I was suddenly aware that this was far more than a child, she was a king's daughter. 'My father,' she said in a clear voice so that others could hear, 'says you are the best warrior in his service. But he does not trust you.'

There was an awkward silence. Egbert cleared his throat and stared at the ground. 'I have never let your father down,' I said harshly.

'He fears your loyalty is for sale,' she said.

'He has my oath,' I replied, my voice still harsh.

'And I want it now,' she demanded and held out a slender hand.

'What oath?' I asked.

'That you keep your oath to my father,' Æthelflaed said, 'and that you swear loyalty to Saxon over Dane, and that you will fight for Mercia when Mercia asks it.'

136

'My lady,' I began, appalled at her list of demands.

'Egbert!' Æthelflaed interrupted me. 'You will give Lord Uhtred no men unless he swears to serve Mercia while I live.'

'No, lady,' Egbert muttered.

While she lived? Why had she said that? I remember wondering about those words, and I remember, too, thinking that my plan to capture Lundene hung in the balance. Æthelred had stripped me of the forces I needed, and Æthelflaed had the power to restore my numbers, but to win my victory I had to lock myself in yet another oath that I did not want to swear. What did I care for Mercia? But I cared that night about taking men through a bridge of death to prove that I could do it. I cared about reputation, I cared about my name, I cared about fame.

I drew Serpent-Breath, knowing that was why she held out her hand, and I gave the blade to her, hilt first. Then I knelt and I folded my hands around hers that, in turn, were clasped about the hilt of my sword. 'I swear it, lady,' I said.

'You swear,' she said, 'that you will serve my father faithfully?'

'Yes, lady.'

'And, as I live, you will serve Mercia?'

'As you live, lady,' I said, kneeling in the mud, and wondering what a fool I was. I wanted to be in the north, I wanted to be free of Alfred's piety, I wanted to be with my friends, yet here I was, swearing loyalty to Alfred's ambitions and to his golden-haired daughter. 'I swear it,' I said, and gave her hands a slight squeeze as a signal of my truthfulness.

'Give him men, Egbert,' Æthelflaed ordered.

He gave me thirty and, to give Egbert his due, he gave me his fit men, the young ones, leaving his older and sick warriors to guard Æthelflaed and the camp. So now I led

137

over seventy men and those men included Father Pyrlig.
'Thank you, my lady,' I said to Æthelflaed.

'You could reward me,' she said, and once again sounded child-like, her solemnity gone and her old mischief back.

'How?'

'Take me with you?'

'Never,' I said harshly.

She frowned at my tone and looked up into my eyes. 'Are you angry with me?' she asked in a soft voice.

'With myself, lady,' I said and turned away.

'Uhtred!' She sounded unhappy.

'I will keep the oaths, lady,' I said, and I was angry that I had taken them again, but at least they had provided me with seventy men to take a city, seventy men on board two boats that pushed away from the creek into the Temes's strong current.

I was on board Ralla's boat, the same ship that we had captured from Jarrel, the Dane whose hanged body had long been reduced to a skeleton. Ralla was at the stern, leaning on the steering-oar. 'Not sure we should be doing this, lord,' he said.

'Why not?'

He spat over the side into the black river. 'Water's running too fast. It'll be spilling through the gap like a waterfall. Even at slack water, lord, that gap can be wicked.'

'Take it straight,' I said, 'and pray to whatever god you believe in.'

'If we can even see the gap,' he said gloomily. He peered behind, looking for a glimpse of Osric's boat, but it was swallowed in the darkness. 'I've seen it done on a falling tide,' Ralla said, 'but that was in daylight, and the river wasn't in spate.'

'The tide's falling?' I asked.

'Like a stone,' Ralla said gloomily.

'Then pray,' I said curtly.

I touched the hammer amulet, then the hilt of Serpent-Breath as the boat gathered speed on the surging current. The riverbanks were far off. Here and there was a glimmer of light, evidence of a fire smouldering in a house, while ahead, under the moonless sky, was a dull glow smeared with a black veil, and that, I knew, was the new Saxon Lundene. The glow came from the sullen fires in the town and the veil was the smoke of those fires, and I knew that somewhere beneath that veil Æthelred would be marshalling his men for their advance across the valley of the Fleot and up to the old Roman wall. Sigefrid, Erik and Haesten would know he was there because someone would have run from the new town to warn the old. Danes, Norsemen and Frisians, even some masterless Saxons, would be rousing themselves and hurrying to the old city's ramparts.

And we swept down the black river.

No one spoke much. Every man in both boats knew the danger we faced. I edged my way forward between the crouching figures, and Father Pyrlig must have sensed my approach or else a gleam of light reflected from the wolf's head that served as the silver crest of my helmet because he greeted me before I saw him. 'Here, lord,' he said.

He was sitting on the end of a rower's bench and I stood beside him, my boots splashing in the bilge water. 'Have you prayed?' I asked him.

'I haven't stopped praying,' he said seriously. 'I sometimes think God must be tired of my voice. And Brother Osferth here is praying.'

'I'm not a brother,' Osferth said sullenly.

'But your prayers might work better if God thinks you are,' Pyrlig said.

Alfred's bastard son was crouching by Father Pyrlig. Finan had equipped Osferth with a mail coat that had been mended

139

after some Dane had been belly-gutted by a Saxon spear. He also had a helmet, tall boots, leather gloves, a round shield and both a long-and a short-sword, so that at least he looked like a warrior. 'I'm supposed to send you back to Wintanceaster,' I told him.

'I know.'

'Lord,' Pyrlig reminded Osferth.

'Lord,' Osferth said, though reluctantly.

'I don't want to send the king your corpse,' I said, 'so stay close to Father Pyrlig.'

'Very close, boy,' Pyrlig said, 'pretend you love me.'

'Stay behind him,' I ordered Osferth.

'Forget about being my lover,' Pyrlig said hurriedly, 'pretend you're my dog instead.'

'And say your prayers,' I finished. There was no other useful advice I could give Osferth, unless it was to strip off his clothes, swim ashore and go back to his monastery. I had as much faith in his fighting skills as Finan, which meant I had none. Osferth was sour, inept and clumsy. If it had not been for his dead uncle, Leofric, I would have happily sent him back to Wintanceaster, but Leofric had taken me as a young raw boy and had turned me into a sword warrior and so I would endure Osferth for Leofric's sake.

We were abreast of the new town now. I could smell the charcoal fires of the smithies, and see the reflected glow of fires flickering deep in alleyways. I looked ahead to where the bridge spanned the river, but all was black there.

'I need to see the gap,' Ralla called from the steering platform.

I worked my way aft again, stepping blindly between the crouching men.

'If I can't see it,' Ralla heard me coming, 'then I can't try it.'

'How close are we?'

'Too close.' There was panic in his voice.

I clambered up beside him. I could see the old city now, the city on the hills surrounded by its Roman wall. I could see it because the fires in the city made a dull glow and Ralla was right. We were close.

'We have to make a decision,' he said. 'We'll have to land upriver of the bridge.'

'They'll see us if we land there,' I said. The Danes would be certain to have men guarding the river wall upstream of the bridge.

'So you either die there with a sword in your hand,' Ralla said brutally, 'or you drown.'

I stared ahead and saw nothing. 'Then I choose the sword,' I said dully, seeing the death of my desperate idea.

Ralla took a deep breath to shout at the oarsmen, but the shout never came because, quite suddenly and far ahead, out where the Temes spread and emptied into the sea, a scrap of yellow showed. Not bright yellow, not a wasp's yellow, but a sour, leprous, dark yellow that leaked through a rent in the clouds. It was dawn beyond the sea, a dark dawn, a reluctant dawn, but it was light, and Ralla neither shouted nor turned the steering-oar to take us into the bank. Instead he touched the amulet at his neck and kept the boat on its headlong course. 'Crouch down, lord,' he said, 'and hold hard to something.'

The boat was quivering like a horse before battle. We were helpless now, caught in the river's grip. The water was sweeping down from far inland, fed by spring rains and subsiding floods, and where it met the bridge it piled itself in great white ragged heaps. It seethed, roared and foamed between the stone pilings, but in the bridge's centre, where the gap was, it poured in a sheeting, gleaming stream that fell a man's height to the new water level beyond where the river swirled and grumbled before becoming calm again.

I could hear the water fighting the bridge, hear the thunder of it loud as wind-driven breakers assaulting a beach.

And Ralla steered for the gap, which he could just see outlined against the dull yellow of the broken eastern sky. Behind us was blackness, though once I did see that sour morning light reflect from the water-glossed stem of Osric's ship and I knew he was close behind us.

'Hold hard!' Ralla called to our crew, and the ship was hissing, still quivering, and she seemed to race faster, and I saw the bridge come towards us and it loomed black over us as I crouched beside the ship's side and gripped the timber hard.

And then we were in the gap, and I had the sensation of falling as though we had tipped into an abyss between the worlds. The noise was deafening. It was the noise of water fighting stone, water tearing, water breaking, water pouring, a noise to fill the skies, a noise louder even than Thor's thunder, and the ship gave a lurch and I thought she must have struck and would slew sideways and tip us to our deaths, but somehow she straightened and flew on. There was blackness above, the blackness of the stub ends of the bridge's broken timbers, and then the noise doubled and spray flew across the deck and we were slamming downwards, ship tipping, and there was a crack like the gates of Odin's hall banging shut and I was spilled forward as water cascaded over us. We had struck stone, I thought, and I waited to drown and I even remembered to grip Serpent-Breath's hilt so I would die with my sword in my hand, but the ship staggered up and I understood the crash had been the bows striking the river beyond the bridge and that we were alive.

'Row!' Ralla shouted. 'Oh you lucky bastards, row!'

Water was deep in the bilge, but we were afloat, and the eastern sky was ragged with rents and in their shadowy

142

light we could see the city, and see the place where the wall was broken. 'And the rest,' Ralla said with pride in his voice, 'is up to you, lord.'

'It's up to the gods,' I said, and looked behind to see Osric's boat fighting up from the maelstrom where the river fell. So both our ships had lived, and the current was sweeping us downstream of the place we wished to land, but the oarsmen turned us and fought against the water so that we came to the wharf from the east, and that was good, because anyone watching would assume we had rowed upriver from Beamfleot. They would think we were Danes who had come to reinforce the garrison that now readied itself for Æthelred's assault.

There was a large sea-going ship moored in the dock where we wanted to land. I could see her clearly because torches blazed on the white wall of the mansion the dock served. The ship was a fine thing, her stem and stern rearing high and proud. There were no beast-heads on the ship, for no Northman would let his carved heads frighten the spirit of a friendly land. A lone man was on board the ship and he watched us approach. 'Who are you?' he shouted.

'Ragnar Ragnarson!' I called back. I heaved him a line woven from walrus hide. 'Has the fighting started?'

'Not yet, lord,' he said. He took the line and twisted it around the other ship's stem. 'And when it does they'll get slaughtered!'

'We're not too late, then?' I said. I staggered as our ship struck the other, then stepped over the sheer-strakes onto one of the empty rowers' benches. 'Whose ship is this?' I asked the man.

'Sigefrid's, lord. The *Wave-Tamer*.'

'She's beautiful,' I said, then turned back. 'Ashore!' I shouted in English and watched as my men retrieved shields and weapons from the flooded bilge. Osric's ship came in behind us, low in the water, and I realised she had been half swamped as she shot the bridge's gap. Men began clambering onto the *Wave-Tamer* and the Northman who had taken my line saw the crosses hanging from their necks.

'You . . .' he began, and found he had nothing more to say. He half turned to run ashore, but I had blocked his escape. There was shock on his face, shock and puzzlement.

'Put your hand on your sword hilt,' I said, drawing Serpent-Breath.

'Lord,' he said, as if about to plead for his life, but then he understood his life was ending because I could not leave him alive. I could not let him go, because then he would warn Sigefrid of our arrival, and if I had tied his hands and feet and left him aboard the *Wave-Tamer* then some other person might have found and released him. He knew all that, and his face changed from puzzlement to defiance and, instead of just gripping his sword's hilt, he began to pull the weapon free of its scabbard.

And died.

Serpent-Breath took him in the throat. Hard and fast. I felt her tip pierce muscle and tough tissue. Saw the blood. Saw his arm falter and the blade drop back into its scabbard, and I reached out with my left hand to grip his sword hand and hold it over his hilt. I made sure that he kept hold of his sword as he died, for then he would be taken to the feasting hall of the dead. I held his hand tight and let him collapse onto my chest where his blood ran down my mail. 'Go to Odin's hall,' I told him softly, 'and save a place for me.'

He could not speak. He choked as blood spilled down his windpipe.

'My name is Uhtred,' I said, 'and one day I will feast with you in the corpse-hall and we shall laugh together and drink together and be friends.'

I let his body drop, then knelt and found his amulet, Thor's hammer, which I cut from his neck with Serpent-Breath. I put the hammer in a pouch, cleaned my sword's tip on the dead man's cloak, then slid the blade back into her fleece-lined scabbard. I took my shield from Sihtric, my servant.

'Let's go ashore,' I said, 'and take a city.'

Because it was time to fight.

Five

Then all, suddenly, was quiet.

Not really quiet, of course. The river hissed where it ran through the bridge, small waves slapped on the boat hulls, the guttering torches on the house wall crackled and I could hear my men's footsteps as they clambered ashore. Shields and spear butts thumped on ships' timbers, dogs barked in the city and somewhere a gander was giving its harsh call, but it seemed quiet. Dawn was now a paler yellow, half concealed by dark clouds.

'And now?' Finan appeared beside me. Steapa loomed beside him, but said nothing.

'We go to the gate,' I said, 'Ludd's Gate.' But I did not move. I did not want to move. I wanted to be back at Coccham with Gisela. It was not cowardice. Cowardice is always with us, and bravery, the thing that provokes the poets to make their songs about us, is merely the will to overcome the fear. It was tiredness that made me reluctant to move, but not a physical tiredness. I was young then and the wounds of war had yet to sap my strength. I think I was tired of Wessex, tired of fighting for a king I did not like, and, standing on that Lundene wharf, I did not understand why I fought for him. And now, looking back over the years, I wonder if that lassitude was caused by the man I had just killed and whom I had promised to join in Odin's hall. I believe the men we kill are inseparably joined to us. Their life threads, turned ghostly, are twisted by the Fates around our own thread and their burden stays to haunt us till the sharp blade cuts our life at last. I felt remorse for his death.

'Are you going to sleep?' Father Pyrlig asked me. He had joined Finan.

'We're going to the gate,' I said.

It seemed like a dream. I was walking, but my mind was somewhere else. This, I thought, was how the dead walked our world, for the dead do come back. Not as Bjorn had pretended to come back, but in the darkest nights, when no one alive can see them, they wander our world. They must, I thought, only half see it, as if the places they knew were veiled in a winter mist, and I wondered if my father was watching me. Why did I think that? I had not been fond of my father, nor he of me, and he had died when I was young, but he had been a warrior. The poets sang of him. And what would he think of me? I was walking through Lundene instead of attacking Bebbanburg, and that was what I should have done. I should have gone north. I should have spent my whole hoard of silver on hiring men and leading them in an assault across Bebbanburg's neck of land and up across the walls to the high hall where we could make great slaughter. Then I could live in my own home, my father's home, for ever. I could live near Ragnar and be far from Wessex.

Except my spies, for I employed a dozen in Northumbria, had told me what my uncle had done to my fortress. He had closed the landside gates. He had taken them away altogether and in their place were ramparts, newly built, high and reinforced with stone, and now, if a man wished to get inside the fortress, he needed to follow a path that led to the northern end of the crag on which the fortress stood. And every step of that path would be under those high walls, under attack, and then, at the northern end, where the sea broke and sucked, there was a small gate. Beyond that gate was a steep path leading to another wall and another gate. Bebbanburg had been sealed, and to take it I would need an army beyond even the reach of my hoarded silver.

'Be lucky!' a woman's voice startled me from my thoughts. The folk of the old city were awake and they saw us pass and took us for Danes because I had ordered my men to hide their crosses.

'Kill the Saxon bastards!' another voice shouted.

Our footsteps echoed from the high houses that were all at least three storeys tall. Some had beautiful stonework over their bricks and I thought how the world had once been filled with these houses. I remember the first time I ever climbed a Roman staircase, and how odd it felt, and I knew that in times gone by men must have taken such things for granted. Now the world was dung and straw and damp-ridden wood. We had stone masons, of course, but it was quicker to build from wood, and the wood rotted, but no one seemed to care. The whole world rotted as we slid from light into darkness, getting ever nearer to the black chaos in which this middle world would end and the gods would fight and all love and light and laughter would dissolve. 'Thirty years,' I said aloud.

'Is that how old you are?' Father Pyrlig asked me.

'It's how long a hall lasts,' I said, 'unless you keep repairing it. Our world is falling apart, father.'

'My God, you're gloomy,' Pyrlig said, amused.

'And I watch Alfred,' I went on, 'and see how he tries to tidy our world. Lists! Lists and parchment! He's like a man putting wattle hurdles in the face of a flood.'

'Brace a hurdle well,' Steapa was listening to our conversation and now intervened, 'and it'll turn a stream.'

'And better to fight a flood than drown in it,' Pyrlig commented.

'Look at that!' I said, pointing to the carved stone head of a beast that was fixed to a brick wall. The beast was like none I had ever seen, a shaggy great cat, and its open mouth was poised above a chipped stone basin suggesting that water had once flowed from mouth to bowl. 'Could we make that?' I asked bitterly.

'There are craftsmen who can make such things,' Pyrlig said.

'Then where are they?' I demanded angrily, and I thought that all these things, the carvings and bricks and marble, had been made before Pyrlig's religion came to the island. Was that the reason for the world's decay? Were the true gods punishing us because so many men worshipped the nailed god? I did not make the suggestion to Pyrlig, but kept silent. The houses loomed above us, except where one had collapsed into a heap of rubble. A dog rooted along a wall, stopped to cock its leg, then turned a snarl on us. A baby cried in a house. Our footsteps echoed from the walls. Most of my men were silent, wary of the ghosts they believed inhabited these relics of an older time.

The baby wailed again, louder. 'Be a young mother in there,' Rypere said happily. Rypere was his nickname and meant 'thief', and he was a skinny Angle from the north, clever and sly, and he at least was not thinking of ghosts.

'I should stick to goats, if I were you,' Clapa said, 'they don't mind your stink.' Clapa was a Dane, one who had taken an oath to me and served me loyally. He was a hulking great boy raised on a farm, strong as an ox, ever cheerful. He and Rypere were friends who never stopped goading each other.

149

'Quiet!' I said before Rypere could make a retort. I knew we had to be getting close to the western walls. At the place where we had come ashore, the city climbed the wide terraced hill to the palace at the top, but that hill was flattening now, which meant we were nearing the valley of the Fleot. Behind us the sky was lightening to morning and I knew Æthelred would think I had failed to make my feint attack just before the dawn and that belief, I feared, might have persuaded him to abandon his own assault. Perhaps he was already leading his men back to the island? In which case we would be alone, surrounded by our enemies, and doomed.

'God help us,' Pyrlig suddenly said.

I held up my hand to stop my men because, in front of us, in the last stretch of the street before it passed under the stone arch called Ludd's Gate, was a crowd of men. Armed men. Men whose helmets, axe blades and spearpoints caught and reflected the dull light of the clouded and newly-risen sun.

'God help us,' Pyrlig said again and made the sign of the cross. 'There must be two hundred of them.'

'More,' I said. There were so many men that they could not all stand in the street, forcing some into the alleyways on either side. All the men we could see were facing the gate, and that made me understand what the enemy was doing and my mind cleared at that instant as if a fog had lifted. There was a courtyard to my left and I pointed through its gateway. 'In there,' I ordered.

I remember a priest, a clever fellow, visiting me to ask for my memories of Alfred, which he wanted to put in a book. He never did, because he died of the flux shortly after he saw me, but he was a shrewd man and more forgiving than most priests, and I recall how he asked me to describe the joy of battle. 'My wife's poets will tell you,' I said to him.

'Your wife's poets never fought,' he pointed out, 'and they just take songs about other heroes and change the names.'

'They do?'

'Of course they do,' he had said, 'wouldn't you, lord?'

I liked that priest and so I talked to him, and the answer I eventually gave him was that the joy of battle was the delight of tricking the other side. Of knowing what they will do before they do it, and having the response ready so that, when they make the move that is supposed to kill you, they die instead. And at that moment, in the damp gloom of the Lundene street, I knew what Sigefrid was doing and knew too, though he did not know it, that he was giving me Ludd's Gate.

The courtyard belonged to a stone-merchant. His quarries were Lundene's Roman buildings and piles of dressed masonry were stacked against the walls ready to be shipped to Frankia. Still more stones were heaped against the gate that led through the river wall to the wharves. Sigefrid, I thought, must have feared an assault from the river and had blocked every gate through the walls west of the bridge, but he had never dreamed anyone would shoot the bridge to the unguarded eastern side. But we had, and my men were hidden in the courtyard while I stood in the entrance and watched the enemy throng at Ludd's Gate.

'We're hiding?' Osferth asked me. His voice had a whine to it, as if he were perpetually complaining.

'There are hundreds of men between us and the gate,' I explained patiently, 'and we are too few to cut through them.'

'So we failed,' he said, not as a question, but as a petulant statement.

I wanted to hit him, but managed to stay patient. 'Tell him,' I said to Pyrlig, 'what is happening.'

151

'God in his wisdom,' the Welshman explained, 'has persuaded Sigefrid to lead an attack out of the city! They're going to open that gate, boy, and stream across the marshes, and hack their way into Lord Æthelred's men. And as most of Lord Æthelred's men are from the fyrd, and most of Sigefrid's are real warriors, then we all know what's going to happen!' Father Pyrlig touched his mail coat where the wooden cross was hidden. 'Thank you, God!'

Osferth stared at the priest. 'You mean,' he said after a pause, 'that Lord Æthelred's men will be slaughtered?'

'Some of them are going to die!' Pyrlig allowed cheerfully, 'and I hope to God they die in grace, boy, or they'll never hear that heavenly choir, will they?'

'I hate choirs,' I growled.

'No, you don't,' Pyrlig said. 'You see, boy,' he looked back to Osferth, 'once they've gone out of the gate, then there'll only be a handful of men guarding it. So that's when we attack! And Sigefrid will suddenly find himself with an enemy in front and another one behind, and that predicament can make a man wish he'd stayed in bed.'

A shutter opened in one of the high windows over the courtyard. A young woman stared out at the lightening sky, then stretched her hands high and yawned hugely. The gesture stretched her linen shift tight across her breasts, then she saw my men beneath her and instinctively clutched her arms to her chest. She was clothed, but must have felt naked. 'Oh, thank you dear Saviour for another sweet mercy,' Pyrlig said, watching her.

'But if we take the gate,' Osferth said, worrying at the problems he saw, 'the men left in the city will attack us.'

'They will,' I agreed.

'And Sigefrid . . .' he began.

'Will probably turn back to slaughter us,' I finished his sentence for him.

'So?' he said, then checked, because he saw nothing but blood and death in his future.

'It all depends,' I said, 'on my cousin. If he comes to our aid then we should win. If he doesn't?' I shrugged, 'then keep good hold of your sword.'

A roar sounded from Ludd's Gate and I knew it had been swung open and that men were streaming down the road that led to the Fleot. Æthelred, if he was still readying his assault, would see them coming and have a choice to make. He could stand and fight in the new Saxon town, or else run. I hoped he would stand. I did not like him, but I never saw a lack of courage in him. I did see a great deal of stupidity, which suggested he would probably welcome a fight.

It took a long time for Sigefrid's men to get through the gate. I watched from the shadows at the courtyard's entrance and reckoned at least four hundred men were leaving the city. Æthelred had over three hundred good troops, most of them from Alfred's household, but the rest of his force was from the fyrd and would never stand against a hard, savage attack. The advantage lay with Sigefrid whose men were warm, rested and fed, while Æthelred's troops had stumbled through the night and would be tired.

'The sooner we do it,' I said to no one in particular, 'the better.'

'Go now, then?' Pyrlig suggested.

'We just walk to the gate!' I shouted to my men. 'You don't run! Look as if you belong here!'

Which is what we did.

And so, with a stroll down a Lundene street, that bitter fight began.

* * *

There were no more than thirty men left at Ludd's Gate. Some were sentries posted to guard the archway, but most were idlers who had climbed to the rampart to watch Sigefrid's sally. A big man with one leg was climbing the uneven stone steps on his crutches. He stopped halfway and turned to watch our approach. 'If you hurry, lord,' he shouted to me, 'you can join them!'

He called me lord because he saw a lord. He saw a warrior lord.

A handful of men could go to war as I did. They were chieftains, earls, kings, lords; the men who had killed enough other men to amass the fortune needed to buy mail, helmet and weapons. And not just any mail. My coat was of Frankish make and would cost a man more than the price of a warship. Sihtric had polished the metal with sand so that it shone like silver. The hem of the coat was at my knees and was hung with thirty-eight hammers of Thor; some made of bone, some of ivory, some of silver, but all had once hung about the necks of brave enemies I had killed in battle, and I wore the amulets so that when I came to the corpse-hall the former owners would know me, greet me and drink ale with me.

I wore a cloak of wool dyed black on which Gisela had embroidered a white lightning flash that ran from my neck to my heels. The cloak could be an encumbrance in battle, but I wore it now, for it made me look larger, and I was already taller and broader than most men. Thor's hammer hung at my neck, and that alone was a poor thing, a miserable amulet made of iron that rusted constantly, and all the scraping and cleaning had worn it thin and misshapen over the years, but I had taken that little iron hammer with my fists when I was a boy and I loved it. I wear it to this day.

My helmet was a glorious thing, polished to an eye-blinding shine, inlaid with silver and crested with a silver wolf's head. The face-plates were decorated with silver spirals. That helmet alone told an enemy I was a man of substance. If a man killed me and took that helmet he would be instantly rich, but my enemies would rather have taken my arm rings, which, like the Danes, I wore over my mail sleeves. My rings were silver and gold, and there were so many that some had to be worn above my elbows. They spoke of men killed and wealth hoarded. My boots were of thick leather and had iron plates sewn around them to deflect the spear thrust that comes under the shield. The shield itself, rimmed with iron, was painted with a wolf's head, my badge, and at my left hip hung Serpent-Breath and at my right Wasp-Sting, and I strode towards the gate with the sun rising behind me to throw my long shadow on the filth-strewn street.

I was a warlord in my glory, I had come to kill, and no one at the gate knew it.

They saw us coming, but assumed we were Danes. Most of the enemy were on the high rampart, but five were standing in the open gate and all were watching Sigefrid's force that streamed down the brief steep slope to the Fleot. The Saxon settlement was not far beyond and I hoped Æthelred was still there. 'Steapa,' I called, still far enough from the gate so that no one there could hear me speak English, 'take your men and kill those turds in the archway.'

Steapa's skull face grinned. 'You want me to close the gate?' he asked.

'Leave it open,' I said. I wanted to lure Sigefrid back to prevent his hardened men getting among Æthelred's fyrd, and if the gate were open Sigefrid would be more inclined to attack us.

The gate was built between two massive stone bastions, each with its own stairway and I remembered how, when I was a child, Father Beocca had once described the Christian heaven to me. It would have crystal stairs, he had claimed, and enthusiastically described a great flight of glassy steps climbing to a white-hung throne of gold where his god sat. Angels would surround that throne, each brighter than the sun, while the saints, as he had called the dead Christians, would cluster about the stairs and sing. It sounded dull then and still does. 'In the next world,' I told Pyrlig, 'we will all be gods.'

He looked at me with surprise, wondering where that statement had come from. 'We will be with God,' he corrected me.

'In your heaven, maybe,' I said, 'but not in mine.'

'There is only one heaven, Lord Uhtred.'

'Then let mine be that one heaven,' I said, and I knew at that moment that my truth was the truth, and that Pyrlig, Alfred and all the other Christians were wrong. They were wrong. We did not go towards the light, we slid from it. We went to chaos. We went to death and to death's heaven, and I began to shout as we drew nearer the enemy. 'A heaven for men! A heaven for warriors! A heaven where swords shine! A heaven for brave men! A heaven of savagery! A heaven of corpse-gods! A heaven of death!'

They all stared at me, friend and enemy alike. They stared and they thought me mad, and perhaps I was mad as I climbed the right-hand stairway where the man on crutches gazed at me. I kicked one of his crutches away so that he fell. The crutch clattered down the stairs and one of my men booted it back to the ground. 'Death's heaven!' I screamed, and every man on the rampart had his eyes on me and still they thought I was a friend because I shouted my weird war cry in Danish.

I smiled behind my twin face-plates, then drew Serpent-Breath. Beneath me, out of my sight, Steapa and his men had begun their killing.

Not ten minutes before I had been in a waking dream, and now the madness had come. I should have waited for my men to climb the stairs and form a shield wall, but some impulse drove me forward. I was screaming still, but screaming my own name now, and Serpent-Breath was singing her hunger-song and I was a lord of war.

The happiness of battle. The ecstasy. It is not just deceiving an enemy, but feeling like a god. I had once tried to explain it to Gisela and she had touched my face with her long fingers and smiled. 'It's better than this?' she had asked.

'The same,' I had said.

But it is not the same. In battle a man risks all to gain reputation. In bed he risks nothing. The joy is comparable, but the joy of a woman is fleeting, while reputation is for ever. Men die, women die, all die, but reputation lives after a man, and that was why I screamed my name as Serpent-Breath took her first soul. He was a tall man with a battered helmet and a long-bladed spear that he instinctively thrust at me and, just as instinctively, I turned his lunge away with my shield and put Serpent-Breath into his throat. There was a man to my right and I shoulder-charged him, driving him down, and stamped on his groin while my shield took a sword swing from my left. I stepped over the man whose groin I had pulped and the rampart's protective wall was on my right now, where I wanted it, and ahead of me was the enemy.

I drove into them. 'Uhtred!' I was shouting, 'Uhtred of Bebbanburg!'

I was inviting death. By attacking alone I let the enemy get behind me, but at that moment I was immortal. Time had slowed so that the enemy moved like snails and I was fast as the lightning on my cloak. I was shouting still as Serpent-Breath lunged into a man's eye, driving hard till the bone of his socket stopped her thrust, and then I swept her left to slam down a sword coming at my face, and my shield lifted to take an axe blow, and Serpent-Breath dropped and I pushed her hard forward to pierce the leather jerkin of the man whose sword I had parried. I twisted her so the blade would not be seized by his belly while she gouged his blood and guts, and then I stepped left and rammed the iron boss of the shield at the axeman.

He staggered back. Serpent-Breath came from the swordsman's belly and flew wide right to crash against another sword. I followed her, still screaming, and saw the terror on that enemy's face, and terror on an enemy breeds cruelty. 'Uhtred,' I shouted, and stared at him, and he saw death coming, and he tried to back from me, but other men came behind to block his retreat and I was smiling as I slashed Serpent-Breath across his face. Blood sprayed in the dawn, and the backswing sliced his throat and two men pushed past him and I parried one with the sword and the other with my shield.

Those two men were no fools. They came with their shields touching and their only ambition was to push me back against the rampart and hold me there, pinned by their shields, so that I could not use Serpent-Breath. And once they had trapped me they would let other men come to jab me with blades until I lost too much blood to stand. Those two knew how to kill me, and they came to do it.

But I was laughing. I was laughing because I knew what they planned, and they seemed so slow and I rammed my own shield forward to crash against theirs and they thought they had trapped me because I could not hope to push two men away. They crouched behind their shields and heaved forward and I just stepped back, snatching my own shield backwards so that they stumbled forward as my resistance vanished. Their shields were slightly lowered as they stumbled and Serpent-Breath flickered like a viper's tongue so that her bloodied tip smashed into the forehead of the man on my left. I felt his thick bone break, saw his eyes glaze, heard the crash of his dropped shield, and I swept her to the right and the second man parried. He rammed his shield at me, hoping to unbalance me, but just then there was a mighty shout from my left. 'Christ Jesus and Alfred!' It was Father Pyrlig, and behind him the wide bastion was now swarming with my men. 'You damned heathen fool,' Pyrlig shouted at me.

I laughed. Pyrlig's sword cut into my opponent's arm, and Serpent-Breath beat down his shield. I remember he looked at me then. He had a fine helmet with raven wings fixed to its sides. His beard was golden, his eyes blue, and in those eyes was the knowledge of his imminent death as he tried to lift his sword with a wounded arm.

'Hold tight to your sword,' I told him. He nodded.

Pyrlig killed him, though I did not see it. I was moving past the man to attack the remaining enemy and beside me Clapa was swinging a huge axe so violently that he was as much a danger to our side as to the enemy, but no enemy wanted to face the two of us. They were fleeing along the ramparts and the gate was ours.

I leaned on the low outer wall and immediately stood upright because the stones shifted under my weight. The masonry was crumbling. I slapped the loose stonework and laughed aloud for joy. Sihtric grinned at me. He had a bloodied sword. 'Any amulets, lord?' he asked.

'That one,' I pointed to the man whose helmet was decorated with raven wings, 'he died well, I'll take his.'

Sihtric stooped to find the man's hammer-image. Beyond him Osferth was staring at the half-dozen dead men who lay in splats of blood across the stones. He was carrying a spear that had a reddened tip. 'You killed someone?' I asked him.

He looked at me wide-eyed, then nodded. 'Yes, lord.'

'Good,' I said and jerked my head towards the sprawling corpses. 'Which one?'

'It wasn't here, lord,' he said. He seemed puzzled for a moment, then looked back at the steps we had climbed. 'It was over there, lord.'

'On the steps?'

'Yes,' he said.

I stared at him long enough to make him uncomfortable. 'Tell me,' I said at last, 'did he threaten you?'

'He was an enemy, lord.'

'What did he do,' I asked, 'wave his one crutch at you?'

'He,' Osferth began, then appeared to run out of words. He stared down at a man I had killed, then frowned. 'Lord?'

'Yes?'

'You told us it was death to leave the shield wall.'

I stooped to clean Serpent-Breath's blade on a dead man's cloak. 'So?'

'You left the shield wall, lord,' Osferth said, almost reprovingly.

I straightened and touched my arm rings. 'You live,' I told him harshly, 'by obeying the rules. You make a reputation, boy, by breaking them. But you do not make a reputation by killing cripples.' I spat those last words, then turned to see that Sigefrid's men had crossed the River Fleot, but had now become aware of the commotion behind them and had stopped to stare back at the gate.

Pyrlig appeared beside me. 'Let's get rid of this rag,' he said, and I saw there was a banner hanging from the wall. Pyrlig hauled it up and showed me Sigefrid's raven badge. 'We'll let them know,' Pyrlig said, 'that the city has a new master.' He hauled up his mail coat and pulled out a banner that had been folded and tucked into his waistband. He shook it loose to reveal a black cross on a dull white field.

'Praise God,' Pyrlig said, then dropped the banner over the wall, securing it by weighting its top edge with dead men's weapons. Now Sigefrid would know that Ludd's Gate was lost. The Christian banner was flaunted in his face.

Yet, for the next few moments, things were quiet. I suppose Sigefrid's men were astonished by what had happened and were recovering from that surprise. They were no longer moving towards the new Saxon town, but were still staring back at the cross-hung gate, while inside the city groups of men gathered in the streets and gazed up at us.

I was staring towards the new town. I could see no sign of Æthelred's men. There was a wooden palisade cresting the low slope where the Saxon town was built and it was possible Æthelred's troops were behind the fence that had decayed in places and was entirely missing in others.

'If Æthelred doesn't come,' Pyrlig said softly.

'Then we're dead,' I finished the remark for him. To my left the river slid grey as misery towards the broken bridge and distant sea. Gulls were white on the grey. Far off, on the southern bank, I could see a few hovels where smoke rose. That was Wessex. In front of me, where Sigefrid's men remained motionless, was Mercia, while behind me, north of the river, was East Anglia.

'Do we shut the gate?' Pyrlig asked.

'No,' I said. 'I told Steapa to leave it open.'

'You did?'

'We want Sigefrid to attack us,' I said, and I thought that if Æthelred had abandoned his attack then I would die in the gate where the three kingdoms met. I still could not see Æthelred's force, yet I was relying on my cousin's men to give us victory. If I could tempt Sigefrid's warriors back to the gate, and hold them there, then Æthelred could assail them from behind. That was why I had to leave the gate open, as an invitation to Sigefrid. If I had shut it then he

161

could have used another entrance to the Roman city, and his men would not be exposed to my cousin's assault.

The more immediate problem was that the Danes who had stayed in the city were at last recovering from their surprise. Some were in the streets while others gathered on the walls either side of Ludd's Gate. The walls were lower than the gate's bastion, which meant any attack on us had to be made up the narrow stone steps which climbed from wall to bastion. Each of those steps would need five men to hold them, as would the twin stairways climbing from the street. I thought about abandoning the bastion's top, but if the fight went badly in the archway, then the high rampart was our best refuge. 'You'll have twenty men,' I told Pyrlig, 'to hold this bastion. And you can have him as well,' I nodded towards Osferth. I did not want Alfred's cripple-killing son in the arch below where the fighting would be fiercest. It was down there that we would make two shield walls, one facing into the city and the other looking out towards the Fleot, and there the shield walls would clash, and there, I thought, we would die because I still could not see Æthelred's army.

I was tempted to run away. It would have been simple enough to have retreated the way we had come, thrusting aside the enemy in the streets. We could have taken Sigefrid's boat, the *Wave-Tamer*, and used her to cross to the West Saxon bank. But I was Uhtred of Bebbanburg, stuffed full of warrior pride, and I had sworn to take Lundene. We stayed.

Fifty of us went down the stairways and filled the gate. Twenty men faced into the city while the rest faced out towards Sigefrid. Inside the gate arch there was just room for eight men to stand abreast with their shields touching and so we made our twin shield walls under the shadows of the stone. Steapa commanded the twenty, while I stood in the front rank of the wall looking west.

I left the shield wall and walked a few paces towards the Fleot valley. The small river, fouled by the tanners' pits upstream, ran dirty and sluggish towards the Temes. Beyond the river Sigefrid, Haesten and Erik had at last turned their force around and what had been their rearmost ranks of northern warriors were now wading back across the shallow Fleot to thrust my little force aside.

I stood on their skyline. The cloud-veiled sun was behind me, but its pale light would be reflecting from the silver of my helmet and from the smoky sheen of Serpent-Breath's blade. I had drawn her again, and now I stood with sword held out to my right and shield to my left. I stood above them, a lord in glory, a man in mail, a warrior inviting warriors to fight, and I saw no friendly troops on the farther hill.

And if Æthelred had gone, I thought, then we would die.

I gripped Serpent-Breath's hilt. I stared at Sigefrid's men, then clashed Serpent-Breath's blade against my shield. I beat her three times and the sound echoed from the walls behind me, and then I turned and went back to my small shield wall.

And, with a roar of anger and the howling of men who see victory, Sigefrid's army came to kill us.

A poet should have written the tale of that fight.

That is what poets are for.

My present wife, who is a fool, pays poets to sing of Christ Jesus, who is her god, but her poets falter into embarrassed silence when I limp into the hall. They know scores of songs about their saints, and they sing melancholy chants about the day their god was nailed to the cross, but when I am present they sing the real poems, those poems that the clever priest told me had been written about other men whose names had been taken out so mine could be inserted.

They are poems about slaughter, poems about warriors, real poems.

Warriors defend the home, they defend children, they defend women, they defend the harvest, and they kill the enemies who come to steal those things. Without warriors the land would be a waste place, desolate and full of laments. Yet a warrior's real reward is not the silver and gold he can wear on his arms, but his reputation, and that is why there are poets. Poets tell the tales of the men who defend the land and kill a land's enemies. That is what poets are for, yet there is no poem about the fight in Ludd's Gate of Lundene.

There is a poem sung in what used to be Mercia that tells of Lord Æthelred's capture of Lundene, and it is a fine poem, yet it does not mention my name, nor Steapa's name, nor Pyrlig's name, nor the names of the men who really fought that day. You would think, listening to that poem, that Æthelred came and those whom the poet calls 'the heathen' just ran.

But it was not like that.

It was not like that at all.

I say that the Northmen came in a rush, and they did, but Sigefrid was no fool when it came to a fight. He could see how few of us blocked that gateway and he knew that if he could break my shield wall quickly then we would all die under that old Roman arch.

I had gone back to my troops. My shield overlapped the shields of the men to my left and right, and it was just as I set myself, ready for their charge, that I saw what Sigefrid planned.

His men had not just been staring at Ludd's Gate, but had been reorganised so that eight warriors had been placed in the van of his attack. Four of them carried massive long spears that needed two hands to hold level. Those four had no shields, but next to each spearman was a massive warrior armed with shield and axe, and behind them were more men with shields, spears and long-swords. I knew just what was about to happen. The four men would come at a run and hammer their spears into four of our shields. The weight of the spears and the power of the charge would drive four of us into the rank behind, and then the axemen would strike. They would not try to batter our shields into splinters, but would instead widen the gaps the four spearmen had made, hook and pull down the shields of our second rank, and so expose us to the long weapons of the men following the axe-warriors. Sigefrid had only one ambition, and that was to break our wall fast, and I had no doubt that the eight men were not only trained to break a shield wall quickly, but had done it before.

'Brace yourselves!' I shouted, though it was a pointless shout. My men knew what they had to do. They had to stand and die. That was what they had sworn in their oaths to me.

And I knew we would die unless Æthelred came. The power of Sigefrid's attack would hammer into our shield wall and I had no spears long enough to counter the four that were coming. We could only try to stand fast, but we were outnumbered and the enemy's confidence was plain. They were shouting insults, promising us death, and death was coming.

'Close the gate, lord?' Cerdic, standing beside me, suggested nervously.

'Too late,' I said.

And the attack came.

The four spearmen screamed as they ran at us. Their weapons were as big as oar shafts and had spearheads the size of short-swords. They held the spears low and I knew they aimed to strike the lower part of our shields to tip the upper rims forward so the axemen could hook more easily and thus strip our defence in an instant.

And I knew it would work because the men attacking us were Sigefrid's breakers of shield walls. This was what they had trained to do, and had done, and the corpse-hall must have been full of their victims. They screamed their incoherent challenge as they ran at us. I could see their distorted faces. Eight men, big men, big-bearded and mail-coated, warriors to fear, and I braced my shield and crouched slightly, hoping a spear would strike the heavy metal boss in the shield's centre. 'Push against us,' I called to my second rank.

I could see one of the spears was aimed at my shield. If it struck low enough then my shield would be tilted forward and the axeman would strike down with his big blade. Death in a spring morning, and so I put my left leg against the shield, hoping that would stop the shield being driven inward, but I suspected the spear would shatter the lime-wood anyway and the blade would gouge into my groin. 'Brace yourselves!' I shouted again.

And the spears came for us. I saw the spearman grimacing as he readied to hurl his weight against my shield. And that crash of metal on wood was just a heartbeat away when Pyrlig struck instead.

I did not know what happened at first. I was waiting for the spear's blow and readying to parry an axe blow with Serpent-Breath, when something fell from the sky to slam into the attackers. The long spears dropped and their blades gouged the roadway just paces in front of me, and the eight men staggered, all cohesion and impetus gone. At first I thought two of Pyrlig's men had jumped from the gate's high rampart, but then I saw that the Welshman had hurled two corpses from the bastion's top. The bodies, both of big men, were still dressed in mail and their weight slammed onto the spear shafts, driving the weapons down and causing chaos in the enemy's front rank. One moment they had been in line, threatening, and now they were stumbling on corpses.

I moved without thinking. Serpent-Breath hissed in a backswing and her blade crashed into an axeman's helmet and I sawed her back, seeing blood show through the broken metal. That axeman went down as I slammed my shield's heavy boss into a spearman's face and felt his bones collapse.

'Shield wall!' I shouted, stepping back.

Finan had gone forward like me and had killed another spearman. The road was obstructed now by three corpses and at least one stunned man, and as I backed towards the gate's arch, two more bodies were hurled from the bastion. The corpses thumped heavily on the roadway, bounced, then lay as extra stumbling blocks to Sigefrid's advance, and it was then that I saw Sigefrid.

He was in the second rank, a baleful figure in his thick bear cloak. That fur alone could stop most sword blows, and beneath it he wore shining mail. He was roaring at his men to advance, but the sudden corpse fall had checked them. 'Forward!' Sigefrid bellowed, and pushed his way into the front rank and came straight for me. He was staring at me and shouting, but what he shouted I do not remember.

Sigefrid's attack had lost all its impetus. Instead of hitting us at a run, they closed on us at a walk and I remember thrusting my shield forward, and the crash as our two shields banged together, and the shock of Sigefrid's weight, though he must have felt the same because neither of us was thrown off balance. He rammed a sword at me and I felt a thudding blow on my shield, and I did the same to him. I had sheathed Serpent-Breath. She was and is a lovely blade, but a long-sword is no use when the shield walls come close as lovers. I had drawn Wasp-Sting, my short-sword, and I felt with her blade for a gap between the enemy's shields and drove her forward. She struck nothing.

Sigefrid heaved at me. We heaved back. A line of shields had crashed against another line, and behind them, on both sides, men pushed and swore, grunted and heaved. An axe came towards my head, swung by the man behind Sigefrid, but behind me Clapa had his shield raised and caught the blow, which was powerful enough to drive his shield down onto my helmet. For a moment I could see nothing, but I shook my head and my vision cleared. Another axe had hooked its blade over my shield's top edge and the man was trying to pull my shield down, but it was crammed so tight against Sigefrid's shield that it would not move. Sigefrid was cursing me, spitting into my face, and I was calling him the son of a goat-humping whore and stabbing at him with Wasp-Sting. She had found something solid behind the enemy wall and I gouged her, then shoved her hard forward and gouged the blade again, but what damage she did I do not know to this day.

The poets tell of those battles, but no poet I know was ever in the front rank of a shield wall. They boast of a warrior's prowess and they record how many men he killed. Bright his blade flashed, they sing, and great was his spear's slaughter, but it was never like that. Blades were not bright, but cramped. Men swore, pushed and sweated. Not many men died once the shields touched and the heaving began because there was not room enough to swing a blade. The real killing began when a shield wall broke, but ours held against that first attack. I saw little because my helmet had been shoved low over my eyes, but I remember Sigefrid's open mouth, all rotten teeth and yellow spittle. He was cursing me, and I was cursing him, and my shield shuddered from blows and men were shouting. One was screaming. Then I heard another scream and Sigefrid suddenly stepped back. His whole line was moving away from us and for a moment I thought they were trying to tempt us out of the gate's archway, but I stayed where I was. I dared not take my little shield wall out of the arch, for the great stone walls on either side protected my flanks. Then there was a third scream and at last I saw why Sigefrid's men had faltered. Big blocks of stone were falling from the ramparts. Pyrlig was evidently not being attacked and so his men were prising away lumps of masonry and dropping them on the enemy, and the man behind Sigefrid had been struck on the head and Sigefrid stumbled on him.

'Stay here!' I shouted at my men. They were tempted to go forward and take advantage of the enemy's disarray, but that would mean leaving the gate's safety. 'Stay!' I bellowed angrily, and they stayed.

It was Sigefrid who retreated. He looked angry and puzzled. He had expected an easy victory, but instead he had lost men while we were unscathed. Cerdic's face was covered in blood, but he shook his head when I asked if he had been badly wounded. Then from behind me I heard a roar of voices and my men, packed together in the archway, shuddered forward as an enemy struck from the streets. Steapa was there and I did not even bother to turn and see the fight because I knew Steapa would hold. I could also hear the clash of blades above me and knew that Pyrlig too was now fighting for his life.

Sigefrid saw Pyrlig's men fighting and deduced he would be spared their shower of masonry and so he shouted at his men to ready themselves. 'Kill the bastards!' he bellowed, 'kill them! But take the big one alive. I want him.' He swept his sword to point at me and I remembered his blade's name; Fear-Giver. 'You're mine!' he shouted at me, 'and I still have

169

to crucify a man! And you're the man!' He laughed, sheathed Fear-Giver and took a long-handled war axe from one his followers. He offered me a malevolent grin, covered his body with his raven-decorated shield, and shouted at his men to advance. 'Kill them all! All but the big bastard! Kill them!'

But this time, instead of pushing close to shove us through the gate like a stopper being forced through a bottle's neck, he made his men pause at sword's length and try to haul our shields down with their long-hafted war axes. And so the work became desperate.

An axe is a vicious weapon in a fight between shield walls. If it does not hook a shield down it can still break the boards into splinters. I felt Sigefrid's blows crashing into the shield, saw the axe blade appear through a rent in the limewood, and all I could do was endure the assault. I dared not go forward because that would break our wall, and if our whole wall stepped forward then the men on the flanks would be exposed and we would die.

A spear was jabbing at my ankles. A second axe crashed on the shield. All along our short line the blows were falling, the shields were breaking and death was looming. I had no axe to swing, for I was never fond of it as a weapon, though I recognised how lethal it was. I kept Wasp-Sting in my hand, hoping Sigefrid would close the gap and I could slide the blade past his shield and deep into his big belly, but Sigefrid stayed an axe's length away, and my shield was broken, and I knew a blow would soon crack my forearm into a useless mess of blood and shattered bone.

I risked one step forward. I made it suddenly so that Sigefrid's next swing was wasted, though the axe shaft bruised my left shoulder. He had to drop his shield to swing the axe and I lunged Wasp-Sting across his body and the blade rammed into his right shoulder, but his expensive mail held. He recoiled. I sliced her at his face, but he rammed

170

his shield into mine, driving me back, and an instant later his axe slammed into my shield again.

He grimaced then, all rotten teeth and angry eyes and bushy beard. 'I want you alive,' he said. He swung the axe sideways and I managed to pull the shield inwards just enough so that the blade crashed against the boss. 'Alive,' he said again, 'and you will die a death fit for a man who breaks his oath.'

'I made no oath to you,' I said.

'But you will die as though you had,' he said, 'with your hands and feet nailed to a cross, and your screams won't stop until I tire of them.' He grimaced again as he drew the axe back for a last shield-splintering stroke. 'And I'll flay your corpse, Uhtred the Betrayer,' he said, 'and cover my shield with your tanned skin. I'll piss in your dead throat and dance on your bones.' He swung the axe, and the sky fell.

A whole length of heavy masonry had been toppled from the rampart and slammed into Sigefrid's ranks. There was dust and screaming and broken men. Six warriors were either on the ground or clutching shattered bones. All were behind Sigefrid, and he turned, astonished, and just then Osferth, Alfred's bastard son, jumped from the gate's top.

He should have broken his ankles in that desperate leap, but somehow he survived. He landed amid the broken stones and shattered bodies that had been Sigefrid's second rank and he screamed like a girl as he swung his sword at the huge Norseman's head. The blade thumped into Sigefrid's helmet. It did not break the metal, but it must have stunned Sigefrid for an instant. I had broken my shield wall by taking two paces forward and I rammed my broken shield at the dazed man and stabbed Wasp-Sting into his left thigh. This time she broke through the links of his mail and I twisted her, ripping muscle. Sigefrid staggered and it was then that Osferth, whose face was a picture of pure terror, stabbed his sword into the small of the Norseman's back. I do not think Osferth was aware of what he was doing. He had pissed himself with fear, he was dazed, he was confused, the enemy was recovering their sense and coming to kill him, and Osferth just stabbed his sword with enough desperate force to pierce the bear-fur cloak, Sigefrid's mail, and then Sigefrid himself.

The big man screamed with agony. Finan was beside me, dancing as he always danced in battle, and he fooled the man next to Sigefrid with a lunge that was a feint, flicked his sword sideways across the man's face, then shouted at Osferth to come to us.

But Alfred's son was frozen by terror. He would have lived no longer than one more heartbeat if I had not shaken off the remnants of my shattered shield and reached past the screaming Sigefrid to haul Osferth towards me. I shoved him back into the second rank and, with no shield to protect myself, waited for the next attack.

'My God, thank you, thank you, Lord God,' Osferth was saying. He sounded pathetic.

Sigefrid was on his knees, whimpering. Two men dragged him away, and I saw Erik staring appalled at his wounded brother. 'Come and die!' I shouted at him, and Erik answered my anger with a sad look. He nodded to me, as if to acknowledge that custom forced me to threaten him, but that the threat in no way diminished his regard for me. 'Come on!' I goaded him, 'come and meet Serpent-Breath!'

'In my own time, Lord Uhtred,' Erik called back, his courtesy a reproof to my snarl. He stooped beside his wounded brother, and Sigefrid's plight had persuaded the enemy to hesitate before attacking us again. They hesitated long enough for me to turn and see that Steapa had beaten off the attack from the inside of the city.

'What's happening on the bastion?' I asked Osferth.

He stared at me with pure terror on his face. 'Thank you, Lord Jesus,' he stammered.

I rammed my left fist into his belly. 'What's happening up there!' I shouted at him.

He gaped at me, stammered again, then managed to speak coherently. 'Nothing, lord. The pagans can't get up the stairs.'

I turned back to face the enemy. Pyrlig was holding the bastion's top, Steapa was holding the inner side of the gate, so I had to hold here. I touched my hammer amulet, brushed my left hand over Serpent-Breath's hilt, and thanked the gods I was still alive. 'Give me your shield,' I said to Osferth. I snatched it from him, put my bruised arm through the leather loops, and saw the enemy was forming a new line.

'Did you see Æthelred's men?' I asked Osferth.

'Æthelred?' he responded as though he had never heard the name.

'My cousin!' I snarled. 'Did you see him?'

'Oh yes, lord, he's coming,' Osferth said, giving the news as though it were utterly unimportant, as if he were telling me that he had seen rain in the distance.

I risked turning to face him. 'He is coming?'

'Yes, lord,' Osferth said.

And so Æthelred was, and so he did. Our fight more or less ended there, because Æthelred had not abandoned his plan to assault the city, and now brought his men across the Fleot to attack the rear of the enemy, and that enemy fled north towards the next gate. We pursued for a while. I drew Serpent-Breath because she was a better weapon for an open fight, and I caught a Dane who was too fat to run hard. He turned, lunged at me with a spear, and I slid the lunge away with my borrowed shield and sent him to the corpse-hall with a lunge of my own. Æthelred's men were howling as they fought up the slope, and I reckoned they might easily mistake my men for the enemy and so I called for my troops to return to Ludd's Gate. The arch was empty now, though on either side were bloodied corpses and broken shields. The sun was higher, but the clouds still made it look a dirty yellow behind their veil.

Some of Sigefrid's men died outside the walls and such was their panic that some were even hacked to death with sharpened hoes. Most managed to get through the next gate and into the old city, and there we hunted them down.

It was a wild and howling hunt. Sigefrid's troops, those who had not sallied beyond the walls, were slow to learn of their defeat. They stayed on their ramparts until they saw death coming, and then they fled into streets and alleys already choked with men, women and children fleeing the Saxon assault. They ran down the terraced hills of the city, going for the boats that were tied to the wharves downstream of the bridge. Some, the fools, tried to save their belongings, and that was fatal for they were burdened by their possessions, caught in the streets and cut down. A young girl screamed as she was dragged into a house by a Mercian spearman. Dead men lay in gutters, sniffed by dogs. Some houses showed a cross, denoting that Christians lived there, but the protection meant nothing if a girl in the house was pretty. A priest held a wooden crucifix aloft outside a low doorway, and shouted that there were Christian women sheltering in his small church, but the priest was cut down by an axe and the screaming began. A score of Northmen were caught in the palace where they guarded the treasury amassed by Sigefrid and Erik and they all died there, their blood trickling between the small tiles of the mosaic floor of the Roman hall.

It was the fyrd that did most destruction. The household troops had discipline and stayed together, and it was those trained troops who chased the Northmen out of Lundene. I stayed on the street next to the river wall, the street that we had followed from our half-swamped ships, and we drove the fugitives as though they were sheep running from wolves. Father Pyrlig had attached his cross banner to a Danish spear and he waved it over our heads to show Æthelred's men that we were friends. Screams and howling sounded from the higher streets. I stepped over a dead child, her golden curls thick with the blood of her father who had died beside her. His last act had been to seize his child's arm and his dead hand was still curled about her elbow. I thought of my daughter, Stiorra. 'Lord!' Sihtric shouted, 'lord!' he was pointing with his sword.

He had seen that one large group of Northmen, presumably cut off as they retreated towards their ships, had taken refuge on the broken bridge. The bridge's northern end was guarded by a Roman bastion through which an arch led, though the arch had long lost its gateway. Instead the passage to the bridge's broken timber roadway was blocked by a shield wall. They were in the same position I had been in Ludd's Gate with their flanks protected by high stonework. Their shields filled the arch, and I could see at least six ranks of men behind the front line of round overlapping shields.

Steapa made a low growling noise and hefted his axe. 'No,' I said, laying a hand on his massive shield arm.

'Make a boar's tusk,' he said vengefully, 'kill the bastards. Kill them all.'

'No,' I said again. A boar's tusk was a wedge of men that would drive into a shield wall like a human spear-point, but no boar's tusk would pierce this Northmen's wall. They were too tightly packed in the archway, and they were desperate, and desperate men will fight fanatically for the chance to live. They would die in the end, that was true, but many of my men would die with them.

'Stay here,' I told my men. I handed my borrowed shield

175

to Sihtric, then gave him my helmet. I sheathed Serpent-Breath. Pyrlig copied me, taking off his helmet. 'You don't have to come,' I told him.

'And why shouldn't I?' he asked, smiling. He handed his makeshift standard to Rypere, laid his shield down, and, because I was glad of the Welshman's company, the two of us walked to the bridge's gate.

'I am Uhtred of Bebbanburg,' I announced to the hard-faced men staring over their shield rims, 'and if you wish to feast in Odin's corpse-hall this night then I am willing to send you there.'

Behind me the city screamed and smoke drifted dense across the sky. The nine men in the enemy's front rank stared at me, but none spoke.

'But if you want to taste the joys of this world longer,' I went on, 'then speak to me.'

'We serve our earl,' one of the men finally said.

'And he is?'

'Sigefrid Thurgilson,' the man said.

'Who fought well,' I said. I had been screaming insults at Sigefrid not two hours before, but now was the time for softer speech. A time to arrange for an enemy to yield and thus save my men's lives. 'Does the Earl Sigefrid live?' I asked.

'He lives,' the man said curtly, jerking his head to indicate that Sigefrid was somewhere behind him on the bridge.

'Then tell him Uhtred of Bebbanburg would speak with him, to decide whether he lives or dies.'

That was not my choice to make. The Fates had already made the decision, and I was but their instrument. The man who had spoken to me called the message to the men behind on the bridge and I waited. Pyrlig was praying, though whether he beseeched mercy for the folk who screamed behind us or death for the men in front of us, I never asked.

176

Then the tight-packed shield wall in the arch shuffled aside as men made a passage down the roadway's centre. 'The Earl Erik will speak with you,' the man told me.

And Pyrlig and I went to meet the enemy.

Six

'My brother says I should kill you,' Erik greeted me. The younger of the Thurgilson brothers had been waiting for me on the bridge and, though his words held menace, there was none in his face. He was placid, calm and apparently unworried by his predicament. His black hair was crammed beneath a plain helmet and his fine mail was spattered with blood. There was a rent at the mail's hem, and I guessed that marked where a spear had come beneath his shield, but he was evidently unwounded. Sigefrid, though, was horribly injured. I could see him on the roadway, lying on his bear-fur cloak, twisting and jerking in pain, and being tended by two men.

'Your brother,' I said, still watching Sigefrid, 'thinks that death is the answer to everything.'

'Then he's like you in that regard,' Erik said with a wan smile, 'if you are what men say you are.'

'What do men say of me?' I asked, curious.

'That you kill like a Northman,' Erik said. He turned to stare downriver. A small fleet of Danish and Norse ships had managed to escape the wharves, but some now rowed back upstream in an attempt to save the fugitives who crowded the river's edge, but the Saxons were already among that doomed crowd. A furious fight was raging on the wharves where men hacked at each other. Some, to escape the fury, were leaping into the river. 'I sometimes think,' Erik said sadly, 'that death is the real meaning of life. We worship death, we give it, we believe it leads to joy.'

'I don't worship death,' I said.

'Christians do,' Erik remarked, glancing at Pyrlig, whose mailed chest displayed his wooden cross.

'No,' Pyrlig said.

'Then why the image of a dead man?' Erik asked.

'Our Lord Jesus Christ rose from the dead,' Pyrlig said energetically, 'he conquered death! He died to give us life and regained his own life in his dying. Death, lord, is just a gate to more life.'

'Then why do we fear death?' Erik asked in a voice that suggested he expected no answer. He turned to look at the downstream chaos. The two ships we had used to shoot the bridge's gap had been commandeered by fleeing men, and one of those ships had foundered just yards from the wharf where it now lay on its side, half sunken. Men had been spilled into the water where many must have drowned, but others had managed to reach the muddy foreshore where they were being hacked to death by gleeful men with spears, swords, axes and hoes. The survivors clung to the wreck, trying to shelter from a handful of Saxon bowmen whose long hunting arrows thudded into the ship's timbers. There was so much death that morning. The streets of the broken city reeked of blood and were filled with the wailing of women beneath the smoke-smeared yellow sky. 'We trusted you, Lord Uhtred,' Erik said bleakly, still staring downriver. 'You were going to bring us Ragnar, you were to be king in Mercia and you were to give us the whole island of Britain.'

'The dead man lied,' I said, 'Bjorn lied.'

Erik turned back to me, his face grave. 'I said we should not try and trick you,' he said, 'but Earl Haesten insisted.' Erik shrugged, then looked at Father Pyrlig, noting his mail coat and the well-worn hilts of his swords. 'But you also tricked us, Lord Uhtred,' Erik went on, 'because I think you knew this man was no priest, but a warrior.'

'He is both,' I said.

Erik grimaced, perhaps remembering the skill with which Pyrlig had defeated his brother in the arena. 'You lied,' he said sadly, 'and we lied, but we still could have taken Wessex together. And now?' he turned and looked along the bridge's roadway, 'now I don't know whether my brother will live or die.' He grimaced. Sigefrid was motionless now and for a moment I thought he might have gone to the corpse-hall already, but then he slowly turned his head to give me a baleful stare.

'I shall pray for him,' Pyrlig said.

'Yes,' Erik said simply, 'please.'

'And what shall I do?' I asked.

'You?' Erik frowned, puzzled by my question.

'Do I let you live, Erik Thurgilson?' I asked. 'Or kill you?'

'You will find us difficult to kill,' he said.

'But kill you I will,' I responded, 'if I must.' That was the real negotiation in those two sentences. The truth was that Erik and his men were trapped and doomed, but to kill them we would need to hack our way through a fearsome shield wall, and then batter down desperate men whose only thought would be to take many of us with them to the next world. I would lose twenty or more men here, and others of my household troops would be crippled for life. That was a price I did not want to pay, and Erik knew it, but he also knew that the price would be paid if he was not reasonable. 'Is Haesten here?' I asked him, looking down the broken bridge.

Erik shook his head. 'I saw him leave,' he said, nodding downriver.

'A pity,' I said, 'because he broke an oath to me. If he had been here I would have let you all go in exchange for his life.'

Erik stared at me for a few heartbeats, judging whether I had spoken the truth. 'Then kill me instead of Haesten,' he said at last, 'and let all these others leave.'

'You broke no oath to me,' I said, 'so you owe me no life.'

'I want these men to live,' Erik said with a sudden passion, 'and my life is a small price for theirs. I will pay it, Lord Uhtred, and in return you give my men their lives, and give them *Wave-Tamer*,' he pointed to his brother's ship that was still tied in the small dock where we had landed.

'Is it a fair price, father?' I asked Pyrlig.

'Who can set a value on life?' Pyrlig asked in return.

'I can,' I said harshly, and turned back to Erik. 'The price is this,' I told him. 'You will leave every weapon you carry on this bridge. You will leave your shields. You will leave your mail coats, and you will leave your helmets. You will leave your arm rings, your chains, your brooches, your coins and your belt buckles. You will leave everything of value, Erik Thurgilson, and then you may take a ship that I choose to give you, and you may go.'

'A ship that you choose,' Erik said.

'Yes.'

He smiled wanly. 'I made *Wave-Tamer* for my brother,' he said. 'I first found her keel in the forest. It was an oak with a trunk straight as an oar shaft and I cut that myself. We used eleven other oaks, Lord Uhtred, for her ribs and her cross-pieces, for her stem and her planking. Her caulking was hair from seven bears I killed with my own spear, and I made her nails on my own forge. My mother made her sail, I wove her lines, and I gave her to Thor by killing a horse I loved and sprinkling his blood on her stem. She has carried my brother and me through storms and fog and ice. She is,' he turned to look at *Wave-Tamer*, 'she is beautiful. I love that ship.'

'You love her more than your life?'

He thought for an instant, then shook his head. 'No.'

'Then it will be a ship of my choice,' I said stubbornly, and that might have ended the negotiation except there was a commotion under the archway where the Northmen's shield wall still faced my troops.

Æthelred had come to the bridge, and was demanding to be allowed through the gate. Erik offered me a quizzical look when the news was brought to us and I shrugged. 'He commands here,' I said.

'So I will need his permission to leave?'

'You will,' I said.

Erik sent word that the shield wall was to let Æthelred onto the roadway and my cousin strutted onto the bridge with his customary cockiness. Aldhelm, the commander of his guard, was his only companion. Æthelred ignored Erik, instead facing me with a belligerent expression. 'You presume to negotiate on my behalf?' he accused me.

'No,' I said.

'Then what are you doing here?'

'Negotiating on my own behalf,' I said. 'This is the Earl Erik Thurgilson,' I introduced the Norseman in English, but now changed to Danish. 'And this,' I said to Erik, 'is the Ealdorman of Mercia, the Lord Æthelred.'

Erik responded to the introduction by offering Æthelred a small bow, but the courtesy was wasted. Æthelred looked around the bridge, counting the men who had taken refuge there. 'Not so many,' he said brusquely. 'They must all die.'

'I have already offered them their lives,' I said.

Æthelred rounded on me. 'We had orders,' he said bitingly, 'to capture Sigefrid, Erik and Haesten, and deliver them as captives to King Æthelstan.' I saw Erik's eyes widen slightly. I had assumed he spoke no English, but now realised he must have learned enough of the language to understand Æthelred's words. 'Are you disobeying my father-in-law?' Æthelred challenged me when I made no response.

I kept my temper. 'You can fight them here,' I explained patiently, 'and you'll lose many good men. Too many. You can trap them here, but at slack water a ship will row to the bridge and rescue them.' That would be a hard thing to do, but I had learned never to underestimate the seamanship of the Northmen. 'Or you can rid Lundene of their presence,' I said, 'and that is what I chose to do.' Aldhelm sniggered at that, implying that I had chosen the coward's option. I looked at him and he challenged my gaze, refusing to look away.

'Kill them, lord,' Aldhelm said to Æthelred, though he continued staring at me.

'If you wish to fight them,' I said, 'then that is your privilege, but I'll have none of it.'

For a moment both Æthelred and Aldhelm were tempted to accuse me of cowardice. I could see the thought on their faces, but they could also see something in my face and they let the thought go unsaid. 'You always loved pagans,' Æthelred sneered instead.

'I loved them so well,' I said angrily, 'that I took two ships through that gap in the black of night,' I pointed to where the jagged stumps of the bridge's planking ended. 'I brought men into the city, cousin, and I captured Ludd's Gate, and I fought a battle in that gate such as I would never wish to fight again, and in that fight I killed pagans for you. And yes, I love them.'

Æthelred looked at the gap. Spray showed continually

there, thrown up by the seethe of water falling through the break with such force that the ancient wooden roadway quivered and the air was filled with the river's noise. 'You had no orders to come by ship,' Æthelred said indignantly, and I knew he resented my actions because they might detract from the glory he expected to garner from his capture of Lundene.

'I had orders to give you the city,' I retorted, 'so here it is!' I gestured at the smoke drifting over the scream-filled hill. 'Your wedding present,' I said, mocking him with a bow.

'And not just the city, lord,' Aldhelm said to Æthelred, 'but everything in it.'

'Everything?' Æthelred asked, as if he could not believe his good fortune.

'Everything,' Aldhelm said wolfishly.

'And if you're grateful for that,' I interjected sourly, 'then thank your wife.'

Æthelred jerked around to stare wide-eyed at me. Something in my words had astonished him for he looked as though I had struck him. There was disbelief on his broad face, and anger, and for a moment he was incapable of speaking. 'My wife?' he finally asked.

'If it had not been for Æthelflaed,' I explained, 'we could not have taken the city. Last night she gave me men.'

'You saw her last night?' he asked incredulously.

I looked at him, wondering if he was mad. 'Of course I saw her last night!' I said. 'We went back to the island to board the ships! She was there! She shamed your men into coming with me.'

'And she made Lord Uhtred give her an oath,' Pyrlig added, 'an oath to defend your Mercia, Lord Æthelred.'

Æthelred ignored the Welshman. He was still staring at me, but now with an expression of hatred. 'You boarded my ship?' he could barely speak for loathing and anger, 'and saw my wife?'

'She came ashore,' I said, 'with Father Pyrlig.'

I meant nothing by saying that. I had merely reported what had happened and hoped that Æthelred would admire his wife for her initiative, but the moment I spoke I saw I had made a mistake. I thought for a heartbeat that Æthelred was going to hit me, so fierce was the sudden fury on his broad face, but then he controlled himself and turned and walked away. Aldhelm hurried after him and managed to check my cousin's haste long enough to speak with him. I saw Æthelred make a furious, careless gesture, then Aldhelm turned back to me. 'You must do what you think best,' he called, then followed his master through the arch where the Northmen's shield wall made a passage for them.

'I always do,' I said to no one in particular.

'Do what?' Father Pyrlig asked, staring at the arch where my cousin had so abruptly vanished.

'What I think is best,' I said, then frowned. 'What happened there?' I asked Pyrlig.

'He doesn't like other men speaking to his wife,' The Welshman said. 'I noticed that when I was on the ship with them, coming down the Temes. He's jealous.'

'But I've known Æthelflaed for ever!' I exclaimed.

'He fears you know her only too well,' Pyrlig said, 'and it drives him to madness.'

'But that's stupid!' I spoke angrily.

'It's jealousy,' Pyrlig said, 'and all jealousy is stupid.'

Erik had also watched Æthelred walk away and was as confused as I was. 'He is your commander?' the Norseman asked.

'He's my cousin,' I said bitterly.

'And he's your commander?' Erik asked again.

'The Lord Æthelred commands,' Pyrlig explained, 'and the Lord Uhtred disobeys.'

Erik smiled at that. 'So, Lord Uhtred, do we have an agreement?' He asked that question in English, hesitating slightly over the words.

'Your English is good,' I said, sounding surprised.

He smiled. 'A Saxon slave taught me.'

'I hope she was beautiful,' I said, 'and yes, we do have an agreement, but with one change.'

Erik bridled, but stayed courteous. 'One change?' he asked cautiously.

'You may take *Wave-Tamer*,' I said.

I thought Erik would kiss me. For a heartbeat he did not believe my words, then he saw that I was sincere and he smiled broadly. 'Lord Uhtred,' he began.

'Take her,' I interrupted him, not wanting his gratitude, 'just take her and go!'

It had been Aldhelm's words that had changed my mind. He had been right; everything in the city now belonged to Mercia, and Æthelred was Mercia's ruler, and my cousin had a lust for anything beautiful and, if he discovered I wanted *Wave-Tamer* for myself, which I did, he would be sure to take it from me, and so I kept the ship from his grasp by giving it back to the Thurgilson brothers.

Sigefrid was carried to his own ship. The Northmen, stripped of their weapons and valuables, were guarded by my men as they walked to the *Wave-Tamer*. It took a long time, but at last they were all on board and they shoved away from the quay, and I watched as they rowed downstream towards the small mists that still hovered above the lower reaches of the river.

And somewhere in Wessex the first cuckoo called.

*   *   *

I wrote Alfred a letter. I have always hated writing, and it has been years since I last used a quill. My wife's priests now scratch letters for me, but they know I can read what they write so they take care to write what I tell them. But on the night of Lundene's fall, I wrote in my own hand to Alfred. 'Lundene is yours, lord King,' I told him, 'and I am staying here to rebuild its walls.'

Writing even that much exhausted my patience. The quill spluttered, the parchment was uneven and the ink, which I had found in a wooden chest containing plunder evidently stolen from a monastery, spat droplets over the parchment. 'Now fetch Father Pyrlig,' I told Sihtric, 'and Osferth.'

'Lord,' Sihtric said nervously.

'I know,' I said impatiently, 'you want to marry your whore. But fetch Father Pyrlig and Osferth first. The whore can wait.'

Pyrlig arrived a moment later and I pushed the letter across the table to him. 'I want you to go to Alfred,' I told him, 'give him that, and tell him what happened here.'

Pyrlig read my message and I saw a small smile flicker on his ugly face, a smile that vanished swiftly so that I would not be offended by his opinion of my handwriting. He said nothing of my short message, but glanced around with surprise as Sihtric brought Osferth into the room.

'I'm sending Brother Osferth with you,' I explained to the Welshman.

Osferth stiffened. He hated being called brother. 'I want to stay here,' he said, 'lord.'

'The king wants you in Wintanceaster,' I said dismissively, 'and we obey the king.' I took the letter back from Pyrlig, dipped the quill in the ink that had faded to a rusty brown, and added more words. 'Sigefrid,' I wrote laboriously, 'was defeated by Osferth, who I would like to keep in my household guard.'

Why did I write that? I did not like Osferth any more than I liked his father, yet he had leaped from the bastion and that had shown courage. Foolish courage, perhaps, but still courage, and if Osferth had not leaped then Lundene might be in Norse or Danish hands to this day. Osferth had earned his place in the shield wall, even if his prospects of surviving there were still desperately low. 'Father Pyrlig,' I said to Osferth as I blew on the ink, 'will tell the king of your actions today, and this letter requests that you be returned to me. But you must leave that decision to Alfred.'

'He'll say no,' Osferth said sullenly.

'Father Pyrlig will persuade him,' I said. The Welshman raised an eyebrow in silent question and I gave him the smallest nod to show I spoke the truth. I gave the letter to Sihtric and watched as he folded the parchment, then sealed it with wax. I pressed my badge of the wolf's head into the seal, then handed the letter to Pyrlig. 'Tell Alfred the truth about what happened here,' I said, 'because he's going to hear a different version from my cousin. And travel fast!'

Pyrlig smiled. 'You want us to reach the king before your cousin's messenger?'

'Yes,' I said. That was a lesson I had learned; that the first news is generally the version that is believed. I had no doubt Æthelred would be sending a triumphant message to his father-in-law, and I had no doubt either that in his telling, our part in the victory would be diminished to nothing. Father Pyrlig would ensure that Alfred heard the truth, though whether the king would believe what he heard was another matter.

Pyrlig and Osferth left before dawn, using two horses out of the many we had captured in Lundene. I walked around the circuit of the walls as the sun rose, noting those places that still needed repair. My men were standing guard. Most were from the Berrocscire fyrd, which had fought under

Æthelred the previous day, and their excitement at their apparently easy victory had still not subsided.

A few of Æthelred's men were also posted on the walls, though most were recovering from the ale and mead they had drunk through the night. At one of the northern gates, which looked towards misted green hills, I met Egbert, the elderly man who had yielded to Æthelflaed's demands and had given me his best men. I rewarded him with the gift of a silver arm ring I had taken from one of the many corpses. Those dead were still unburied and, in the dawn, ravens and kites were feasting. 'Thank you,' I said.

'I should have trusted you,' he said awkwardly.

'You did trust me.'

He shrugged. 'Because of her, yes.'

'Is Æthelflaed here?' I asked.

'Still at the island,' Egbert said.

'I thought you were guarding her?'

'I was,' Egbert said dully, 'but Lord Æthelred had me replaced last night.'

'Had you replaced?' I asked, then saw that his silver chain, the symbol that he commanded men, had been taken from him.

He shrugged as if to tell me he did not understand the decision. 'Ordered me to come here,' he said, 'but when I arrived he wouldn't see me. He was sick.'

'Something serious, I hope?'

A half-smile flickered and died on Egbert's face. 'He was vomiting, I'm told. Probably nothing.'

My cousin had taken the palace at the top of Lundene's hill as his quarters, while I stayed in the Roman house by the river. I liked it. I have always liked Roman buildings because their walls possess the great virtue of keeping out wind, rain and snow. That house was large. You entered through an arch leading from the street into a courtyard surrounded by a pillared arcade. On three sides of the court-yard were small rooms that must have been used by servants or for storage. One was a kitchen and had a brick bread oven so large that you could bake enough loaves to feed three crews at one time. The courtyard's fourth side led into six rooms, two of them big enough to assemble my whole bodyguard. Beyond those two big rooms was a paved terrace that overlooked the river and at evening time that was a pleasant place, though at low tide the stench of the Temes could be overwhelming.

I could have gone back to Coccham, but I stayed anyway and the men of Berrocscire's fyrd also stayed, though they were unhappy because it was springtime and there was work to do on their farms. I kept them in Lundene to strengthen the city's walls. I would have gone home if I thought Æthelred would have done that work, but he seemed blithely unaware of the sad state of the city's defences. Sigefrid had patched a few places and he had strengthened the gates, but there was still much to do. The old masonry was crumbling and had even fallen into the outer ditch in places, and my men cut and trimmed trees to make new palisades wherever the wall was weak. Then we cleared the ditch outside the wall, scraping out matted filth and planting sharpened stakes to welcome any attacker.

Alfred sent orders that the whole of the old city was to be rebuilt. Any Roman building in good repair was to be kept, while dilapidated ruins were to be pulled down and replaced with sturdy timber and thatch, but there were neither the men nor the funds to attempt such work. Alfred's idea was that the Saxons of the undefended new town would move into old Lundene and be safe behind its ramparts, but those Saxons still feared the ghosts of the Roman builders and they stubbornly resisted every invitation to take over the deserted properties. My men of the Berrocscire fyrd were

190

just as frightened of the ghosts, but they were still more frightened of me and so they stayed and worked.

Æthelred took no notice of what I did. His sickness must have passed for he busied himself hunting. Every day he rode to the wooded hills north of the city where he pursued deer. He never took fewer than forty men, for there was always a chance that some marauding Danish band might come close to Lundene. There were many of those bands, but fate decreed that none went near Æthelred. Every day I would see horsemen to the east, picking their way through the desolate dark marshes that lay seawards of the city. They were Danes, watching us, and doubtless reporting back to Sigefrid.

I got news of Sigefrid. He lived, the reports said, though he was so crippled by his wound that he could neither walk nor stand. He had taken refuge at Beamfleot with his brother and with Haesten, and from there they sent raiders into the mouth of the Temes. Saxon ships dared not sail to Frankia, for the Northmen were in a vengeful mood after their defeat in Lundene. One Danish ship, dragon-prowed, even rowed up the Temes to taunt us from the churning water just below the gap in the broken bridge. They had Saxon prisoners aboard and the Danes killed them, one by one, making sure we could see the bloody executions. There were also women captives aboard and we could hear them screaming. I sent Finan and a dozen men to the bridge and they carried a clay pot of fire, and once on the bridge they used hunting bows to shoot fire-arrows at the intruder. All shipmasters fear fire, and the arrows, most of which missed altogether, persuaded them to drop downriver until the arrows could no longer reach them, but they did not go far and their oarsmen held the ship against the current as more prisoners were killed. They did not leave until I had assembled a crew to man one of the captured boats tied at the wharves, and only then did they turn and row downriver into the darkening evening.

Other ships from Beamfleot crossed the wide estuary of the Temes and landed men in Wessex. That part of Wessex was an alien place. It had once been the kingdom of Cent until it was conquered by the West Saxons and, though the men of Cent were Saxons, they spoke in a strange accent. It had always been a wild place, close to the other lands across the sea, and ever liable to be raided by Vikings. Now Sigefrid's men launched ship after ship across the estuary and pillaged deep into Cent. They took slaves and burned villages. A messenger came from Swithwulf, Bishop of Hrofeceastre, to beg for my help. 'The heathen were at Contwaraburg,' the messenger, a young priest, told me gloomily.

'Did they kill the archbishop?' I asked cheerfully.

'He was not there, lord, thank God.' The priest made the sign of the cross. 'The pagans are everywhere, lord, and no one is safe. Bishop Swithwulf begs your help.'

But I could not help the bishop. I needed men to guard Lundene, not Cent, and I needed men to guard my family too for, a week after the city's fall, Gisela, Stiorra and a half-dozen maids arrived. I had sent Finan and thirty men to escort them safely down the river and the house by the Temes seemed to grow warmer with the echoes of women's laughter. 'You might have swept the house,' Gisela chided me.

'I did!'

'Ha!' she pointed to a ceiling, 'what are those?'

'Cobwebs,' I said, 'they're holding the beams in place.'

The cobwebs were swept away and the kitchen fires were lit. In the courtyard, under a corner where the tiled arcade roofs met, there was an old stone urn that was choked with rubbish. Gisela cleaned the filth out, then she and two maids scrubbed the outside of the urn to reveal white marble carved with delicate women who appeared to be chasing each other and waving harps. Gisela loved those carvings. She crouched beside them, tracing a finger over the hair of the Roman women, and then she and the maids tried to copy the hairstyle. She loved the house too, and even endured the river's stench to sit on the terrace in the evening and watch the water slide by. 'He beats her,' she told me one evening.

I knew of whom she spoke and said nothing.

'She's bruised,' Gisela said, 'and she's pregnant, and he beats her.'

'She's what?' I asked in surprise.

'Æthelflaed,' Gisela said patiently, 'is pregnant.' Almost every day Gisela went to the palace and spent time with Æthelflaed, though Æthelflaed was never allowed to visit our house.

I was surprised by Gisela's news of Æthelflaed's pregnancy. I do not know why I should have been surprised, but I was. I suppose I still thought of Æthelflaed as a child. 'And he hits her?' I asked.

'Because he thinks she loves other men,' Gisela said.

'Does she?'

'No, of course she doesn't, but he fears she does.' Gisela paused to gather more wool that she was spinning onto a distaff. 'He thinks she loves you.'

I thought of Æthelred's sudden anger on Lundene's bridge. 'He's mad!' I said.

'No, he's jealous,' Gisela said, laying a hand on my arm. 'And I know he has nothing to be jealous about.' She smiled at me, then went back to gathering her wool. 'It's a strange way to show love, isn't it?'

Æthelflaed had come to the city the day after it fell. She travelled by boat to the Saxon town, and from there an ox cart had carried her across the Fleot and so up to her husband's new palace. Men lined the route waving leafy green boughs, a priest walked ahead of the oxen scattering holy water while a choir of women followed the cart, which, like the oxen's horns, was hung with spring flowers. Æthelflaed, clutching the cart's side to steady herself, had looked uncomfortable, but she had given me a wan smile as the oxen dragged her over the uneven stones inside the gate.

Æthelflaed's arrival was celebrated by a feast in the palace. I am certain Æthelred had not wanted to invite me, but my rank had given him little choice and a grudging message had arrived on the afternoon before the celebration. The feast had been nothing special, though the ale was plentiful enough. A dozen priests shared the top table with Æthelred and Æthelflaed, and I was given a stool at the end of that long board. Æthelred glowered at me, the priests ignored me, and I left early, pleading that I had to walk the walls and make certain the sentries were awake. I remember my cousin had looked pale that night, but it was soon after his vomiting fit. I had asked after his health and he had waved the question away as though it were irrelevant.

Gisela and Æthelflaed became friends in Lundene. I repaired the wall and Æthelred hunted while his men plundered the city for his palace's furnishings. I went home one day to find six of his followers in the courtyard of my house. Egbert, the man who had given me the troops on the eve of the attack, was one of the six and his face showed no expression as I came into the courtyard. He just watched me. 'What do you want?' I asked the six men. Five were in mail and had swords, the sixth wore a finely embroidered jerkin that showed hounds chasing deer. That sixth man also wore a silver chain, a sign of noble rank. It was Aldhelm, my cousin's friend and the commander of his household troops.

'This,' Aldhelm answered. He was standing by the urn

that Gisela had cleaned. It served now to catch rainwater that fell from the roof, and that water was sweet and clean-tasting, a rarity in any city.

'Two hundred silver shillings,' I told Aldhelm, 'and it's yours.'

He sneered at that. The price was outrageous. The four younger men had succeeded in tipping the urn so that its water had flowed out and now they were struggling to right it again, though they had stopped their efforts when I appeared.

Gisela came from the main house and smiled at me. 'I told them they couldn't have it,' she said.

'Lord Æthelred wants it,' Aldhelm insisted.

'You're called Aldhelm,' I said, 'just Aldhelm, and I am Uhtred, Lord of Bebbanburg, and you call me "Lord".'

'Not this one,' Gisela spoke silkily. 'He called me an inter-fering bitch.'

My men, there were four of them, moved to my side and put hands on sword hilts. I gestured for them to step back and unbuckled my own sword belt. 'Did you call my wife a bitch?' I asked Aldhelm.

'My lord requires this statue,' he said, ignoring my question.

'You will apologise to my wife,' I told him, 'and then to me.' I laid the belt with its two heavy swords on the flag-stones.

He pointedly turned away from me. 'Leave it on its side,' he told the four men, 'and roll it out to the street.'

'I want two apologies,' I said.

He heard the menace in my voice and turned back to me, alarmed now. 'This house,' Aldhelm explained, 'belongs to the Lord Æthelred. If you live here it is by his gracious permission.' He became even more alarmed as I drew closer. 'Egbert!' he said loudly, but Egbert's only response was a calming motion with his right hand, a signal that his men should keep their swords scabbarded. Egbert knew that if a single blade left its long scabbard there would be a fight between his men and mine, and he had the sense to avoid that slaughter, but Aldhelm had no such sense. 'You impertinent bastard,' he said, and snatched a knife from a sheath at his waist and lunged it at my belly.

I broke Aldhelm's jaw, his nose, both his hands and maybe a couple of his ribs before Egbert hauled me away. When Aldhelm apologised to Gisela he did so while spitting teeth through bubbling blood, and the urn stayed in our courtyard. I gave his knife to the girls who worked in the kitchen, where it proved useful for cutting onions.

And the next day, Alfred came.

The king came silently, his ship arriving at a wharf upstream of the broken bridge. The *Haligast* waited for a river trader to pull away, then ghosted in on short, efficient oar strokes. Alfred, accompanied by a score of priests and monks, and guarded by six mailed men, came ashore unheralded and unannounced. He threaded the goods stacked on the wharf, stepped over a drunken man sleeping in the shade and ducked through the small gate in the wall leading to a merchant's courtyard.

I heard he went to the palace. Æthelred was not there, he was hunting again, but the king went to his daughter's chamber and stayed there a long time. Afterwards he walked back down the hill and, still with his priestly entourage, came to our house. I was with one of the groups making repairs to the walls, but Gisela had been warned of Alfred's presence in Lundene and, suspecting he might come to our house, had prepared a meal of bread, ale, cheese and boiled lentils. She offered no meat, for Alfred would not touch flesh. His stomach was tender and his bowels in perpetual torment and he had somehow persuaded himself that meat was an abomination.

Gisela had sent a servant to warn me of the king's arrival, yet even so I arrived at the house long after Alfred to find my elegant courtyard black with priests, among whom was Father Pyrlig and, next to him, Osferth, who was once again dressed in monkish robes. Osferth gave me a sour look, as if blaming me for his return to the church, while Pyrlig embraced me. 'Æthelred said nothing of you in his report to the king,' he murmured those words, gusting ale-smelling breath over my face.

'We weren't here when the city fell?' I asked.

'Not according to your cousin,' Pyrlig said, then chuckled. 'But I told Alfred the truth. Go on, he's waiting for you.'

Alfred was on the river terrace. His guards stood behind him, lined against the house, while the king was seated on a wooden chair. I paused in the doorway, surprised because Alfred's face, usually so pallid and solemn, had an animated look. He was even smiling. Gisela was seated next to him and the king was leaning forward, talking, and Gisela, whose back was to me, was listening. I stayed where I was, watching that rarest of sights, Alfred happy. He tapped a long white finger on her knee once to stress some point. There was nothing untoward in the gesture, except it was so unlike him.

But then, of course, maybe it was very like him. Alfred had been a famous womaniser before he was caught in the snare of Christianity, and Osferth was a product of that early princely lust. Alfred liked pretty women, and it was obvious he liked Gisela. I heard her laugh suddenly and Alfred, flattered by her amusement, smiled shyly. He seemed not to mind that she was no Christian and that she wore a pagan amulet about her neck, he was simply happy to be in her company and I was tempted to leave them alone. I had never seen him happy in the company of Ælswith, his weasel-tongued, stoat-faced, shrike-voiced wife. Then he happened to glance over Gisela's shoulder and saw me.

His face changed immediately. He stiffened, sat upright and reluctantly beckoned me forward.

I picked up a stool that our daughter used and heard a hiss as Alfred's guards drew swords. Alfred waved the blades down, sensible enough to know that if I had wanted to attack him then I would hardly use a three-legged milking stool. He watched as I gave my swords to one of the guards, a mark of respect, then as I carried the stool across the terrace flagstones. 'Lord Uhtred,' he greeted me coldly.

'Welcome to our house, lord King.' I gave him a bow, then sat with my back to the river.

He was silent for a moment. He was wearing a brown cloak that was drawn tight around his thin body. A silver cross hung at his neck, while on his thinning hair was a circlet of bronze, which surprised me, for he rarely wore symbols of kingship, thinking them vain baubles, but he must have decided that Lundene needed to see a king. He sensed my surprise for he clawed the circlet off his head. 'I had hoped,' he said coldly, 'that the Saxons of the new town would have abandoned their houses. That they would live here instead. They could be protected here by the walls! Why won't they move?'

'They fear the ghosts, lord,' I said.

'And you do not?'

I thought for a while. 'Yes,' I said after thinking about my answer.

'Yet you live here?' he waved at the house.

'We propitiate the spirits, lord,' Gisela explained softly and, when the king raised an eyebrow, she told how we

198

placed food and drink in the courtyard to greet any ghosts who came to our house.

Alfred rubbed his eyes. 'It might be better,' he said, 'if our priests exorcise the streets. Prayer and holy water! We shall drive the ghosts away.'

'Or let me take three hundred men to sack the new town,' I suggested. 'Burn their houses, lord, and they'll have to live in the old city.'

A half-smile flickered on his face, gone as quickly as it had showed. 'It is hard to force obedience,' he said, 'without encouraging resentment. I sometimes think the only true authority I have is over my family, and even then I wonder! If I release you with sword and spear onto the new town, Lord Uhtred, then they will learn to hate you. Lundene must be obedient, but it must also be a bastion of Christian Saxons, and if they hate us then they will welcome a return of the Danes, who left them in peace.' He shook his head abruptly. 'We shall leave them in peace, but don't build them a palisade. Let them come into the old city of their own accord. Now, forgive me,' those last two words were to Gisela, 'but we must speak of still darker things.'

Alfred gestured to a guard who pushed open the door from the terrace. Father Beocca appeared and with him a second priest; a black-haired, pouchy-faced, scowling creature called Father Erkenwald. He hated me. He had once tried to have me killed by accusing me of piracy and, though his accusations had been entirely true, I had slipped away from his bad-tempered clutches. He gave me a sour look while Beocca offered a solemn nod, then both men stared attentively at Alfred.

'Tell me,' Alfred said, looking at me, 'what Sigefrid, Haesten and Erik do now?'

'They're at Beamfleot, lord,' I said, 'strengthening their

199

camp. They have thirty-two ships, and men enough to crew them.'

'You've seen this place?' Father Erkenwald demanded. The two priests, I knew, had been fetched onto the terrace to serve as witnesses to this conversation. Alfred, ever careful, liked to have a record, either written or memorised, of all such discussions.

'I've not seen it,' I said coldly.

'Your spies, then?' Alfred resumed the questions.

'Yes, lord.'

He thought for a moment. 'The ships can be burned?' he asked.

I shook my head. 'They're in a creek, lord.'

'They must be destroyed,' he said vengefully, and I saw his long thin hands clench on his lap. 'They raided Contwaraburg!' he said, sounding distraught.

'I heard of it, lord.'

'They burned the church!' he said indignantly, 'and stole everything! Gospel books, crosses, even the relics!' he shuddered. 'The church possessed a leaf of the fig tree that our Lord Jesus withered! I touched it once, and felt its power.' He shuddered again. 'It is all gone to pagan hands.' He sounded as if he might weep.

I said nothing. Beocca had started writing, his pen scratching on a parchment held awkwardly in his lamed hand. Father Erkenwald was holding a pot of ink and had a look of disdain as if such a chore was belittling him. 'Thirty-two ships, did you say?' Beocca asked me.

'That was the last I heard.'

'Creeks can be entered,' Alfred said acidly, his distress suddenly gone.

'The creek at Beamfleot dries at low tide, lord,' I explained, 'and to reach the enemy ships we must pass their camp, which is on a hill above the mooring. And the last report I received, lord, said a ship was permanently moored across the channel. We could destroy that ship and fight our way through, but you'll need a thousand men to do it and you'll lose at least two hundred of them.'

'A thousand?' he asked sceptically.

'The last I heard, lord, said Sigefrid had close to two thousand men.'

He closed his eyes briefly. 'Sigefrid lives?'

'Barely,' I said. I had received most of this news from Ulf, my Danish trader, who loved the silver I paid him. I had no doubt Ulf was receiving silver from Haesten or Erik for telling them what I did in Lundene, but that was a price worth paying. 'Brother Osferth wounded him badly,' I said.

The king's shrewd eyes rested on me. 'Osferth,' he said tonelessly.

'Won the battle, lord,' I said just as tonelessly. Alfred just watched me, still expressionless. 'You heard from Father Pyrlig?' I asked, and received a curt nod. 'What Osferth did, lord, was brave,' I said, 'and I am not certain I would have had the courage to do it. He jumped from a great height and attacked a fearsome warrior, and he lived to remember the achievement. If it was not for Osferth, lord, Sigefrid would be in Lundene today and I would be in my grave.'

'You want him back?' Alfred asked.

The answer, of course, was no, but Beocca gave an almost imperceptible nod of his grey head and I understood Osferth was not wanted in Wintanceaster. I did not like the youth and, judging from Beocca's silent message, no one liked him in Wintanceaster either, yet his courage had been exemplary. Osferth was, I thought, a warrior at heart. 'Yes, lord,' I said, and saw Gisela's secret smile.

'He's yours,' Alfred said shortly. Beocca rolled his good eye to heaven in gratitude. 'And I want the Northmen out of the Temes estuary,' Alfred went on.

I shrugged. 'Isn't that Guthrum's business?' I asked. Beamfleot lay in the kingdom of East Anglia with which, officially, we were at peace.

Alfred looked irritated, probably because I had used Guthrum's Danish name. 'King Æthelstan has been informed of the problem,' he said.

'And does nothing?'

'He makes promises.'

'And Vikings use his land with impunity,' I observed.

Alfred bridled. 'Are you suggesting I declare war on King Æthelstan?'

'He allows raiders to come to Wessex, lord,' I said, 'so why don't we return the favour? Why don't we send ships to East Anglia to hurt King Æthelstan's holdings?'

Alfred stood, ignoring my suggestion. 'What is most important,' he said, 'is that we do not lose Lundene.' He held a hand towards Father Erkenwald who opened a leather satchel and took out a scroll of parchment sealed with brown wax. Alfred held the parchment to me. 'I have appointed you as Military Governor of this city. Do not let the enemy retake it.'

I took the parchment. 'Military Governor?' I asked pointedly.

'All troops and fyrd members will be under your command.'

'And the city, lord?' I asked.

'Will be a godly place,' Alfred said.

'We shall cleanse it of its iniquity,' Father Erkenwald interjected, 'and wash it whiter than snow.'

'Amen,' Beocca said fervently.

'I am naming Father Erkenwald as Bishop of Lundene,' Alfred said, 'and the civil governance will reside with him.'

I felt a lurch in my heart. Erkenwald? Who hated me? 'And what about the Ealdorman of Mercia?' I asked, 'does he not have civil governance here?'

'My son-in-law,' Alfred said distantly, 'will not countermand my appointments.'

'And how much authority does he have here?' I asked.

'This is Mercia!' Alfred said, tapping the terrace with a foot, 'and he rules Mercia.'

'So he can appoint a new military governor?' I asked.

'He will do as I tell him,' Alfred said, and there was a sudden anger in his voice. 'And in four days' time we shall all gather,' he had recovered his poise quickly, 'and discuss what needs to be done to make this city safe and full of grace.' He nodded brusquely to me, inclined his head to Gisela and turned away.

'Lord King,' Gisela spoke softly, checking Alfred's departure, 'how is your daughter? I saw her yesterday and she was bruised.'

Alfred's gaze flickered to the river where six swans rode the water beneath the tumult of the broken bridge. 'She's well,' he said distantly.

'The bruising . . .' Gisela began.

'She was always a mischievous child,' Alfred interrupted her.

'Mischievous?' Gisela's response was tentative.

'I love her,' Alfred said, and there could have been no doubt of that from the unexpected passion in his voice, 'but while mischief in a child is amusing, in an adult it is sinful. My dear Æthelflaed must learn obedience.'

'So she learns to hate?' I asked, echoing the king's earlier words.

'She's married now,' Alfred said, 'and her duty before God is to be obedient to her husband. She will learn that, I am sure, and be grateful for the lesson. It is hard to inflict punishment on a child you love, but it is a sin to withhold such punishment. I pray God she comes to a state of good grace.'

'Amen,' Father Erkenwald said.

'Praise God,' Beocca said.

Gisela said nothing and the king left.

I should have known that the summons to the palace on top of Lundene's low hill would involve priests. I had expected a council of war and a hard-headed discussion on how best to scour the Temes of the brigands who infested the estuary, but instead, once I had been relieved of my swords, I was shown into the pillared hall where an altar had been erected. Finan and Sihtric were with me. Finan, a good Christian, made the sign of the cross, but Sihtric, like me, was a pagan and he looked at me with alarm as though he feared some religious magic.

I endured the service. Monks chanted, priests prayed, bells were rung and men genuflected. There were some forty men in the room, most of them priests, but only one woman. Æthelflaed was seated beside her husband. She was dressed in a white robe, gathered at her waist by a blue sash, and her corn-gold hair had speedwell woven into its bun. I was behind her, but once, when she turned to look at her father, I saw the purplish bruise around her right eye. Alfred did not look at her, but stayed on his knees. I watched him, watched Æthelflaed's slumped shoulders, and thought about Beamfleot, and how that wasps' nest could be burned out. First, I thought, I needed to take a ship downriver and see Beamfleot for myself.

Alfred suddenly stood up and I assumed the service was at last over, but instead the king turned to us and delivered a mercifully brief homily. He encouraged us to ponder the words of the prophet Ezekiel, whoever he was. '"Then the heathen that are left round about you,"' the king read to us, '"shall know that I the Lord build the ruined places, and plant that which was desolate". Lundene,' the king put down the parchment with Ezekiel's words, 'is again a Saxon city, and though it is in ruins, with God's help we shall rebuild it. We shall make it a place of God, a light to the pagans.' He paused, smiled gravely and beckoned to Bishop Erkenwald who, draped in a white cape hung with red strips on which silver crosses had been embroidered, stood to deliver a sermon. I groaned. We were supposed to be discussing how to rid the Temes of our enemies, and instead were being tortured with dull piety.

I had long learned to ignore sermons. It has been my unhappy fate to hear many, and the words of most have passed over me like rain running down newly laid thatch, but some minutes into Erkenwald's hoarse harangue I began to take notice.

Because he was not preaching about remaking ruined cities, nor even about the heathen who threatened Lundene, instead he was preaching to Æthelflaed.

He stood by the altar and he shouted. He was ever an angry man, but on that spring day in the old Roman hall, he was filled with a passionate fury. God, he said, was speaking through him. God had a message, and God's word could not be ignored or else the brimstone fires of hell would consume all mankind. He never used Æthelflaed's name, but he stared at her, and no man in the room could doubt the message that the Christian's god was sending to the poor girl. God, it seemed, had even written the message down in a gospel book, and Erkenwald snatched a copy from the altar, held it up so that the light from the smoke-hole in the roof caught the page, and read aloud.

'"To be discreet,"' he looked up to glare at Æthelflaed, '"chaste! Keepers of the home! Good! Obedient to their husbands!" Those are God's own words! That is what God demands of a woman! To be discreet, to be chaste, to be home-keepers, to be obedient! God spoke to us!' He almost writhed in ecstasy as he said those last four words. 'God still speaks to us!' he gazed up at the roof as if he could glimpse his god peering through the ceiling. 'God speaks to us!'

He preached for over an hour. His spittle spun through the ray of sunlight cast through the smoke-hole. He cringed, he shouted, he shuddered. And time and again he went back to the words in the gospel book that wives must be obedient to their husbands.

'Obedient!' he shouted, and paused.

I heard a thump from the outer hall as a guard rested his shield.

'Obedient!' Erkenwald shrieked again.

Æthelflaed's head was held high. From my view behind her it seemed as if she were staring straight at that mad, vicious priest who was now the bishop and ruler of Lundene. Æthelred, beside her, fidgeted, but the few glimpses I got of his face showed a smug, self-satisfied look. Most of the men there looked bored and only one, Father Beocca, seemed to disapprove of the bishop's sermon. He caught my eye once and made me smile by raising an indignant eyebrow. I am certain Beocca did not dislike the message, but he doubt-less believed it should not have been preached in so public a manner. As for Alfred, he just gazed serenely at the altar as the bishop ranted, yet his passivity disguised involvement because that bitter sermon could never have been preached without the king's knowledge and permission.

'Obedient!' Erkenwald cried again, and stared up at heaven as though that one word was the solution to all mankind's troubles. The king nodded approval, and it occurred to me that Alfred had not only approved Erkenwald's rant, but must have requested it. Perhaps he thought that a public admonition would save Æthelflaed from private beatings?

The message certainly matched Alfred's philosophy, for he believed that a kingdom could only thrive if it was ruled by law, was ordered by government and was obedient to the will of God and the king. Yet he could look at his daughter, see her bruises and approve? He had always loved his children. I had watched them grow, and I had seen Alfred play with them, yet his religion could allow him to humiliate a daughter he loved? Sometimes, when I pray to my gods, I thank them fervently that they let me escape Alfred's god.

Erkenwald at last ran out of words. There was a pause, then Alfred stood and turned to face us. 'The word of God,' he said, smiling. The priests murmured brief prayers, then Alfred shook his head as though clearing it of pious matters. 'The city of Lundene is now a proper part of Mercia,' he said, and a louder murmur of approval echoed through the room. 'I have entrusted its civil government to Bishop Erkenwald,' he turned and smiled at the bishop, who smirked and bowed, 'while Lord Uhtred will be responsible for the defence of the city,' Alfred said, looking at me. I did not bow.

Æthelflaed turned then. I think she had not known I was in the room, but she turned when my name was spoken and stared at me. I winked at her, and her bruised face smiled. Æthelred did not see the wink. He was pointedly ignoring me.

'The city, of course,' Alfred went on, his voice suddenly ice cold because he had seen my wink, 'falls under the authority and rule of my beloved son-in-law. In time it will become a valuable part of his possessions, yet for the moment he has graciously agreed that Lundene must be administered by men experienced in government.' In other words Lundene might be part of Mercia, but Alfred had no intention of allowing it out of West Saxon hands. 'Bishop Erkenwald has the authority to set dues and raise taxes,'

Alfred explained, 'and one third of the money will be spent on civil government, one third on the church, and one third on defending the city. And I know that under the bishop's guidance and with the help of Almighty God we can raise a city that glorifies Christ and His church.'

I did not know most of the men in the room because they were almost all Mercian thegns who had been summoned to Lundene to meet Alfred. Aldhelm was among them, his face still black and bloodied from my hands. He had glanced at me once and twisted fast away. The summons had been unexpected and only a few thegns had made the journey to Lundene, and those men now listened politely enough to Alfred, but almost all were torn between two masters. Northern Mercia was under Danish rule, and only the southern part, which bordered Wessex, could be called free Saxon land and even that land was under constant harassment. A Mercian thegn who wished to stay alive, who wished his daughters safe from slavers and his livestock free of cattle-raiders, did well to pay tribute to the Danes as well as pay taxes to Æthelred who, because of his inherited land-holdings, marriage and lineage, was acknowledged as the most noble of the Mercian thegns. He might call himself king if he wished, and I had no doubt he did so wish, but Alfred did not, and Æthelred without Alfred was nothing.

'It is our intention,' Alfred said, 'to rid Mercia of its pagan invaders. To do that we needed to secure Lundene and so put a stop to the Northmen's ships raiding up the Temes. Now we must hold Lundene. How is that to be done?'

The answer to that was obvious, though it did not stop a general discussion that meandered aimlessly as men argued about how many troops would be needed to defend the walls. I took no part. I leaned against the back wall and noted which of the thegns were enthusiastic and which were guarded. Bishop Erkenwald glanced at me occasionally, plainly wondering why I did not contribute my grain of wheat to the threshing floor, but I kept silent. Æthelred listened intently and finally summed up the discussion. 'The city, lord King,' he said brightly, 'needs a garrison of two thousand men.'

'Mercians,' Alfred said. 'Those men must come from Mercia.'

'Of course,' Æthelred agreed quickly. I noted that many of the thegns looked dubious.

Alfred saw it too and glanced at me. 'This is your responsibility, Lord Uhtred. Have you no opinion?'

I almost yawned, but managed to resist the impulse. 'I have better than an opinion, lord King,' I said, 'I can give you fact.'

Alfred raised an eyebrow and managed to look disapproving at the same time. 'Well?' he asked irritably when I paused too long.

'Four men for every pole,' I said. A pole was six paces, or thereabouts, and the allocation of four men to a pole was not mine, but Alfred's. When he ordered the burhs built he had worked out in his meticulous way how many men would be needed to defend each, and the distance about the walls determined the final figure. Coccham's walls were one thousand four hundred paces in length and so my household guards and the fyrd had to supply a thousand men for its defence. But Coccham was a small burh, Lundene a city.

'And the distance about Lundene's walls?' Alfred demanded.

I looked at Æthelred, as though expecting him to answer and Alfred, seeing where I looked, also gazed at his son-in-law. Æthelred thought for a heartbeat and, instead of telling the truth which was that he did not know, made a guess. 'Eight hundred poles, lord King?'

'The landward wall,' I broke in harshly, 'is six hundred

and ninety-two poles. The river wall adds a further three hundred and fifty-eight. The defences, lord King, stretch for one thousand and fifty poles.'

'Four thousand, two hundred men,' Bishop Erkenwald said immediately, and I confess I was impressed. It had taken me a long time to discover that number, and I had not been certain my computation had been correct until Gisela also worked the problem out.

'No enemy, lord King,' I said, 'can attack everywhere at once, so I reckon the city can be defended by a garrison of three thousand, four hundred men.'

One of the Mercian thegns made a hissing noise, as though such a figure was an impossibility. 'Only one thousand men more than your garrison in Wintanceaster, lord King,' I pointed out. The difference, of course, was that Wintanceaster lay in a loyal West Saxon shire that was accustomed to its men serving their turn in the fyrd.

'And where do you find those men?' a Mercian demanded.

'From you,' I said harshly.

'But . . .' the man began, then faltered. He was going to point out that the Mercian fyrd was a useless thing, grown weak by disuse, and that any attempt to raise the fyrd might draw the malevolent attention of the Danish earls who ruled in northern Mercia, and so these men had learned to lie low and keep silent. They were like deerhounds who shiver in the undergrowth for fear of attracting the wolves.

'But nothing,' I said, louder and harsher still. 'For if a man does not contribute to his country's defence then that man is a traitor. He should be dispossessed of his land, put to death, and his family reduced to slavery.'

I thought Alfred might object to those words, but he kept silent. Indeed, he nodded agreement. I was the blade inside his scabbard and he was evidently pleased that I had shown the steel for an instant. The Mercians said nothing.

'We also need men for ships, lord King,' I went on.

'Ships?' Alfred asked.

'Ships?' Erkenwald echoed.

'We need crewmen,' I explained. We had captured twenty-one ships when we took Lundene, of which seventeen were fighting boats. The others were wider beamed, built for trading, but they could be useful too. 'I have the ships,' I went on, 'but they need crews, and those crews have to be good fighters.'

'You defend the city with ships?' Erkenwald asked defiantly.

'And where will your money come from?' I asked him. 'From customs dues. But no trader dare sail here, so I have to clear the estuary of enemy ships. That means killing the pirates, and for that I need crews of fighting men. I can use my household troops, but they have to be replaced in the city's garrison by other men.'

'I need ships,' Æthelred suddenly intervened.

Æthelred needed ships? I was so astonished that I said nothing. My cousin's job was to defend southern Mercia and push the Danes northwards from the rest of his country, and that would mean fighting on land. Now, suddenly, he needed ships? What did he plan? To row across pasture-land?

'I would suggest, lord King,' Æthelred was smiling as he spoke, his voice smooth and respectful, 'that all the ships west of the bridge be given to me, for use in your service,' and he bowed to Alfred when he said that, 'and my cousin be given the ships east of the bridge.'

'That . . .' I began, but was cut off by Alfred.

'That is fair,' the king said firmly. It was not fair, it was ridiculous. There were only two fighting ships in the stretch of river east of the bridge, and fifteen upstream of the obstruction. The presence of those fifteen ships suggested that Sigefrid had been planning a major raid on Alfred's territory before we struck him, and I needed those ships to scour the estuary clear of enemies. But Alfred, eager to be seen supporting his son-in-law, swept my objections aside. 'You will use what ships you have, Lord Uhtred,' he insisted, 'and I will put seventy of my household guard under your command to crew one ship.'

So I was to drive the Danes from the estuary with two ships? I gave up, and leaned against the wall as the discussion droned on, mostly about the level of customs to be charged, and how much the neighbouring shires were to be taxed, and I wondered yet again why I was not in the north where a man's sword was free and there was small law and much laughter.

Bishop Erkenwald cornered me when the meeting was over. I was strapping on my sword belt when he peered up at me with his beady eyes. 'You should know,' he greeted me, 'that I opposed your appointment.'

'As I would have opposed yours,' I said bitterly, still angry at Æthelred's theft of the fifteen warships.

'God may not look with blessing on a pagan warrior,' the newly appointed bishop explained himself, 'but the king, in his wisdom, considers you a soldier of ability.'

'And Alfred's wisdom is famous,' I said blandly.

'I have spoken with the Lord Æthelred,' he went on, ignoring my words, 'and he has agreed that I can issue writs of assembly for Lundene's adjacent counties. You have no objection?'

Erkenwald meant that he now had the power to raise the fyrd. It was a power that might better have been given me, but I doubted Æthelred would have agreed to that. Nor did I think that Erkenwald, nasty man though he was, would be anything but loyal to Alfred. 'I have no objection,' I said.

'Then I shall inform Lord Æthelred of your agreement,' he said formally.

'And when you speak with him,' I said, 'tell him to stop hitting his wife.'

Erkenwald jerked as though I had just struck him in the face. 'It is his Christian duty,' he said stiffly, 'to discipline his wife, and it is her duty to submit. Did you not listen to what I preached?'

'To every word,' I said.

'She brought it on herself,' Erkenwald snarled. 'She has a fiery spirit, she defies him!'

'She's little more than a child,' I said, 'and a pregnant child at that.'

'And foolishness is deep in the heart of a child,' Erkenwald responded, 'and those are the words of God! And what does God say should be done about the foolishness of a child? That the rod of correction shall beat it far away!' He shuddered suddenly. 'That is what you do, Lord Uhtred! You beat a child into obedience! A child learns by suffering pain, by being beaten, and that pregnant child must learn her duty. God wills it! Praise God!'

I heard only last week that they want to make Erkenwald into a saint. Priests come to my home beside the northern sea where they find an old man, and they tell me I am just a few paces from the fires of hell. I only need repent, they say, and I will go to heaven and live for evermore in the blessed company of the saints.

And I would rather burn till time itself burns out.

Seven

Water dripped from oar-blades, the drips spreading ripples in a sea that was shining slabs of light that slowly shifted and parted, joined and slid.

Our ship was poised on that shifting light, silent.

The sky to the east was molten gold pouring around a bank of sun-drenched cloud, while the rest was blue. Pale blue to the east and dark blue to the west where night fled towards the unknown lands beyond the distant ocean.

To the south I could see the low shore of Wessex. It was green and brown, treeless and not that far away, though I would go no closer for the light-sliding sea concealed mudbanks and shoals. Our oars were resting and the wind was dead, but we moved relentlessly eastwards, carried by the tide and by the river's strong flow. This was the estuary of the Temes; a wide place of water, mud, sand and terror.

Our ship had no name and she carried no beast-heads on her prow or stern. She was a trading ship, one of the two I had captured in Lundene, and she was wide-beamed, sluggish, big-bellied and clumsy. She carried a sail, but the sail was furled on the yard, and the yard was in its crutches. We drifted on the tide towards the golden dawn.

I stood with the steering-oar in my right hand. I wore mail, but no helmet. My two swords were strapped to my waist, but they, like my mail coat, were hidden beneath a dirty brown woollen cloak. There were twelve rowers on the benches, Sihtric was beside me, one man was on the bow platform and all those men, like me, showed neither armour nor weapons.

We looked like a trading ship drifting along the Wessex shore in hope that no one on the northern side of the estuary would see us.

But they had seen us.

And a sea-wolf was stalking us.

She was rowing to our north, slanting south and eastwards, waiting for us to turn and try to escape upriver against the tide. She was perhaps a mile away and I could see the short black upright line of her stemhead, which ended in a beast's head. She was in no hurry. Her shipmaster could see we were not rowing and he would take that inactivity as a sign of panic. He would think we were discussing what to do. His own oar banks were dipping slow, but every stroke surged that distant boat forward to cut off our seaward escape.

Finan, who was manning one of the stern oars of our ship, glanced over his shoulder. 'Crew of fifty?' he suggested.

'Maybe more,' I said.

He grinned. 'How many more?'

'Could be seventy?' I guessed.

We numbered forty-three, and all but fifteen of us were hidden in the place where the ship would normally have carried goods. Those hidden men were covered by an old sail, making it look as though we carried salt or grain, some cargo that needed to be protected from any rain or spray. 'Be a rare fight if it's seventy,' Finan said with relish.

'Won't be any fight at all,' I said, 'because they won't be ready for us,' and that was true. We looked like an easy victim, a handful of men on a tubby ship, and the sea-wolf would come alongside and a dozen men would leap aboard while the rest of the crew just watched the slaughter. That, at least, was what I hoped. The watching crew would be armed, of course, but they would not be expecting battle, and my men were more than ready.

'Remember,' I called loudly so the men beneath the sail would hear me, 'we kill them all!'

'Even women?' Finan asked.

'Not women,' I said. I doubted there would be women aboard the far ship.

Sihtric was crouching beside me and now squinted up. 'Why kill them all, lord?'

'So they learn to fear us,' I said.

The gold in the sky was brightening and fading. The sun was above the cloud bank and the sea shimmered with its new brilliance. The reflected image of the enemy was long on the light-flickering, slow-moving water.

'Steorbord oars!' I called, 'back water. Clumsy now!'

The oarsmen grinned as they deliberately churned the water with clumsy strokes that slowly turned our prow upriver so that it appeared as though we were trying to escape. The sensible thing for us to have done, had we been as innocent and vulnerable as we looked, would have been to row to the southern shore, ground the boat and run for our lives, but instead we turned and started rowing against tide and current. Our oars clashed, making us look like incompetent, scared fools.

'He's taken the bait,' I said to our rowers, though, because our bows now pointed westwards, they could see for themselves that the enemy had started rowing hard. The Viking was coming straight for us, her oar banks rising and falling like wings and the white water swelling and shrinking at her stem as each blade-beat surged the ship.

216

We kept feigning panic. Our oars banged into each other so that we did little except stir the water around our clumsy hull. Two gulls circled our stubby mast, their cries sad in the limpid morning. Far to the west, where the sky was darkened by the smoke of Lundene that lay beyond the horizon, I could just see a tiny dark streak, which I knew to be the mast of another ship. She was coming towards us, and I knew the enemy ship would have seen her too and would be wondering whether she was friend or foe.

Not that it mattered, for it would take the enemy only five minutes to capture our small, under-manned cargo ship and it would be the best part of an hour before the ebbing tide and steady rowing could bring that western ship to where we struggled. The Viking boat came on fast, her oars working in lovely unison, but the ship's speed meant that her oarsmen would be tired as well as unprepared by the time she reached us. Her beast-head, proud on her high stem, was an eagle with an open beak painted red as if the bird had just ripped bloody flesh from a victim, while beneath the carved head a dozen armed men were crowded on the bow platform. They were the men supposed to board and kill us.

Twenty oars a side made forty men. The boarding party added a dozen, though it was hard to count the men who were crowded so close together, and two men stood beside the steering-oar. 'Between fifty and sixty,' I called aloud. The enemy rowers were not in mail. They did not expect to fight, and most would have their swords at their feet and their shields stacked in the bilge.

'Stop oars!' I called. 'Rowers, get up!'

The eagle-prowed ship was close now. I could hear the creak of her oar tholes, the splash of her blades and the hiss of the sea at her cutwater. I could see bright axe blades, the helmeted faces of the men who thought they would kill us,

217

and the anxiety on the steersman's face as he attempted to lay his bows directly on ours. My rowers were milling about, feigning panic. The Viking oarsmen gave a last heave and I heard their shipmaster order them to cease rowing and ship oars. She ran on towards us, water sliding away from her stem and she was very close now, close enough to smell, and the men on her bow platform hefted their shields as the steersman aimed her bows to slide along our flank. Her oars were drawn inboard as she swooped to her kill.

I waited a heartbeat, waited until the enemy could no longer avoid us, then sprang our ambush. 'Now!' I shouted.

The sail was dragged away and suddenly our little ship bristled with armed men. I threw off my cloak and Sihtric brought me my helmet and shield. A man shouted a warning on the enemy ship and the steersman threw his weight on his long oar and his vessel turned slightly, but she had turned away too late, and there was a splintering sound as her bows cracked through our oar shafts. 'Now!' I shouted again.

Clapa was my man in our bows and he hurled a grapnel to haul the enemy into our embrace. The grapnel slammed over her sheer-strake, Clapa heaved and the impetus of the enemy ship made her swing on the line to crash against our flank. My men immediately swarmed over her side. These were my household troops, trained warriors, dressed in mail and hungry for slaughter, and they leaped among unarmoured oarsmen who were utterly unprepared for a fight. The enemy boarders, the only men armed and keyed for a battle, hesitated as the two ships crashed together. They could have attacked my men who were already killing, but instead their leader shouted at them to jump across onto our ship. He hoped to take my men in the rear, and it was a shrewd enough tactic, but we still had enough men left aboard to thwart them. 'Kill them all!' I shouted.

One Dane, I assume he was a Dane, tried to jump onto

my platform and I simply banged my shield into him and he disappeared between the ships where his mail took him instantly to the sea's bed. The other Viking boarders had reached the stern rowers' benches where they hacked and cursed at my men. I was behind and above them, and only had Sihtric for company, and the two of us could have stayed safe by remaining on the steering platform, but a man does not lead by staying out of a fight. 'Stay where you are,' I told Sihtric, and jumped.

I shouted a challenge as I jumped and a tall man turned to face me. He had an eagle's wing on his helmet, and his mail was fine, and his arms were bright with rings, and his shield was painted with an eagle, and I knew he must be the owner of the enemy ship. He was a Viking lord, fair-bearded and brown-eyed, and he carried a long-handled axe, its blade already reddened, and he swept it at me and I parried with the shield and his axe dropped at the last moment to cut at my ankles and, by the gift of Thor, the ship lurched and the axe lost its force in a rib of the trading ship. He kept my sword lunge away with his shield as he raised the axe again and I shield-charged him, throwing him back with my weight.

He should have fallen, but he staggered back into his own men and so stayed on his feet. I cut at his ankle and Serpent-Breath rasped on metal. His boots were protected as mine were by metal strips. The axe hurtled around and thumped into my shield, and his shield crashed into my sword and I was hurled back by the double blow. I hit the edge of the steering platform with my shoulderblades and he charged me again, trying to drive me down, and I was half aware of Sihtric still standing on the small stern platform and beating a sword at my enemy, but the blade glanced off the Dane's helmet and wasted itself on the man's mailed shoulders. He kicked at my feet, knowing I was unbalanced, and I fell.

219

'Turd,' he snarled, then took one backwards step. Behind him his men were dying, but he had time to kill me before he died himself. 'I am Olaf Eagleclaw,' he told me proudly, 'and I will meet you in the corpse-hall.'

'Uhtred of Bebbanburg,' I said, and I was still on the deck as he lifted his axe high.

And Olaf Eagleclaw screamed.

I had fallen on purpose. He was heavier than me, and he had me cornered, and I knew he would go on beating at me and I would be helpless to push him away, and so I had fallen. Sword blades were wasted on his fine mail and on his shining helmet, but now I thrust Serpent-Breath upwards, under the skirt of his mail, up into his unarmoured groin, and I followed her up, ripping the blade into him and through him as the blood drenched the deck between us. He was staring at me, wide-eyed and mouth open, as the axe fell from his hand. I was standing now, still hauling on Serpent-Breath, and he fell away, twitching, and I yanked her out of his body and saw his right hand scrabbling for his axe handle, and I kicked it towards him and watched his fingers curl around the haft before I killed him with a quick thrust into the throat. More blood spilled across the ship's timbers.

I make that small fight sound easy. It was not. It is true I fell on purpose, but Olaf made me fall, and instead of resisting, I let myself drop. Sometimes, in my old age, I wake shivering in the night as I remember the moments I should have died and did not. That is one of those moments. Perhaps I remember it wrong? Age clouds old things. There must have been the sound of feet scraping on the deck, the grunt of men making a blow, the stench of the filthy bilge, the gasps of wounded men. I remember the fear as I fell, the gut-souring, mind-screaming panic of imminent death. It was but a moment of life, soon gone, a flurry of blows and panic, a fight hardly worth remembering, yet still Olaf Eagleclaw can wake me in the darkness and I lie, listening to the sea beat on the sand, and I know he will be waiting for me in the corpse-hall where he will want to know whether I killed him by pure luck or whether I planned that fatal thrust. He will also remember that I kicked the axe back into his grasp so that he could die with a weapon in his hand, and for that he will thank me.

I look forward to seeing him.

By the time Olaf was dead his ship was taken and his crew slaughtered. Finan had led the charge onto the *Sea-Eagle*. I knew she was called that, for her name was cut in runic letters on her stem-post. 'It was no fight,' Finan reported, sounding disgusted.

'I told you,' I said.

'A few of the rowers found weapons,' he said, dismissing their effort with a shrug. Then he pointed down into the *Sea-Eagle*'s bilge that was sodden with blood. Five men crouched there, shivering, and Finan saw my questioning look. 'They're Saxons, lord,' he explained why the men still lived.

The five men were fishermen who told me they lived at a place called Fughelness. I hardly understood them. They spoke English, but in such a strange way that it was like a foreign language, yet I understood them to say that Fughelness was a barren island in a waste of marshes and creeks. A place of birds, emptiness, and a few poor folk who lived in the mud by trapping birds, catching eels and netting fish. They said Olaf had captured them a week before and forced them to his rowing benches. There had been eleven of them, but six had died in the fury of Finan's assault before these survivors had managed to convince my men that they were prisoners, not enemies.

We stripped the enemy of everything, then piled their mail, weapons, arm rings and clothes at the foot of *Sea-Eagle*'s mast. In time we would divide those spoils. Each man would receive one share, Finan would take three and I would take five. I was supposed to yield one third to Alfred and another third to Bishop Erkenwald, but I rarely gave them the plunder I took in battle.

We threw the naked dead into the trading ship where they made a grisly cargo of blood-spattered bodies. I remember thinking how white those bodies looked, yet how dark their faces were. A cloud of gulls screamed at us, wanting to come down and peck the corpses, but the birds were too nervous of our proximity to dare try. By now the ship that had been coming downtide from the west had reached us. She was a fine fighting ship, her bow crowned with a dragon's head, her stern showing a wolf's head and her masthead decorated with a raven wind-vane. She was one of the two warships we had captured in Lundene and Ralla had christened her *Sword of the Lord*. Alfred would have approved. She slewed to a stop and Ralla, her ship-master, cupped his hands. 'Well done!'

'We lost three men,' I called back. All three had died in the fight against Olaf's boarders, and those men we carried aboard *Sea-Eagle*. I would have dropped them into the sea and let them sink to the sea-god's embrace, but they were Christians and their friends wanted them carried back to a Christian graveyard in Lundene.

'You want me to tow her?' Ralla shouted, gesturing at the trading ship.

I said yes, and there was a pause while he fixed a line to the stem-post of the cargo ship. Then, in consort, we rowed northwards across the estuary of the Temes. The gulls, emboldened now, were plucking at the dead men's eyes.

It was close to midday and the tide had gone slack. The

estuary heaved oily and sluggish under the high sun as we rowed slowly, conserving our strength, sliding across the sun-silvered sea. And slowly, too, the estuary's northern shore came into view.

Low hills shimmered in the day's heat. I had rowed that shore before and knew that wooded hills lay beyond a flat shelf of waterlogged land. Ralla, who knew the coast much better than I, guided us, and I memorised the landmarks as we approached. I noted a slightly higher hill, a bluff and a clump of trees, and I knew I would see those things again because we were rowing our ships towards Beamfleot. This was the den of sea-wolves, the sea-serpent's haunt, Sigefrid's refuge.

This was also the old kingdom of the East Saxons, a kingdom that had long vanished, though ancient stories said they had once been feared. They had been a sea-people, raiders, but the Angles to their north had conquered them and now this coast was a part of Guthrum's realm, East Anglia.

It was a lawless coast, far from Guthrum's capital. Here, in the creeks that dried at low tide, ships could wait and, as the tide rose, they could slip out of their inlets to raid the merchants whose goods were carried up the Temes. This was a pirates' nest, and here Sigefrid, Erik and Haesten had their camp.

They must have seen us approach, but what did they see? They saw the *Sea-Eagle*, one of their own ships, and with her another Danish ship, both boats proudly decorated with beast-heads. They saw a third ship, a tubby cargo ship, and would have assumed Olaf was returning from a successful foray. They would have thought *Sword of the Lord* a Northmen's ship newly come to England. In short, they saw us, but they suspected nothing.

As we neared the land I ordered the beast-heads taken

223

from stern and stem-posts. Such things were never left on display as a boat entered its home waters, for the animals were there to frighten hostile spirits and Olaf would have assumed that the spirits inhabiting the creeks at Beamfleot were friendly, and he would have been loath to frighten them. And so the watchers from Sigefrid's camp saw the carved heads heaved off and they would have thought we were friends rowing homewards.

And I stared at that shore, knowing that fate would bring me back, and I touched the hilt of Serpent-Breath, for she had a fate too, and I knew she would come to this place again. This was a place for my sword to sing.

Beamfleot lay beneath a hill that sloped steeply down to the creek. One of the fishermen, a younger man who seemed blessed with more wit than his companions, stood beside me and named the places as I pointed at them. The settlement beneath the hill, he confirmed, was Beamfleot, and the creek he insisted was a river, the Hothlege. Beamfleot lay on the Hothlege's northern bank while the southern bank was a low, dark, wide and sullen island. 'Caninga,' the fisherman told me.

I repeated the names, memorising them as I memorised the land I saw.

Caninga was a sodden place, an island of marsh and reeds, wildfowl and mud. The Hothlege, which looked to me more like a creek than a river, was a tangle of mudbanks through which a channel twisted towards the hill above Beamfleot, and now, as we rounded the eastern tip of Caninga, I could see Sigefrid's camp crowning that hill. It was a green hill, and his walls, made of earth and topped with a timber palisade, lay like a brown scar on its domed summit. The slope from his southern wall was precipitous, dropping to where a crowd of ships lay canted on the mud exposed by low tide. The Hothlege's mouth was guarded by a ship that blocked the channel. She lay athwart the waterway, held against the tides by chains at stem and stern. One chain led to a massive post sunk on Caninga's shore, while the other was attached to a tree that grew lonely on the smaller island that formed the northern bank of the channel's mouth. 'Two-Tree Island,' the fisherman saw where I was looking and named the islet.

'But there's only one tree there,' I pointed out.

'In my father's day there were two, lord.'

The tide had turned. The flood had begun, and the great waters were surging into the estuary so that our three ships were being carried towards the enemy's camp. 'Turn!' I shouted to Ralla, and saw the relief on his face, 'but put the dragon's head back first!'

And so Sigefrid's men saw the dragon's head replaced, and the eagle's beaked head put high on *Sea-Eagle*'s stem, and they must have known something was wrong, not just because we displayed our beasts, but because we turned our ships and Ralla cut the smaller cargo boat loose. And, as they watched from their high fort, they would have seen my banner unfurled from *Sea-Eagle*'s mast. Gisela and her women had made that flag of the wolf's head, and I flew it so that the watching men would know who had killed the *Sea-Eagle*'s crew.

Then we rowed away, pulling hard against that flooding tide. We turned south and west about Caninga, then let the strong new tide carry us upriver towards Lundene.

And the cargo ship, its hold filled with blood-laced gull-pecked corpses, rode the same tide up the creek to bump against the longship moored athwart the channel.

I had three fighting ships now while my cousin possessed fifteen. He had moved those captured boats upriver where, for all I knew, they rotted. If I had possessed ten more ships and had the crews to man them I could have taken

Beamfleot, but all I had was three ships and the creek beneath the high fort was crammed with masts.

Still, I was sending a message.

That death was coming to Beamfleot.

Death visited Hrofeceastre first. Hrofeceastre was a town close to Lundene on the southern bank of the Temes estuary in the old kingdom of Cent. The Romans had made a fort there, and now a sizeable town had grown in and around the old stronghold. Cent, of course, had long been a part of Wessex and Alfred had ordered the town's defences to be strengthened, which was easily done for the old earth walls of the Roman fort still stood, and all that had to be added was a deepening of the ditch, the making of an oak palisade and the destruction of some buildings that were outside and too close to the ramparts. And it was well that the work had been completed because, early that summer, a great fleet of Danish ships came from Frankia. They found refuge in East Anglia, from where they sailed south, rode the tide up the Temes and then beached their ships on the River Medwæg, the tributary on which Hrofeceastre stood. They had hoped to storm the town, sacking it with fire and terror, but the new walls and the strong garrison defied them.

I had news of their coming before Alfred. I sent a messenger to tell him of the attack and, that same day, took Sea-Eagle down the Temes and up the Medwæg to find that I was helpless. At least sixty warships were beached on the river's muddy bank, and two others had been chained together and moored athwart the Medwæg to deter any attack by West Saxon ships. On shore I could see the invaders throwing up an earthen embankment, suggesting that they intended to ring Hrofeceastre with their own wall.

226

The leader of the invaders was a man called Gunnkel Rodeson. I learned later he had sailed from a lean season in Frankia in hope of taking the silver reputed to be in Hrofeceastre's big church and monastery. I rowed away from his ships and, in a brisk south-east wind, hoisted *Sea-Eagle*'s sail and crossed the estuary. I hoped to find Beamfleot deserted, but though it was obvious that many of Sigefrid's ships and men had gone to join Gunnkel, sixteen vessels remained and the fort's high wall still bristled with men and spear-points.

And so we went back to Lundene.

'Do you know Gunnkel?' Gisela asked me. We spoke in Danish as we almost always did.

'Never heard of him.'

'A new enemy?' she asked, smiling.

'They come from the north endlessly,' I said. 'Kill one and two more sail south.'

'A very good reason to stop killing them, then,' she said. That was as close as Gisela ever came to chiding me for killing her own people.

'I am sworn to Alfred,' I said in bleak explanation.

Next day I woke to find ships coming through the bridge. A horn alerted me. The horn was blown by a sentry on the walls of a small burh I was building at the bridge's southern end. We called that burh Suthriganaweorc, which simply meant the southern defence, and it was being built and guarded by men of the Suthrige fyrd. Fifteen warships were coming downstream, and they rowed through the gap at high water when the tumult in the broken middle was at its calmest. All fifteen ships came through safely and the third, I saw, flew my cousin Æthelred's banner of the prancing white horse. Once below the bridge the ships rowed for the wharves where they tied up three abreast. Æthelred, it seemed, was returning to Lundene. At the beginning of

227

summer he had taken Æthelflaed back to his estates in western Mercia, there to fight against the Welsh cattle thieves who loved riding into Mercia's fat lands. Now he was back.

He went to his palace. Æthelflaed, of course, was with him for Æthelred refused to allow her out of his sight, though I do not think that was love. It was jealousy. I half expected to receive a summons to his presence, but none came and, next morning, when Gisela walked to the palace, she was turned away. The Lady Æthelflaed, she was informed, was unwell. 'They weren't rude to me,' she said, 'just insistent.'

'Maybe she is unwell?' I suggested.

'Even more reason to see a friend,' Gisela said, staring through the open shutters to where the summer sun splattered the Temes with glinting silver. 'He has put her in a cage, hasn't he?'

We were interrupted by Bishop Erkenwald, or rather by one of his priests, who announced the bishop's imminent arrival. Gisela, knowing that Erkenwald would never speak openly in front of her, went to the kitchens while I greeted him at my door.

I never liked that man. In time we were to hate each other, but he was loyal to Alfred and he was efficient and he was conscientious. He did not waste time with small talk, but told me he had issued a writ for raising the local fyrd. 'The king,' he said, 'has ordered the men of his bodyguard to join your cousin's ships.'

'And me?'

'You will stay here,' he said brusquely, 'as will I.'

'And the fyrd?'

'Is for the city's defence. They replace the royal troops.'

'Because of Hrofeceastre?'

'The king is determined to punish the pagans,' Erkenwald said, 'but while he is doing God's work at Hrofeceastre there is a chance that other pagans will attack Lundene. We will prevent any such attack succeeding.'

No pagans did attack Lundene, and so I sat in the city while the events at Hrofeceastre unfolded and, strangely, those events have become famous. Men often come to me these days and they ask me about Alfred for I am one of the few men alive who remember him. They are all churchmen, of course, and they want to hear of his piety, of which I pretend to know nothing, and some, a few, ask about his wars. They know of his exile in the marshes and the victory at Ethandun, but they also want to hear of Hrofeceastre. That is strange. Alfred was to gain many victories over his enemies and Hrofeceastre was undoubtedly one of them, but it was not the great triumph that men now believe it to have been.

It was, of course, a victory, but it should have been a great victory. There was a chance to destroy a whole fleet of Vikings and to turn the Medwæg dark with their blood, but the chance was lost. Alfred trusted the defences at Hrofeceastre to hold the invaders in place, and those walls and the garrison did their job while he assembled an army of horsemen. He had the troops of his own royal household, and to that he added the household warriors of every ealdorman between Wintanceaster and Hrofeceastre, and they all rode eastwards, the army getting larger as they travelled, and they gathered at the Mæides Stana, just south of the old Roman fort that was now the town of Hrofeceastre.

Alfred had moved fast and well. The town had defeated two Danish attacks, and now Gunnkel's men found themselves threatened not just by Hrofeceastre's garrison, but by over a thousand of Wessex's finest warriors. Gunnkel, knowing he had lost his gamble, sent an envoy to Alfred, who agreed to talk. What Alfred was waiting for was the arrival of Æthelred's ships at the mouth of the Medwæg, for then Gunnkel would be trapped, and so Alfred talked and talked, and still the ships did not come. And when Gunnkel realised that Alfred would not pay him to leave, and that the talking was a ruse and that the West Saxon king planned to fight, he ran away. At midnight, after two days of evasive negotiations, the invaders left their camp-fires burning bright to suggest they were still on land, then boarded their ships and rode the ebb tide to the Temes. And so the siege of Hrofeceastre ended, and it was a great victory in that a Viking army had been ignominiously expelled from Wessex, but the waters of the Medwæg were not thickened by blood. Gunnkel lived, and the ships that had come from Beamfleot returned there, and some other ships went with them so that Sigefrid's camp was strengthened with new crews of hungry fighters. The rest of Gunnkel's fleet either went to look for easier prey in Frankia or found refuge on the East Anglian coast.

And, while all this happened, Æthelred was still in Lundene.

He complained that the ale on his ships was sour. He told Bishop Erkenwald that his men could not fight if their bellies were churning and their bowels spewing, and so he insisted that the barrels were emptied and refilled with freshly brewed ale. That took two days, and on the next he insisted on giving judgment in court, a job that properly belonged to Erkenwald, but which Æthelred, as Ealdorman of Mercia, had every right to do. He might not have wished to see me, and Gisela might have been turned away from the palace when she had tried to visit Æthelflaed, but no free citizen could be barred from witnessing judgments and so we joined the crowd in the big pillared hall.

Æthelred sprawled in a chair that could well have been a throne. It had a high back, ornately carved arms and was cushioned with fur. I do not know if he saw us, and if he did he took no notice of us, but Æthelflaed, who was sitting in a lower chair beside him, certainly saw us. She stared at us with an apparent lack of recognition, then turned her face away as if she was bored. The cases occupying Æthelred were trivial, but he insisted on listening to every oath-taker. The first complaint was about a miller who was accused of using false weights, and Æthelred questioned the oath-takers relentlessly. His friend, Aldhelm, sat just behind him and kept whispering advice into Æthelred's ear. Aldhelm's once handsome face was scarred from the beating I had given him, his nose crooked and one cheekbone flattened. It seemed to me, who had often judged such matters, that the miller was plainly guilty, but it took Æthelred and Aldhelm a long time to reach the same conclusion. The man was sentenced to the loss of one ear and a brand-mark on one cheek, then a young priest read aloud an indictment against a prostitute accused of stealing from the poor box in the church of Saint Alban. It was while the priest was still speaking that Æthelflaed suddenly griped. She jerked forward with one hand clutching at her belly. I thought she was going to vomit, but nothing came from her open mouth except a low moan of pain. She stayed bent forward, mouth open and with the one hand clasped to her stomach that still showed no sign of any pregnancy.

The hall had gone silent. Æthelred stared at his young wife, apparently helpless in the face of her distress, then two women came from an open archway and, after going on one knee to Æthelred and evidently receiving his permission, helped Æthelflaed away. My cousin, his face pale, gestured at the priest. 'Start again at the beginning of the indictment, father,' Æthelred said, 'my attention wandered.'

'I had almost finished, lord,' the priest said helpfully, 'and have oath-takers who can describe the crime.'

'No, no, no!' Æthelred held up a hand. 'I wish to hear the indictment. We must be seen to be thorough in our judgment.'

So the priest began again. Folk shuffled their feet in boredom as he droned on, and it was then that Gisela touched my elbow.

A woman had just spoken to Gisela who, twitching my tunic, turned and followed the woman through the door at the back of the hall. I went too, hoping that Æthelred was too involved in his pretence of being the perfect judge to see our departure.

We followed the woman down a corridor that had once been the cloistered side of a courtyard, but at some time the pillars of the open arcade had been filled with screens of wattle and mud. At the corridor's end a crude wooden door had been hung in a stone frame. Carved vines writhed up the masonry. On the far side was a room with a floor of small tiles that showed some Roman god casting a thunderbolt and beyond that was a sunlit garden where three pear trees cast shade on a patch of grass bright with daisies and buttercups. Æthelflaed waited for us beneath the trees.

She showed no sign of the distress that had sent her crouching and dry-retching from the hall. Instead she was standing tall, her back straight and with a solemn expression, though that solemnity brightened into a smile when she saw Gisela. They hugged, and I saw Æthelflaed's eyes close as if she was fighting back tears.

'You're not ill, lady?' I asked.

'Just pregnant,' she said, her eyes still shut, 'not ill.'

'You looked ill just now,' I said.

'I wanted to talk with you,' she said, pulling away from Gisela, 'and pretending to be ill was the only way to have privacy. He can't stand it when I'm sick. He leaves me alone when I vomit.'

'Are you often sick?' Gisela asked.

'Every morning,' Æthelflaed said, 'sick like a hound, but isn't everyone?'

'Not this time,' Gisela said, and touched her amulet. She wore a small image of Frigg, wife of Odin and Queen of Asgard where the gods live. Frigg is the goddess of pregnancy and childbirth, and the amulet was supposed to give Gisela a safe delivery of the child she carried. The little image had worked well with our first two children and I prayed daily that it would work again with the third.

'I vomit every morning,' Æthelflaed said, 'then feel fine for the rest of the day.' She touched her belly, then stroked Gisela's stomach that was now distended with her child. 'You must tell me about childbirth,' Æthelflaed said anxiously. 'It's painful, isn't it?'

'You forget the pain,' Gisela said, 'because it's swamped by joy.'

'I hate pain.'

'There are herbs,' Gisela said, trying to sound convincing, 'and there is so much joy when the child comes.'

They talked of childbirth and I leaned on the brick wall and stared at the patch of blue sky beyond the pear tree leaves. The woman who had brought us had gone away and we were alone. Somewhere beyond the brick wall a man was shouting at recruits to keep their shields up and I could hear the bang of staves on wood as they practised. I thought of the new city, the Lundene outside the walls where the Saxons had made their town. They wanted me to make a new palisade there, and defend it with my garrison, but I was refusing because Alfred had ordered me to refuse and because, with the new town enclosed by a wall, there would be too many ramparts to protect. I wanted those Saxons to move into the old city. A few had come, wanting the protection of the old Roman wall and my garrison, but most stubbornly stayed in the new town. 'What are you thinking?' Æthelflaed suddenly interrupted my thoughts.

'He's thanking Thor that he's a man,' Gisela said, 'and that he doesn't have to give birth.'

'True,' I said, 'and I was thinking that if people prefer to die in the new town rather than live in the old, then we should let them die.'

Æthelflaed smiled at that callous statement. She crossed to me. She was barefoot and looked very small. 'You don't hit Gisela, do you?' she asked, gazing up at me.

I glanced at Gisela and smiled. 'No, lady,' I said gently.

Æthelflaed went on staring at me. She had blue eyes with brown flecks, a slightly snub nose, and her lower lip was larger than her top lip. Her bruises had gone, though a faint dark blush on one cheek showed where she had last been struck. She looked very serious. Wisps of golden hair showed around her bonnet. 'Why didn't you warn me, Uhtred?' she asked.

'Because you didn't want to be warned,' I said.

She thought about that, then nodded abruptly. 'No, I didn't, you're right. I put myself in the cage, didn't I? Then I locked it.'

'Then unlock it,' I said brutally.

'Can't,' she said curtly.

'No?' Gisela asked.

'God has the key.'

I smiled at that. 'I never did like your god,' I said.

'No wonder my husband says you're a bad man,' Æthelflaed retorted with a smile.

'Does he say that?'

'He says you are wicked, untrustworthy and treacherous.'

I smiled, said nothing.

'Pig-headed,' Gisela kept the litany going, 'simple-minded and brutal.'

'That's me,' I said.

'And very kind,' Gisela finished.

Æthelflaed still looked up at me. 'He fears you,' she said, 'and Aldhelm hates you,' she went on. 'He'll kill you if he can.'

'He can try,' I said.

'Aldhelm wants my husband to be king,' Æthelflaed said.

'And what does your husband think?' I asked.

'He would like it,' Æthelflaed said and that did not surprise me. Mercia lacked a king, and Æthelred had a claim, but my cousin was nothing without Alfred's support and Alfred wanted no man to be called king in Mercia.

'Why doesn't your father just declare himself King of Mercia?' I asked Æthelflaed.

'I think he will,' she said, 'one day.'

'But not yet?'

'Mercia is a proud country,' she said, 'and not every Mercian loves Wessex.'

'And you're there to make them love Wessex?'

She touched her belly. 'Perhaps my father wants his first grandchild to be king in Mercia,' she suggested. 'A king with West Saxon blood?'

'And Æthelred's blood,' I said sourly.

She sighed. 'He's not a bad man,' she said wistfully, almost as if she were trying to persuade herself.

'He beats you,' Gisela said drily.

'He wants to be a good man,' Æthelflaed said. She touched my arm. 'He wants to be like you, Uhtred.'

'Like me!' I said, almost laughing.

'Feared,' Æthelflaed explained.

'Then why,' I asked, 'is he wasting time here? Why isn't he taking his ships to fight the Danes?'

Æthelflaed sighed. 'Because Aldhelm tells him not to,' she said. 'Aldhelm says that if Gunnkel stays in Cent or East

235

Anglia,' she went on, 'then my father has to keep more forces here. He has to keep looking eastwards.'

'He has to do that anyway,' I said.

'But Aldhelm says that if my father has to worry all the time about a horde of pagans in the Temes estuary, then he might not notice what happens in Mercia.'

'Where my cousin will declare himself king?' I guessed.

'It will be the price he demands,' Æthelflaed said, 'for defending the northern frontier of Wessex.'

'And you'll be queen,' I said.

She grimaced at that. 'You think I want that?'

'No,' I admitted.

'No,' she agreed. 'What I want is the Danes gone from Mercia. I want the Danes gone from East Anglia. I want the Danes gone from Northumbria.' She was little more than a child, a thin child with a snub nose and bright eyes, but she had steel in her. She was talking to me, who loved the Danes because I had been raised by them, and to Gisela, who was a Dane, but Æthelflaed did not try to soften her words. There was a hatred of the Danes in her, a hatred she had inherited from her father. Then, suddenly, she shuddered and the steel vanished. 'And I want to live,' she said.

I did not know what to say. Women died giving birth. So many died. I had sacrificed to Odin and Thor both times that Gisela had given birth and I had still been scared, and I was frightened now because she was pregnant again.

'You use the wisest women,' Gisela said, 'and you trust the herbs and charms they use.'

'No,' Æthelflaed said firmly, 'not that.'

'Then what?'

'Tonight,' Æthelflaed said, 'at midnight. In St Alban's church.'

'Tonight?' I asked, utterly confused, 'in the church?'

She stared up at me with huge blue eyes. 'They might kill me,' she said.

236

'No!' Gisela protested, not believing what she heard.

'He wants to be sure the child is his!' Æthelflaed interrupted her, 'and of course it is! But they want to be sure and I'm frightened!'

Gisela gathered Æthelflaed into her arms and stroked her hair. 'No one will kill you,' she said softly, looking at me.

'Be at the church, please,' Æthelflaed said in a voice made small because her head was crushed against Gisela's breasts.

'We'll be with you,' Gisela said.

'Go to the big church, the one dedicated to Alban,' Æthelflaed said. She was crying softly. 'So how bad is the pain?' she asked. 'Is it like being torn in two? That's what my mother says!'

'It is bad,' Gisela admitted, 'but it leads to a joy like no other.' She stroked Æthelflaed and stared at me as though I could explain what was to happen at midnight, but I had no idea what was in my cousin's suspicious mind.

Then the woman who had led us to the pear tree garden appeared at the door. 'Your husband, mistress,' she said urgently, 'he wants you in the hall.'

'I must go,' Æthelflaed said. She cuffed her eyes with her sleeve, smiled at us without joy, and fled.

'What are they going to do to her?' Gisela asked angrily.

'I don't know.'

'Sorcery?' she demanded. 'Some Christian sorcery?'

'I don't know,' I said again, nor did I, except that the summons was for midnight, the darkest hour, when evil appears and shape-shifters stalk the land and the Shadow-Walkers come. At midnight.

Eight

The church of Saint Alban was ancient. The lower walls were of stone, which meant the Romans had built it, though at some time the roof had fallen in and the upper masonry had crumbled, so that now almost everything above head height was made of timber, wattle and thatch. The church lay on the main street of Lundene, which ran north and south from what was now called the Bishop's Gate down to the broken bridge. Beocca once told me that the church had been a royal chapel for the Mercian kings, and perhaps he was right. 'And Alban was a soldier!' Beocca had added. He always got enthusiastic when he talked about the saints whose stories he knew and loved, 'So you should like him!'

'I should like him simply because he was a soldier?' I had asked sceptically.

'Because he was a brave soldier!' Beocca told me, 'and,' he paused, snuffling excitedly because he had important information to impart, 'and when he was martyred the eyes of his executioner fell out!' He beamed at me with his own one good eye. 'They fell out, Uhtred! Just popped out of his head! That was God's punishment, you see? You kill a holy man and God pulls out your eyes!'

'So Brother Jænberht wasn't holy?' I had suggested. Jænberht was a monk I had killed in a church, much to the horror of Father Beocca and a crowd of other watching churchmen. 'I've still got my eyes, father,' I pointed out.

'You deserve to be blinded!' Beocca had said, 'but God is merciful. Strangely merciful at times, I must say.'

I had thought about Alban for a while. 'Why,' I had then asked, 'if your god can pull out a man's eyes, didn't he just save Alban's life?'

'Because God chose not to, of course!' Beocca had answered sniffily, which is just the kind of answer you always get when you ask a Christian priest to explain another inexplicable act of their god.

'Alban was a Roman soldier?' I had asked, choosing not to query his god's capriciously cruel nature.

'He was a Briton,' Beocca told me, 'a very brave and very holy Briton.'

'Does that mean he was Welsh?'

'Of course it does!'

'Maybe that's why your god let him die,' I said, and Beocca had made the sign of the cross and rolled his good eye to heaven.

So, though Alban was a Welshman, and we Saxons have no love for the Welsh, there was a church named for him in Lundene, and that church appeared as dead as the dead saint's corpse when Gisela, Finan and I arrived. The street was night black. Some small firelight escaped past the window shutters of a few houses, and a tavern was loud with singing in a nearby street, but the church was black and silent. 'I don't like it,' Gisela whispered, and I knew she had touched the amulet around her neck. Before we left the house she had cast her runesticks, hoping to see some pattern to this night, but the random fall of the sticks had mystified her.

Something moved in a nearby alleyway. It might have been nothing more than a rat, but both Finan and I turned, swords hissing out of our scabbards, and the noise in the alleyway immediately stopped. I let Serpent-Breath slide back into her fleece-lined scabbard.

The three of us were wearing dark cloaks with hoods so, if anyone was watching, they must have thought we were priests or monks as we stood outside Saint Alban's dark and silent door. No light showed past that door's edges. I tried to open it, pulling on the short rope that lifted the latch inside, but the door was apparently barred. I pushed hard, rattling the locked door, then beat on its timbers with a fist, but there was no response. Then Finan touched my arm and I heard the footsteps. 'Over the street,' I whispered, and we crossed to the alleyway where we had heard the noise. The small, tight passage stank of sewage.

'They're priests,' Finan whispered to me.

Two men were walking down the street. They were momentarily visible in the small light cast by a loosely shuttered window and I saw their black robes and the glint from the silver crosses they wore on their breasts. They stopped at the church and one knocked hard on the barred door. He gave three knocks, paused, gave a single rap, paused again, then knocked three times more.

We heard the bar lifted and the creak of hinges as the door was swung open, then light flooded into the street as a curtain inside the doorway was pulled aside. A priest or monk let the two men step into the candlelit church, then peered up and down the roadway and I knew he was searching for whoever had rattled the door a few moments earlier. A question must have been called to him, for he turned and gave an answer. 'No one here, lord,' he said, then pulled the door shut. I heard the locking bar drop and, for an instant, light showed about the doorframe until the curtain inside was pulled closed and the church was dark again.

'Wait,' I said.

We waited, listening to the wind rustle across the thatched roofs and moan in the ruined houses. I waited a long time, letting the memory of the rattled door subside.

'It must be close to midnight,' Gisela whispered.

'Whoever opens the door,' I said softly, 'has to be silenced.' I did not know what was happening inside the church, but I did know it was so secret that the church was locked and a coded knock was needed to enter, and I also knew that we were uninvited, and that if the man who opened the door made a protest at our arrival then we might never discover Æthelflaed's danger.

'Leave him to me,' Finan said happily.

'He's a churchman,' I whispered, 'does that worry you?'

'In the dark, lord, all cats are black.'

'Meaning?'

'Leave him to me,' the Irishman said again.

'Then let's go to church,' I said, and the three of us crossed the street and I knocked hard on the door. I knocked three times, gave a single rap, then knocked three times again.

It took a long time for the door to be opened, but at last the bar was lifted and the door was pushed outwards. 'They've started,' a robed figure whispered, then gasped as I seized his collar and pulled him into the street where Finan hit him in the belly. The Irishman was a small man, but had extraordinary strength in his lithe arms, and the robed figure bent double with a sudden gasp. The door's inner curtain had fallen across the opening and no one inside the church could see what happened outside. Finan punched the man again, felling him, then knelt on the fallen figure. 'You go away,' Finan whispered, 'if you want to live. You just go a

241

very long way from the church and you forget you ever saw us. Do you understand?'

'Yes,' the man said.

Finan tapped the man on the head to reinforce the order, then stood up and we saw the dark figure scrabble to his feet and stumble away downhill. I waited a brief while to make sure he had really gone, then the three of us stepped inside and Finan pulled the door shut and dropped the bar into its brackets.

And I pushed the curtain aside.

We were in the darkest part of the church, but I still felt exposed because the far end, where the altar stood, was ablaze with rushlights and wax candles. A line of robed men stood facing the altar and their shadows shrouded us. One of those priests turned towards us, but he just saw three cloaked and hooded figures and must have assumed we were more priests because he turned back to the altar.

It took me a moment to see who was on the altar's wide shallow dais because they were hidden by the priests and monks, but then the churchmen all bowed to the silver crucifix and I saw Æthelred and Aldhelm standing on the left-hand side of the altar while Bishop Erkenwald was on the right. Between them was Æthelflaed. She wore a white linen shift belted just beneath her small breasts and her fair hair was hanging loose, as if she were a girl again. She looked frightened. An older woman stood behind Æthelred. She had hard eyes and her grey hair was rolled into a tight scroll on the crown of her skull.

Bishop Erkenwald was praying in Latin and every few minutes the watching priests and monks, there were nine of them altogether, echoed his words. Erkenwald was dressed in red and white robes on which jewelled crosses had been sewn. His voice, always harsh, echoed from the stone walls, while the responses of the churchmen were a dull murmur.

Æthelred looked bored, while Aldhelm seemed to be taking a quiet delight in whatever mysteries unfolded in that flame-lit sanctuary.

The bishop finished his prayers, the watching men all said amen, and then there was a slight pause before Erkenwald took a book from the altar. He unwrapped the leather covers, then turned the stiff pages to a place he had marked with a seagull's feather. 'This,' he spoke in English now, 'is the word of the Lord.'

'Hear the word of the Lord,' the priests and monks muttered.

'If a man fears his wife has been unfaithful,' the bishop spoke louder, his grating voice repeated by the echo, 'he shall bring her before the priest! And he shall bring an offering!' He stared pointedly at Æthelred who was dressed in a pale green cloak over a full coat of mail. He even wore his swords, something most priests would never allow in a church. 'An offering!' the bishop repeated.

Æthelred started as if he had been woken from a half-sleep. He fumbled in a pouch hanging from his sword belt and produced a small bag that he held towards the bishop. 'Barley,' he said.

'As the Lord God commanded it,' Erkenwald responded, but did not take the offered barley.

'And silver,' Æthelred added, hurriedly taking a second bag from his pouch.

Erkenwald took the two offerings and laid them in front of the crucifix. He bowed to the bright-gleaming image of his nailed god, then picked up the big book again. 'This is the word of the Lord,' he said fiercely, 'that we take holy water in an earthen vessel, and of the dust that is on the floor of the tabernacle the priest shall take, and he shall put that dust in the water.'

The book was put back on the altar as a priest offered

the bishop a crude pottery cup that evidently held holy water, for Erkenwald bowed to it, then stooped to the floor and scraped up a handful of dirt and dust. He poured the dirt into the water, then placed the cup on the altar before taking up the book again.

'I charge thee, woman,' he said savagely, looking from the book to Æthelflaed, 'if no man hath lain with thee, and if thou hast not gone aside to uncleanness with another man instead of thy husband, then be thou free of the curse of this bitter water!'

'Amen,' one of the priests said.

'The word of the Lord!' another said.

'But if thou hast gone aside to another man,' Erkenwald spat the words as he read them, 'and be defiled, then the Lord shall make thy thigh to rot and thy belly to swell.' He put the book back on the altar. 'Speak, woman.'

Æthelflaed just stared at the bishop. She said nothing. Her eyes were wide with fear.

'Speak, woman!' The bishop snarled. 'You know what words you must say! So say them!'

Æthelflaed seemed too frightened to speak. Aldhelm whispered something to Æthelred who nodded, but did nothing. Aldhelm whispered again, and again Æthelred nodded, and this time Aldhelm took a pace forward and hit Æthelfaed. It was not a hard blow, just a slap around the head, but it was enough to force me to take an involuntary step forward. Gisela snatched my arm, checking me. 'Speak, woman,' Aldhelm ordered Æthelflaed.

'Amen,' Æthelflaed managed to whisper, 'amen.'

Gisela's hand was still on my arm. I patted her fingers as a signal that I was calm. I was angry, I was astonished, but I was calm. I stroked Gisela's hand, then dropped my fingers to Serpent-Breath's hilt.

Æthelflaed had evidently spoken the right words because

Bishop Erkenwald took the earthen cup from the altar. He raised it high in front of the crucifix, as if showing it to his god, then he carefully poured a little of its dust-fouled water into a silver chalice. He held the pottery cup high again, then ceremoniously offered it to Æthelflaed. 'Drink the bitter water,' he ordered her.

Æthelflaed hesitated, then saw Aldhelm's mailed arm ready to strike her again and so she obediently reached for the cup. She took it, held it poised by her mouth for a brief moment, then closed her eyes, screwed up her face and drank the contents. The men watched intently, making certain she drained the cup. The candle flames flickered in a draught from the smoke-hole in the roof and somewhere in the city a dog suddenly howled. Gisela was clutching my arm now, her fingers tight as claws.

Erkenwald took the cup and, when he was satisfied that it was empty, nodded to Æthelred. 'She drank it,' the bishop confirmed. Æthelflaed's face glistened where her tears reflected the wavering light from the altar on which, I now saw, was a quill pen, a pot of ink and a piece of parchment. 'What I do now,' Erkenwald said solemnly, 'is in accordance with the word of God.'

'Amen,' the priests said. Æthelred was watching his wife as if he expected her flesh to start rotting before his eyes, while Æthelflaed herself was trembling so much that I thought she might collapse.

'God commands me to write the curses down,' the bishop announced, then bent to the altar. The quill scratched for a long time. Æthelred was still staring intently at Æthelflaed. The priests also watched her as the bishop scratched on. 'And having written the curses,' Erkenwald said, capping the ink pot, 'I wipe them out according to the commands of Almighty God, our Father in heaven.'

'Hear the word of the Lord,' a priest said.

'Praise his name,' another said.

Erkenwald picked up the silver chalice into which he had poured a small amount of the dirty water and dribbled the contents onto the newly written words. He scrubbed at the ink with a finger, then held up the parchment to show that the writing had been smeared into oblivion. 'It is done,' he said pompously, then nodded at the grey-haired woman. 'Do your duty!' he commanded her.

The old, bitter-faced woman stepped to Æthelflaed's side. The girl shrank away, but Aldhelm seized her by the shoulders. Æthelflaed shrieked in terror, and Aldhelm's response was to cuff her hard around the head. I thought Æthelred must respond to that assault on his wife by another man, but he evidently approved for he did nothing except watch as Aldhelm took Æthelflaed by her shoulders again. He held her motionless as the old woman stooped to seize the hem of Æthelflaed's linen shift. 'No!' Æthelflaed protested in a wailing, despairing voice.

'Show her to us!' Erkenwald snapped. 'Show us her thighs and her belly!'

The woman obediently lifted the shift to reveal Æthelflaed's thighs.

'Enough!' I shouted that word.

The woman froze. The priests were stooping to gaze at Æthelflaed's bare legs and waiting for the dress to be lifted to reveal her belly. Aldhelm still held her by the shoulders, while the bishop was gaping towards the shadows at the church door from where I had spoken. 'Who is that?' Erkenwald demanded.

'You evil bastards,' I said as I walked forward, my steps echoing from the stone walls, 'you filthy earslings.' I remember my anger from that night, a cold and savage fury that had driven me to intervene without thinking of the consequences. My wife's priests all preach that anger is a sin, but a warrior who does not have anger is no true warrior. Anger is a spur, it is a goad, it overcomes fear to make a man fight, and I would fight for Æthelflaed that night. 'She is a king's daughter,' I snarled, 'so drop the dress!'

'You will do as God tells you,' Erkenwald snarled at the woman, but she dared neither drop the hem nor raise it further.

I pushed my way through the stooping priests, kicking one in the arse so hard that he pitched forward onto the dais at the bishop's feet. Erkenwald had seized his staff, its silver finial curved like a shepherd's crook, and he swung it towards me, but checked his swing when he saw my eyes. I drew Serpent-Breath, her long steel scraping and hissing on the scabbard's throat. 'You want to die?' I asked Erkenwald, and he heard the menace in my voice and his shepherd's staff slowly went down. 'Drop the dress,' I told the woman. She hesitated. 'Drop it, you filthy bitch-hag,' I snarled, then sensed the bishop had moved and whipped Serpent-Breath around so that her blade shimmered just beneath his throat. 'One word, bishop,' I said, 'just one word, and you meet your god here and now. Gisela!' I called, and Gisela came to the altar. 'Take the hag,' I told her, 'and take Æthelflaed, and see whether her belly has swollen or whether her thighs have rotted. Do it in decent privacy. And you!' I turned the blade so that it pointed at Aldhelm's scarred face, 'take your hands off King Alfred's daughter, or I will hang you from Lundene's bridge and the birds will peck out your eyes and eat your tongue.' He let go of Æthelflaed.

'You have no right . . .' Æthelred said, finding his tongue.

'I come here,' I interrupted him, 'with a message from Alfred. He wishes to know where your ships are. He wishes you to set sail. He wishes you to do your duty. He wants to know why you are skulking here when there are Danes

247

to kill.' I put the tip of Serpent-Breath's blade into the scabbard and let her fall home. 'And,' I went on when the sound of the sword had finished echoing in the church, 'he wishes you to know that his daughter is precious to him, and he dislikes things that are precious to him being maltreated.' I invented that message, of course.

Æthelred just stared at me. He said nothing, though there was a look of indignation on his jaw-jutting face. Did he believe I came with a message from Alfred? I could not tell, but he must have feared such a message for he knew he had been shirking his duty.

Bishop Erkenwald was just as indignant. 'You dare to carry a sword in God's house?' he demanded angrily.

'I dare do more than that, bishop,' I said. 'You've heard of Brother Jænberht? One of your precious martyrs? I killed him in a church and your god neither saved him nor stopped my blade.' I smiled, remembering my own astonishment as I had cut Jænberht's throat. I had hated that monk. 'Your king,' I said to Erkenwald, 'wants his god's work done, and that work is killing Danes, not amusing yourself by looking at a young girl's nakedness.'

'This is God's work!' Æthelred shouted at me.

I wanted to kill him then. I felt the twitch as my hand went to Serpent-Breath's hilt, but just then the hag came back. 'She's . . .' the woman started, then fell silent as she saw the look of hatred I was giving Æthelred.

'Speak, woman!' Erkenwald commanded.

'She shows no signs, lord,' the woman said grudgingly. 'Her skin is unmarked.'

'Belly and thighs?' Erkenwald pressed the woman.

'She is pure,' Gisela spoke from a recess at the side of the church. She had an arm around Æthelflaed and her voice was bitter.

Erkenwald seemed discomfited by the report, but drew

himself up and grudgingly acknowledged that Æthelflaed was indeed pure. 'She is evidently undefiled, lord,' he said to Æthelred, pointedly ignoring me. Finan was standing behind the watching priests, his presence a threat to them. The Irishman was smiling and watching Aldhelm who, like Æthelred, wore a sword. Either man could have tried to cut me down, but neither touched their weapon.

'Your wife,' I said to Æthelred, 'is not undefiled. She's defiled by you.'

His face jerked up as though I had slapped him. 'You are . . .' he began.

I unleashed the anger then. I was much taller and broader than my cousin, and I bullied him back from the altar to the side wall of the church, and there I spoke to him in a hiss of fury. Only he could hear what I said. Aldhelm might have been tempted to rescue Æthelred, but Finan was watching him, and the Irishman's reputation was enough to ensure that Aldhelm did not move. 'I have known Æthelflaed since she was a small child,' I told Æthelred, 'and I love her as if she was my own child. Do you understand that, earsling? She is like a daughter to me, and she is a good wife to you. And if you touch her again, cousin, if I see one more bruise on Æthelflaed's face, I shall find you and I shall kill you.' I paused, and he was silent.

I turned and looked at Erkenwald. 'And what would you have done, bishop,' I sneered, 'if the Lady Æthelflaed's thighs had rotted? Would you have dared kill Alfred's daughter?'

Erkenwald muttered something about condemning her to a nunnery, not that I cared. I had stopped close beside Aldhelm and looked at him. 'And you,' I said, 'struck a king's daughter.' I hit him so hard that he spun into the altar and staggered for balance. I waited, giving him a chance to fight back, but he had no courage left so I hit him again and then stepped away and raised my voice so that everyone in the church could hear. 'And the King of Wessex orders the Lord Æthelred to set sail.'

Alfred had sent no such orders, but Æthelred would hardly dare ask his father-in-law whether he had or not. As for Erkenwald, I was sure he would tell Alfred that I had carried a sword and made threats inside a church, and Alfred would be angry at that. He would be more angry with me for defiling a church than he would be with the priests for humiliating his daughter, but I wanted Alfred to be angry. I wanted him to punish me by dismissing me from my oath and thus releasing me from his service. I wanted Alfred to make me a free man again, a man with a sword, a shield and enemies. I wanted to be rid of Alfred, but Alfred was far too clever to allow that. He knew just how to punish me.

He would make me keep my oath.

It was two days later, long after Gunnkel had fled from Hrofeceastre, that Æthelred at last sailed. His fleet of fifteen warships, the most powerful fleet Wessex had ever assembled, slid downriver on the ebb tide, propelled by an angry message that was delivered to Æthelred by Steapa. The big man had ridden from Hrofeceastre, and the message he carried from Alfred demanded to know why the fleet lingered while the defeated Vikings fled. Steapa stayed that night at our house. 'The king is unhappy,' he told me over supper, 'I've never seen him so angry!' Gisela was fascinated by the sight of Steapa eating. He was using one hand to hold pork ribs that he flensed with his teeth, while the other fed bread into a spare corner of his mouth. 'Very angry,' he said, pausing to drink ale. 'The Sture,' he added mysteriously, picking up a new slab of ribs.

'The Sture?'

'Gunnkel made a camp there, and Alfred thinks he's probably gone back to it.'

The Sture was a river in East Anglia, north of the Temes. I had been there once and remembered a wide mouth protected from easterly gales by a long spit of sandy land. 'He's safe there,' I said.

'Safe?' Steapa asked.

'Guthrum's territory.'

Steapa paused to pull a scrap of meat from between his teeth. 'Guthrum sheltered him there. Alfred doesn't like it. Thinks Guthrum has to be smacked.'

'Alfred's going to war with East Anglia?' Gisela asked, surprised.

'No, lady. Just smacking him,' Steapa said, crunching his jaws on some crackling. I reckoned he had eaten half a pig and showed no signs of slowing down. 'Guthrum doesn't want war, lady. But he has to be taught not to shelter pagans. So he's sending the Lord Æthelred to attack Gunnkel's camp on the Sture, and while he's at it to steal some of Guthrum's cattle. Just smack him.' Steapa gave me a solemn look. 'Pity you can't come.'

'It is,' I agreed.

And why, I wondered, had Alfred chosen Æthelred to lead an expedition to punish Guthrum? Æthelred was not even a West Saxon, though he had sworn an oath to Alfred of Wessex. My cousin was a Mercian, and the Mercians have never been famous for their ships. So why choose Æthelred? The only explanation I could find was that Alfred's eldest son, Edward, was still a child with an unbroken voice and Alfred himself was a sick man. He feared his own death, and he feared the chaos that could descend on Wessex if Edward took the throne as a child. So Alfred was offering Æthelred a chance to redeem himself for his failure to trap

251

Gunnkel's ships in the Medwæg, and an opportunity to make himself a reputation large enough to persuade the thegns and ealdormen of Wessex that Æthelred, Lord of Mercia, could rule them if Alfred died before Edward was old enough to succeed.

Æthelred's fleet carried a message to the Danes of East Anglia. If you raid Wessex, Alfred was saying, then we shall raid you. We shall harry your coast, burn your houses, sink your ships and leave your beaches stinking of death. Alfred had made Æthelred into a Viking, and I was jealous. I wanted to take my ships, but I had been ordered to stay in Lundene, and I obeyed. Instead I watched the great fleet leave Lundene. It was impressive. The largest of the captured warships had thirty oars a side, and there were six of those, while the smallest had banks of twenty. Æthelred was leading almost a thousand men on his raid, and they were all good men; warriors from Alfred's household and from his own trained troops. Æthelred sailed in one of the large ships that had once carried a great raven's head, scorched black, on her stem, but that beaked image was gone and now the ship was named *Rodbora*, which meant 'carrier of the cross', and her stem-post was now decorated with a massive cross and she sailed with warriors aboard, and with priests, and, of course, with Æthelflaed, for Æthelred would go nowhere without her.

It was summer. Folk who have never lived in a town during the summer cannot imagine the stench of it, nor the flies. Red kites flocked in the streets, living off carrion. When the wind was north the smell of the urine and animal dung in the tanners' pits mixed with the city's own stench of human sewage. Gisela's belly grew, and my fear for her grew with it.

I went to sea as often as I could. We took *Sea-Eagle* and *Sword of the Lord* down the river on the ebb tide and came back with the flood. We hunted ships from Beamfleot, but Sigefrid's men had learned their lesson and they never left their creek with fewer than three ships in company. Yet, though those groups of ships hunted prey, trade was at last reaching Lundene, for the merchants had learned to sail in large convoys. A dozen ships would keep each other company, all with armed men aboard and so Sigefrid's pickings were scanty, but so were mine.

I waited two weeks for news of my cousin's expedition, and learned its fate on a day when I made my usual excursion down the Temes. There was always a blessed moment as we left the smoke and smells of Lundene and felt the clean sea winds. The river looped about wide marshes where herons stalked. I remember being happy that day because there were blue butterflies everywhere. They settled on the *Sea-Eagle* and on the *Sword of the Lord* that followed in our wake. One insect perched on my outstretched finger where it opened and closed its wings.

'That means good luck, lord,' Sihtric said.

'It does?'

'The longer it stays there, the longer your luck lasts,' Sihtric said, and held out his own hand, but no blue butterfly settled there.

'Looks like you've no luck,' I said lightly. I watched the butterfly on my finger and thought of Gisela and of childbirth. Stay there, I silently ordered the insect, and it did.

'I'm lucky, lord,' Sihtric said, grinning.

'You are?'

'Ealhswith's in Lundene,' he said. Ealhswith was the whore whom Sihtric loved.

'There's more trade for her in Lundene than in Coccham,' I said.

'She stopped doing that,' Sihtric said fiercely.

I looked at him, surprised. 'She has?'

253

'Yes, lord. She wants to marry me, lord.'

He was a good-looking young man, hawk-faced, black-haired and well built. I had known him since he was almost a child, and I supposed that altered my impression of him, for I still saw the frightened boy whose life I had spared in Cair Ligualid. Ealhswith, perhaps, saw the young man he had become. I looked away, watching a tiny trickle of smoke rising from the southern marshes and I wondered whose fire it was and how they lived in that mosquito-haunted swamp. 'You've been with her a long time,' I said.

'Yes, lord.'

'Send her to me,' I said. Sihtric was sworn to me and he needed my permission to marry because his wife would become a part of my household and thus my responsibility. 'I'll talk to her,' I added.

'You'll like her, lord.'

I smiled at that. 'I hope so,' I said.

A flight of swans beat between our boats, their wings loud in the summer air. I was feeling content, all but for my fears about Gisela, and the butterfly was allaying that worry, though after a while it launched itself from my finger and fluttered clumsily in the southwards wake of the swans. I touched Serpent-Breath's hilt, then my amulet, and sent a prayer to Frigg that Gisela would be safe.

It was midday before we were abreast of Caninga. The tide was low and the mudflats stretched into the calm estuary where we were the only ships. I took Sea-Eagle close to Caninga's southern shore and stared towards Beamfleot's creek, but I could see nothing useful through the heat haze that shimmered above the island. 'Looks like they've gone,' Finan commented. Like me he was staring northwards.

'No,' I said, 'there are ships there.' I thought I could see the masts of Sigefrid's ships through the wavering air.

'Not as many as there should be,' Finan said.

'We'll take a look,' I said, and so we rowed around the island's eastern tip, and discovered that Finan was right. Over half of Sigefrid's ships had left the little River Hothlege.

Only three days before there had been thirty-six masts in the creek and now there were just fourteen. I knew the missing ships had not gone upriver towards Lundene, for we would have seen them, and that left only two choices. Either they had gone east and north about the East Anglian coast, or else they had rowed south to make another raid into Cent. The sun, so hot and high and bright, winked reflected dazzling light from the spear-points on the ramparts of the high camp. Men watched us from that high wall, and they saw us turn and hoist our sails and use a small north-east wind that had stirred since dawn to carry us south across the estuary. I was looking for a great smear of smoke that would tell me a raiding party had landed to attack, plunder and burn some town, but the sky over Cent was clear. We dropped the sail and rowed east towards the Medwæg's mouth, and still saw no smoke, and then Finan, sharp-eyed and posted in our bows, saw the ships.

Six ships.

I was looking for a fleet of at least twenty boats, not some small group of ships, and at first I took no notice, assuming the six were merchant ships keeping company as they rowed towards Lundene, but then Finan came hurrying back between the rowers' benches. 'They're warships,' he said.

I peered eastwards. I could see the dark flecks of the hulls, but my eyes were not so keen as Finan's and I could not make out their shapes. The six hulls flickered in the heat haze. 'Are they moving?' I asked.

'No, lord.'

'Why anchor there?' I wondered. The ships were on the far side of the Medwæg's mouth, just off the point called Scerhnesse, which means 'bright headland', and it was a

255

strange place to anchor for the currents swirled strong off the low point.

'I think they're grounded, lord,' Finan said. If the ships had been anchored I would have assumed they were waiting for the flood tide to carry them upriver, but grounded boats usually meant men had gone ashore, and the only reason to go ashore was to find plunder.

'But there's nothing left to steal on Scaepege,' I said, puzzled. Scerhnesse lay at the western end of Scaepege, which was an island on the southern side of the Temes's estuary, and Scaepege had been harried and harrowed and harried again by Viking raids. Few folk lived there, and those that did hid in the creeks. The channel between Scaepege and the mainland was known as the Swealwe, and whole Viking fleets had sheltered there in bad weather. Scaepege and the Swealwe were dangerous places, but not places to find silver or slaves.

'We'll go closer,' I said. Finan went back to the prow as Ralla, in *Sword of the Lord*, pulled abreast of the *Sea-Eagle*. I pointed at the distant ships. 'We're taking a look at those six boats!' I called across the gap. Ralla nodded, shouted an order, and his oars bit into the water.

I saw Finan was right as we crossed the Medwæg's wide mouth; the six were warships, all of them longer and leaner than any cargo-carrying vessel, and all six had been beached. A trickle of smoke drifted south and west, suggesting the crews had lit a fire ashore. I could see no beast-heads on the prows, but that meant nothing. Viking crews might well regard the whole of Scaepege as Danish territory and so take down their dragons, eagles, ravens and serpents to prevent frightening the spirits of the island.

I called Clapa to the steering-oar. 'Take her straight towards the ships,' I ordered him, then went forward to join Finan in the prow. Osferth was on one of the oars, sweating and glowering. 'Nothing like rowing to put on muscle,' I told him cheerfully, and was rewarded with a scowl.

I clambered up beside the Irishman. 'They look like Danes,' he greeted me.

'We can't fight six crews,' I said.

Finan scratched his groin. 'They making a camp there, you think?' That was a nasty thought. It was bad enough that Sigefrid's ships sailed from the northern side of the estuary, without another vipers' nest being built on the southern bank.

'No,' I said, because for once my eyes had proved sharper than the Irishman's. 'No,' I said, 'they're not making a camp.' I touched my amulet.

Finan saw the gesture and heard the anger in my voice. 'What?' he asked.

'The ship on the left,' I said, pointing, 'that's *Rodbora*.' I had seen the cross mounted on the stem-post.

Finan's mouth opened, but he said nothing for a moment. He just stared. Six ships, just six ships, and fifteen had left Lundene. 'Sweet Jesus Christ,' Finan finally spoke. He made the sign of the cross. 'Perhaps the others have gone upriver?'

'We'd have seen them.'

'Then they're coming behind?'

'You'd better be right,' I said grimly, 'or else it's nine ships gone.'

'God, no.'

We were close now. The men ashore saw the eagle's head on my boat and took me for a Viking and some ran into the shallows between two of the stranded ships and made a shield wall there, daring me to attack. 'That's Steapa,' I said, seeing the huge figure at the centre of the shield wall. I ordered the eagle taken down, then stood with my arms outstretched, empty-handed, to show I came in peace. Steapa recognised me, and the shields went down and the weapons

257

were sheathed. A moment later *Sea-Eagle*'s bows slid soft onto the sandy mud. The tide was rising, so she was safe.

I dropped over the side into water that came to my waist and waded ashore. I reckoned there were at least four hundred men on the beach, far too many for just six ships and, as I neared the shore, I could see that many of those men were wounded. They lay with blood-soaked bandages and pale faces. Priests knelt among them while, at the top of the beach, where pale grass topped the low dunes, I could see that crude driftwood crosses had been driven into newly dug graves.

Steapa waited for me, his face grimmer than ever. 'What happened?' I asked him.

'Ask him,' Steapa said, sounding bitter. He jerked his head along the beach and I saw Æthelred sitting close to the fire on which a cooking pot bubbled gently. His usual entourage was with him, including Aldhelm, who watched me with a resentful face. None of them spoke as I walked towards them. The fire crackled. Æthelred was toying with a piece of bladderwrack and, though he must have been aware of my approach, he did not look up.

I stopped beside the fire. 'Where are the other nine ships?' I asked.

Æthelred's face jerked up, as though he were surprised to see me. He smiled. 'Good news,' he said. He expected me to ask what that news was, but I just watched him and said nothing. 'We have won,' he said expansively, 'a great victory!'

'A magnificent victory,' Aldhelm interjected.

I saw that Æthelred's smile was forced. His next words were halting, as if it took a great effort to string them together. 'Gunnkel,' he said, 'has been taught the power of our swords.'

'We burned their ships!' Aldhelm boasted.

'And made great slaughter,' Æthelred said, and I saw that his eyes were glistening.

I looked up and down the beach where the wounded lay and where the uninjured sat with bowed heads. 'You left with fifteen ships,' I said.

'We burned their ships,' Æthelred said, and I thought he was going to cry.

'Where are the other nine ships?' I demanded.

'We stopped here,' Aldhelm said, and he must have thought I was being critical of their decision to beach the boats, 'because we could not row against the falling tide.'

'The other nine ships?' I asked again, but received no answer. I was still searching the beach and what I sought I could not find. I looked back at Æthelred, whose head had dropped again, and I feared to ask the next question, but it had to be asked. 'Where is your wife?' I demanded.

Silence.

'Where,' I spoke louder, 'is Æthelflaed?'

A gull sounded its harsh, forlorn cry. 'She is taken,' Æthelred said at last in a voice so small that I could barely hear him.

'Taken?'

'A captive,' Æthelred said, his voice still low.

'Sweet Jesus Christ,' I said, using Finan's favourite expletive. The wind stirred the bitter smoke into my face. For a moment I did not believe what I had heard, but all around me was evidence that Æthelred's magnificent victory had really been a catastrophic defeat. Nine ships were gone, but ships could be replaced, and half of Æthelred's troops were missing, yet new men could be found to replace those dead, but what could replace a king's daughter? 'Who has her?' I asked.

'Sigefrid,' Aldhelm muttered.

Which explained where the missing ships from Beamfleot had gone.

And Æthelflaed, sweet Æthelflaed, to whom I had made an oath, was a captive.

Our eight ships rode the flooding tide back up the Temes to Lundene. It was a summer's evening, limpid and calm, in which the sun seemed to linger like a giant red globe suspended in the veil of smoke that clouded the air above the city. Æthelred made the voyage in *Rodbora* and, when I let *Sea-Eagle* drop back to row alongside that ship, I saw the black streaks where blood had stained her timbers. I quickened the oar strokes and pulled ahead again.

Steapa travelled with me in the *Sea-Eagle* and the big man told me what had happened in the River Sture.

It had, indeed, been a magnificent victory. Æthelred's fleet had surprised the Vikings as they made their encampment on the river's southern bank. 'We came at dawn,' Steapa said.

'You stayed all night at sea?'

'Lord Æthelred ordered it,' Steapa said.

'Brave,' I commented.

'It was a calm night,' Steapa said dismissively, 'and at first light we found their ships. Sixteen ships.' He stopped abruptly. He was a taciturn man and found it difficult to speak more than a few words together.

'Beached?' I asked.

'They were anchored,' he said.

That suggested the Danes had wanted their vessels to be ready at any state of the tide, but it also meant the ships could not be defended because their crews had been mostly ashore where they were throwing up earth walls to make a camp. Æthelred's fleet had made short work of the few men aboard the enemy vessels, and then the great rope-wrapped stones that served as anchors had been hauled up and the sixteen ships were towed to the northern bank and beached there. 'He was going to keep them there,' Steapa explained, 'till he was finished, then bring them back.'

'Finished?' I asked.

'He wanted to kill all the pagans before we left,' Steapa said, and explained how Æthelred's fleet had marauded up the Sture and its adjacent river, the Arwan, landing men along the banks to burn Danish halls, slaughter Danish cattle and, when they could, to kill Danes. The Saxon raiders had caused panic. Folk had fled inland, but Gunnkel, left ship-less in his encampment at the mouth of the Sture, had not panicked.

'You didn't attack the camp?' I asked Steapa.

'Lord Æthelred said it was too well protected.'

'I thought you said it was unfinished?'

Steapa shrugged. 'They hadn't built the palisade,' he said, 'at least on one side, so we could have got in and killed them, but we'd have lost a lot of our own men too.'

'True,' I admitted.

'So we attacked farms instead,' Steapa went on, and while Æthelred's men raided the Danish settlements, Gunnkel had sent messengers southwards to the other rivers of the East Anglian coast. There, on those riverbanks, were other Viking encampments. Gunnkel was summoning reinforcements.

'I told Lord Æthelred to leave,' Steapa said gloomily, 'I told him on the second day. I said we'd stayed long enough.'

'He wouldn't listen to you?'

'He called me a fool,' Steapa said with a shrug. Æthelred had wanted plunder, and so he had stayed in the Sture and his men brought him anything they could find of value, from cooking pots to reaping knives. 'He found some silver,' Steapa said, 'but not much.'

And while Æthelred stayed to enrich himself, the sea-wolves gathered.

Danish ships came from the south. Sigefrid's ships had sailed from Beamfleot, joining other boats that rowed from the mouths of the Colaun, the Hwealf and the Pant. I had passed those rivers often enough and imagined the lean fast boats sliding out through the mudbanks on the ebbing tides, with their high prows fiercely decorated with beasts and their hulls filled with vengeful men, shields and weapons.

The Danish ships gathered off the island of Horseg, south of the Sture in the wide bay that is haunted by wildfowl. Then, on a grey morning, under a summer rainstorm that blew in from the sea, and on a flooding tide made stronger by a full moon, thirty-eight ships came from the ocean to enter the Sture.

'It was a Sunday,' Steapa said, 'and the Lord Æthelred insisted we listen to a sermon.'

'Alfred will be pleased to hear that,' I said sarcastically.

'It was on the beach,' Steapa said, 'where the Danish boats were grounded.'

'Why there?'

'Because the priests wanted to drive the evil spirits from the boats,' he said, and told me how the beast-heads from the captured ships had been stacked in a great pile on the sand. Driftwood had been packed around them, along with straw from a nearby thatch, and then, to loud prayers from the priests, the heap had been set alight. Dragons and eagles, ravens and wolves had burned, their flames leaping high, and the smoke of the great fire must have blown inland as the rain spat and hissed on the burning wood. The priests had prayed and chanted, crowing their victory over the pagans, and no one had noticed the dark shapes coming through the seawards drizzle.

I can only imagine the fear, the flight and the slaughter. Danes leaping ashore. Sword-Danes, spear-Danes, axe-Danes. The only reason so many men had escaped was that so many were dying. The Danes had started their killing, and found so many men to kill that they could not reach those who fled to the ships. Other Danish boats were attacking the Saxon fleet, but *Rodbora* had held them off. 'I'd left men aboard,' Steapa said.

'Why?'

'Don't know,' he said bleakly. 'I just had a feeling.'

'I know that feeling,' I said. It was the prickle at the back of the neck, the vague unformed suspicion that danger was close, and it was a feeling that should never be ignored. I have seen my hounds suddenly raise their heads from sleep and growl softly, or whine piteously with their eyes staring at me in mute appeal. I know when that happens that thunder is coming, and it always does, but how the dogs sense it I cannot tell. But it must be the same feeling, the discomfort of hidden danger.

'It was a rare fight,' Steapa said dully.

We were rounding the last bend in the Temes before the river reached Lundene. I could see the city's repaired wall, the new timber raw against the older Roman stone. Banners were hung from those ramparts, most of the flags showing saints or crosses; bright symbols to defy the enemy who came every day to inspect the city from the east. An enemy, I thought, who had just won a victory that would stun Alfred.

Steapa was sparing with details of the fight and I had to prise what little I learned out of him. The enemy boats, he said, had mostly landed on the eastern end of the beach, drawn there by the great fire, and *Rodbora* and seven other Saxon boats had been farther west. The beach was a place of screaming chaos as pagans howled and killed. The Saxons tried to reach the western ships and Steapa had made a shield wall to protect those boats as the fugitives scrambled aboard.

'Æthelred reached you,' I commented sourly.

'He can run fast,' Steapa said.

'And Æthelflaed?'

'We couldn't go back for her,' he said.

'No, I'm sure,' I said, and knew he spoke the truth. He told me how Æthelflaed had been trapped and surrounded by the enemy. She had been with her maids close to the great fire, while Æthelred had been accompanying the priests who sprinkled holy water on the prows of the captured Danish ships.

'He did want to go back for her,' Steapa admitted.

'So he should,' I said.

'But it couldn't be done,' he said, 'so we rowed away.'

'They didn't try and stop you?'

'They tried,' he said.

'And?' I prompted him.

'Some got on board,' he said, and shrugged. I imagined Steapa, axe in hand, cutting down the boarders. 'We managed to row past them,' he said, as if it had been easy. The Danes, I thought, should have stopped every boat escaping, but the six ships had managed to escape to sea. 'But eight boats left altogether,' Steapa added.

So two Saxon boats had been successfully boarded, and I flinched at the thought of the axe-work and sword strokes, of the bottom timbers sloppy with blood. 'Did you see Sigefrid?' I asked.

Steapa nodded. 'He was in a chair. Strapped in.'

'And do you know if Æthelflaed lives?' I asked.

'She lives,' Steapa said. 'As we left, we saw her. She was on that ship that was in Lundene? The ship you let go?'

'The *Wave-Tamer*,' I said.

'Sigefrid's ship,' Steapa said, 'and he showed her to us. He made her stand on the steering platform.'

'Clothed?'

'Clothed?' he asked, frowning as though my question was somehow improper. 'Yes,' he said, 'she was clothed.'

'With any luck,' I said, hoping I spoke the truth, 'they won't rape her. She's more valuable unharmed.'

'Valuable?'

'Brace yourself for the ransom,' I said as we smelt Lundene's filthy stench.

Sea-Eagle slid into her dock. Gisela was waiting and I gave her the news, and she gave a small cry as though she were in pain, and then she waited for Æthelred to come ashore, but he ignored her just as he ignored me. He walked uphill towards his palace and his face was pale. His men, those that survived, closed protectively around him.

And I found the stale ink, sharpened a quill and wrote another letter to Alfred.

PART THREE

The Scouring

Nine

We were forbidden to sail down the Temes.

Bishop Erkenwald gave me the order and my instinctive response was to snarl at him, saying that we should have every Saxon ship in the wide estuary harrying the Danes mercilessly. He listened to me without comment and, when I had finished, he appeared to ignore everything I had said. He was writing, copying some book that was propped on his upright desk. 'And what would your violence achieve?' he finally asked in an acid voice.

'It would teach them to fear us,' I said.

'To fear us,' he echoed, saying each word very distinctly and imbuing them with mockery. His quill scratched on the parchment. He had summoned me to his house, which was next to Æthelred's palace and was a surprisingly comfortless place, with nothing in the main large room except an empty hearth, a bench and the upright desk on which the bishop was writing. A young priest sat on the bench, saying nothing, but watching the two of us anxiously. The priest, I was certain, was simply there to be a witness so that, should an argument arise over what was said in this meeting, the bishop would have someone to back his version. Not that much was being said, for Erkenwald ignored me again for another long period, bending low over the desk with his eyes fixed on the words he laboriously scratched. 'If I am right,' he suddenly spoke, though he continued to peer at his work, 'the Danes have just destroyed the largest fleet ever to be deployed from Wessex. I hardly think they will take fright if you stir the water with your few oars.'

'So we leave the water calm?' I asked angrily.

'I dare say,' he said, then paused as he made another letter, 'that the king will want us to do nothing that might aggravate,' another pause as still another letter was formed, 'an unfortunate situation.'

'The unfortunate situation,' I said, 'being that his daughter is being raped daily by the Danes? And you expect us to do nothing?'

'Precisely. You have seized upon the essence of my orders. You are to do nothing to make a bad situation worse.' He still did not look at me. He dipped the quill in his pot and carefully drained the excess ink from the tip. 'How do you prevent a wasp from stinging you?' he asked.

'By killing it first,' I said.

'By remaining motionless,' the bishop said, 'and that is how we shall behave now, by doing nothing to aggravate the situation. Do you have any evidence that the lady is being raped?'

'No.'

'She is valuable to them,' the bishop said, repeating the argument I had myself used to Steapa, 'and I surmise they will do nothing to lessen that value. No doubt you are more informed than I of pagan ways, but if our enemies possess even a scrap of good sense they will treat her with the proper respect due to her rank.' He at last looked at me, offering a sideways glance of pure loathing. 'I will need soldiers,' he said, 'when the time comes to raise the ransom.'

Meaning my men were to threaten every other man who

might possess a battered coin. 'And how much will that be?' I asked sourly, wondering what contribution would be expected of me.

'Thirty years ago in Frankia,' the bishop was writing again, 'the Abbot Louis of the monastery of Saint Denis was captured. A pious and good man. The ransom for the abbot and his brother amounted to six hundred and eighty-six pounds of gold and three thousand, two hundred and fifty pounds of silver. The Lady Æthelflaed might be a mere woman, but I cannot imagine our enemies will settle for a dissimilar sum.' I said nothing. The ransom the bishop had quoted was unimaginable, yet he was surely right in thinking that Sigefrid would want the same or, more likely, a greater amount. 'So you see,' the bishop went on coldly, 'the lady's value is of considerable significance to the pagans, and they will not wish to devalue her. I have assured the Lord Æthelred on this point, and I would be grateful if you do not disabuse him of that hope?'

'Have you heard from Sigefrid?' I asked, thinking that Erkenwald seemed very certain that Æthelflaed was being well treated.

'No, have you?' The question was a challenge, implying that I might be in secret negotiations with Sigefrid. I did not answer and the bishop did not expect me to. 'I foresee,' he continued, 'that the king will wish to supervise the negotiations himself. So until he arrives here, or until he offers me contrary orders, you are to stay in Lundene. Your ships will not sail!'

Nor did they. But the Northmen's ships were sailing. Trade, which had increased through the summer, died to nothing as swarms of beast-headed boats rowed out from Beamfleot to scour the estuary. My best sources of information died with the traders, though a few men did find their way upriver. They were usually fishermen bringing their catch to Lundene's

271

fish market, and they claimed that over fifty ships now grounded their keels in the drying creek beneath Beamfleot's high fort. Vikings were flocking to the estuary.

'They know Sigefrid and his brother will be rich,' I told Gisela the night after the bishop had ordered me to do nothing provocative.

'Very rich,' she said drily.

'Rich enough to assemble an army,' I went on bitterly because, once the ransom was paid, the Thurgilson brothers would be gold-givers and ships would come from every sea, swelling into a horde that could drive into Wessex. The brothers' dream of conquering all the Saxon lands, which had once depended on Ragnar's help, now looked as though it might come true without any northern help, and all thanks to Æthelflaed's capture.

'Will they attack Lundene?' Gisela asked.

'If I were Sigefrid,' I said, 'I would cross the Temes and slash into Wessex through Cent. He'll have enough ships to carry an army across the river and we have nowhere near enough to stop him.'

Stiorra was playing with a wooden doll I had carved out of beechwood and which Gisela had clothed with scraps of linen. My daughter looked so intent on her play and so happy, and I tried to imagine losing her. I tried to imagine Alfred's distress, and found my heart could not even endure the mere thought. 'The baby's kicking,' Gisela said, stroking her belly.

I felt the panic I always experienced when I thought of the approaching childbirth. 'We must find a name for him,' I said, hiding my thoughts.

'Or her?'

'Him,' I said firmly, though without joy because the future, that night, seemed so bleak.

* * *

Alfred came, as the bishop had foreseen, and once again I was summoned to the palace, though this time we were spared any sermon. The king came with his bodyguard, what was left of it after the disaster on the Sture, and I greeted Steapa in the outer courtyard where a steward collected our swords. The priests had come in force, a flock of cawing crows, but among them were the friendly faces of Father Pyrlig, Father Beocca and, to my surprise, Father Willibald. Willibald, all bounce and cheerfulness, scurried across the courtyard to embrace me. 'You're taller than ever, lord!' he said.

'And how are you, father?'

'The Lord sees fit to bless me!' he said happily. 'I minister to souls in Exanceaster these days!'

'I like that town,' I said.

'You had a house nearby, didn't you? With your . . .' Willibald paused, embarrassed.

'With that pious misery I married before Gisela,' I said. Mildrith still lived, though these days she was in a nunnery and I had long forgotten most of the pain of that unhappy union. 'And you?' I asked. 'You're married?'

'To a lovely woman,' Willibald said brightly. He had been my tutor once, though he had taught me little, yet he was a good man, kind and dutiful.

'Does the Bishop of Exanceaster still keep the whores busy?' I asked.

'Uhtred, Uhtred!' Willibald chided me, 'I know you only say these things to shock me!'

'I also tell the truth,' I said, which I did. 'There was a red-headed one,' I went on, 'who he really liked. The story was that he liked her to dress in his robes and then . . .'

'We have all sinned,' Willibald interrupted me hurriedly, 'and fallen short of God's expectations.'

'You too? Was she red-headed?' I asked, then laughed at his discomfort. 'It's good to see you, father. So what brings you from Exanceaster to Lundene?'

'The king, God bless him, wanted the company of old friends,' Willibald said, then shook his head. 'He is in a bad way, Uhtred, a bad way. Do not, I pray you, say anything to upset him. He needs prayers!'

'He needs a new son-in-law,' I said sourly.

'The Lord Æthelred is a faithful servant of God,' Willibald said, 'and a noble warrior! Perhaps he does not have your reputation yet, but his name inspires fear among our enemies.'

'It does?' I asked. 'What are they frightened of? That they might die laughing if he attacks them again?'

'Lord Uhtred!' he chided me again.

I laughed, then followed Willibald into the pillared hall where thegns, priests and ealdormen gathered. This was not an official witanegemot, that royal council of great men that met twice a year to advise the king, but almost every man present was in the Witan. They had travelled from all across Wessex, while others had come from southern Mercia, all summoned to Lundene so that whatever Alfred decided would have the support of both kingdoms. Æthelred was already inside, meeting no one's eye and slumped in a chair below the dais where Alfred would preside. Men avoided Æthelred, all except Aldhelm who crouched beside his chair and whispered in his ear.

Alfred arrived, accompanied by Erkenwald and Brother Asser. I had never seen the king look so haggard. He had one hand clutched to his belly, suggesting that his sickness was bad, but I do not think that was what gave his face the deep lines and the wan, almost hopeless look. His hair was thinning and, for the first time, I saw him as an old man. He was thirty-six years old that year. He took his chair on the dais, waved a hand to show that men might be seated, but said nothing. It was left to Bishop Erkenwald to say a brief prayer, then ask for any man who had a suggestion to speak up.

They talked, and they talked and then they talked some more. The mystery that gripped them was why no message had come from the camp at Beamfleot. A spy had reported to Alfred that his daughter lived, even that she was being treated with respect as Erkenwald had surmised, but no messenger had come from Sigefrid. 'He wants us to be the supplicant,' Bishop Erkenwald suggested, and no one had a better idea. It was pointed out that Æthelflaed was being held prisoner on territory that belonged to King Æthelstan of East Anglia, and surely that Christianised Dane would help? Bishop Erkenwald said a delegation had already travelled to meet the king.

'Guthrum won't fight,' I said, making my first contribution.

'King Æthelstan,' Bishop Erkenwald said, stressing Guthrum's Christian name, 'is proving a constant ally. He will, I am sure, offer us succour.'

'He won't fight,' I said again.

Alfred waved a weary hand towards me, indicating he wanted to hear what I had to say.

'Guthrum is old,' I said, 'and he doesn't want war. Nor can he take on the men near Beamfleot. They get stronger every day. If Guthrum fights them, then he might well lose, and if he loses then Sigefrid will be king in East Anglia.' No one liked that thought, but nor could they argue with it. Sigefrid, despite the wound that Osferth had given him, was becoming ever more powerful and already had enough followers to challenge Guthrum's forces.

'I would not want King Æthelstan to fight,' Alfred said

unhappily, 'for any war will risk my daughter's life. We must, instead, contemplate the necessity of a ransom.'

There was silence as the men in the room imagined the vast sum that would be needed. Some, the wealthiest, avoided Alfred's gaze, while all, I am sure, were wondering where they could hide their wealth before Alfred's tax-collectors and troops came to visit. Bishop Erkenwald broke the silence by observing, with regret, that the church was impoverished or else he would have been happy to contribute. 'What small sums we have,' he said, 'are dedicated to the work of God.'

'They are, indeed,' a fat abbot whose chest gleamed with three silver crosses agreed.

'And the Lady Æthelflaed is now a Mercian,' a thegn from Wiltunscir growled, 'so the Mercians must carry the greater burden.'

'She is my daughter,' Alfred said quietly, 'and I will, of course, contribute all I can afford.'

'But how much will we need?' Father Pyrlig enquired energetically. 'We need to know that first, lord King, and that means someone must travel to meet the pagans. If they will not talk to us, then we must talk to them. As the good bishop says,' and here Pyrlig bowed gravely in Erkenwald's direction, 'they want us to be the suppliants.'

'They wish to humiliate us,' a man growled.

'They do indeed!' Father Pyrlig agreed. 'So we must send a delegation to suffer that humiliation.'

'You would go to Beamfleot?' Alfred asked Pyrlig hopefully.

The Welshman shook his head. 'Lord King,' he said, 'those pagans have cause to hate me. I am not the man to send. The Lord Uhtred, though,' Pyrlig indicated me, 'did Erik Thurgilson a favour.'

'What favour?' Brother Asser demanded quickly.

'I warned him about the treachery of Welsh monks,' I said, and there was a rustle of laughter as Alfred shot me a disapproving look. 'I let him take his own ship from Lundene,' I explained.

'A favour,' Asser retorted, 'that has enabled this unhappy situation to occur. If you had killed the Thurgilsons as you should have, then we would not be here.'

'What brought us here,' I said, 'was the stupidity of lingering in the Sture. If you collect a fat flock you don't leave it grazing beside a wolf's den.'

'Enough!' Alfred said harshly. Æthelred was shuddering with anger. He had not spoken a word so far, but now he turned in his chair and pointed at me. He opened his mouth and I waited for his angry retort, but instead he twisted away and vomited. It was sudden and violent, his stomach voiding itself in a thick, stinking rush. He was jerking as his vomit splashed noisily on the dais. Alfred, appalled, just watched. Aldhelm stepped hastily away. Some of the priests made the sign of the cross. No one spoke or moved to help him. The vomiting appeared to have ceased, but then he twitched again and another spate poured from his mouth. Æthelred spat the last remnants out, wiped his lips on his sleeve and leaned back in his chair with closed eyes and a pale face.

Alfred had watched his son-in-law's sudden attack, but now turned back to the room and said nothing of what had happened. A servant hovered at the edge of the room, plainly tempted to go to Æthelred's assistance, but was frightened of trespassing on the dais. Æthelred was groaning slightly, one hand held across his belly. Aldhelm was staring at the pool of vomit as though he had never seen such a thing.

'Lord Uhtred,' the king broke the embarrassed silence.

'Lord King,' I answered, bowing.

277

Alfred frowned at me. 'There are those, Lord Uhtred, who say you are too friendly with the Northmen?'

'I gave you an oath, lord King,' I said harshly, 'and I renewed that oath to Father Pyrlig and then again to your daughter. If the men who say I am too friendly with the Northmen wish to accuse me of breaking that triple oath then I will meet them at sword's length in any place they wish. And they will face a sword that has killed more Northmen than I can count.'

That brought silence. Pyrlig smiled slyly. Not one man there wanted to fight me, and the only one who might have beaten me, Steapa, was grinning, though Steapa's grin was a deathly rictus that could have frightened a demon back into its lair.

The king sighed as if my display of anger had been tiresome. 'Will Sigefrid talk to you?' he asked.

'The Earl Sigefrid hates me, lord King.'

'But will he talk to you?' Alfred insisted.

'Either that or kill me,' I said, 'but his brother likes me, and Haesten is in debt to me so, yes, I think they'll talk.'

'You must also send a skilled negotiator, lord King,' Erkenwald said unctuously, 'a man who will not be tempted to do further favours to pagans. I would suggest my treasurer? He is a most subtle man.'

'He's also a priest,' I said, 'and Sigefrid hates priests. He also has a burning ambition to watch a priest being crucified.' I smiled at Erkenwald. 'Maybe you should send your treasurer. Or maybe come yourself?'

Erkenwald stared at me blankly. I assumed he was praying that his god send a thunderbolt to punish me, but his god failed to oblige. The king sighed again. 'You can negotiate yourself?' he asked me patiently.

'I've purchased horses, lord,' I said, 'so yes, I can negotiate.'

'Bargaining for a horse is not the same as . . .' Erkenwald began angrily, then subsided as the king waved a weary hand towards him.

'The Lord Uhtred sought to annoy you, bishop,' the king said, 'and it is best not to give him the satisfaction of showing that he has succeeded.'

'I can negotiate, lord King,' I said, 'but in this case I'm bargaining for a mare of very great value. She will not be cheap.'

Alfred nodded. 'Perhaps you should take the bishop's treasurer?' he suggested hesitantly.

'I want only one companion, lord,' I said, 'Steapa.'

'Steapa?' Alfred sounded surprised.

'When you face an enemy, lord,' I explained, 'then it is well to take a man whose very presence is a threat.'

'You will take two companions,' the king corrected me. 'Despite Sigefrid's hatred I want my daughter to receive the blessings of the sacraments. You must take a priest, Lord Uhtred.'

'If you insist, lord,' I said, not bothering to hide my scorn.

'I do insist,' Alfred's voice regained some of its force. 'And be back here quickly,' he went on, 'for I would have news of her.' He stood, and everyone else scrambled to their feet and bowed.

Æthelred had not spoken a word.

And I was going to Beamfleot.

One hundred of us rode. Only three of us would go to Sigefrid's camp, but three men could not ride through the countryside between Lundene and Beamfleot unprotected. This was frontier land, the wild flat land of East Anglia's border, and we rode in mail, with shields and weapons, letting folk know we were ready to fight. It would have been faster to go by ship, but I had persuaded Alfred that there was an advantage in taking horses. 'I've seen Beamfleot from the sea,' I had told him the previous evening, 'and it's impregnable. A steep hill, lord, and a fort on its summit. I haven't seen that fort from inland, lord, and I need to.'

'You need to?' It had been Brother Asser who answered. He was standing close by Alfred's chair as though he protected the king.

'If it comes to a fight,' I had said, 'we might have to attack from the landward side.'

The king had looked at me wearily. 'You want there to be a fight?' he had asked.

'The Lady Æthelflaed will die if there's a fight,' Asser had said.

'I want to return your daughter to you,' I had said to Alfred, ignoring the Welsh monk, 'but only a fool, lord, would assume we will not have to fight them before the summer is over. Sigefrid is becoming too powerful. If we let his power grow we will have an enemy that can threaten all Wessex, and we have to break him before he becomes too strong.'

'No fighting now,' Alfred had insisted. 'Go there by land if you must, speak to them and bring me news quickly.'

He had insisted on sending a priest, but to my relief it was Father Willibald who was chosen. 'I'm an old friend of the Lady Æthelflaed,' Willibald explained as we rode from Lundene. 'She's always been fond of me,' he went on, 'and I of her.'

I rode Smoca. Finan and my household warriors were with me, as were fifty of Alfred's picked men who were commanded by Steapa. We carried no banners, instead Sihtric held a leafy alder branch as a signal that we came seeking a truce.

It was an awful country to the east of Lundene, a flat and desolate place of creeks, ditches, reeds, bog grass and wildfowl. To our right, where sometimes the Temes was visible as a grey sheet, the marshland looked dark even under the summer sun. Few folk lived in this wet wasteland, though we did pass some low hovels thatched with reed. No people were apparent. The eel fishermen who lived in the hovels would have seen us coming and hurried their families to safe hiding places.

The track, it was hardly a road, followed slightly higher ground at the edge of the marsh and led across small, thorn-hedged fields that were heavy with clay. The few trees were stunted and wind bent. The further east we went, the more houses we saw, and gradually those buildings became larger. At midday we stopped at a hall to water and rest the horses. The hall had a palisade, and a servant came cautiously from the gate to ask our business. 'Where are we?' I demanded of him before answering his question.

'Wocca's Dun, lord,' he answered. He spoke English.

I laughed grimly at that for dun meant hill and there was no hill that I could see, though the hall did stand on a very slight mound. 'Is Wocca here?' I asked.

'His grandson owns the land now, lord. He is not here.'

I slid out of Smoca's saddle and tossed the reins to Sihtric. 'Walk him before you let him drink,' I told Sihtric, then turned back to the servant. 'So this grandson,' I asked, 'to whom does he owe oath-duty?'

'He serves Hakon, lord.'

'And Hakon?' I asked, noting that a Saxon owned the hall, but had sworn an oath to a Dane.

'Is sworn to King Æthelstan, lord.'

'To Guthrum?'

'Yes, lord.'

'Has Guthrum summoned men?'

'No, lord,' the servant said.

'And if Guthrum did,' I asked, 'would Hakon and your master obey?'

The servant looked cautious. 'They have gone to Beamfleot,' he said, and that was a truly interesting answer. Hakon, the servant told me, held a wide swathe of this clay-heavy land, which he had been granted by Guthrum, but Hakon was now torn between his oath-sworn allegiance to Guthrum and his fear of Sigefrid.

'So Hakon will follow the Earl Sigefrid?' I asked.

'I think so, lord. A summons came from Beamfleot, lord, I know that much, and my master went there with Hakon.'

'Did they take their warriors?'

'Only a few, lord.'

'The warriors weren't summoned?'

'No, lord.'

So Sigefrid was not gathering an army yet, but rather assembling the richer men of East Anglia to tell them what was expected of them. He would want their warriors when the time came, and doubtless he was now enticing them with visions of the riches that would be theirs when Æthelflaed's ransom was paid. And Guthrum? Guthrum, I supposed, was simply staying silent, while his oath-men were seduced by Sigefrid. He was certainly making no attempt to stop that process and had probably reckoned he was powerless to prevent it in the face of the Norseman's lavish promises. Better, in that case, to let Sigefrid lead his forces against Wessex than to tempt him to usurp the throne of East Anglia. 'And Wocca's grandson,' I asked even though I knew the answer, 'your master, he is a Saxon?'

'Yes, lord. Though his daughter is married to a Dane.'

So it seemed that the Saxons of this dull land would fight for the Danes, perhaps because they had no choice or perhaps because, with marriages, their allegiance was changing.

The servant gave us ale, smoked eel and hard bread and, when we had eaten, we rode on as the sun slid into the west to shine on a great line of hills that rose abruptly out of the flat country. The sun-facing slopes were steep so that the hills looked like a green rampart. 'That's Beamfleot,' Finan said.

'It's up there,' I agreed. Beamfleot would lie at the southern end of the hills though, at this distance, it was impossible to discern the fort. I felt my spirits sinking. If we had to attack Sigefrid then the clear course would have been to lead troops from Lundene, but I had no wish to fight my way up those steep slopes. I could see Steapa eyeing the escarpment with the same foreboding. 'If it comes to a fight, Steapa!' I called cheerfully, 'I'll send you and your troops up there first!'

I got a sour look as the only reply.

'They'll have seen us,' I said to Finan.

'They've been watching us for an hour, lord,' he said.

'They have?'

'I've been watching the glint from their spear-points,' the Irishman said. 'They aren't trying to hide from us.'

It was the beginning of a long summer's evening as we climbed the hill. The air was warm and the slanting light was beautiful among the leaves that shrouded the slope. A road zig-zagged its way to the heights and, as we slowly climbed, I saw the splinters of light from high above and knew they were reflections from spear-points or helmets. Our enemies had been watching us and were ready for us.

There were just three horsemen waiting. All three were in mail, all wore helmets and the helmets had long horse-hair plumes that made their wearers look savage. They had seen Sihtric's alder branch and, as we neared the summit, the three men spurred towards us. I held up my hand to stop my troops and, accompanied only by Finan, rode to greet the three plumed riders.

'You come at last,' one of them called in heavily accented English.

'We come in peace,' I said in Danish.

The man laughed. I could not see his face because his helmet had cheek-pieces and all I could make out was his bearded mouth and the glint of his shadowed eyes. 'You come in peace,' he said, 'because you daren't come any other way. Or do you want us to disembowel your king's daughter after we've all rutted between her thighs?'

'I would speak with the Earl Sigefrid,' I said, ignoring his provocation.

'But does he want to speak with you?' the man asked. He touched a spur to his horse and the stallion turned prettily, not to any purpose, but merely to show off his rider's skill in horsemanship. 'And who are you?' he asked.

'Uhtred of Bebbanburg.'

'I've heard the name,' the man allowed.

'Then tell it to the Earl Sigefrid,' I said, 'and say I bring him greetings from King Alfred.'

'I've heard that name too,' the man said. He paused, playing with our patience. 'You may follow the road,' he finally said, pointing to where the track disappeared over the brow of the hill, 'and you will come to a great stone. Beside the stone is a hall and that is where you and all your men will wait. Earl Sigefrid will inform you tomorrow if he wishes to speak with you, or whether he wishes you to leave, or whether he desires the amusement of your deaths.' He touched the spur to his horse's flank again and all three men rode swiftly away, their hoofbeats loud in the still summer air.

And we rode on to find the hall beside the great stone.

*   *   *

The hall, very ancient, was made from oak that had turned almost black over the years. Its thatched roof was steep, and the building was surrounded by tall oaks that shielded it from the sun. In front of the hall, standing in a patch of rank grass, was a pillar of uncut stone taller than a man. The stone had a hole through it, and in the hole were pebbles and scraps of bone, tokens from the folk who believed that the boulder had magical properties. Finan made the sign of the cross. 'The old people must have put it there,' he said.

'What old people?'

'The ones who lived here when the world was young,' he said, 'the ones who came before us. They put such stones all across Ireland.' He eyed the stone warily and made his horse pass as far away from it as possible.

A single lame servant waited outside the hall. He was a Saxon and he said the place was named Thunresleam, and that name was old too. It meant Thor's Grove and it told me that the hall must have been built in a place where the old Saxons, the Saxons who did not acknowledge the Christian's nailed god, had worshipped their more ancient god, my god, Thor. I bent from Smoca's saddle to touch the stone, and I sent a prayer to Thor that Gisela would survive childbirth and that Æthelflaed would be rescued. 'There is food for you, lord,' the lame servant said, taking Smoca's reins.

There was not just food and ale, there was a feast, and there were Saxon women slaves to prepare the feast and pour the ale, mead and birch wine. There was pork, beef, duck, dried cod and dried haddock, eels, crabs and goose. There was bread, cheese, honey and butter. Father Willibald feared the food might be poisoned and watched fearfully as I ate a leg of goose. 'There,' I said, wiping the grease from my lips onto the back of my hand, 'I'm still alive.'

'Praise God,' Willibald said, still watching me anxiously.

'Praise Thor,' I said, 'this is his hill.'

Willibald made the sign of the cross, then gingerly speared his knife into a piece of duck. 'I am told,' he said nervously, 'that Sigefrid hates Christians.'

'He does. Especially priests.'

'Then why does he feed us so well?'

'To show that he despises us,' I said.

'Not to poison us?' Willibald asked, still worried.

'Eat,' I said, 'enjoy.' I doubted the Northmen would poison us. They might want us dead, but not before they had humiliated us, yet even so I set a careful guard on the paths leading to the hall. I half feared that Sigefrid's chosen humiliation would be to burn the hall at dead of night, with us sleeping inside. I had watched a hall-burning once, and it is a terrible thing. Warriors wait outside to drive the panicked occupants back into the inferno of falling, burning thatch in which folk scream before they die. Next morning, after the hall-burning, the victims had been small as little children, their corpses shrunken and blackened, their hands curled, and their burned lips drawn back from their teeth in a terrible and eternal scream of pain.

But no one tried to kill us in that short summer night. I stood guard for a time, listening to the owls, then watching as the sun rose through the thick tangle of trees. Some time later I heard a horn blowing. It made a mournful wail that was repeated three times, then sounded three times again, and I knew Sigefrid must be summoning his men. He would send for us soon, I thought, and I dressed carefully. I chose to wear my best mail, and my fine war helmet and, though the day promised to be warm, my black cloak with its lightning bolt streaking down the long back. I pulled on my boots and strapped on my swords. Steapa also wore mail, though his armour was dirty and tarnished, while his boots were scuffed and his scabbard-covering torn, yet somehow he looked much more fearsome than I did. Father Willibald was dressed in his black gown and carried a small bag, which contained a gospel book and the sacraments. 'You will translate for me, won't you?' he asked earnestly.

'Why didn't Alfred send a priest who spoke Danish?' I asked.

'I do speak some!' Willibald said, 'but not as much as I'd like. No, the king sent me because he thought I might be a comfort to the Lady Æthelflaed.'

'Make sure you are,' I said, then turned because Cerdic had come running down the track that led through the trees from the south.

'They're coming, lord,' he said.

'How many?'

'Six, lord. Six horsemen.'

The six men rode into the clearing about the hall. They stopped and looked around them. Their helmet masks restricted their vision, forcing them to move their heads extravagantly in order to see our picketed horses. They were counting heads, making sure I had not sent a scouting party to explore the country. Finally, satisfied that no such party existed, their leader deigned to look at me. I thought he was the same man who had greeted us on the hilltop the previous day. 'You alone must come,' he said, pointing at me.

'Three of us are coming,' I said.

'You alone,' he insisted.

'Then we leave for Lundene now,' I said, and turned. 'Pack up! Saddles! Hurry! We're going!'

The man made no fight of it. 'Three, then,' he said carelessly, 'but you do not ride to Earl Sigefrid's presence. You walk.'

I made no fight of that. I knew it was part of Sigefrid's purpose to humiliate us, and how better than to make us walk to his camp? Lords rode while common men walked, but Steapa, Father Willibald and I meekly walked behind the six horsemen as they followed a track through the trees and out onto a wide grassy down that overlooked the sun-shimmering Temes. The down was covered by crude shelters, places built by the new crews who had come to support Sigefrid in anticipation of the treasure he would soon possess and distribute.

I was sweating fiercely by the time we climbed the slope to Sigefrid's encampment. I could see Caninga now, and the eastern part of the creek, both places I knew intimately from their seaward side, but which I had never seen from this eagle's height. I could see, too, that there were now many more ships crammed into the drying Hothlege. The Vikings roamed the world in search of a weak spot into which they could pour with axe, sword and spear, and Æthelflaed's capture had revealed just such an opportunity and so the Northmen gathered.

Hundreds of men waited inside the gate. They made a passageway towards the fort's great hall and the three of us had to walk between those twin grim lines of bearded, armed men towards two big farm wagons that had been placed together to make a long platform. In the centre of that makeshift stage was a chair in which Sigefrid slouched. He was in his black bear robe despite the heat. His brother Erik stood to one side of the big chair while Haesten, grinning slyly, stood on the other. A row of helmeted guards was behind the trio, while in front of them, hanging from the wagons' beds, were banners of ravens, eagles and wolves. On the ground in front of Sigefrid were the standards captured from Æthelred's fleet. The Lord of Mercia's own great banner of a prancing horse was there, and beside it were flags showing crosses and saints. The standards were soiled, and I guessed the Danes had taken it in turns to piss on the captured flags. There was no sign of Æthelflaed. I had half expected that we should see her paraded in public, but she must have been under guard in one of the dozen buildings on the hilltop.

'Alfred has sent his puppies to yelp at us!' Sigefrid announced as we reached the fouled banners.

I took off my helmet. 'Alfred sends you greetings,' I said. I had half expected to be met by Sigefrid inside his hall, then realised he had wanted to greet me in the open air so that as many of his followers as possible could see my humiliation.

'You whine like a puppy,' Sigefrid said.

'And he wishes you joy of the Lady Æthelflaed's company,' I went on.

He scowled in puzzlement. His broad face looked fatter, indeed his body looked fatter because the wound Osferth had given him had taken away the use of his legs but not his appetite, and so he sat, a cripple, slumped and gross, staring indignantly at me. 'Joy of her, puppy?' he growled. 'What are you yapping about?'

'The King of Wessex,' I said loudly, letting the audience hear me, 'has other daughters! There is the lovely Æthelgifu, and her sister, Æfthryth, so what need does he have of Æthelflaed? And what use are daughters anyway? He is a king and he has sons, Edward and Æthelweard, and sons are a man's glory, while daughters are his burden. So he wishes you joy of her, and sent me to bid her farewell.'

'The puppy tries to amuse us,' Sigefrid said scornfully. He did not believe me, of course, but I hoped I had sown a small seed of doubt, just enough to justify the low ransom I was going to offer. I knew, and Sigefrid knew, that the final price would be huge, but maybe, if I repeated it often enough, I could persuade him that Alfred did not care deeply about Æthelflaed. 'Perhaps I shall take her for my lover?' Sigefrid suggested.

I noticed Erik, beside his brother, shifting uncomfortably.

'She would be fortunate in that,' I said carelessly.

'You lie, puppy,' Sigefrid said, but there was just the smallest note of uncertainty in his voice. 'But the Saxon bitch is pregnant. Perhaps her father will buy her child?'

'If it's a boy,' I said dubiously, 'perhaps.'

'Then you must make an offer,' Sigefrid said.

'Alfred might pay a small sum for a grandchild,' I began.

'Not to me,' Sigefrid interrupted me. 'You must persuade Weland of your good faith.'

'Wayland?' I asked, thinking he meant the blacksmith to the gods.

'Weland the Giant,' Sigefrid said and, smiling, nodded past me. 'He's a Dane,' Sigefrid went on, 'and no man has ever out-wrestled Weland.'

I turned and facing me was the biggest man I have ever seen. A huge man. A warrior, doubtless, though he wore neither weapons nor mail. He wore leather trews and boots, but above the waist he was naked to reveal muscles like twisted cord under a skin that had been scored and coloured with ink so that his wide chest and massive arms writhed with black dragons. His forearms were thick with rings larger than any I had seen, for no normal ring would have fitted Weland. His beard, black as the dragons on his body, was tied with small amulets, while his skull was bald. His face was malevolent, scarred, brutish, though he smiled when I caught his eye.

'You must persuade Weland,' Sigefrid said, 'that you do not lie, puppy, or else I will not talk with you.'

I had expected something of this sort. In Alfred's mind

290

we would have come to Beamfleot, conducted a civilised discussion and reached a moderate compromise that I would duly report back to him, but I was more used to the Northmen. They needed amusement. If I were to negotiate then I must first show my strength. I must needs prove myself, but as I stared at Weland I knew I would fail. He was a head taller than me, and I was a head taller than most men, but the same instinct that had warned me of an ordeal had also persuaded me to bring Steapa.

Who smiled his death's-head smile. He had not understood anything I had said to Sigefrid, or Sigefrid to me, but he understood Weland's stance. 'He has to be beaten?' he asked me.

'Let me do it,' I said.

'Not while I live,' Steapa answered. He unbuckled his sword belt and gave the weapons to Father Willibald, then hauled the heavy mail coat over his head. The watching men, anticipating the fight, gave a raucous cheer.

'You had best hope your man wins, puppy,' Sigefrid said behind me.

'He will,' I said, with a confidence I did not feel.

'In the spring, puppy,' Sigefrid growled, 'you stopped me from crucifying a priest. I am still curious, so if your man loses I shall crucify that piece of priestly piss beside you.'

'What's he saying?' Willibald had seen the malevolent glance Sigefrid had shot in his direction and, unsurprisingly, sounded nervous.

'He says you're not to use your Christian magic to influence the fight,' I lied.

'I shall pray anyway,' Father Willibald said bravely.

Weland was stretching his huge arms and flexing his thick fingers. He stamped his feet, then settled into a wrestler's stance, though I doubted this fight would keep

291

to the grappling rules of wrestling. I had been watching him carefully. 'He's favouring his right leg,' I said quietly to Steapa, 'which could mean his left leg was wounded once.'

I might have saved my breath because Steapa was not listening to me. His eyes were narrow and furious, while his face, always stark, was now a taut mask of concentrated anger. He looked like a madman. I remembered the one time I had fought him. It had been on a day just before Yule, the same day that Guthrum's Danes had descended unexpectedly on Cippanhamm, and Steapa had been calm before that fight. He had seemed to me, on that far-off winter's day, like a workman going about his trade, confident in his tools and skill, but that was not how he looked now. Now he was in a private fury, and whether it was because he fought a hated pagan, or whether because, in Cippanhamm, he had underestimated me, I did not know. Nor did I care. 'Remember,' I tried again, 'Wayland the Smith was lame.'

'Start!' Sigefrid called behind me.

'God and Jesus,' Steapa bellowed, 'hell and Christ!' He was not reacting to Sigefrid's command, indeed I doubt he even heard it. Instead he was summoning his last tension, like a bowman drawing the cord of a hunting bow an extra inch to give the arrow deadly force, then Steapa howled like an animal and charged.

Weland charged too and they met like stags in the rutting season.

The Danes and Norsemen had crowded around, making a circle that was limited by the spears of Sigefrid's body-guard, and the watching warriors gave a gasp as those two men-animals crashed together. Steapa had lowered his head, hoping to drive his skull into Weland's face, but Weland had moved at the last instant and instead their bodies slammed together and there was a flurry as they sought holds on each other. Steapa had a handful of Weland's trews, Weland was pulling on Steapa's hair, and both were using their free hands to flail at each other with clenched fists. Steapa tried to bite Weland, Weland butted him, then Steapa reached down in an attempt to crush Weland's groin, and there was another desperate flurry as Weland brought a massive knee hard up between Steapa's thighs.

'Dear Jesus,' Willibald murmured beside me.

Weland broke away from Steapa's grip and punched hard at Steapa's face and the sound of the fist landing was like the splintering wet noise of a butcher's axe striking meat. There was blood pouring from Steapa's nose now, but he seemed oblivious to it. He traded blows, driving his fists at Weland's ribs and head, then straightened his fingers and jabbed hard at the Dane's eyes. Weland managed to avoid the gouging thrust and landed a knuckle-crunching blow on Steapa's throat so that the Saxon staggered back, suddenly unable to breathe.

'Oh, my God, my God,' Willibald whispered, making the sign of the cross.

Weland followed fast, punching, then using his heavy arm rings to clout Steapa's skull so that the metal ornaments raked across the Saxon's scalp. More blood showed. Steapa was reeling, staggering, gasping, choking, and suddenly he dropped to his knees and the watching crowd gave a great jeer at his weakness. Weland drew back a mighty fist, but, before the blow was even launched, Steapa threw himself forward and seized the Dane's left ankle. He pulled and twisted, and Weland went down like a felled oak. He crashed onto the turf and Steapa, snarling and bleeding, threw himself on top of his enemy and started punching again.

'They'll kill each other,' Father Willibald said in a frightened voice.

'Sigefrid won't allow his champion to die,' I said, though having said it I wondered if that was true. I turned to look at Sigefrid and found that he was watching me. He gave me a sly smile, then looked back to the fighters. This was his game, I thought. The outcome of the battle would make no difference to the discussions. Nothing, except perhaps Father Willibald's life, depended on the savage display. It was just a game.

Weland managed to turn Steapa so they lay side by side on the grass. They exchanged ineffective blows and then, as if by mutual consent, rolled away from each other and stood again. There was a pause as both men drew breath, then they crashed together a second time. Steapa's face was a pulp of blood, Weland's bottom lip and left ear were bleeding, one eye was almost closed and his ribs had taken a pounding. For a moment the two men grappled, seeking holds, feet shifting, grunting, then Weland managed to grasp Steapa's trews and threw him so that the big Saxon turned on the Dane's left hip and thumped down to the turf. Weland raised his foot to stamp Steapa's groin, and Steapa seized the foot and twisted.

Weland yelped. It was an odd, small sound from such a big man, and the damage being done to him seemed trivial after the hammering he had already taken, but Steapa had at last remembered that Wayland the Smith had been lamed by Nidung, and his twisting of the Dane's foot was aggravating an ancient injury. Weland tried to pull away, but lost his balance and fell again, and Steapa, breathing thick and spitting blood, crawled towards him and began hitting again. He was hitting blindly, his hammer fists thumping on arms, chest and head. Weland responded by trying to gouge out Steapa's eyes, but the Saxon snapped at the groping hand with his teeth and I distinctly heard the crunch as he bit off Weland's small finger. Weland twitched away, Steapa spat the finger out and dropped his huge hands onto the Dane's neck. He started to squeeze and Weland, choking for breath, began to jerk and flap like a banked trout.

'Enough!' Erik called.

No one moved. Weland's eyes were widening while Steapa, blood blinded and teeth bared, had his hands around the Dane's neck. Steapa was making mewing noises, then grunting as he tried to drive his fingers into the Dane's gullet.

'Enough!' Sigefrid roared.

Steapa's blood dripped onto Weland's face as the Saxon throttled the Dane. I could hear Steapa growling and knew he would never stop until the huge man was dead and so I pushed past one of the horizontal spears that held the spectators back. 'Stop!' I shouted at Steapa, and when he ignored me I drew Wasp-Sting and slapped the flat of her short blade hard across his bloodied skull. 'Stop!' I shouted again.

He snarled at me and I thought, for an instant, he was going to attack me, but then sense came to his half-closed eyes and he let go of Weland's neck and stared up at me. 'I won,' he said angrily. 'Tell me I won!'

'Oh, you won,' I said.

Steapa got to his feet. He stood unsteadily, then he braced himself on spread legs and punched both arms into the summer air. 'I won!' he shouted.

Weland was still gasping for breath. He tried to stand, but fell back again.

I turned to Sigefrid. 'The Saxon won,' I said, 'and the priest lives.'

'The priest lives,' it was Erik who answered. Haesten was

295

grinning, Sigefrid looked amused, and Weland was making a grating noise as he tried to breathe.

'Then make your offer,' Sigefrid said to me, 'for Alfred's bitch.'

And the haggling could begin.

Ten

Sigefrid was carried from the wagon platform by four men who struggled to lift his chair and lower it safely to the ground. He shot me a resentful scowl, as if I were to blame for his crippled condition, which, I suppose, I was. The four men carried the chair to his hall and Haesten, who had neither greeted me nor even acknowledged my presence other than by smiling slyly, gestured that we should follow.

'Steapa needs help,' I said

'A woman will mop his blood,' Haesten said carelessly, then laughed suddenly. 'So you discovered Bjorn was an illusion?'

'A good one,' I acknowledged grudgingly.

'He's dead now,' Haesten said, with as much feeling as if he spoke of a hound that had died. 'He caught a fever about two weeks after you saw him. And now he can't come from his grave any more, the bastard!' Haesten wore a gold chain now, a rope of thick links that hung heavy on his broad chest. I remembered him as a young man, he had been scarce more than a boy when I had rescued him, but now I saw the adult in Haesten and I did not like what I saw. His eyes were friendly enough, but they had a guarded quality as if, behind them, was a soul ready to strike like a snake. He punched my arm familiarly. 'You know this royal Saxon bitch is going to cost you a lot of silver?'

'If Alfred decides he wants her back,' I said airily, 'then I suppose he might pay something.'

Haesten laughed at that. 'And if he doesn't want her back? We'll take her around Britain, around Frankia and back to our homeland, and we'll strip her naked and strap her to a frame with her legs open, and let everyone come and see the King of Wessex's daughter. You want that for her, Lord Uhtred?'

'You want me for an enemy, Earl Haesten?' I asked.

'I think we're enemies already,' Haesten said, for once allowing the truth to show, but he immediately smiled as if to prove he was not serious. 'Folk will pay good silver to see the daughter of the King of Wessex, don't you think? And men will pay gold to enjoy her.' He laughed. 'I think your Alfred will want to prevent that humiliation.'

He was right, of course, though I dared not acknowledge it. 'Has she been harmed?' I asked.

'Erik won't let us near her!' Haesten said, evidently amused. 'No, she's unscratched. If you're selling a sow you don't beat her with a holly stick, do you?'

'True,' I said. Beating a pig with a stick made from a branch of holly left bruises so deep that the beast's compacted flesh could never be properly salt-cured. Haesten's entourage waited nearby and among them I recognised Eilaf the Red, the man whose hall had been used to show me Bjorn, and he gave me a small bow. I ignored the courtesy.

'We'd best go in,' Haesten said, gesturing towards Sigefrid's hall, 'and see how much gold we can squeeze out of Wessex.'

'I must see Steapa first,' I said, though by the time I found Steapa he was surrounded by Saxon women slaves, who

298

were using a lanolin salve on his cuts and bruises. He did not need me and so I followed Haesten into the hall.

A ring of stools and benches had been placed around the hall's central hearth. Willibald and I were given two of the lowest stools, while Sigefrid glared at us from his chair on the far side of the empty hearth. Haesten and Erik took their places on either side of the cripple, then other men, all of them with lavish arm rings, filled the circle. These, I knew, were the more important Northmen, the ones who had brought two or more ships, and the men who, if Sigefrid succeeded in conquering Wessex, would be rewarded with rich grants of land. Their followers crowded at the hall's edges where women distributed horns of ale. 'Make your offer,' Sigefrid commanded me abruptly.

'She is a daughter, not a son,' I said, 'so Alfred is not minded to pay a great sum. Three hundred pounds of silver would seem adequate.'

Sigefrid stared at me for a long while, then stared around the hall where the men watched and listened. 'Did I hear a Saxon fart?' he demanded, and was rewarded with laughter. He sniffed ostentatiously, then wrinkled his nose, while the spectators erupted into a chorus of farting noises. Then Sigefrid slammed a huge fist onto the arm of his chair and the hall went immediately silent. 'You insult me,' he said, and I saw the anger in his eyes. 'If Alfred is minded to offer so little, then I am minded to bring the girl here now and make you watch while we tup her. Why shouldn't I!' He struggled in the chair as if he wanted to get to his feet, then slumped back. 'Is that what you want, you Saxon fart? You want to see her raped?'

The anger, I thought, had been feigned. Just as I had to try and diminish Æthelflaed's value, so Sigefrid had to exaggerate the threat to her, but I had noticed a flicker of disgust on Erik's face when Sigefrid suggested rape, and that disgust had been aimed at his brother, not at me. I kept my voice calm. 'The king,' I said, 'gave me some discretion to increase his offer.'

'Oh, what a surprise!' Sigefrid said sarcastically, 'so let me discover the limits of your discretion. We wish to be given ten thousand pounds of silver and five thousand pounds of gold.' He paused, wanting a response from me, but I kept silent. 'And the money,' Sigefrid finally went on, 'is to be brought here by Alfred himself. He is to pay it in person.'

That was a long day, a very long day, lubricated by ale, mead and birch wine, and the negotiations were punctuated by threats, anger and insults. I drank little, just some ale, but Sigefrid and his captains drank heavily and that, perhaps, is why they yielded more than I expected. The truth is they wanted money; they wanted a boatload of silver and gold so they could hire more men and more weapons and so begin their conquest of Wessex. I had made a rough estimate of the numbers in that high fort and reckoned Sigefrid could assemble an army of about three thousand men, and that was nowhere near sufficient to invade Wessex. He needed five or six thousand men, and even that many might not be sufficient, but if he could raise eight thousand warriors then he would win. With such an army he could conquer Wessex and become the crippled king of her fertile fields, and to get those extra warriors he needed silver, and if he did not receive the ransom then even the men he now possessed would quickly melt away in search of other lords who could give them bright gold and shining silver.

By mid afternoon they had settled for three thousand pounds of silver and five hundred pounds of gold. They still insisted Alfred deliver the money in person, but I resolutely refused that demand, even going so far as to stand and pluck Father Willibald's arm, telling him we were leaving because

300

we could reach no agreement. Many of the spectators were bored, and more than a few were drunk, and they growled with anger when they saw me stand so that, for a moment, I thought we would be attacked, but then Haesten intervened.

'What about the bitch's husband?' he asked.

'What about him?' I asked, turning back as the hall slowly quietened.

'Doesn't her husband call himself the Lord of Mercia?' Haesten enquired, mocking the title with laughter. 'So let the Lord of Mercia bring the money.'

'And let him beg me for his wife,' Sigefrid added, 'on his knees.'

'Agreed,' I said, surprising them by the ease of my surrender to their suggestion.

Sigefrid frowned, suspecting I had given in much too easily. 'Agreed?' he asked, not sure he had heard me correctly.

'Agreed,' I said, sitting again. 'The Lord of Mercia will deliver the ransom and he will go on his knees to you.' Sigefrid was still suspicious. 'The Lord of Mercia is my cousin,' I explained, 'and I hate the little bastard,' and at that even Sigefrid laughed.

'The money is to be here before the full moon,' he said, then pointed a blunt finger at me, 'and you come the day before to tell me the silver and gold is on its way. You will fly a green branch at your masthead as a signal you come in peace.'

He wanted the full day's warning of the ransom's arrival so he could assemble as many men as possible to witness his triumph, and so I agreed to come the day before the treasure ship sailed, but explained that he could not expect that to happen soon because such a vast sum would take time to collect. Sigefrid growled at that, but I hurried on, assuring him that Alfred was a man who kept his word and that, by the next full moon, as large a down payment as could be assembled would be brought to Beamfleot. Æthelflaed was to be released then, I insisted, and the rest of the silver and gold would arrive before the following full moon. They haggled over those demands, but by now the bored men in the hall were getting restless and angry, so Sigefrid yielded the point that the ransom could be paid in two parts, and I yielded that Æthelflaed would not be freed until the second part had been delivered. 'And I wish to see the Lady Æthelflaed now,' I said, making my last demand.

Sigefrid waved a careless hand. 'Why not? Erik will take you.' Erik had hardly spoken all day. Like me he had stayed sober, and had neither joined in the insults nor the laughter. Instead he had sat, serious and withdrawn, his watchful eyes going from his brother to me. 'You will eat with us tonight,' Sigefrid said. He smiled suddenly, showing some of the charm I had felt when I had first met him in Lundene. 'We shall celebrate our agreement with a feast,' he went on, 'and your men at Thunresleam will also be fed. You can talk to the girl now! Go with my brother.'

Erik led Father Willibald and me towards a smaller hall that was guarded by a dozen men in long mail coats, all of them carrying shields and weapons. It was plainly the place where Æthelflaed was being held captive and it lay close to the seawards rampart of the camp. Erik did not speak as we walked, indeed he seemed almost oblivious of my company, keeping his eyes fixed so firmly on the ground at his feet that I had to steer him around some trestles on which men were shaping new oars. The long curling wood-shavings peeled off and smelt oddly sweet in the late afternoon warmth. Erik stopped just beyond the trestles and turned on me with a frown. 'Did you mean what you said today?' he demanded angrily.

302

'I said a lot today,' I answered cautiously.

'About King Alfred not wanting to pay much for the Lady Æthelflaed? Because she's a girl?'

'Sons are worth more than daughters,' I said truthfully enough.

'Or were you just bargaining?' he asked fiercely.

I hesitated. It struck me as a strange question because Erik was surely clever enough to have seen through that feeble attempt to lower Æthelflaed's value, but there was real passion in his voice and I sensed he needed to hear the truth. Besides, nothing I said now could change the arrangements I had made with Sigefrid. The two of us had drunk the scot-ale to show that we had reached agreement, we had spat on our hands and touched palms, then sworn on a hammer amulet to keep faith with each other. That agreement was made, and that meant I could now tell the truth to Erik. 'Of course I was bargaining,' I said. 'Æthelflaed is dear to her father, very dear. He's suffering because of all this.'

'I thought you had to be bargaining,' Erik said, sounding wistful. He turned and stared across the wide estuary of the Temes. A dragon ship was sliding on the flooding tide towards the creek, her oar-blades rising and falling to catch and reflect the settling sun with every lazy stroke. 'How much would the king have paid for his daughter?' he asked.

'Whatever was necessary,' I said.

'Truly?' He sounded eager now. 'He set no limit?'

'He told me,' I answered truthfully, 'to pay whatever was necessary to take Æthelflaed home.'

'To her husband,' he said flatly.

'To her husband,' I agreed.

'Who should die,' Erik said, and he shuddered uncontrollably, a swift shudder, but something that told me he had a touch of his brother's anger in his soul.

'When the Lord Æthelred comes with the gold and silver,' I warned Erik, 'then you cannot touch him. He will come under a banner of truce.'

'He hits her! Is that true?' The question was abrupt.

'Yes,' I said.

Erik stared at me for a heartbeat and I could see him struggling to control that sudden burst of anger. He nodded and turned. 'This way,' he said, leading me towards the smaller hall. The hall's guards, I noticed, were all older men, and I guessed they were trusted not just to guard Æthelflaed, but not to molest her either. 'She has not been harmed,' Erik said, perhaps reading my thoughts.

'So I've been assured.'

'She has three of her own maids here,' Erik went on, 'and I gave her two Danish girls, both nice girls. And I put these guards on the house.'

'Men you trust,' I said.

'My men,' he said warmly, 'and yes, trustworthy.' He held out a hand to check me. 'I'll bring her out here to meet you,' he explained, 'because she likes being in the open air.'

I waited while Father Willibald looked nervously back at the Northmen who watched us from outside Sigefrid's hall. 'Why are we meeting her out here?' he asked.

'Because Erik says she likes being in the fresh air,' I explained.

'But will they kill me if I give her the sacrament here?'

'Because they think you're doing Christian magic?' I asked. 'I doubt it, father.' I watched as Erik pulled aside the leather curtain that served as the hall's door. He had said something to the guards first, and those warriors now moved to each side, leaving an open space between the building's facade and the fort's walls. Those ramparts were a thick bank of earth, only some three feet high, but I knew their farther side would fall a much greater depth.

The bank was topped by a palisade of stout oak logs that had been sharpened into points. I could not imagine climbing the hill from the creek and then trying to cross that formidable wall. But nor could I envisage attacking from the fort's landwards side, climbing in the open down to the ditch, wall, and palisade that protected this place. It was a good camp, not impregnable, but its capture would be unimaginably expensive in men's lives.

'She lives,' Father Willibald breathed, and I looked back to the hall to see Æthelflaed ducking under the leather curtain that was being held aside by an unseen hand. She looked smaller and younger than ever and, though her pregnancy had at last begun to show, she still looked lissom. Lissom and vulnerable, I thought, and then she saw me, and a smile came to her face. Father Willibald started towards her, but I held him back by gripping his shoulder. Something in Æthelflaed's demeanour made me detain him. I had half expected Æthelflaed to run to me in relief, but instead she hesitated by the door and the smile she had offered me was merely dutiful. She was pleased to see me, that was certain, but there was a wariness in her eyes until she turned to watch Erik follow her through the curtain. He gestured that she should greet me, and only then, when she had received his encouragement, did she come towards me.

And now her face was radiant.

And I remembered her face on the day she had been married in her father's new church in Wintanceaster. She looked the same today as she had then. She looked happy. She glowed. She walked as lightly as a dancer, and she smiled so beautifully, and I recalled how I had thought, in that church, that she had been in love with love, and that, I suddenly realised, was the difference between that day and this.

Because the radiant smile was not for me. She looked

behind once more and caught Erik's eye, and I just stared. I should have known from everything Erik had said. I should have known, for it was as plain as new-shed blood on virgin snow.

Æthelflaed and Erik were in love.

Love is a dangerous thing.

It comes in disguise to change our life. I had thought I loved Mildrith, but that was lust, though for a time I had believed it was love. Lust is the deceiver. Lust wrenches our lives until nothing matters except the one we think we love, and under that deceptive spell we kill for them, give all for them, and then, when we have what we have wanted, we discover that it is all an illusion and nothing is there. Lust is a voyage to nowhere, to an empty land, but some men just love such voyages and never care about the destination.

Love is a voyage too, a voyage with no destination except death, but a voyage of bliss. I loved Gisela, and we were fortunate because our threads had come together and stayed together and were twined about each other, and the three Norns, for a time at least, were kind to us. Love even works when the threads do not lie comfortably side by side. I had come to see that Alfred loved his Ælswith, though she was like a streak of vinegar in his milk. Perhaps he just got used to her, and perhaps love is friendship more than it is lust, though the gods know the lust is always there. Gisela and I had gained that contentment, as Alfred did with Ælswith, though I think our voyage was happier because our boat danced on sunlit seas and was driven by a brisk warm wind.

And Æthelflaed? I saw it in her face. I saw in her radiance all her sudden love and all the unhappiness that was to come, and all the tears, and all the heartbreak. She was on a voyage, and it was a journey of love, but it was sailing into a storm so bleak and dark that my own heart almost broke for her.

'Lord Uhtred,' she said as she came close.

'My lady,' I said, and bowed to her, and then we said nothing.

Willibald chattered, but I do not think either of us heard him. I looked at her and she smiled at me and the sun shone on that springy high turf beneath the singing skylarks, but all I could hear was thunder wrecking the sky and all I could see were waves shattering in white-whipping fury and a ship swamping and her crew drowning in despair. Æthelflaed was in love.

'Your father sends his affection,' I said, finding my voice.

'Poor Father,' she said. 'Is he angry with me?'

'He shows no anger to anybody,' I said, 'but he should be furious with your husband.'

'Yes,' she agreed calmly, 'he should.'

'And I am here to arrange your release,' I told her, ignoring my certainty that release was the very last thing she now desired, 'and you will be pleased to know, my lady, that all is agreed and you will be home soon.'

She showed no pleasure at that news. Father Willibald, blind to her true feelings, beamed at her, and Æthelflaed rewarded him with a wry smile. 'I am here to give you the sacraments,' Willibald said.

'I would like that,' Æthelflaed answered gravely, then looked up at me and, for an instant, there was despair on her face. 'Will you wait for me?' she asked.

'Wait for you?' I asked, puzzled by the question.

'Out here,' she explained, 'and dear Father Willibald can pray with me inside.'

'Of course,' I said.

She smiled her thanks and led Willibald back to the hall while I went to the ramparts and climbed the brief bank so that I could lean on the sun-warmed palisade and stare down into the creek so far below. The dragon ship, her carved head dismounted, was rowing into the channel and I watched as men unchained the moored guard-ship that blocked the Hothlege. The blocking ship was tethered at bow and stern by heavy chains connected to massive posts sunk into the muddy banks and the crew slipped the ship's stern chain and then paid it out with a long rope. The chain sank to the creek bed as the ship swung on her bow chain to open like a gate on the incoming tide to clear the passage. The newly-arrived boat was rowed past, then the blocking ship's crew hauled on the rope to retrieve the chain and so dragged the ship back to bar the creek again. There were at least forty men on that blocking ship, and they were not just there to haul on lines and chains. The flanks of the ship had been built up with extra strakes, all of heavy timber, so that her sheerline was well above the height of any vessel that might attack her. To assault that blocking ship would be like tackling the palisade of a fortress. The dragon ship glided up the Hothlege, passing the boats hauled high on the muddy creek bank where men were caulking the planks with hair and tar. Smoke from the fires under the tar pots drifted up the slope where gulls circled, their cries raucous in the afternoon's warmth.

'Sixty-four ships,' Erik said. He had climbed up beside me.

'I know,' I said, 'I counted them.'

'And by next week,' Erik said, 'we will have a hundred crews here.'

'And you'll run out of food with so many mouths to feed.'

'There's plenty of food here,' Erik said dismissively. 'We have fish traps and eel traps, we net wildfowl and eat well.

And the prospect of silver and gold buys a lot of wheat, barley, oats, meat, fish and ale.'

'It will buy men too,' I said.

'It will,' he agreed.

'And thus,' I said, 'Alfred of Wessex pays for his own destruction.'

'So it would seem,' Erik said quietly. He stared southwards to where great clouds piled over Cent, their tops silver white and their bases dark above the distant green land.

I turned to look at the encampment inside its ring of ramparts and saw Steapa, walking with a slight limp and with his head bandaged, appear from a hut. He looked slightly drunk. He saw me, waved and sat in the shade of Sigefrid's hall where he appeared to fall asleep. 'Do you think,' I said, my back still turned on Erik, 'that Alfred has not thought of what you'll buy with the ransom money?'

'But what can he do about it?'

'That's not for me to tell you,' I said, trying to imply that there was an answer. In truth, if seven or eight thousand Northmen appeared in Wessex then we would have no choice but to fight, and the battle, I thought, would be horrendous. It would be a blood-letting even greater than Ethandun, and at its end there would most likely be a new king in Wessex and a new name for the kingdom. Norseland, perhaps.

'Tell me about Guthred,' Erik asked abruptly.

'Guthred!' I turned back to him, surprised by the question. Guthred was Gisela's brother and King of Northumbria, and what he had to do with Alfred, Æthelflaed or Erik I could not imagine.

'He's a Christian, isn't he?' Erik asked.

'So he says.'

'Is he?'

'How would I know?' I asked. 'He claims to be a Christian, but I doubt he's given up his worship of the true gods.'

'You like him?' Erik asked anxiously.

'Everyone likes Guthred,' I said, and that was true, yet it constantly astonished me that a man so affable and indecisive had held on to his throne for so long. Mainly, I knew, that was because my brother-in-law had the support of Ragnar, my soul brother, and no man would want to fight Ragnar's wild forces.

'I was thinking,' Erik said, and then fell silent, and in his silence I suddenly understood what he was dreaming.

'You were thinking,' I told him the brutal truth, 'that you and Æthelflaed can take a ship, maybe your brother's ship, and go to Northumbria and live under Guthred's protection?'

Erik stared at me as though I were a magician. 'She told you?' he asked.

'Your faces told me,' I said.

'Guthred would protect us,' Erik said.

'How?' I asked. 'You think he'll summon his army if your brother comes after you?'

'My brother?' Erik asked, as if Sigefrid would forgive him anything.

'Your brother,' I said harshly, 'who is expecting a payment of three thousand pounds of silver and five hundred pounds of gold, and if you take Æthelflaed away, then he loses that money. You think he won't want her back?'

'Your friend, Ragnar,' Erik suggested hesitantly.

'You want Ragnar to fight for you?' I asked. 'Why should he?'

'Because you ask him to,' Erik said firmly. 'Æthelflaed says you love each other like brothers.'

'We do.'

'Then ask him,' he demanded.

I sighed and stared at those distant clouds and thought how love wrenches our lives and drives us to such sweet insanity. 'And what will you do,' I asked, 'against the murderers who come in the night? Against the vengeful men who will burn your hall?'

'Guard against them,' he said stubbornly.

I watched the clouds pile higher and thought that Thor would be sending his thunderbolts down to the fields of Cent before the summer evening was over. 'Æthelflaed is married,' I said gently.

'To a vicious bastard,' Erik said angrily.

'And her father,' I went on, 'regards marriage as sacred.'

'Alfred won't fetch her back from Northumbria,' Erik said confidently, 'no West Saxon army could reach that far.'

'He will send priests to gnaw her conscience, though,' I said, 'and how do you know he won't send men to fetch her? It doesn't have to be an army. One crew of determined men might be enough.'

'All I ask,' Erik said, 'is a chance! A hall in some valley, fields to till, beasts to raise, a place to be at peace!'

I said nothing for a while. Erik, I thought, was building a ship in his dreams, a beautiful ship, a swift-hulled ship of elegance, but it was all a dream! I closed my eyes, trying to frame my words. 'Æthelflaed,' I finally said, 'is a prize. She has value. She is a king's daughter and her marriage portion was land. She's rich, she's beautiful, she's valuable. Any man who wants to be rich will know where she is. Any scavenger wanting a fast ransom will know where to find her. You will never have peace.' I turned and looked at him. 'Every night when you bar your door you will fear the enemies in the dark and every day you will look for enemies. There will be no peace for you, none.'

'Dunholm,' he said flatly.

I half smiled. 'I know the place,' I said.

'Then you know that it is a fortress that cannot be captured,' Erik said stubbornly.

311

'I captured it,' I said.

'And no one else will do what you did,' Erik said, 'not till the world falls. We can live in Dunholm.'

'Ragnar holds Dunholm.'

'Then I will swear oaths to him,' Erik said fervently, 'I will become his man, I will swear my life to him.'

I thought about that for a moment, testing Erik's wild dream against the harsh realities of this life. Dunholm, cradled in its loop of the river and poised on its high crag, was indeed almost unassailable. A man might think of dying in his bed if he held Dunholm, because even a handful of troops was sufficient to defend the steep rocky path that was its only approach. And Ragnar, I knew, would be amused by Erik and Æthelflaed, and so I felt myself being seduced by Erik's passion. Maybe his dream was not as crazy as I thought? 'But how,' I asked, 'do you take Æthelflaed from here without your brother knowing?'

'With your help,' he said.

And with that answer I could hear the three Norns laughing. A horn blew in the camp, a summons, I supposed, to the feast that Sigefrid had promised. 'I am sworn to Alfred,' I said flatly.

'I don't ask you to break that oath,' Erik said.

'Yes, you do!' I said sharply. 'Alfred gave me a mission. I have fulfilled half of it. The other half is to retrieve his daughter!'

Erik's big fists curled and uncurled on the palisade's top. 'Three thousand pounds of silver,' he said, 'and five hundred pounds of gold. Think how many men that will buy.'

'I have thought of it.'

'A crew of seasoned warriors can be purchased for a pound of gold,' Erik said.

'True.'

'And we have enough men now to challenge Wessex.'

'You can challenge Wessex, but not defeat it.'

312

'But we will, when we have the gold and the men.'

'True,' I allowed again.

'And the gold will bring more men,' Erik went on relentlessly, 'and more ships, and either this autumn or next spring we will lead a horde into Wessex. We will make the army you defeated at Ethandun look small. We shall blacken the land. We shall bring spears and axes and swords to Wessex. We will burn your towns, enslave your children, use your women, take your land and kill your men. Is that what serving Alfred means to you?'

'That is what your brother plans?'

'And to do it,' Erik said, ignoring my question for he knew I already knew its answer, 'he must sell Æthelflaed back to her father.'

'Yes,' I acknowledged. If no ransom was paid then the men already encamped in and around Beamfleot would vanish like dew on a hot morning. No more ships would come and Wessex would not be threatened.

'Your oath, as I understand it,' Erik said respectfully, 'is to serve Alfred of Wessex. Do you serve him, Lord Uhtred, by allowing my brother to become rich enough to destroy him?'

So love, I thought, had turned Erik against his brother. Love would make him slash a blade through every oath he had ever sworn. Love has power over power itself. The horn blew again, more urgently. Men were hurrying towards the great hall. 'Your brother,' I said, 'knows you love Æthelflaed?'

'He believes I love her for now, but will lose her for silver. He thinks I use her for my pleasure and he is amused by that.'

'And do you use her?' I asked harshly, looking into his honest eyes.

'Is that your business?' he asked defiantly.

'No,' I said, 'but you do want my help.'

He hesitated, then nodded. 'I would not call it that,' he said, sounding defensive, 'but we love each other.'

So Æthelflaed had drunk the bitter water before the sin and that, I thought, was very clever of her. I smiled for her, then went to Sigefrid's feast.

Æthelflaed was seated in the place of honour to Sigefrid's right, and I was next to her. Erik was on the farther side of Sigefrid, with Haesten beside him. Æthelflaed, I noticed, never looked at Erik. No one watching, and plenty of men in the hall were curious about the King of Wessex's daughter, could surely have guessed that she had become his lover.

The Northmen know how to give a feast. The food was plentiful, the ale was generous and the entertainment diverting. There were jugglers and stilt walkers, musicians and acrobats, and lunatics who dissolved the lower tables into gusts of laughter. 'We should not laugh at the mad,' Æthelflaed told me. She had hardly eaten, except to nibble at a bowl of seethed cockles.

'They get treated well,' I said, 'and it's surely better to be fed and housed than left to the beasts.' I was watching a naked madman convulsively search his groin. He kept peering around at the laughing tables, unable to understand the noise. A tangle-haired woman, egged on by raucous shouts, took off her clothes one by one, not knowing why she did it.

Æthelflaed stared at the table. 'There are monasteries that will look after the insane,' she said.

'Not where the Danes rule,' I said.

She was silent for a while. Two dwarves were dragging the now naked woman to the naked man and the watching men were collapsing with laughter. Æthelflaed looked up

314

briefly, shuddered and stared down at the table again. 'You talked to Erik?' she asked. We could talk English safely for no one could overhear us, and even if they could they would not have understood most of what we said.

'As you meant me to,' I observed, realising that was why she had insisted on taking Father Willibald into the hall. 'Did you make a proper confession?'

'Is that any business of yours?'

'No,' I said, then laughed.

She looked at me and offered a very shy grin. She blushed. 'So will you help us?'

'To do what?'

She frowned. 'Erik didn't tell you?'

'He said you wanted my help, but what sort of help?'

'Help us to leave here,' she said.

'And what will your father do to me if I help you?' I asked, and got no answer. 'I thought you hated the Danes.'

'Erik is Norse,' she said.

'Danes, Norse, Northmen, Vikings, pagans,' I said, 'they're all your father's enemies.'

She glanced down at the open space beside the hearth where the two naked lunatics were now wrestling instead of making love as the audience had doubtless anticipated. The man was much bigger, but more stupid, and the woman, to huge cheers, was beating him on the head with a handful of floor rushes. 'Why do they let them do that?' Æthelflaed asked.

'Because it amuses them,' I said, 'and because they don't have a pack of black-robed clergy telling them what's right and what's wrong, and that, my lady, is why I like them.'

She looked down again. 'I didn't want to like Erik,' she said in a very small voice.

'But you did.'

There were tears in her eyes. 'I couldn't help it,' she said.

315

'I prayed that it wouldn't happen, but the more I prayed the more I thought about him.'

'And so you love him,' I said.

'Yes.'

'He's a good man,' I assured her.

'You think so?' she asked eagerly.

'I do, truly.'

'And he's going to become a Christian,' she went on enthusiastically. 'He's promised me that. He wants to. Really!'

That did not surprise me. Erik had long shown a fascination with Christianity, and I doubted it had taken much persuasion on Æthelflaed's part. 'And what of Æthelred?' I asked her.

'I hate him,' she hissed those words so vehemently that Sigefrid turned to stare at her. He shrugged, unable to comprehend her, then looked back at the naked fight.

'You will lose your family,' I warned her.

'I will make a family,' she said firmly. 'Erik and I will make a family.'

'And you'll live among the Danes whom you told me you hate.'

'You live among the Christians, Lord Uhtred,' she said with a flash of her old mischief.

I smiled at that. 'You're sure about this?' I asked her, 'about Erik?'

'Yes,' she said intensely, and that was love speaking, of course.

I sighed. 'If I can,' I said, 'I will help you.'

She laid a small hand on mine. 'Thank you.'

Two dogs had begun to fight now and the guests were cheering the beasts on. Rushlights were lit and candles brought to the top table as the summer evening dimmed outside. More ale came, and birch wine too, and the first

316

drunks were singing raucously. 'They'll start fighting soon,'
I told Æthelflaed, and they did. Four men suffered broken
bones before the feast was over, while another had an eye
gouged out before his angry drunken assailant was pulled
away from him. Steapa was seated next to Weland, and the
two men, though they spoke different languages, were
sharing a silver-rimmed drinking horn and appeared to be
making disparaging comments about the brawlers who spilt
across the floor in drunken rage. Weland was obviously
drunk himself, for he draped a huge arm around Steapa's
shoulders and began to sing.

'You sound like a calf being gelded!' Sigefrid roared at
Weland, then demanded that a real singer be fetched, and
so a blind skald was given a chair by the hearth and he
struck his harp and chanted a song of Sigefrid's prowess. He
told of the Franks whom Sigefrid had killed, of the Saxons
cut down by Sigefrid's sword, Fear-Giver, and of the Frisian
women who had been widowed by the bear-cloaked
Norseman. The poem mentioned many of Sigefrid's men by
name, recounting their heroism in battle, and as each new
name was chanted the man would stand and his friends
would cheer him. If the named hero was dead then the
listening men beat three times on the tables so that the dead
man would hear the solemn ovation in Odin's hall. But the
biggest cheers were for Sigefrid, who hoisted an ale-horn
every time his name was mentioned.

I stayed sober. That was hard, for I was tempted to match
Sigefrid horn for horn, but I knew I had to return to Lundene
next morning and that meant Erik had to finish his talk
with me that same night, though in truth the eastern sky
was already lightening by the time I left the hall. Æthelflaed,
escorted by sober and older guards, had left for her bed
hours before. Drunken men were sprawled in noisy sleep
beneath the benches as I walked out, while Sigefrid was

slumped on the table. He had opened one eye and frowned as I left. 'We have agreement?' he asked sleepily.

'We have an agreement,' I confirmed.

'Bring the money, Saxon,' he growled, and fell back to sleep.

Erik was waiting for me outside Æthelflaed's quarters. I had expected him to be there, and we took our old places on the rampart from where I watched the grey light spread like a stain across the calm waters of the estuary.

'That's *Wave-Tamer*,' Erik said, nodding down at the ships drawn up on the muddy beach. He might have been able to discern the beautiful boat he had made, but to me the whole fleet was nothing but black shapes in the grey. 'I have scraped her hull clean,' he told me, 'caulked her, and made her swift again.'

'Your crew can be trusted?'

'They are my oath-men. They can be trusted.' Erik paused. A small wind lifted his dark hair. 'But what they will not do,' he went on in a low voice, 'is fight my brother's men.'

'They might have to.'

'They will defend themselves,' he said, 'but not attack. There are kinsmen on both sides.'

I stretched, yawned, and thought of the long ride home to Lundene. 'So your problem,' I said, 'is the ship that blocks the channel?'

'Which is manned by my brother's men.'

'Not Haesten's?'

'I would kill his men,' he said bitterly, 'there's no kinship there.'

Nor affection either, I noted. 'So you want me to destroy the ship?' I asked him.

'I want you to open the channel,' he corrected me.

I stared at that dark blocking ship with her reinforced sheerline. 'Why don't you just demand that they get out of your way?' I asked. That seemed to me to be the least complicated and safest way for Erik to escape. The chained ship's crew was accustomed to moving the heavy hull to allow vessels to enter or leave the creek, so why would they stop Erik?

'No ships are to sail before the ransom arrives,' Erik explained.

'None?'

'None,' he said flatly.

And that made some sense, because what was to stop some enterprising man taking three or four ships upriver to wait in a reed-shrouded creek for Alfred's treasure fleet to pass, then slide out, oars beating, swords drawn and men howling? Sigefrid had pinned his monstrous ambition on the arrival of the ransom and he would not risk losing it to some Viking even more scoundrelly than himself, and that thought suggested the person who probably embodied Sigefrid's fear. 'Haesten?' I asked Erik.

He nodded. 'A sly man.'

'Sly,' I agreed, 'and untrustworthy. An oath-breaker.'

'He will share the ransom, of course,' Erik said, ignoring the fact that if he got his wish then no ransom would ever be paid, 'but I'm certain he would rather have it all.'

'So no ships sail,' I said, 'until you sail. But can you take Æthelflaed to your ship without your brother knowing?'

'Yes,' he said. He drew a knife from its sheath on his belt. 'It's a fortnight till the next full moon,' he went on, then scored a deep mark in the sharpened top of an oak log. 'That's today,' he said, tapping the fresh cut, then carved another deep mark with the blade's sharp edge. 'Tomorrow's dawn,' he continued, indicating the new cut, then went on slashing the palisade's top until he had made seven raw scars in the timbers. 'Will you come at dawn one week from now?'

I nodded cautiously. 'But the moment I attack,' I pointed out, 'someone blows a horn and wakes the camp.'

'We'll be afloat,' he said, 'ready to go. No one can reach you from the camp before you're back out at sea.' He looked worried at my doubts. 'I'll pay you!'

I smiled at those words. Dawn was bleaching the world, colouring the low long wisps of cloud with streaks of pale gold and edges of shining silver. 'Æthelflaed's happiness is my pay,' I said. 'And one week from today,' I went on, 'I'll open your channel for you. You can sail away together, make landfall at Gyruum, ride hard to Dunholm and give Ragnar my greetings.'

'You'll send him a message?' Erik asked anxiously, 'to warn him of our coming?'

I shook my head. 'Carry the message for me,' I said, and some instinct made me turn to see that Haesten was watching us. He was standing with two companions outside the big hall where he was strapping on his swords, brought by Sigefrid's steward from the place where we had all surrendered our weapons before the feast. There was nothing strange in what Haesten did, except my senses prickled because he seemed so watchful. I had a horrid suspicion that he knew what Erik and I talked about. He went on looking at me. He was very still, but at last he gave me a low, mocking bow and walked away. Eilaf the Red, I saw, was one of his two companions. 'Does Haesten know about you and Æthelflaed?' I asked Erik.

'Of course not. He just thinks I'm responsible for guarding her.'

'He knows you like her?'

'That's all he knows,' Erik insisted.

Sly, untrustworthy Haesten, who owed me his life. Who had broken his oath. Whose ambitions probably outstretched even Sigefrid's dreams. I watched him until he went through the doorway of what I assumed was his own hall. 'Be careful with Haesten,' I warned Erik, 'I think he is easily under-estimated.'

'He's a weasel,' Erik said, dismissing my fears. 'What message do I take to Ragnar?' he asked.

'Tell Ragnar,' I said, 'that his sister is happy and let Æthelflaed give him news of her.' There was no point in writing anything, even if I had possessed parchment or ink, because Ragnar could not read, but Æthelflaed knew Thyra and her news of Beocca's wife would convince Ragnar that the runaway lovers told the truth. 'And one week from now,' I said, 'as the upper edge of the sun touches the world's rim, be ready.'

Erik thought for a heartbeat, making a fast computation in his head. 'It will be low tide,' he said, 'slack water. We'll be ready.'

For madness, I thought, or for love. Madness. Love. Madness.

And how the three sisters at the world's root must have been laughing.

I spoke little as we rode home. Finan chattered happily, saying how generous Sigefrid had been with his food, ale and female slaves. I half listened until the Irishman finally sensed my mood and fell into a companionable silence. It was not till we were in sight of the banners on Lundene's eastern ramparts that I gestured he should ride ahead with me, leaving my other men out of earshot. 'Six days from now,' I said, 'you must have the *Sea-Eagle* ready for a voyage. We'll need ale and food for three days.' I did not expect to be away that long, but it was good to be prepared. 'Clean her hull between tides,' I went on, 'and make sure every man is sober when we leave. Sober, with weapons sharpened, and battle-ready.'

Finan half smiled, but said nothing. We were riding through hovels that had sprung up on the edges of the marshlands beside the Temes. Many of the folk who lived here were slaves who had escaped their Danish masters in East Anglia, and they made a living by scratching through the refuse of the city, though a few had planted tiny fields of rye, barley or oats. The meagre harvest was being gathered and I listened to the scrape of blades cutting through the handfuls of stalks.

'No one in Lundene is to know we're sailing,' I told Finan.

'They won't,' the Irishman said grimly.

'Battle-ready,' I told him again.

'They'll be that, so they will.'

I rode in silence for a while. People saw my mail and scuttled out of our way. They touched their foreheads or knelt in the mud, then scrambled when I threw pennies to them. It was evening and the sun was already behind the great cloud of smoke rising from Lundene's cooking fires, and the stench of the city drifted sour and thick in the air. 'Did you see that ship blocking the channel at Beamfleot?' I asked Finan.

'I took a squint at her, lord.'

'If we attacked her,' I said, 'they'd see us coming. They'd be behind that raised sheerline.'

'Almost a man's height above us,' Finan agreed, revealing that he had done more than just take a squint.

'So think how we might get that ship out of the channel.'

'Not that we're thinking of doing that, lord, are we?' he asked slyly.

'Of course not,' I said, 'but think on it anyway.'

Then a squeal of ungreased hinges announced the opening of the nearest gate and we rode into the city's gloom.

Alfred had been waiting for us, and messengers had already informed him of our return so that, even before I could greet Gisela, I was summoned to the high palace. I went with Father Willibald, Steapa and Finan. The king waited for us in the great hall that was lit with the high candles by which he reckoned the passing time. Wax ran thick down the banded shafts and a servant was trimming the wicks so that the light stayed steady. Alfred had been writing, but he stopped as we entered. Æthelred was also there, as were Brother Asser, Father Beocca and Bishop Erkenwald.

'Well,' Alfred snapped. It was not anger, but worry that made his voice so sharp.

'She lives,' I said, 'she is unharmed, she is treated with the respect due to her rank, she is properly and well guarded, and they will sell her back to us.'

'Thank God,' Alfred said, and made the sign of the cross. 'Thank God,' he repeated, and I thought he was going to drop to his knees. Æthelred said nothing, but just stared at me with serpent eyes.

'How much?' Bishop Erkenwald demanded.

'Three thousand pounds of silver and five hundred of gold,' I said, and explained that the first metal had to be delivered by the next full moon and the balance was to be taken down-river one month later. 'And the Lady Æthelflaed will not be released until the last coin is paid,' I finished.

Bishop Erkenwald and Brother Asser both winced at the amount of the ransom, though Alfred showed no such reaction. 'We will be paying for our own destruction,' Bishop Erkenwald growled.

'My daughter is dear to me,' Alfred said mildly.

'With that money,' the bishop warned, 'they will raise thousands of men!'

'And without that money?' Alfred turned to me, 'what will happen to her?'

'Humiliation,' I said. In truth Æthelflaed might have found

happiness with Erik if the ransom was not paid, but I could hardly say as much. Instead I described the fate that Haesten had suggested so wolfishly. 'She'll be taken to every place where Northmen live,' I said, 'and she will be shown naked to mocking crowds.' Alfred winced. 'Then,' I went on remorselessly, 'she'll be whored to the highest bidders.'

Æthelred gazed at the floor, the churchmen were silent. 'It is the dignity of Wessex that is at stake,' Alfred said quietly.

'So men must die for the dignity of Wessex?' Bishop Erkenwald asked.

'Yes!' Alfred was suddenly angry. 'A country is its history, bishop, the sum of all its stories. We are what our fathers made us, their victories gave us what we have, and you would make me leave my descendants a tale of humiliation? You want men to tell how Wessex was made a laughing stock to howling heathens? That is a story, bishop, that would never die, and if that tale is told then whenever men think of Wessex they will think of a Princess of Wessex paraded naked to pagans. Whenever they think of England, they will think of that!' And that, I thought, was interesting. We rarely used that name in those days; England. That was a dream, but Alfred, in his anger, had lifted a curtain on his dream and I knew then he wanted his army to continue north, ever north, until there was no more Wessex, no more East Anglia, no more Mercia and no more Northumbria, only England.

'Lord King,' Erkenwald said with unnatural humility, 'I do not know if there will be a Wessex if we pay the pagans to raise an army.'

'Raising an army takes time,' Alfred said firmly, 'and no pagan army can attack until after the harvest. And once the harvest is gathered we can raise the fyrd. We will have the men to oppose them.' That was true, but most of our men would be untrained farmers, while Sigefrid would bring howling, hungry Northmen who had been bred to the sword. Alfred turned on his son-in-law. 'And I will expect the fyrd of southern Mercia to be at our side.'

'It will be, lord,' Æthelred said enthusiastically. There was no sign on his face of the sickness that had assailed him the last time I had seen him in this hall. His colour was back, and his jaunty confidence seemed undiminished.

'Maybe this is God's doing,' Alfred said, speaking again to Erkenwald. 'In His mercy He has offered our enemies a chance to gather in their thousands so that we can defeat them in one great battle.' His voice strengthened with that thought. 'The Lord is on my side,' he said firmly, 'I will not fear!'

'The word of the Lord,' Brother Asser said piously, making the sign of the cross.

'Amen,' Æthelred said, 'and amen. We shall defeat them, lord!'

'But before you win that great victory,' I said to Æthelred, taking a malicious pleasure in what I was about to say, 'you have a duty to perform. You are to deliver the ransom in person.'

'By God, I will not!' Æthelred said indignantly, then caught Alfred's eye and subsided back into his chair.

'And you are to kneel to Sigefrid,' I said, twisting the knife.

Even Alfred looked appalled at that. 'Sigefrid insists on that condition?' he asked.

'He does, lord,' I said, 'even though I argued with him! I appealed, lord, and I argued and I pleaded, but he would not yield.'

Æthelred was just staring at me with horror on his face.

'Then so be it,' Alfred said. 'Sometimes the Lord God asks more than we can bear, but for His glorious sake we must endure it.'

'Amen,' I said fervently, deserving and receiving a sceptical look from the king.

They talked for as long as it took one of Alfred's banded candles to burn through two hours' worth of wax, and it was all wasted talk; talk of how the money was to be raised, and how it was to be transported to Lundene and how it was to be delivered to Beamfleot. I made suggestions while Alfred wrote notes on the margin of his parchment, and it was all useless effort because if I was successful then no ransom would be paid and Æthelflaed would not return and Alfred's throne would be safe.

And I was to make it all possible.

In one week's time.

Eleven

Darkness. The last light of day was just gone, and a new darkness now shrouded us.

There was moonlight, but the moon was hidden so that the cloud edges were silvered, and beneath that vast sky of silver, black and starlight, the *Sea-Eagle* slid down the Temes.

Ralla was at the steering-oar. He was a far better seaman than I could ever hope to be, and I trusted him to take us around the river's sweeping bends in the blackness. Most of the time it was impossible to tell where the water ended and the marshes began, but Ralla seemed unconcerned. He stood with legs spread and one foot tapping the deck in time to the slow beat of the oars. He said little, but now and then made tiny course corrections with the oar's long loom and never once did a blade touch the shelving mud at the river's margins. Occasionally the moon would slither out from behind a cloud and the water would suddenly gleam a glittering silver before us. There were red sparks on the banks that came and went, small fires in the marsh hovels.

We were using the last of the ebb to take us downriver. The intermittent sheen of moon on water showed the banks going ever farther apart as the river widened imperceptibly into the sea. I kept glancing northwards, waiting to see the glow in the sky that would betray the fires in and around the high camp at Beamfleot.

'How many pagan ships at Beamfleot?' Ralla suddenly asked me.

'Sixty-four a week ago,' I said, 'but probably nearer eighty by now. Maybe a hundred or more?'

'And just us, eh?' he asked, amused.

'Just us,' I agreed.

'And there'll be more ships up the coast,' Ralla said. 'I heard they were making a camp at Sceobyrig?'

'They've been there a month now,' I said, 'and there's at least fifteen crews there. Probably thirty by now.' Sceobyrig was a desolate spit of mud and muddy land a few miles east of Beamfleot and the fifteen Danish ships had landed there and made a fort of earth walls and wooden posts. I suspected they had chosen Sceobyrig because there was scarcely any room left in Beamfleot's creek any more, and because their proximity to Sigefrid's fleet offered them his protection. Doubtless they paid him silver, and doubtless they hoped to follow him into Wessex to snap up what plunder they could. On the banks of every sea, and in camps upriver, and all across the Northmen's world, the news was spreading that the kingdom of Wessex was vulnerable and so the warriors were gathering.

'But we're not going to fight today?' Ralla asked.

'I hope not,' I said, 'fighting's very dangerous.'

Ralla chuckled, but said nothing.

'There shouldn't be any fighting,' I said, after a pause.

'Because if there is,' Ralla pointed out, 'we have no priest aboard.'

'We never do have a priest aboard,' I said defensively.

'But we should, lord,' he remonstrated.

'Why?' I asked belligerently.

'Because you want to die with a sword in your hand,' Ralla said reprovingly, 'and we like to die shriven.'

His words chided me. My duty was to these men, and if they died without the benefit of whatever a priest did to the dying, then I had failed them. For a moment I did not know what to say, then an idea sprang unbidden into my head. 'Brother Osferth can be our priest today,' I said.

'I will,' Osferth said from a rower's bench, and I was pleased with that reply because at last he was willing to do something I knew he did not wish to do. I later discovered that, as a man who had only ever been a failed novice monk, he had no power to administer the Christian sacraments, but my men believed he was closer to their god than they were and that, as it turned out, was good enough.

'But I don't expect to fight,' I said firmly.

A dozen men, those closest to the steering platform, were listening. Finan was with me, of course, and Cerdic and Sihtric and Rypere and Clapa. They were my house-hold troops, my house carls, my companions, my blood brothers, my oath-men, and they had followed me to sea this night and they trusted me, even though they did not know where we sailed or what we did.

'So what are we doing?' Ralla asked.

I paused, knowing the answer would excite them. 'We're rescuing the Lady Æthelflaed,' I finally said.

I heard gasps from the listening men, then the murmur of voices as that news was passed up the benches to the *Sea-Eagle*'s bows. My men knew this voyage meant trouble, and they had been intrigued by my savage imposition of secrecy, and they must have guessed that we sailed in connection with Æthelflaed's plight, but now I had confirmed it.

The steering-oar creaked as Ralla made a slight correction. 'How?' he asked.

'Any day now,' I said, ignoring his question and speaking loudly enough for every man in the boat to hear me, 'the king starts to collect the ransom for his daughter. If you have ten arm rings, he will want four of them! If you have silver hoarded, the king's men will find it and take their share! But what we do today could stop that!'

Another murmur. There was already a deep unhappiness in Wessex at the thought of the money that would be forced from landowners and merchants. Alfred had pledged his own wealth, but he would need more, much more, and the only reason the collection had not already begun was the arguments that raged among his advisers. Some wanted the church to contribute because, despite the clergy's insistence that they had no treasure, every man knew that the monasteries were stuffed with wealth. The church's response had been to threaten excommunication on anyone who dared touch so much as one silver penny that belonged to God or, more particularly, to God's bishops and abbots. I, even though I secretly hoped that no ransom would be necessary, had recommended raising the whole amount from the church, but that wise advice, of course, had been ignored.

'And if the ransom is paid,' I went on, 'then our enemies will be rich enough to hire ten thousand swords! We will have war all across Wessex! Your houses will be burned, your women raped, your children stolen and your wealth confiscated. But what we do today could stop that!'

I exaggerated a little, but not by much. The ransom could certainly raise five thousand more spears, axes and swords and that was why the Vikings were gathering in the estuary of the Temes. They smelt weakness, and weakness meant blood, and blood meant wealth. The longships were coming south, their keels ploughing the sea as they headed for Beamfleot and then for Wessex.

'But the Northmen are greedy!' I continued. 'They know that in Æthelflaed they have a girl of high value, and they are snarling at each other like hungry dogs! Well, one of them is ready to betray the others! At dawn today he will bring Æthelflaed out of the camp! He will give her to us and he will accept a much lower ransom! He would rather keep that smaller ransom all to himself than take a share of the larger! He will become wealthy! But he will not be wealthy enough to buy an army!'

That was the story I had decided to tell. I could not return to Lundene and say I had helped Æthelflaed run away with her lover, so instead I would pretend that Erik had offered to betray his brother and that I had sailed to assist that treachery, and that Erik had then betrayed me by breaking the agreement we had made. Instead of giving me Æthelflaed, I would claim he had just sailed away with her. Alfred would still be furious with me, but he could not accuse me of betraying Wessex. I had even brought a big wooden chest aboard. It was filled with sand, and locked with two great hasps secured with iron pins that had been hammered into circles so that the lid could not be opened. Every man had seen the chest brought onto the *Sea-Eagle* and there stowed under her steering platform, and they would surely think that big box carried Erik's price.

'Before dawn,' I went on, 'the Lady Æthelflaed will be taken to a ship! As the sun touches the sky's edge, that ship will bring her out! But in their way is a blocking ship, a ship chained so she lies from shore to shore across the creek's mouth. Our job is to clear that ship out of the way! That is all! We just have to move that one ship and the Lady Æthelflaed will be free, and we shall take her back to Lundene and we'll be celebrated as heroes! The king will be grateful!'

They liked that. They liked the thought that they would

be rewarded by the king, and I felt a pang because I knew we would only provoke Alfred's anger, though we would also save him the necessity of raising the ransom.

'I did not tell you this before,' I said, 'nor did I tell Alfred, because if I had told you then one of you or one of the king's men would have got drunk and blabbered the news in a tavern and Sigefrid's spies would have told Sigefrid and we would reach Beamfleot to find an army waiting to greet us! Instead they're asleep! And we shall rescue Æthelflaed!'

They cheered that. Only Ralla was silent and, when the clamour ended, he asked a soft question. 'And how do we move that ship?' he asked. 'She's bigger than us, her sides have been raised, she carries a fighting crew, and they won't be asleep.'

'We don't do it,' I said. 'I do it. Clapa? Rypere? You two will help me. The three of us will move the ship.'

And Æthelflaed would be free, and love would win, and the wind would always blow warm, and there would be food all winter, and none of us would ever grow old, and silver would grow on trees, and gold would appear like dew on grass, and the lovers' bright stars would dazzle for ever.

It was all so simple.

As we rowed on eastwards.

Before leaving Lundene we had taken down the *Sea-Eagle*'s mast that now lay in crutches along the ship's centre-line. I had not put her beast-heads on her stem or stern because I wanted her to lie low in the water. I wanted her to be a black shape against blackness, and with no rearing eagle's head or high mast to show above the horizon. We came in stealth before the dawn. We were the Shadow-Walkers of the sea.

And I touched Serpent-Breath's hilt and felt no tingle there, no singing, no hunger for blood and I took comfort from that. I thought we would open the creek and watch Æthelflaed sail to freedom and that Serpent-Breath would sleep silently in her fleece-lined scabbard.

Then, at last, I saw the higher glow in the sky, the dull red glow that marked where fires burned in Sigefrid's hilltop encampment. The glow grew brighter as we rowed through the slack water of high tide, and beyond it, on the hills that slowly fell away to the east, were more reflections of fire on clouds. Those red glows marked the sites of the new encampments that stretched from high Beamfleot to low Sceobyrig. 'Even without the ransom,' Ralla remarked to me, 'they might be tempted to attack.'

'They might,' I agreed, though I doubted Sigefrid had enough men yet to feel sure of success. Wessex, with its newly built burhs, was a hard place to attack, and I guessed Sigefrid would want at least three thousand more men before he rolled the dice of war, and to get those men he needed the ransom. 'You know what to do?' I asked Ralla.

'I know,' he said patiently, also knowing that my question had been provoked by nervousness rather than by necessity. 'I'll go seaward of Caninga,' he said, 'and collect you at the eastern end.'

'And if the channel isn't open?' I asked.

I sensed that he grinned in the darkness. 'Then I'll collect you,' he said, 'and you make that decision.'

Because if I failed to move the ship that blocked the channel then Æthelflaed would be trapped in the creek and I would have to decide whether to commit Sea-Eagle to a fight against a ship with higher sides and an angry crew. It was not a fight I wanted and I doubted we could win it, which meant I had to open the channel before such a fight became necessary.

'Slow!' Ralla called to the oarsmen. He had turned the ship northwards and now we rowed slow and cautious towards Caninga's black shore. 'You'll get wet,' he told me.

'How long till dawn?'

'Five hours? Six?' he guessed.

'Long enough,' I said, and just then the Sea-Eagle's bows touched the shelving mud and her long hull shivered.

'Back oars!' Ralla shouted, and the oar banks churned the shallow water to pull the bows away from that treacherous shore. 'Go quickly,' he told me, 'tide falls fast here. Don't want to be stranded.'

I led Clapa and Rypere to the bows. I had debated whether to wear mail, hoping that I would need to do no fighting in the approaching summer dawn, but in the end caution had prevailed and I wore a mail coat, two swords but had no helmet. I feared my helmet, with its bright wolf-symbol, would reflect the night's small light, and so I wore a dark leather helmet liner instead. I also wore the black cloak that Gisela had woven for me, that dark night-hiding cloak with its savage stab of lightning running down the back from nape to hem. Rypere and Clapa also wore dark cloaks that covered their mail and each of them had swords, while Clapa carried a huge, beard-bladed war axe strapped to his back.

'You should let me come,' Finan said to me.

'You're in charge here,' I told him. 'And if we get into trouble you might have to abandon us. That will be your decision.'

'Back oars!' Ralla shouted again, and the Sea-Eagle retreated another few feet from the threat of being grounded on the falling tide.

'We won't abandon you,' Finan said, and held out a hand. I clasped it, then let him lower me over the ship's side where I splashed into a soggy mess of mud and water.

'See you at dawn,' I called up to Finan's dark shape, then led Clapa and Rypere across the wide mudflats. I heard the creak and splashing of *Sea-Eagle*'s oars as Ralla backed her offshore, but when I turned she had already vanished.

We had landed at the western end of Caninga, the island that bordered Beamfleot's creek, and we had come ashore a long way from where Sigefrid's ships were moored or beached. We were far enough away so that the sentries on the fort's high walls would not have seen our dark dismasted ship come to the dark land, or so I prayed, and now we had a long walk. We crossed the wide, glistening, moon-rippled stretch of mud that widened as the tide receded, and in places we could not walk, but only struggle. We waded and tripped, fought the sucking mud, we cursed and splashed. That foreshore was neither land nor water, but a sticky, clinging morass, and so I hurried on until, at last, there was more land than water and the shrieks of woken birds surrounded us. The night air was filled with the beat of their wings and the shrillness of their protests. That noise, I thought, would surely alert the enemy, but all I could do was strike inland, praying for higher ground, and at last the going became easier, though still the land smelled of salt. At the highest tides, Ralla had told me, Caninga could vanish entirely beneath the waves and I thought of the Danes I had drowned on the western sea-marshes when I had lured them into just such a rising tide. That had been before Ethandun when Wessex had seemed doomed, but Wessex still lived and the Danes had died.

We found a path. Sheep were sleeping among the tussocks and this was a sheep track, though it was a crude and treacherous path for it was constantly interrupted by ditches through which the tendrils of the falling tide gurgled. I wondered if a shepherd was close by. Perhaps these sheep, being on an island, did not need guarding from wolves, which would mean no shepherd and, better, no dogs to wake and bark. But if there were dogs, they slept as we moved eastwards. I looked for the *Sea-Eagle*, but though there was moonshine glittering wide on the estuary, I could not see her.

After a while we rested, first kicking three sleeping sheep awake so we could occupy their patches of warm dry earth. Clapa was soon asleep and snoring, while I gazed out to the Temes trying once more to see the *Sea-Eagle*, but she was a shadow among shadows. I was thinking of Ragnar, my friend, and how he would react when Erik and Alfred's daughter turned up at Dunholm. He would be amused, I knew, but how long would that amusement last? Alfred would send envoys to Guthred, King of Northumbria, demanding his daughter's return, and every Northman with a sword would eye Dunholm's crag hungrily. Madness, I thought, as the wind rustled across the stiff marsh grasses.

'What's happening there, lord?' Rypere asked, startling me. He had sounded alarmed and I turned from searching the water to see a huge blaze springing from Beamfleot's hilltop. Flames were leaping into the dark sky, outlining the ramparts of the fort, and above those tortuous flames bright sparks whirled in the thick pillar of fire-lit smoke that churned above Sigefrid's hall.

I swore, kicked Clapa awake and stood.

Sigefrid's hall was ablaze, and that meant the whole encampment was awake, but whether the fire was an accident or deliberate, I could not tell. Perhaps this was the diversion that Erik had planned so he could smuggle Æthelflaed from her smaller hall, but somehow I did not think Erik would risk burning his brother to death. 'Whatever caused that fire,' I said grimly, 'is bad news.'

The fire had only just taken hold, but the thatch must

have been dry because the flames were spreading with extraordinary swiftness. The blaze grew larger, lighting the hilltop and throwing garish shadows across Caninga's low, marshy land. 'They'll see us, lord,' Clapa said nervously.

'We have to risk that,' I said, and hoped that the men on the ship that blocked the channel would be watching the fire instead of looking for enemies on Caninga.

I planned to reach the creek's southern bank where the great chain that held the ship against the currents was looped about its huge post. Cut or release that chain and the ship must drift with the outgoing tide and so swing open like a great gate as her bow chain held her fast to the post on the northern bank.

'Let's go,' I said, and we followed the sheep track, our journey now made easy by the light thrown by the great fire. I kept glancing eastwards where the sky was turning pale. Dawn was close, but the sun would not show for a long time. I thought I saw *Sea-Eagle* once, her low shape stark against the shimmer of grey and black, but I could not be certain of what I saw.

As we drew closer to the moored guard-ship we moved off the sheep track to push our way through reed beds that grew high enough to conceal us. Birds screamed again. We stopped every few paces and I would look over the reeds and see the crew of the blocking ship staring up at the high burning hill. The fire was vast now, an inferno in the sky, scorching the high clouds red. We reached the edge of the reeds, and crouched there, a hundred paces from the huge post that tethered the ship's stern.

'We might not need your axe,' I told Clapa. We had brought the axe to try to chop through the heavy iron links.

'You're going to bite the chain, lord?' Rypere asked, amused.

I gave him a friendly cuff around the head. 'If you stand

on Clapa's shoulders,' I said, 'you should be able to lift that chain clean off the post. It'll be quicker.'

'We should do it before it gets light,' Clapa said.

'Mustn't give them time to re-moor the ship,' I said, and wondered if I should have brought more men ashore, and then knew I should.

Because we were not alone on Caninga.

I saw the other men and laid a hand on Clapa's arm to silence him. And everything that had seemed easy became difficult.

I saw men running down the southern bank of the creek. There were six men armed with swords and axes, six men who ran towards the post that was our goal. And I understood what happened then, or I hoped I did, but it was a moment when all the future hung in the balance. I had an instant to make a decision, and I thought of the three Norns sitting at Yggdrasil's roots and I knew that if I made the wrong choice, the choice they already knew I would make, then I could ruin all that I wanted of that morning.

Perhaps, I thought, Erik had decided to open the channel himself.

Perhaps he believed I would not come. Or perhaps he had realised that he could open the channel without attacking his brother's men. Perhaps the six men were Erik's warriors.

Or perhaps they were not.

'Kill them,' I said, hardly aware that I spoke, hardly aware of the decision I had made.

'Lord?' Clapa asked.

'Now!' I was already moving. 'Fast, come on!'

The guard-ship's crew were hurling spears at the six men, but none struck home as the three of us raced towards the post. Rypere, lithe and quick, ran ahead of me and I hauled him back with my left hand before drawing Serpent-Breath.

And so death came in the wolf-light before dawn. Death on a muddy bank. The six men reached the post before we did and one of them, a tall man, swung a war axe at the looped chain, but a spear flung from the ship thudded into his thigh and he staggered back, cursing, as his five companions turned in astonishment to face us. We had surprised them.

I screamed a huge challenge, an incoherent challenge, and leaped at the five men. It was a mad attack. A sword could have pierced my belly and left me writhing in blood, but the gods were with me. Serpent-Breath struck a shield plumb centre and the man went backwards, knocked off his feet and I followed him, trusting that Rypere and Clapa would keep his four comrades busy. Clapa was swinging his huge axe, while Rypere danced the sword-dance Finan had taught him. I slashed Serpent-Breath at the fallen man and her blade crashed on his helmet so that he fell back again and then I twisted to lunge Serpent-Breath at the tall man who had been trying to sever the chain.

He turned, his axe swinging, and there was enough light in the sky to let me see the bright red hair under his helmet's rim and the bright red beard jutting beneath the helmet's cheek-plates. He was Eilaf the Red, Haesten's oath-man, and I knew then what must have happened in this treacherous morning.

Haesten had set the fire.

And Haesten must have taken Æthelflaed.

And now he wanted the channel opened so that his ships could escape.

So now we had to keep the channel closed. We had come to open it, and now we would fight on Sigefrid's side to keep it shut up, and I rammed the sword at Eilaf who somehow sidestepped the blade, and his axe struck me at the waist, but there was no power in his blow and I scarce felt the blade's impact through my cloak and mail. A spear hissed past me, thrown from the ship, then another thudded hard into the post and stayed there, quivering. I had stumbled past Eilaf, my footing uncertain in the marshy ground.

He was quick and I had no shield. The axe swung and I ducked as I turned back to him, then thrust Serpent-Breath two-handed at his belly, but his shield took the lunge. I heard splashing behind me and I guessed the guard-ship's crew were coming to our aid. A man screamed where Clapa and Rypere fought, but I had no time to discover what happened there. I thrust again, and a sword is a faster weapon than an axe and Eilaf the Red was still drawing his right arm back and had to move the shield to deflect my blade and I flicked it up and slid it scraping and ringing across his shield's iron rim and banged her tip into his skull beneath his helmet's edge.

I felt bone break. The axe was coming, but slowly, and I caught the haft with my left hand and hauled on it as Eilaf staggered, his eyes glazed from the wound I had given him. I kicked his spear-pierced leg, wrenched Serpent-Breath free, then stabbed her down. She punctured his mail to make him jerk like an eel on a spear, then he thumped into the mud and tried to pull his axe free of my grasp. He was snarling at me, his forehead a mass of blood. I swore at him, kicked his hand free of the axe's handle, slashed Serpent-Breath down on his neck and watched him quiver. Men from the guard-ship's crew ran past me to kill Eilaf's men and I snatched Eilaf's helmet off his bloody head. It dripped with gore, but I rammed it over my leather headgear and hoped the cheek-plates would conceal my face.

The men who had come from the ship might well have seen me at Sigefrid's feast, and if they recognised me they would turn their swords on me. There were ten or eleven of the crewmen and they had killed Eilaf the Red's five companions, but not before Clapa had been given his last wound. Poor Clapa, so slow in thought, so gentle in manner, so strong in war, and now he lay, mouth open, blood spilling down his beard, and I saw a tremor in his body and jumped to him and found a fallen sword that I put into his empty right hand and closed his fingers about the hilt. His chest had been mangled by an axe blow so that ribs and lung and mail were tangled in a bloody, bubbling mess.

'Who are you?' a man shouted.

'Ragnar Olafson,' I invented a name.

'Why are you here?'

'Our ship stranded on the coast,' I said, 'we were coming to find help.'

Rypere was in tears. He was holding Clapa's left hand, saying his friend's name over and over.

We make friends in battle. We tease each other, jeer at each other and insult each other, yet we also love each other. In battle you become closer than brothers, and Clapa and Rypere were friends who had known that closeness, and now Clapa, who was Danish, was dying and Rypere, who was Saxon, was weeping. Yet his tears were not from weakness, but from rage, and as I held Clapa's dying hand tight on the sword hilt I watched Rypere turn and lift his own sword. 'Lord,' he said, and I swivelled to see still more men coming down the bank.

Haesten had sent a whole crew to open the channel. Their ship had been beached fifty paces down the bank and, beyond it, I could see a mass of other ships waiting to row out to sea when the channel was cleared. Haesten and all his men were fleeing Beamfleot, and they were taking Æthelflaed with them, and beyond the creek, on the steep hill beneath the burning hall, I could see Sigefrid and Erik's men running recklessly down the precipitous slope to assault the treacherous Haesten.

Whose men now came at us in overwhelming numbers.

'Shield wall!' a voice roared. I have no idea who shouted and only remember that I thought we must die here on this muddy bank and I patted Clapa's bloody cheek and saw his axe lying in the mud and I felt the same rage that Rypere felt. I sheathed Serpent-Breath and snatched up the huge, wide-bladed, long-bearded war axe.

Haesten's crew came screaming, driven by an urgency to escape the creek before Sigefrid's men came to slaughter them. Haesten was doing his best to slow that pursuit by burning Sigefrid's ships where they were beached on the far side of the creek. I was only dimly aware of those new fires, of flames rippling quick up tarred rigging, of smoke blowing across the incoming tide, but I had no time to watch, only to brace myself as the screaming men came closer.

And then they charged the last few paces, and we should have died there, but whoever had shouted at us to form a shield wall had chosen his place well, for one of Caninga's many ditches snaked across our front. It was not much of a ditch, scarce a muddy rivulet, but our attackers stumbled on its slippery sides and we went forward, our turn to scream, and the fury in me became the red rage of battle. I swung the huge axe at a man recovering from his stumble and my war shout rose to a scream of triumph as my blade slashed through a helmet, chopped into a skull and sliced a brain in two. Blood sluiced black into the air as I still screamed and jerked the axe free and swung it again. I knew nothing but madness, anger and desperation. Battle-joy. Blood-mad. Warriors to the slaughter, and our whole shield wall had moved to the ditch's edge where our enemy was floundering and we had a moment's furious slaughter, blades in the moonlight, blood black as pitch, and men's screams as wild as the wild birds' screams in the darkness.

Yet we were outnumbered and we were outflanked. We should have died there about the post that held the guard-ship's chain, except that more men dropped overboard from that tethered ship and came running through the shallows to assail our attackers' left flank. But Haesten's men still outnumbered us, and the men in the ranks behind pushed past their dying comrades to attack us. We were forced slowly back, as much by their weight as by their weapons. I had no shield. I was swinging the axe two-handed, snarling, keeping men at bay with the heavy blade, though a spearman, out of reach of my axe blade, jabbed repeatedly at me. Rypere, beside me, had found a fallen shield and did his best to cover me, but the spearman managed to dodge the shield and stabbed low to slice open my left calf. I hurled the axe and the heavy blade smashed into his face as I slid Serpent-Breath from her scabbard and let her scream her war song. My wound was trivial, the wounds Serpent-Breath gave were not. A demented man, mouth agape to reveal toothless gums, flailed an axe at me and Serpent-Breath took his soul with elegant ease, so elegant that I laughed in triumph as I wrenched the blade from his upper belly. 'We're holding them!' I bellowed, and no one noticed I shouted in English, but though our small shield wall was indeed hold-ing firm just in front of the great post, our attackers had outflanked the left of our line and the men there, attacked from two sides, broke and ran. We stumbled backwards to follow them. Blades crashed into our shields, axes splintered boards, swords rang on swords, and back we went, unable to hold our ground against so many, and we were driven past the great mooring post and now there was light enough in the sky for me to see the green slime clinging to the post's base where the huge chain lay rusted.

Haesten's men screamed a great howl of victory. Their mouths were distended, their eyes were bright with light reflected from the east and they knew they had won, and we just ran away. There is no other way to describe that moment just before the full dawn. Sixty or seventy men were trying to kill us, and they had already killed some of the crewmen from the moored guard-ship, and the rest of us ran back onto the foreshore where the mud was thick and I thought again that I must die there where the sea ran in slithering ripples across the slick flats, but our attackers, content that they had driven us off, turned back to the post and chain. Some watched us, daring us to go back to the firmer ground and challenge them, while the others slashed at the chain with axes. Beyond them, dark against the darkest part of the sky where the last stars faded, I could see Haesten's ships waiting to slide out to sea.

The axes rang and chopped, and then a cheer sounded and I saw the heavy chain slither snake-like across the mud. The tide had turned now and the new flood was running strong, and the blocking ship was being swung westwards, carried into the creek by that surge of water, and I could do nothing but watch as Haesten's escape was made possible.

Our attackers were running back to their own ship. The chain had vanished into the low water as the blocking ship slowly dragged it away. I remember stumbling forward through the mud, one hand on Rypere's shoulder and my left foot squelching the blood in my boot. I held Serpent-Breath and knew I was powerless to stop Æthelflaed being carried away to a worse captivity.

The ransom, I thought, would be doubled now, and Haesten would become a lord of warriors, a man wealthy beyond even his inordinate greed. He would assemble an army. He would come to destroy Wessex. He would be king, and all because that chain had been severed and the Hothlege at last was being unblocked.

I saw Haesten then. He was standing in the bows of his ship, which I knew was named the *Dragon-Voyager*, and she was the first ship waiting for the creek mouth to be fully clear. Haesten stood in cloak and armour, stood proud beneath the raven's head that crowned his ship's prow, and his helmet glinted with the new dawn, and his drawn blade was shining, and he was smiling. He had won. Æthelflaed, I was certain, was in that ship, and behind him were twenty other ships; his fleet, his men.

Sigefrid and Erik's men had reached the creek and had launched some of the boats that had been spared the fire. They had begun to fight Haesten's rearward ships and in the glare of the burning ships I saw the glint of weapons and knew that more men were dying, but it was all too late. The creek was opening.

The blocking ship, held now by its bow chain alone, swung faster and faster. In a few heartbeats, I knew, the narrow channel would be wide open. I watched Haesten's oars dip to keep the *Dragon-Voyager* steady against the flooding tide and knew that at any moment the oars would pull hard instead and I would see his lean vessel speed past the stranded guard-ship. He would row away eastwards, away to a new encampment, away to a future that would bring him a kingdom that had once been called Wessex.

None of us spoke. I did not know the men beside whom I had fought, and they did not know me, and we just stood there, disconsolate strangers, watching the channel widen and the sky brighten. The sun had almost touched the world's rim and the east was ablaze with red, gold and silver light. And that sunlight flashed off Haesten's wet oar-blades as his men brought them far forward. For a moment the sun slashed into my eyes from all those reflections, then Haesten shouted a command and the blades vanished in the water and his longship surged forward.

And it was then I realised that there had been panic in Haesten's voice. 'Row!' he was shouting, 'pull!'

I did not understand his panic. None of Sigefrid's hastily manned ships were anywhere near him and the open sea lay before him, yet his voice sounded desperate. 'Row!' he screamed, 'row!' and the *Dragon-Voyager* slid still faster towards the gold-bright east. Her dragon's head, snout raised and teeth bared, defied the rising sun.

And then I saw why Haesten panicked.

The *Sea-Eagle* was coming.

Finan had made the decision. Later he explained it to me, but even days afterwards he found it hard to justify the choice he had made. It was instinct as much as anything. He knew I wanted the channel open, yet by bringing *Sea-Eagle* into the Hothlege he would bar the passage again, yet still he decided to come. 'I saw your cloak,' he explained.

'My cloak?'

'The bolt of lightning, lord. And you were defending the chain-post, not attacking it.'

'Suppose I'd been killed?' I suggested. 'Suppose an enemy had taken my cloak?'

'And I recognised Rypere, too,' Finan said, 'you can't mistake that ugly little man, can you?' And so Finan had told Ralla to bring the *Sea-Eagle* into the channel. They had been lurking at the eastern end of Two-Tree Island, the patch of marsh and mud that formed the northern bank of the channel's entrance, and Ralla had ridden the incoming tide into the Hothlege. Just before they entered the channel he ordered the oars to be shipped inboard, then he had steered the *Sea-Eagle* so that she struck one bank of the *Dragon-Voyager*'s oars.

I watched. The *Sea-Eagle* was in the channel's centre while Haesten's ship was nearer to me so I did not see the long oar looms snap, though I heard them shatter. I heard the splintering sound as shaft after shaft broke, and I heard the screams from Haesten's men as the oar handles were driven back to crush their chests, and that is a horrible injury. Those screams were still sounding as the *Dragon-Voyager* jarred to a sudden stop. Ralla had thrust on the steering-oar to push Haesten's ship onto Caninga's mud shelving bank, and then the *Sea-Eagle* also stopped abruptly as she was trapped between the stranded blocking ship and the newly beached *Dragon-Voyager*. The channel was closed again, plugged now by three ships.

And the sun rose full above the sea, brilliant as gold, flooding the earth with a dazzling new light.

And Beamfleot's creek became the killing place.

Haesten ordered his men to board the mastless *Sea-Eagle* and kill its crew. I doubt he knew whose ship it was, only that it had thwarted him, and his men screamed as they leaped aboard to find Finan leading my household warriors to meet them, and the two shield walls met on the forward rowing benches. Axe and spear, sword and shield. For a moment I could only watch. I heard the crack of shields slamming together, saw that new light flicker from raised blades, and saw more of Haesten's men crowding onto *Sea-Eagle*'s bows.

That fight filled the creek's entrance. Behind those three ships the flooding tide was drifting the rest of Haesten's fleet back towards the burning boats on the shore, but not all of Sigefrid's boats were burning, and more and more were being manned and rowed towards Haesten's rearward vessels. The fighting had started there too. Above me, on

Beamfleot's looming green hill, the hall still burned, and on Hothlege's shore the ships burned too, and so the new golden light was veiled with palls of smoke beneath which men died while wisps of black ash, fluttering like moths, drifted from the sky.

Haesten's men ashore, the ones who had driven us onto the mud and released the guard-ship's chain, splashed through the shallow water to haul themselves onto *Dragon-Voyager* so they could join the fight aboard *Sea-Eagle*. 'Follow them,' I shouted.

There was no reason for Sigefrid's men to obey me. They did not know who I was, only that I had fought beside them, but they understood what I wanted and they were infused with a fighting-man's rage. Haesten had betrayed his agreement with Sigefrid, and these were Sigefrid's men, and so Haesten's men must die.

Those men, the ones who had driven us to ignominious flight, had forgotten us. They were on board *Dragon-Voyager* now and scrambled towards the *Sea-Eagle*, intent on killing the crew that had frustrated Haesten's escape, and we were unopposed as we climbed aboard their ship. The men I led were my enemies, but they did not know that and they followed me willingly, eager to serve their lord, and we struck Haesten's men from the rear and, for an instant, we were the lords of killing. Our blades took men in the spine, they died without knowing they were under attack, and then the survivors turned and we were nothing but a handful of men facing a hundred.

There were far too many men aboard Haesten's ship, and there was not nearly room enough in the *Sea-Eagle*'s bows for all of them to join that fight. But the men on *Dragon-Voyager* now had their own enemy. They had us.

But a ship is narrow. Our shield wall, that had easily been outflanked on land, here stretched from side to side of the

Dragon-Voyager, and the rowing benches made obstacles that stopped a man charging home. They had to come slowly or else risk tripping on the knee-high benches, but they still came eagerly. They had Æthelflaed, and every man was fighting for a dream of riches, and all they needed to do to become wealthy was kill us. I had picked up a shield from one of the men I had struck down in our first sudden assault, and now I stood, Rypere on my right and a stranger on my left, and let them come.

I used Serpent-Breath. My short-sword, Wasp-Sting, was usually better in a shield wall fight, but here the enemy could not close on us because we stood behind a rowing bench. At the ship's centreline, where I stood, there was no bench, but a mast crutch served as an obstacle, and I had to keep looking left and right, past the high crutch, to see where the worst danger threatened. A wild-bearded man climbed onto the bench in front of Rypere, meaning to hack an axe down onto his head, but the man held his shield too high and Serpent-Breath pierced his belly from beneath and I turned her, ripped her sideways and his axe fell behind Rypere as the Northman screamed and twisted on my blade. Something, axe or sword, was beating on my shield, then the stomach-ripped man fell sideways across that weapon, and blood ran down Serpent-Breath's blade to warm my hand.

A spear slashed beside me, the lunge deflected by my shield. The blade vanished, pulled back, and I overlapped my shield on Rypere's just before the spear struck again. Let it, I remember thinking. They could thrust spears at shields all morning and get nowhere. To break us they had to cross the obstructing bench and fight us face to face, and I looked over the shield's rim to see the bearded faces. They were shouting, I have no idea what insults they hurled at us, I only knew that they would come again, and they did, and I thrust the shield up at a man on the bench to my left and stabbed Serpent-Breath at his leg, a puny stroke, but my shield boss caught his belly and hurled him backwards, and a blade rammed my lower belly, but the mail did not break. They were crowding down the ship now, the men behind forcing the men in front onto our blades, but the sheer weight of the attack was driving us backwards, and I was dimly aware that some of our men were defending our spines against a counter attack from those of Haesten's men who had boarded *Sea-Eagle* and now tried to get back on board *Dragon-Voyager*. Two men managed to get past the crutch and shield-charged me, their slamming impact staggering me sideways and back and I tripped on something and sat heavily on the edge of a rower's bench and, in blind panic, stabbed Serpent-Breath past the edge of my shield and felt her puncture mail, leather, skin, muscle and flesh. Things crashed on my shield and I heaved forward, sword still trapped in an enemy's flesh, and miraculously there was no enemy to keep me down and I touched shields right and left and roared a challenge as I ripped and twisted Serpent-Breath free. An axe hooked on my shield's upper rim and tried to haul it down, but I dropped the shield, lost the axe, and raised the shield and my sword was free again and I could lunge her at the axeman. All instinct, all rage, all screaming hate, all a blur in my mind now.

How long did that fight last?

It might have been a moment or an hour. To this day I do not know. I listen to my poets sing of age-old fights and I think no, it was not like that, and certainly that fight aboard Haesten's ship was nothing like the version my poets warble. It was not heroic and grand, and it was not a lord of war giving out death with unstoppable sword-skill. It was panic. It was abject fear. It was men shitting themselves with fright, men pissing, men bleeding, men grimacing and men crying as pathetically as whipped children. It was a chaos of flying blades, of shields breaking, of half-caught glimpses, of despairing parries and blind lunges. Feet slipped on blood and the dead lay with curling hands and the injured clutched awful wounds that would kill them and they cried for their mothers and the gulls cried, and all that the poets celebrate, because that is their job. They make it sound marvellous. And the wind blew soft across the flooding tide that filled Beamfleot's creek with swirling water in which the new-shed blood twisted and faded, faded and twisted, until the cold green sea diluted it.

There had been two battles at the beginning. My crew aboard *Sea-Eagle*, led by Finan and helped by the remnants of Sigefrid's warriors who had been manning the stranded blocking ship, fought a desperate defence against Haesten's household troops. We helped them by boarding *Dragon-Voyager* while, at the creek's far end, where the ships burned bright, Sigefrid and Erik's men attacked the rearward boats of Haesten's fleet.

But now it changed. Erik had seen what happened at the creek's mouth and, instead of boarding a ship, he led his men up the southern bank, splashed through the small channel that led to Two-Tree Island, and then swarmed onto the beached blocking ship. From there they jumped onto *Sea-Eagle* and so added their weight to Finan's shield wall. And they were needed, for Haesten's leading ships had at last rowed to their lord's rescue and still more men were trying to board the *Sea-Eagle*, while others were climbing aboard the *Dragon-Voyager*. It was chaos. And when Sigefrid's men saw what Erik did, many followed, and Sigefrid himself, aboard a smaller longship, found water enough to row against the tide and was bringing that ship towards the fight at the channel's mouth where the three boats were locked together, and men fought in ignorance of who they fought. Everyone, it seemed, was against everyone. This, I remember thinking, was like the battles that wait for us in Odin's corpse-hall, that eternity of joy in which warriors will fight all day and are resurrected to drink and eat and to love their women all night.

Erik's men, flooding aboard the *Sea-Eagle*, helped Finan drive Haesten's boarders back. Some jumped into the creek, which was just deep enough to drown a man, others escaped onto the newly arrived ships of Haesten's fleet, while a stubborn rearguard made a defiant shield wall in the *Sea-Eagle*'s bows. Finan, helped by Erik, had won his battle, and that meant many of his men could come aboard *Dragon-Voyager* to stiffen our beleaguered shield wall, and the fight on Haesten's ship lessened in intensity as his men saw nothing but death. They backed away, stepping over benches and leaving their dead, and snarled at us from a safe distance. Now they waited for us to attack.

And it was then, in that small pause as men on both sides balanced the probabilities of life and death, that I saw Æthelflaed.

She was crouched beneath the steering platform of *Dragon-Voyager* from where she stared at the tangle of death and blades in front of her, but there was no fear on her face. She had her arms around two of her maidservants and she watched, wide-eyed, but with no apparent fear. She had to have been terrified, for the last few hours had been nothing but fire, death and panic. Haesten, we later learned, had ordered the fire set to Sigefrid's thatch and, in the ensuing chaos, his men had rushed the guards Erik had placed on Æthelflaed's hall. Those guards had died, and Æthelflaed had been snatched from her chamber and dragged precipitately down the hill to the waiting *Dragon-Voyager*. It had been well done; a clever, simple and brutal plan, and it might have worked except that *Sea-Eagle* had been waiting just beyond the creek's mouth, and now hundreds of men hacked and stabbed at each other in a wild fight where no man knew exactly who his enemy was, and men just fought because fighting was their joy.

'Kill them! Kill them!' That was Haesten, urging his men back to the slaughter. He only had to kill our men and Erik's men and he would be free of the creek, but behind him, coming fast, Sigefrid's ship surged past Haesten's other vessels. Her steersman aimed her at the three ships blocking the channel, and there was room enough for the oars to get three hard strokes so that the smaller ship crashed hard into the fight. She rammed *Sea-Eagle*'s bows, just where the last of Haesten's boarders had their shield wall, and I saw those warriors stagger sideways under the shock of the impact, and I also saw *Sea-Eagle*'s planks driven inwards as Sigefrid's stem-post drove hard into my ship. Sigefrid was almost thrown from his chair by the impact, but he struggled back upright, bear-cloaked, sword in hand, and bellowed at his enemies to come and be killed by his sword, Fear-Giver.

Sigefrid's men leaped into the battle, while Erik, tousle-haired and sword in hand, had already crossed the *Sea-Eagle*'s stern to board *Dragon-Voyager* and was hacking his wild way towards Æthelflaed. The fight was turning. The arrival of Erik and his men and the impact of Sigefrid's ship had put Haesten's warriors on the defensive. The remnant on board *Sea-Eagle* gave up first. I saw them struggling to board *Dragon-Voyager* and thought Sigefrid's men must have attacked with a howling intensity to put them to flight so quickly, but then I saw that my ship was sinking. Sigefrid's ship had splintered her side and the sea was flooding through the broken planks.

'Kill them!' Erik was screaming. 'Kill them!' and under his leadership we went forward and the men in front of us gave way, yielding a row of benches. We followed, clambering over the obstacle to receive a rain of blows on our shields.

I stabbed Serpent-Breath forward and struck nothing but shield-wood. An axe hissed over my head, the blow missing only because the *Dragon-Voyager* lurched at that moment and I realised the rising tide had lifted her from the mud. We were afloat.

'Oars!' I heard a huge shout.

An axe buried itself in my shield, splitting the wood apart, and I saw a man with mad eyes staring at me as he tried to retrieve his blade. I pushed the shield wide and lunged Serpent-Breath at his chest, using all my force so that her steel went through his mail and he went on staring at me as the sword found his heart.

'Oars!' It was Ralla, shouting at those of my men who no longer had to defend themselves against Haesten's attackers. 'Oars, you bastards,' he shouted, and I thought he must be mad to try and row a sinking ship.

But Ralla was not mad. He was thinking sensibly. *Sea-Eagle* was sinking, but *Dragon-Voyager* was floating, and *Dragon-Voyager*'s bows were pointing to the open estuary. But Ralla had splintered one bank of her oars and now he forced some of my men to carry *Sea-Eagle*'s oars across the gap. He was planning to take Haesten's ship.

Except the *Dragon-Voyager* was now a maelstrom of desperate men. Sigefrid's crew had crossed *Sea-Eagle*'s sinking bows to gain a lodgement on the steering platform above Æthelflaed and from there they were hacking at Haesten's men, who were being pushed back by my companions and by Erik's crew, who fought with a maniacal fury. Erik had no shield, just his long-sword, and I thought he must die a dozen times as he hurled himself on his enemies, but the gods loved him at that moment and Erik lived while his enemies died. And still more of Sigefrid's men came from the stern so that Haesten and his crew were squeezed between us.

'Haesten!' I shouted, 'come and die!'

He saw me, and looked astonished, but whether he heard me, I do not know, for Haesten wanted to live to fight again. *Dragon-Voyager* was floating, but in water so shallow that I could feel her keel bumping on the mud, and behind her were more of Haesten's ships. He jumped overboard, landing in the knee-deep water, and his crew followed, running down Caninga's bank to the safety of their next ship. The fighting, that had been so furious, died in an eyeblink.

'I have the bitch!' Sigefrid shouted. He had somehow boarded Haesten's ship. His men had not carried him, for his chair with its lifting poles was still on the ship that had sunk *Sea-Eagle*, but the massive strength in Sigefrid's arms had hauled him across the sinking boat and up into *Dragon-Voyager*, and now he lay on useless legs, a sword in one hand and Æthelflaed's unbound hair in his other.

His men grinned. They had won. They had retrieved the prize.

Sigefrid smiled at his brother. 'I have the bitch,' he said again.

'Give her to me,' Erik said.

'We'll take her back,' Sigefrid said, still not understanding.

Æthelflaed was staring at Erik. She had been wrenched down to the deck, her golden hair in Sigefrid's huge hand.

'Give her to me,' Erik said again.

I will not say there was silence. There could not have been silence for the battle still raged along the line of Haesten's ships, and the fires roared and the wounded moaned, but it seemed like silence, and Sigefrid's eyes looked along the line of Erik's men and settled on me. I was taller than the others, and though my back was to the rising sun, he must have seen something he recognised for he lifted his sword to point the blade at me. 'Take off the helmet,' he ordered in his curiously high voice.

'I am not your man to be commanded,' I said.

I still had some of Sigefrid's men with me, the same men who had come from the blocking ship to thwart Haesten's first attempt to open the channel, and those men now turned towards me with weapons rising, but Finan was also there, and with him were my household troops.

'Don't kill them,' I said, 'just drop them overboard. They fought beside me.'

Sigefrid let go of Æthelflaed's hair, shoving her back towards his men, and heaved his huge, black-swathed cripple's body forward. 'You and the Saxon, eh?' he said to Erik. 'You and that treacherous Saxon? You betray me, brother?'

'I will pay your share of the ransom,' Erik said.

'You? Pay? In what? Piss?'

'I will pay the ransom,' Erik insisted.

'You couldn't pay a goat to lick the sweat off your balls!' Sigefrid bellowed. 'Take her ashore!' This last command was to his men.

And Erik charged. He did not need to. There was no way that Sigefrid's men could take Æthelflaed ashore for the *Dragon-Voyager* had been carried by the incoming tide past the half-sunken *Sea-Eagle* and now we were drifting down onto Haesten's next boats, and I feared we would be boarded any minute. Ralla had the same fear and was dragging some of my men to the forward rowers' benches. 'Pull,' he shouted, 'pull!'

And Erik charged, meaning to cut down the men who now held Æthelflaed, and he had to pass his brother who squatted dark and angry on the blood-slicked deck, and I saw Sigefrid lift the sword and saw Erik's look of astonishment that his own brother would raise a blade against him, and I heard Æthelflaed's scream as her lover ran onto Fear-Giver. Sigefrid's face showed nothing, neither rage nor

356

sorrow. He held the sword as his brother folded on the blade, and then, without an order, the rest of us charged. Erik's men and my men, shoulder to shoulder, wènt to start the killing again and I paused only long enough to seize one of my warriors by the shoulder. 'Keep Sigefrid alive,' I ordered him, and never saw who it was, then carried Serpent-Breath to the last slaughter of that bloody morning.

Sigefrid's men died fast. There were few of them and many of us. They stood for a moment, meeting our rush with a locked shield wall, but we came with a fury born of bitter anger and Serpent-Breath sang like a screaming gull. I had thrown down my shield, wanting only to hack into these men, and my first stroke beat down a shield and sliced off the jaw of a man who tried to scream and only spat blood as Sihtric drove a blade into the open red maw of his mouth. The shield wall broke under our fury. Erik's men fought to avenge their lord, and my men fought for Æthelflaed who crouched, arms over her head, as Sigefrid's men died around her. She was shrieking, screaming inconsolably like a woman at the burial of the dead, and perhaps that was what kept her alive because, in that slaughter on the *Dragon-Voyager*'s stern, men feared those awful shrieks. The noise was terrifying, over-whelming, a sadness to fill the world, and it went on even after the last of Sigefrid's men had leaped overboard to escape our swords and axes.

And only Sigefrid remained, and the *Dragon-Voyager* was under way, pulling against the tide to creep out of the channel under her few oars.

I draped my blood-soaked cloak over Æthelflaed's shoul-ders. The ship was moving faster as Ralla's oarsmen found their rhythm and as more men, dropping shields and weapons, snatched up the long oars and fitted them through the holes in *Dragon-Voyager*'s flanks. 'Row!' Ralla called as

357

he came down the blood-slopping deck to take the steering-oar. 'Row!'

Sigefrid remained and Sigefrid lived. He was on the deck, his useless legs curled beneath him, his sword hand empty, and with a blade held at his throat. Osferth, Alfred's son, held that sword, and he looked at me nervously. Sigefrid was cursing and spitting. His brother's body, with Fear-Giver still piercing the belly, lay beside him. Small waves broke on Caninga's point as the new tide raced across the wide mudflats.

I went to stand over Sigefrid. I stared down at him, not hearing his insults. I looked at Erik's corpse and thought that was a man I could have loved, could have fought beside, could have known like a brother, and then I looked at Osferth's face, so like his father's. 'I told you once,' I said, 'that killing a cripple was no way to make a reputation.'

'Yes, lord,' he said.

'I was wrong,' I said, 'kill him.'

'Give me my sword!' Sigefrid demanded.

Osferth hesitated as I looked back to the Norseman. 'I will spend my life beyond death,' I told him, 'in Odin's hall. And there I shall feast with your brother, and neither he nor I wishes your company.'

'Give me my sword!' Sigefrid was pleading now. He reached for Fear-Giver's hilt, but I kicked his hand away from Erik's corpse. 'Kill him,' I told Osferth.

We dropped Sigefrid Thurgilson overboard somewhere on the sun-dancing sea beyond Caninga, then turned westwards so that the flooding tide could carry us upriver. Haesten had managed to board another of his ships and, for a time, he pursued us, but we had the longer and faster boat, and we drew away from him and, after a time, his ships abandoned the chase and the smoke of Beamfleot receded until it looked like a long low cloud. And Æthelflaed still wept.

'What do we do?' a man asked me. He was one of Erik's men, the leader now of the twenty-two survivors who had escaped with us.

'Whatever you wish,' I said.

'We hear that your king hangs all Northmen,' the man said.

'Then he will hang me first,' I said. 'You will live,' I promised him, 'and in Lundene I shall give you a ship and you may go wherever you want.' I smiled. 'You can even stay and serve me.'

Those men had laid Erik's body reverently on a cloak. They pulled Sigefrid's sword from their lord's belly and gave it to me, and I in turn handed it to Osferth. 'You earned it,' I said, and so he had, for in that welter of death Alfred's son had fought like a man. Erik held his own sword in his dead hand and I thought he would already be at the feasting hall, waiting for me.

I took Æthelflaed away from her lover's corpse and led her to the stern and there I held her as she cried in my arms. Her golden hair brushed my beard. She clung to me and cried till she had no more tears, and then she whimpered and hid her face against my bloody mail coat.

'The king will be pleased with us,' Finan said.

'Yes,' I said, 'he will.' No ransom would be paid. Wessex was safe. The Northmen had fought and killed each other, and their ships were burning and their dreams were ashes.

I felt Æthelflaed's body shaking against mine and I stared eastwards to where the sun dazzled above the smoke of burning Beamfleot. 'You're taking me back to Æthelred, aren't you?' she said accusingly.

'I'm taking you to your father,' I said. 'Where else can I take you?' She did not answer because she knew there was no choice. Wyrd bið ful āræd. 'And no one must ever know,' I went on quietly, 'about you and Erik.'

359

Again she did not answer, but now she could not answer. She was sobbing too heavily and I held my arms around her as though I could hide her from the watching men and from the world and from the husband who awaited her.

The long oars dipped, the riverbanks closed on us and in the west the smoke of Lundene smudged the summer sky.

As I took Æthelflaed home.

Historical Note

There is more fiction in *Sword Song* than in the previous novels about Uhtred of Bebbanburg. If Æthelflaed ever was captured by the Vikings then the chroniclers were curiously silent about the incident, so that strand of the story is my invention. What is true is that Alfred's eldest daughter did marry Æthelred of Mercia, and there is a good deal of evidence that the marriage was not made in heaven. I suspect I have been extremely unfair to the real Æthelred, but fairness is not the historical novelist's first duty.

The records of Alfred's reign are comparatively rich, partly because the king was a scholar and wanted such records kept, but even so there are mysteries. We know that his forces captured London, but there is controversy over the exact year in which that city was essentially incorporated into Wessex. Legally it remained in Mercia, but Alfred was an ambitious man, and he was evidently determined to keep kingless Mercia subservient to Wessex. With the capture of Lundene he has begun the inexorable northwards expansion that will eventually, after Alfred's death, transmute the Saxon kingdom of Wessex into the land we know as England.

Much of the rest of the story is based on truth. There

363

was a determined Viking attack on Rochester (Hrofeceastre) in Kent that ended in utter failure. That failure vindicated Alfred's defensive policy of ringing Wessex with burhs that were fortified towns, permanently garrisoned by the fyrd. A Viking chieftain could still invade Wessex, but few Viking armies travelled with siege equipment, and any such invasion thus risked leaving a strong enemy in its rear. The burh system was immaculately organised, a reflection, I suspect, of Alfred's own obsession with order, and we are fortunate to possess a sixteenth-century copy of an eleventh-century copy of the original document describing the burh's organisation. The Burghal Hildage, as the document is known, prescribes how many men would be needed in each burh, and how those men were to be raised, and it reflects an extraordinary defensive effort. Ancient ruined towns were revived and ramparts rebuilt. Alfred even planned some of those towns and, to this day, if you walk the streets of Wareham in Dorset or Wallingford in Oxford you are following the streets his surveyors laid out and passing property lines that have endured for twelve centuries.

If Alfred's defensive scheme was a brilliant success, then his first efforts at offensive warfare were less remarkable. I have no evidence that Æthelred of Mercia led the fleet that attacked the Danes in the River Stour, indeed I doubt that foray was any of Æthelred's business, but other than that the tale is essentially true and the expedition, after its initial success, was overwhelmed by the Vikings. Nor do I have a shred of evidence that Æthelred ever subjected his young wife to the ordeal of bitter water, but anyone fascinated by such ancient and malicious sorcery can find God's instructions for the ceremony in the Old Testament (Numbers 5).

Alfred the Great, as *Sword Song* ends, still has some years to reign, Æthelflaed of Mercia has glory to find, and Uhtred of Bebbanburg, a fictional character, though based on a real man who happens to be one of my paternal ancestors, has a long road to travel. England, in the late ninth century, is still a dream in the minds of a few visionaries. Yet dreams, as the more fortunate of my characters discover, can come true, and so Uhtred and his story will continue.

The Last Kingdom
Bernard Cornwell

Uhtred is an English boy, born into the aristocracy of ninth-century Northumbria. Orphaned at ten, he is captured and adopted by a Dane and taught the Viking ways. Yet Uhtred's fate is indissolubly bound up with Alfred, King of Wessex, who rules over the only English kingdom to survive the Danish assault.

The struggle between the English and the Danes and the strife between Christianity and paganism is the background to Uhtred's growing up. Marriage ties him to the Saxon cause but when his wife and child vanish in the chaos of the Danish invasion, he is driven to face the greatest of Viking chieftains in a battle beside the sea. There, he discovers his true allegiance.

'Cornwell is a virtuoso of historical fiction'   *Sunday Telegraph*

'Bernard Cornwell is a literary miracle, producing the most entertaining and readable historical novels of his generation.'
Daily Mail

ISBN 978 0 00 7149917

The Pale Horseman
Bernard Cornwell

Uhtred, Northumbrian-born, raised a Viking and now married to a Saxon, is already a formidable figure and warrior. But at twenty he is still arrogant, pagan and headstrong, so not a comfortable ally for the thoughtful, pious Alfred. But these two, with Alfred's family and a few of Uhtred's companions, are apparently all that remains of the Wessex leadership after a disastrous truce.

It is the lowest time for the Saxons. Defeated comprehensively by the Vikings who now occupy most of England, Alfred and his surviving followers seek refuge in Athelney, a tidal swamp to which Alfred's kingdom has shrunk. There, using the marsh mists for cover, they travel in small boats from one island to another, hoping to regroup and find more strength and support.

Uhtred is still attracted to rejoining his Danish foster brother and the victorious Vikings. But he finds a growing respect for the stubborn leadership of Alfred, to whom Uhtred's support is essential if the Saxon strength is to be rebuilt and battle joined with the enemy.

The Pale Horseman is a splendid story of divided loyalties and desperate heroism. Uhtred and Alfred, Vikings and Saxons, are a winning combination for Bernard Cornwell.

ISBN 978 000 7149933

The Lords of the North
Bernard Cornwell

The year is 857 and Wessex is free from the Vikings. Uhtred, the dispossessed son of a Northumbrian lord helped Alfred win that victory, but now, as the Lords of the North begins, he is disgusted by Alfred's lack of generosity and repelled by the king's insistent piety. He flees Wessex, going back north to seek revenge for the killing of his foster father and to rescue his stepsister, captured by the same raid. He needs to find his old enemy Kjartan, a renegade Danish lord who lurks in the formidable stronghold of Dunholm.

Uhtred arrives in the north to discover rebellion, chaos and fear. His only ally is Hild, a West Saxon nun fleeing her calling, and his best hope is his sword, with which he has made a formidable reputation as a warrior. He will need the assistance of other warriors if he is to attack Dunholm and he finds Guthred, a slave who believes he is a king.

If Guthred is to rule Northumbria he needs Uthred and Ragnar the Dane who is Uthred's sworn brother. Guthred, though, is weak and yields to treachery. Uthred ends up a slave on a voyage to Iceland. His rescue comes through an unlikely alliance of his friends and enemies. In the end it is Alfred the great of Wessex who sees profit in Northumbria's despair and looses Uthred and Ragnor on to Dunholm, the invincible fortress on its great spur of rock in the lawless north.

'Beautifully crafted story-telling, complete with splendid set-piece battles and relentless derring-do, so gripping that it rarely stops to catch a breath. It demonstrates once again Cornwell's enormous skill as a historical narrator. He would have graced Alfred's court entertaining the guests with his stories.'   *Daily Mail*

'Cornwell's narration is quite masterly and supremely well-researched.'   *Observer*

ISBN 978 000 721970 4

Harlequin
The Grail Quest

Bernard Cornwell

It was the time when the English came across the Channel to take the battle to the French. The army was led by the King, the great lords and knights, but it is the archers, the common men, who are to be England's secret weapon.

Thomas of Hookton is one of those archers. But he is also on a personal mission – one he frequently forgets in the joy of fighting – to avenge his father's killing by a French raider and to retrieve his family's treasure. But the journey is far more complex and treacherous that he had expected, and the enemy who awaits him could harness the power of Christendom's greatest relic, the Grail itself.

The first book in the *Grail Quest* series ends in the great battle of Crecy, the beginning of what became known as the Hundred Years' War.

'A rich mix of bloody conflict amid political and religious turmoil – what a very fine writer Mr Cornwell has become.'
The Economist

ISBN 978 000 6513841